Open Dreams

BY

Neville M. Chesses

Autofiction

Open Dreams

Neville M. Chesses

Autofiction

Copyright©Neville M..Chesses2014

Neville M. Chesses has asserted his right under the Copyright and Designs Act 1988 to be identified as the author of this work.

All rights reserved. Without limiting the rights under copyright reserved above, no part of this publication may be reproduced, stored in or introduced into a retrieval system, or transmitted, in any form, or by any means (electronic, mechanical, photocopying, recording, or otherwise) without the prior written permission of both the copyright owner and the above publisher of this book.

This eBook is licensed for your personal enjoyment only. This eBook may not be re-sold or given away to other people. If you would like to share this book with another person, please purchase an additional copy for each person you share it with

Thank you for respecting the author's hard work.

First published on Amazon Kindle Direct in 2014

This ebook is a work of autobiographically inspired fiction. All names, business organisations, places and events are either the product of the author's imagination or are used fictitiously. The author's use of any actual persons (living or dead), places and characters is not intended to change the entirely fictional character of this work, or to disparage any person or any company or its products or services.

Biography

Neville Chesses was one of the best junior golfers the UK had ever produced; at 17 years of age he defeated the reigning US amateur champion, Jerry Pate at Hoylake and reached the semi finals of the British Boys championships. Many of his contemporaries became feted professionals and Ryder Cup players but his destiny was never to travel this road as his early promise ultimately developed into a constant, bitter struggle. Even though by chance he discovered the secret of golf when he was around 24, enabling him to finally win many county, area and national championships, by then the desire, mixed with the ambition to dedicate and devote his life to the game, had long dissipated and gone.

Neville retired from golf in his late twenties; married, had two children, moved to the North West and did not touch a club for over 20 years. Eventually he returned to the Midlands where he rekindled his passion for the sport and, between his business interests, now teaches professionally, part time at a local driving range for pleasure, satisfaction and fun.

He finds it an obligation, honour and a privilege to pass on the knowledge he has gleaned and learned from such luminaries as Sir Henry Cotton or more importantly in many ways, his own errors.

Neville considers that preventing his pupils making the same mistakes he did is undoubtedly a blessing and, through this cathartic process has rediscovered the same love for golf once more that he first had as a child.

This story had been in his active mind for many years but finally as he had the time he wanted to write and share it.

He sincerely hopes the people that read this adventure are illuminated and informed in some of the realities and sacrifices needed to be made to achieve in sport, and enjoy his combined reminiscences and imagination.

A Message from the Author.

This book is only partially about golf.

In truth it is more about hope, work; the quest for knowledge in a chosen field, achievement and sometimes dealing equally with success, disappointment and occasional disaster.

More than that and most importantly, it is about family and love.

I have listed below an *idiots guide to golf* so anyone reading the book will understand the game and not be put off reading this tale… after all… it is easy! Well not easy to play but I'm sure you get my point!

Golf is played around 18 holes; each hole is a different distance and has an allowed score, dependant on this length, of 3, 4 or 5. This figure is referred to as a par.

A par of a course which is the 18 holes added together is normally around 72. A handicap is then given to the golfers that play; 18, is often the highest and scratch the lowest handicap.

Therefore if a scratch golfer scores 72 and the 18 handicap golfer scores 90; then they have tied on the *net* score (The score with the handicap removed) of 72.

A *birdie* is 1 under par i.e. getting a 3 on par 4 hole.

An *eagle* is 2 under par i.e. getting a 2 on a par 4 hole.

A *bogey* is 1 over par i.e. getting a 5 on a par 4 hole.

A *double bogey* is 2 over par i.e. getting a 6 on a par 4 hole.

The turn is referred to as having reached the end of the 9th hole, half way round the course.

A *shank* is where the ball is hit disastrously at right angles off the club.

Dormie is a reference to when a match cannot be lost; i.e. 1 up with 1 to play or 2 up with 2 to play etc.

The 10 shot rule is a term relating to the cut in a major competition; all competitors after the first 2 rounds, if they are within 10 shots of the leader, qualify for the last 2 rounds.

The Borrow is a term relating to the way the slope of a green affects the roll and path of the ball.

Winning or losing 2/1 is the result when you are 2 holes up or down with only 1 to play etc as is 3/2 etc.

There I told you it was easy!

Dedications

To my father, Freddy, mother Daphne and my children, Sam and Oliver.

My companions and teammates from Warwickshire Golf and to all the friends I knew as a young boy at Shirley Golf club.

And Marion for helping to edit and pull it all together.

Chapter 1

In the fading, bright dazzle of the late afternoon a fresh, warm, light zephyr blew in from the west and covered a sprinkling, sparkling, shimmering fountain of freshly mown grass over the small boy who was just standing and waiting patiently.

Perhaps it was as if to anoint him, as the fabled prophets of the bible once did with honey or perfumed oil to only the chosen few. The practice area of the golf course stretched out before him like the richest, green baize and the tree lined area sloped gently down to a small, dark, greenkeeper's hut that seemed to be waiting permanently for somebody to hit golf balls towards it, as if in that instant, that was its sole and only function.

There was a tall Goliath of a man standing beside the young child; he spoke softly in a quaint, evocative, rich, Irish brogue and drew lazily on a small cigarette that glowed, bright red at the tip as he did so. He looked down at the boy from a fearsome height, balancing his arms precariously on the thick, twisted, black, leather grip of a huge, silver golf club that in itself was bigger and higher than the young boy he was addressing.

"What's your name, Son?"

The child stared up at him with clear, innocent, blue eyes, in equal emotions of awe and trepidation; the man was like an enormous, gentle giant from the treasured pages of the Roald Dahl monster stories he loved to read at bedtime.

"Sam...Sam Chester... I am very pleased to meet you, Mr Thompson."

The wizened, old professional smiled inwardly at the politeness and correctness of the young child; his keen, green eyes observed and closely inspected him up and down as if intently assessing his quality.

He was no more than 11 years old, dressed smartly in short, grey trousers, a black roll neck jumper and a pair of new, white trainers that were already a little scuffed.

He could clearly see the boy was nervous and his feet were moving as if he was dancing absentmindedly to an unheard, up-tempo beat and could not keep still.

He had a round, almost plump, friendly face and his azure blue, gleaming and glinting eyes contrasted sharply with his mop of thick, brown, silken, straight hair.

Len Thompson liked him straight away and smiled, hardly moving his mouth but a fraction, so as not to interfere with the smoking cigarette that was now dangling precariously from his, rough, red and yellow faintly stained lips.

"Let's see what you can do then, Son!"

He unzipped a small, black, bulging bag lying on the earthen, dry floor and a tumbling selection of pristine, shiny white golf balls cascaded out onto the newly manicured length of ground that seemed like an endless, green, magnificent carpet to the amazed and impressionable boy.

Len knelt down and the biggest, broadest, hugest hand Sam had ever seen selected a couple of the cleanest and most perfect spheres then gently tossed them across the lawn to his fascinated pupil.

Sam exhaled in barely concealed anxiety but separated one of the gleaming, small globes with the cut-down 7 iron in his right hand and placed it nervously and tantalisingly in front of him.

The opposite hand was then meaningfully placed onto the club; he breathed in deeply and shaped up to hit it towards the tantalising, magnetic shed that had entreated or beckoned him previously and privately.

His bright eyes focused, he held his breath then swung the small club with all the grace and power he could muster and sensed the club go backwards then through to a full, flourishing finish.

However and unfortunately, when his head returned to the position in which it started he realised the impish, small, white irritating object still remained annoyingly between his feet as if only to belittle him and make him seem foolish.

A mature, teasing male voice called out loudly and suddenly in good humour and mischief from behind them.

"Sam…you can do better than that…!"

Len turned around to see a smiling, bulky, balding man come striding towards them talking constantly and animatedly as he did so.

"…What do you think then, Len… have we got a Champ or not?"

The professional laughed out loudly at this intruder's good humour, audacity and cheek.

"What are you like, Frankie? The, Poor Lad's only had one shot!"

The rotund spectator smiled then sidled up to the tall, ungainly professional and they both once again returned their full and undivided focus to Sam.

He had hastily, already prepared another ball and on this occasion he managed to make some uninspired connection, resulting in the mercurial small, round globe rolling a few, leisurely yards down the perfectly cut and prepared, surface of the ground.

Len stretched over to him and placed his frightening hand on top of his youthful, delicate head, almost capturing it in his expansive, rough palm and spoke gently but firmly to him.

"This…needs to stay still, Son… perfectly still, now… place a ball in front of you and try it again!"

The boy did as he was told and felt the weight of his teacher's, dynamic touch holding his body as if it was in some barbaric, human trap or immovable vice.

The small, circular, shimmering ball on the floor suddenly became the very centre of his attention, and to his great surprise he watched and felt for, the first time in his young life, the club he was swinging make solid contact with the unreasonable, divisive, sphere!

Sam instantly sensed the terrible, downward pressure on his head and hair release, and he looked up immediately in undisguised glee to see his shot floating sweetly in the air and returning to the colourful surface some hundred yards down the fairway.

The old professional picked up the cigarette he had so nonchalantly discarded and thrown onto the short grass then, after bringing it up to his dry mouth, drew the smoke in satisfaction and drawled irresistibly.

"That, Frankie…is a thing of beauty!"

The other man was amused but unconvinced.

"But, does that mean he's got potential?"

Len placed one of his enormous, elongated arms around the shoulders of the chubby companion standing a good 12 inches below him, whilst still instructing the child by gesture, to try another effort.

"Take a good look at your son…"

He chuckled almost silently.

"…And just appreciate the moment… there's no such thing as potential in this game!"

Frankie took a step back to consider what this Mellow Monster of a man had told him as he watched his child's latest effort have less success without the gargantuan, guiding hand of his instructor.

Over the next half hour Len patiently shoved and cajoled the boy into a variety of positions with varying degrees of success, and the trio eventually left the practice area to return to the sanctity of the ancient, golf shop, changing room and storage area.

The main source of the professional man's income, including the stowing of the clubs for the members, was contained within the antiquated, black and white timber building which stood sadly in the shadow of the modern, brick built clubhouse directly opposite.

Len opened the front door and led Sam and his father through into the shop section at the front that was filled haphazardly with an enormous and varied selection of golf equipment.

They then walked slowly into a middle room and central area of the structure where he purposefully sat himself tiredly on an old, wooden bench alongside the black painted but fading, rotten frame of the square, four-panel, timber and glass, solitary window, that looked out over the 13th tee and murmured out loudly.

"Make us a cup of tea, Son!"

The tall professional addressed the remark to

the slim, lanky, anaemic looking young assistant who dutifully clicked on the glinting, sliver kettle that was perched on an ancient workbench, seemingly lost amongst a selection of tins, tools, attachments and vices.

Sam was overwhelmed and enveloped in the almost mystical atmosphere contained within the clutter of the area and wandered between the shop and the workroom fascinated by both the equipment or the multitude and variety of unknown, amazing things that surrounded him.

It was as though he had stumbled into some type of Aladdin's cave and he began busily counting the boxes of golf balls piled so high in front of him as if only to distract his wandering mind, when he was brought back to reality by the sound of his father's, sharp voice.

"Sam… come in here, Mr Thompson wants to ask you a question."

The boy returned to the rear room to find his father and new teacher drinking tea and engaging in some spiky, friendly banter and heard his recent mentor mumble to his rotund, paternal parent.

"Let me ask him myself…"

His dark, green, sparkling eyes were suddenly focussed directly upon him making him feel unsure.

"…Did you enjoy the lesson, Son?"

Sam did not hesitate for a millisecond.

"Yes, Mr Thompson!"

The man asked a rhetorical question as the answer was written all over the young man's engaged and enthused face

"Would you like to come again?"

Sam looked as always towards his father for approval and permission.

"Can I?"

Frankie simply winked at his son, his rounded, chubby, full face seemingly always beaming mischief.

"How about…every Friday…at 5 O'clock, after school?"

Sam literally, shone and radiated happiness and enthusiasm, as the tall professional then actually felt mildly embarrassed that a proposed weekly lesson with him was a cause for such an outpouring and demonstration of expressive joy.

After the two men had finished their drink,

father and son walked back through the shop and Frankie went to the cracked, marked and dirty glass counter to dutifully pay the assistant the fee for the half hour, golf lesson.

He turned to leave and noticed his precious offspring gazing longingly at a small, white pair of golf shoes fighting to be shown through the clear but filthy frontage at the very bottom of the display cabinet.

Instinctively he spoke with his normal effusion and joviality.

"If you are going to play the game… I suppose you've got to look the part… let's see if they fit!"

The footwear and centre of the boy's avarice and desire were duly removed, tried on and purchased before Len put them on a high shelf in the back room in readiness for next week's tuition.

The boy thanked his father for the gift, and Frankie expressed his appreciation to the professional for his time, having revelled in their conviviality and jokey exchanges, as he truly liked the engaging and amusing man.

"We've both enjoyed it…"

His brown, earthy eyes shone at him teasingly,

as he stood weightily in the faded, wooden, weather beaten, black frame of the main entrance door.

"…One thing though, Len…has he got potential or not?"

Len shook his head in long, slow, mock exasperated motion, smiled and chuckled in his normal, velvety, Irish tone.

"You're incorrigible, Frankie, go home!"

Sam was sure he could still hear him laughing as they left the shop and it surprised him that it appeared, just his selfish pleasure was the cause of such good humour or joviality in everyone.

The walk to the car was short; the new, grandiose, red Jaguar quickly sparked into understated, powerful life and started comfortably to propel them slowly up the long, gracefully curved drive to the busy road.

Sam placed his nose against the clear, transparent, passenger window and saw, Len Thompson with his next lesson sauntering and almost loitering, out again towards the immaculate, perfect, practice ground.

His teacher had the same club that he'd leant on in his own lesson, slung casually over his shoulder and this was counterbalanced with the swelling bag of practice balls in his opposite hand, as if he was some talented acrobat or performer and Sam mused that in some way he was!

He whispered out to the enigmatic, tall teacher, as if he would actually hear him.

"See you next week!"

To his surprise and as if he could, Len raised his large head then waved briefly at their car as it disappeared along the tree lined drive towards the main entrance.

Both Sam and his father were quiet on the 15 minute journey home, each seemingly tired by their own particular exertions of the day.

Sam had been busy at his school lessons and his father, with the pressures of his small business, prior to picking up his son to take him to the golf lesson as he had promised.

Frankie did not really understand why his boy took such an interest in the sport; he had only taken the game up himself less than a year ago and at best played poorly and extremely sporadically.

However from the first instant Sam saw his golf clubs he was engaged, interested and continually pestered him to be shown how to play this mercurial, aggravating pastime.

Initially he had humoured the child, allowing him to swing his irons in the garden and then buying him his own, specific, junior club that he had in fact used that very afternoon for his lesson.

Frankie assumed that his interest in this historic, uncommon sport would pass given the allure of football or cricket, but Sam's requests and pleadings to learn this particular recreation and activity only increased, culminating in today's instruction which as promised, was a much appreciated and belated birthday present to him.

If he was honest he had half expected today to be an end to the matter, as he presumed the undoubted difficulty of the game would dull his son's enthusiasm.

However Frankie could clearly see that this was not the case, as not only was it apparent Sam had a natural aptitude to hit the annoying, little ball, but he had been amazed on reflection, just how involved he personally became in the progression of the lesson.

The feeling he got when Sam had hit that one perfect shot was... *memorable* and he had noticed, surprisingly and unexpectedly, that it had made his blood run!

He recalled again to his mind the vision and memory of when he connected sweetly with that first good hit and was visualising in his mind's eye its soaring flight and path through the air, when his imaginative thought processes were interrupted by the sound of his boy's, soft voice.

"Thanks, Dad…we're back."

Home was a modern four- bedroom house in the respectable, affluent suburb of Moseley and they were both pleased to leave the car in the pitted, gravel path and enter.

A warm, engaging, friendly voice soon welcomed and acknowledged them from the kitchen.

"Dinner will be 5 minutes…please go and wash your hands."

Sam responded immediately and raced up the stairs; his father dutifully followed enabling them to enter the dining room shortly afterwards somewhat cleaned and refreshed.

Frankie went over to the slim, dark-haired woman at the cooker then gave her a hug by way of a greeting and she responded with an affectionate, playful, loving peck on the cheek.

He then sat and joined his children, Sam with the teenage and rapidly maturing, Anna who was quiet and moody as was her disposition or inclination most of the time.

Dinner was steaming hot spaghetti and as she served it, the lively, mature woman and cook teased her two men not to get the sauce all over their shirts this time!

They all laughed even though, Dorothy was being half serious, and she soon sat down to join them as well for the simple but extremely well cooked and prepared meal.

No one was very chatty so it was not until the last of the garlic bread had magically vanished and Frankie had wiped his plate clean, that he enquired whether they had had been busy in the shop.

His wife stared at him with the same, brown coloured eyes as he had, then responded that it had been reasonable and they would need to go up to the warehouse tonight to prepare some extra stock for the following day's trading.

Everyone listening to her groaned at the prospect of more work, especially Sam's sister, Anna, whom up to now had been, very quiet as she distractedly and discontentedly had used her fork to tease or toy with her pasta.

But now she rose like a small, dark, temperamental whirlwind and her bright voice swirled then whistled in agitation and frustration.

"Mum, I am going out tonight…I just won't get myself in a mess in that disgusting warehouse, besides… David will be here at 8 and I'm not going to be back in time…. Mum, *Pleeease!*"

Sam sat back in his chair then watched this familiar, emerging, theatrical game; he had seen it so many endless times before, and knew distinctly and exactly what was coming.

It was what always prevailed when his sibling initiated her crying and prima donna routine; abject capitulation or surrender from his normally, eminently sensible parents!

His mother spoke to him softly, even with utter empathy, submission and understanding towards his endlessly infuriating, older sister

"We'll manage, Sam, won't we? We wouldn't want her to miss her big date…would we?"

Sam looked at the focus of his frustration vacuously and blankly; he wondered how it was possible for her to evade every obligation, chore or minimal piece of responsibility for all of his short life?

He felt for certain and sure in the whole of her 17 years there was nothing Anna did that she didn't want to; he therefore just blinked and nodded in agreement and deference to his mother, simply not wishing to make a fuss or upset her.

As if to add insult to injury his Dad then decided to pass comment, which in Sam's less than important or listened to opinion, tended to be somewhat biased and one sided when it came to his sibling.

"Besides…Sam…You've had a treat today and it's only fair… isn't it…isn't it, Son?"

The young boy looked up then smiled weakly at his father, and thought privately to himself that when it came to his mercurial and selfish, closest relation, nothing was ever fair!

Dinner concluded, Anna explained that she had to get herself ready while, as normal, it was left to Sam to clear the table as his mother filled the sink then washed the marked, stained and dirty plates.

The small boy stood beside her then started to dry the dishes and cutlery as her busy hands softly and purposefully placed them on the soapy, draining board.

Sam truly loved both his parents and his

mother especially; he was always pleased to help her as even at his tender age, appreciated how incredibly hard she had to work.

He commented very concernedly and quietly to her, noticing to his unease, how she had more than a trace of weariness in the way she jadedly held herself.

"Dad and I can sort the stock, Mum...you rest!"

Her deep, chocolate, sparkling eyes smiled down at him in amusement, understanding, mischief, and of course unbreakable love; Sam and her strongest eternal feelings of affection were inseparable as they had been from the first second she held him in her slender arms.

"You might be able to, Sam..."

She laughed in her own private, secret irony.

"...But I'm not so sure about your, Dad!"

Dorothy was well aware that whatever were the merits of her husband, attention to detail was not one of them, and she wanted to be sure she had the correct replacement lines or products for the following day's customers.

She changed the subject; her concerns with the struggling business were not for her special, gorgeous, young baby.

"How was your golf?"

Sam was instantly enthused and engaged as he replied with immature, fervent, enthusiasm.

"It was great...Mr Thompson, my teacher was really nice, and Dad bought me a new pair of golf shoes... for next week's lesson!"

She revelled at the sparkle in her boy's, bright, blue eyes; if anything was ever the apple of her own, apart from her husband of course ...then this child undoubtedly was, and she teased him gently!

"Getting very serious this golf?"

Her remark was an intended joke but Sam at his tender age completely, missed the veiled humour and responded casually.

"No, Mum... it's just a bit of fun!"

Dorothy ruffled his velvety hair and thought nothing more of the conversation as she busied herself finishing tidying up in readiness for the trip to get the stock she needed from their store.

However it was their first conversation about this unknown and strange game of golf, and the irony of her son's innocuous description of his approach to the sport, was never lost on her in the evolving months then years that followed.

The dinner service was eventually cleaned then placed away; Anna's man arrived on time, which was 15 minutes late, and Sam pondered dryly to himself that the *delicious,* David wasn't up to that much, as his sister ran eagerly out to the old, navy, tatty, sports car that gave the false impression that her potential boyfriend had some money!

The three, working members of the family then headed to the stockroom on the outskirts of town to do what was necessary for the prosperity and survival of all of the family.

This warehouse was labelled by them all as, *The Place*; it was in fact a large rundown, ramshackle, derelict, old house that had long since seen better and more significant days.

The building was double storey and had large windows that were now boarded up with brick and timber; Frankie played with the multitude of keys eventually opening the various locks that abounded the unsightly, steel fronted entrance.

Finally and ultimately the large, heavy, main door creaked then groaned, slowly ajar, like something from a tacky, horror movie revealing only the inky, blackness and darkness inside.

They all then jumped as the alarm went into mode as a further, more rounded key was turned to silence the imminent explosion of noise.

Diffused lights were then put on placing the previously darkened property and the stock contained within it, at the convenience and discretion of Dorothy's list.

Sam was always both bemused or horrified by the warehouse, the property was a seemingly never ending maze of rooms each one strewn with various products or goods and it always surprised him how anything was ever discovered or found.

It was also beginning to be something of a torture chamber, as ever more frequently he was being asked to help sort out stock, or unload huge, enormous lorries that seemed to stretch out forever with countless, endless boxes.

Fortunately however, tonight his mother knew exactly what she required as she sailed majestically through the mayhem and chaos, swiftly separating the articles, products and lines that she wanted and felt necessary.

Sam quickly put the various items in thin, black, polythene sacs that were then placed in the boot of the car in preparation and readiness for the following day's retail trade.

Everyone was tired suddenly as they drove away; Sam yawned loudly from the back of the luxurious car and Dorothy picked up on his fatigue and exhaustion.

"You've had a busy day, Son, haven't you?"

The boy replied almost silently as if only talking to himself, and made a small, innocent, dry joke.

"Yes… I suppose I have…but apart from this…it's been fun!"

Bed beckoned the young man quickly on his return home as he slept deeply and soundly until the morning, although he could vaguely remember the sound of a slamming car door at some stage, in the middle of the black, mysterious dead of night.

His father quizzed Anna pointedly over breakfast in the emerging light of the new day.

"What time were you home, Young Lady?"

She responded aggressively and without the faintest charm or respect.

"Don't start, Dad…I'm not a Baby!"

Sam stared surreptitiously at his sister and

concluded that in this respect she certainly was right.

Her long, dark, black hair was brushed back in a ponytail and her cherubic, innocent, round face was caked in make up in readiness for her working day in the large, expensive, exclusive store behind one of the cosmetic counters.

She was smartly dressed in a tailored, navy suit or uniform that accentuated her feminine, developing, female shape and, if Sam did not know her to be the undeniable *pain* that she was, he would have assumed her to be an admirable, attractive, young lady.

However he comprehended and understood her far too well as unfortunately for him her character detracted from her presentation; the two seemed strangely separate, distinct and unconnected.

Dorothy drifted about, ensuring her brood had everything they needed to meet the challenging, new day and whispered encouragingly to her daughter.

"Have something to eat, Darling."

As normal however the best, Anna could manage was a mere slice of toast with a quick sip of tea, before she ran and scurried to catch her bus, shouting as she went rushing out of the front door.

"Don't make dinner…I'm meeting, Suzy after work for a drink!"

Sam watched his father and mother exchange, concerned, frustrated glances at each other but he found it hard to understand why, given that his sister's performance was fairly typical of her morning antics.

She was undoubtedly a creature of habit, even her bad one's, and everyday around her was permanently, consistently and un-enjoyably the same as far as he was concerned!

Breakfast concluded the remaining family piled into the expensive, garish car and Frankie dropped his wife at the shop, located at the front entrance to the market, on the way to taking Sam to school then encouraged her as he kissed her quickly on the cheek.

"Have a busy day, Darling."

Dorothy responded with a squeeze of his arm and a warm embrace as she then waved at her special, little man in the back of the vehicle.

"Bye, Sam…see you later!"

His mother then began to drag the heavy bags of stock, selected the previous evening, out of the boot as her son pressed a button and opened the window and smiled lovingly as she did so.

"Bye, Mum!"

School was upon them shortly and Sam slipped out of the vehicle at the traffic lights to enable his father not to get caught in the early morning queue of doting, dashing parents.

There was no time for the normal niceties between them and he ran in through the dark, open, metal gates just as the bell was sounding for assembly.

Sam was intelligent without being naturally academic, and with the 11 plus coming up in a few months time he felt the pressure of exams weighing heavily on his youthful shoulders.

Sometimes when his parents could not pick him up, he would catch the bus home and his focus and attention was always worryingly captured by the large, evil looking, moody, grey, concrete, Comprehensive school he always passed.

He felt it was specifically there to incarcerate or to punish him if he failed to reach the required pass rate and it was undeniably a tremendous incentive and motivation to study.

Sam therefore was normally extremely attentive to his lessons and determined to achieve his highly prized place at one of the sought after grammar schools.

However today he was unusually thinking more about his forthcoming golf lesson on Friday and privately hoping that it would not be raining.

He kept seeing the hypnotic, dark shed at the bottom of the long, manicured, sloping practice area and, in his ever present imagination he was hitting crisp, powerful shots that were still climbing and soaring into the clear, cloudless, blue sky as they flew so high above it.

His introspective fantasy was suddenly and rudely interrupted by a quiet, probing, sensible, salient voice

"And the answer is? Sam... please...inform the class!"

He looked up then uneasily saw that Mr Clarinet, his teacher was gazing enquiringly straight at him and knew that he had been caught out daydreaming; he spoke truthfully, as he always did, even in his confusion, much to everyone's entertainment and amusement.

"I'm sorry, Sir...I wasn't listening!"

The elderly, educational instructor was a small, plump, stooped man, with an engaging, intelligent, charming face, lined and heavily wrinkled with age and worldly wisdom.

His chubby body was well past its best but his slate, grey eyes still retained a spark, richness and sparkle of youth and energy; he was undoubtedly greatly admired, loved and respected by all of his young pupils and charges.

He was amused and intrigued by this child's genuineness but chided then rebuked him very gently and with mock disappointment.

"I can see that, Sam, what on earth were you thinking about?"

Honesty once again seemed the best policy for the trusting and engaging, young boy.

"My golf lesson…on Friday!"

Mr Clarinet's face softened in obvious humour; he laughed out loudly and suggested to his inattentive pupil with some justification and sarcasm, that he *just may* have more chance of a career through his education.

Sam was too naive for such covert irony and just replied with respect and deference to his favourite teacher, although he knew for a fact that he, just perhaps, may one day prove him wrong.

"Yes, Sir, I am sure you are correct...I'm sorry!"

The week duly passed and on Friday at exactly 4p.m. Sam ran out of the entrance gates where his father was patiently waiting as promised; he jumped into the car and instructed him to hurry as he did not want to be late.

His parent tried to soothe, calm or kerb him in his childish enthusiasm and ebullience.

"Relax, Son...we've got plenty of time!"

Sure enough, the school traffic abated as within half an hour, Sam had his new, white, steel-studded golf shoes on and was now waiting on the rickety bench in the dusty, changing room for his new instructor to finish his present lesson.

Sam wandered over to the window and watched with keen interest through the peeling timber as some of the members of the club were driving off on the flat tee of the 13th hole.

In truth the men he was observing were ordinary, middle aged, middle handicap golfers but to Sam, at this point in his experience, they were talented sportsmen and the young boy genuinely marvelled as one by one the four players hit their respective balls up the fairway into the near distance.

The foursome had just reached their tiny, bright spheres on the way to the hole around the dog leg right, when Sam heard the bell on the entrance to the shop ring and jangle; sure enough, his lofty, tall tutor came sauntering into the room with a broad smile on his leathery, weather beaten face and teased him immediately.

"So we didn't frighten you off last week, Son? How are the shoes?"

The youngster replied with great zest and enthusiasm.

"Great…are you ready to go?"

Len laughed again at the boy's, fresh, boundless energy and told him when he reached his age he'd be glad of a breather too!

Within a few minutes however they were once again firmly set on the practice area where the divisive, greenkeeper's hut seemed a far distant and impossible challenge.

Sam mused, fretted and thought to himself, as shot after shot from his small, thin club dribbled embarrassingly but a few feet down the green slope, that *surely no one could ever hit the ball that far!*

Len Thompson went through the same procedure as the previous week but immediately noticed and observed straight away how Sam had tried to take on board his previous instructions as he questioned him interestedly.

"Where have you been practising, Son?"

Sam was irritated as he did not see any improvement at all; he was patently frustrated with his demonstrable inability to hit the blessed but accursed ball as he desired and wished.

"In the garden…with air balls!"

The professional was secretly amazed and impressed at the progress of his small pupil in such a miniscule space of time.

Good shots were still few and far between but more often than not, Sam made a connection with the tiny globe and it was quite clear that his hand and eye coordination was more than excellent.

Frankie, at this lesson watched from nearby but stayed very quiet and was pondering less on his son's progression than on his various burgeoning or pressing, financial and business problems.

The lanky professional challenged him politely but mockingly.

"Are you with us today, Frankie?"

The sound of Len's silky toned question seemed to bring the portly man around and out of his private, fiscal thoughts as he answered him brusquely and with infusive humour.

"I'm not going to speak, Len... until he's hit that *blinking* shed at the bottom of that hill!"

Len stared at the distant, small, innocuous building and chuckled at him in controlled hilarity.

"I don't think you could keep quiet that long, Frankie!"

The half-hour lesson finished far too quickly for Sam and shortly the three of them were sitting once again in the distinctive but strangely cosy, shoe changing room; the men were drinking tea while Sam bit eagerly into one of the shop's chocolate bars as his teacher spoke about him in an enthusiastic and complimentarily fashion.

"The Boy's doing well!"

Frankie was extremely pleased and both father

and son left the golf club in positively, good spirits to make the short journey home.

On this occasion however Frankie did not go straight to the house, but parked his car in one of the poorer and less salubrious areas of town before entering into a shop with the huge image and picture of a white, horse's head adorning its black, uninviting frontage.

Sam sat quietly in the vehicle then waited for his father, as patiently as he could, to complete his business; he absolutely detested and hated this routine and was invariably either bored or increasingly concerned at being abandoned by himself in such a strange, disconcerting location.

He was not quite sure what his Dad did on these far too frequent occasions, but invariably when he came back he was either extremely, animatedly jovial, or red and crimson faced and more often in an all consuming, fearful temper.

Either way it was always unsettling and disquieting for him!

Frankie left the shop to return to the car after fully 25 minutes and the boy could see straight away that his father was uncomfortably flushed as he had patently and obviously not had a good time.

He yanked the door open then literally threw himself into the luxurious, tan leather seat before slamming the door behind him almost violently with all of his force and anger; his son noticeably quivered and shook beside him in utter discomfort and apprehension.

Sam had learned at these moments to keep exceptionally quiet and silent; he did not utter a single word, as his paternal parent literally frothed and seethed in agitation for the remainder of their journey home.

Dorothy immediately sensed Frankie's mood as they walked into the house then also followed her son's example by keeping hushed or out of his way by busying herself preparing the evening meal.

Eventually the four family members seated themselves around the table and somewhere around the main course Frankie began to finally regain his calm and composure.

Dorothy's soft, brown eyes focused on her husband and the faint worry lines around her maturing but still beautiful face showed life with him had often not been easy; the stress and strain was etched on her fraught, taut skin making her look temporarily older than her 37 years.

She unfortunately knew exactly where her

inveterate Frankie had been; where he had visited and been drawn to consistently since she first met him as a love struck teenager, seemingly a million days ago.

The bookies, the turf accountant, the bookmaker had been as much a part of Dorothy's life as her own family, but without any of the good times; simply none at all with regard to this insidious, horrible, odious habit and fetid compulsion.

Her beloved husband, Frankie was irrefutably an addicted gambler and, like all illicit gamblers, would not and never admit that he was, even for a solitary, salutary moment!

Year in, and year out Dorothy had lived with her family on the very pecuniary, tipping point of their survival and existence.

They had all the appearance of affluence but the truth was that her habitual partner had very little regard or respect for money as both the business and their home finances were precariously balanced seemingly always and forever on a jagged, knife's edge.

Her eternal love had obviously not had a good day on his cursed horse or *nags* and like always, Dorothy had to bite her lip then pretend that she was not aware of the obvious reasons for his foul, unacceptable behaviour or demeanour.

As if to add insult to injury her husband now spoke casually as if she was foolish and somehow unaware of his, *little hobby,* as he liked to describe it, and murmured to her lowly as he finished eating.

"I'll need to borrow some money from the day's takings!"

His wife could only nod in timid, passive acquiescence; one day was much the same as another for her as she felt utterly powerless to deal with her husband's ongoing addiction and problem that seemed to destroy or invade every part of their domestic existence.

However this was nothing new; it was just a further event in another second, hour or week of her frustration and disappointment.

In spite of her disquiet and malaise, she recognised there was nothing she could do but ignore the *elephant in the room* and let her treasured, family life stumble along.

Final school exams then summer holidays were approaching and Frankie informed both Sam and Dorothy that the professional, Len Thompson had agreed to let Sam use the practice ground at the golf club, and possibly the course, as long as no one was about.

He also commented one evening that he was considering paying for a membership for, Sam if his golf improved and progressed over the summer causing Dorothy to ask him cautiously then suspiciously a pertinent question.

"How much will it cost?"

Her husband was unilaterally in charge of all fiscal matters and sharply marked his territory with his dismissive, curt answer.

"I'll worry about that, Darling!"

He murmured a sweetener for his wife, as if only to soothe her ruffled feathers and made firm, meaningful comment directly to his son.

"You've got to pass your, *11 Plus,* though!"

Privately he knew from Sam's reports and teachers already, that this would not present a problem for his young man.

The next few weeks were however indeed a pressured time for Sam; a private tutor came to help him on the final preparations for the tortuous, vital test of his academic abilities and much to his disappointment and disgust, he was even forced to cancel one of his beloved, golf lessons with, Mr Thompson.

Eventually the first fateful hour of the exams

arrived and it was almost with relief he found himself sitting in the school hall with the rest of his classmates turning the first, maths paper over.

The same procedure continued the following days with both English and General Studies until finally the dreaded investigations of his youthful intelligence were concluded.

Sam ran down to his father's, resplendent car but as he saw the anxious and concerned look on his full, multi chinned face just laughed contentedly and confidently to him.

"Don't worry, Dad…just send off the subscription for my golf club fees as you promised!"

Soon after, the boy's time at his preparatory, junior school was finished and, one sunny afternoon, after saying his excited, final goodbyes to all his friends and teachers, he walked down the steep school drive for the very last time.

He felt mixed emotions; sadness in leaving somewhere that he had been so happy, anticipation mixed with fear of the unknown, and the joy of the summer, holiday months stretching out before him to practice or even perfect his chosen sport and calling.

Sam sensed, even then at his immature, tender age that this tantalising game of golf was more than a mere distraction or a passing interest.

He had worked out the bus route to the club and he was soon a regular feature on the small, practice range, or in Mr Thompson's fascinating and intriguing shop.

The tall professional lent Sam a couple of old, short clubs to provide him with a make do set, and occasionally in the evening, after his normal lessons had finished, he would take his enthusiastic pupil to play the 3 hole loop starting at the 10th and finishing in front of his archaic and antiquated shop and store.

Len took great enjoyment and pleasure in their improvised, little games ever gleaning extreme satisfaction from the remarkable and rapid improvement of the boy.

On one particular occasion they were playing the 12th, a short 170 yards par 3, where Sam took an almighty swing with his borrowed, somewhat cumbersome, cut down driver.

To his glee and pride the ball sailed majestically into the air and after landing on the very front of the green between the cavernous, dangerous bunkers, ran forward to finish only *6 feet* from the lofty, red pin.

His father, who was waiting by the back of the green to pick up his son, applauded enthusiastically loudly, as Len slapped Sam firmly on his developing back and shoulders.

"Good shot, Son!"

He then had his own attempt, watched as it came to rest much further away from the flag than the child's ball and eventually they walked the short distance to the fine surface together.

Sam finally stood over the tantalising, testing putt and placed an old, golden centre shafted putter, determinedly behind it.

His father commented and spoke loudly, then teased or joked with him as he always did.

"This is for *The Open!*"

Frankie knew nothing at all about golf but even he understood what *The Open* was; everyone always comprehended what the simple words and description of *The Open* represented.

Sam ignored him as he was concentrating intently and, only when he was completely ready, did he strike the ball before looking up to see it roll and tumble with perfect, forward rotation and spin, then literally dive in the small, black hole.

Both men yelled in joyous celebration as he leant forward, picked the bright sphere out of the cup then mumbled with true elation, pride and some disbelief.

"My first birdie!"

Sam was still overjoyed with his notable achievement for the whole journey home and could not wait to tell his mother about his talent and success; Dorothy was pleased but she was too tired from her day's labour and work to get overly excited.

About a *birdie* especially, as she didn't really or honestly understand, what one even was!

She listened with as much interest as she could muster then quickly changed the subject and spoke brightly.

"I had a card from, Anna today…say's that she's having a wonderful and excellent time."

Her daughter was in Israel on Kibbutz and Sam concluded that if Anna was having a good time it was normally at someone else's expense, but kept his opinion closely to himself then replied politely as if he was concerned or even interested.

"Great…give her my love when you write back!"

He spoke graciously for the sake of his mother's feelings but secretly he was unworthily pleased that that she was away; somehow life was ever more difficult and expensive for everyone when she was about!

The three of them sat around the table to eat and the conversation, as normal, revolved mainly around stock and money.

Sam heard his mother mention something about a phone call from the bank and his Dad told her acidly not to concern herself; amazingly nothing ever seemed to bother or worry his father, he just had that type of unique, fearless, brazen attitude to life.

By now the boy had his junior membership from the golf club; it was not expensive at his young age, and he amazed the regulars with his dedication or diligence of trudging then playing the same holes over and over again.

One of the more aged, eccentric and humorous members spoke to him sternly one, blustery afternoon

"Be careful, Young Man...you'll wear the course out!"

Sam looked at him concernedly and wondered for moment if he would and, it was only when he saw the older gentleman's, gaunt, lined face break into a broad smile that he realised he was only joking!

He did tend to take things far too seriously!

August was hot, dry and went, rushing by; Sam, as he had assertively promised his father had passed to a good grammar school and his mum was happier and more exultant than he had ever seen her.

The growing, little man still helped when asked, and was quite prepared to unload the big, mammoth, delivery wagons all for the promise of an extra few practice balls.

Every spare minute he could, Sam was at the entreating and beguiling, golf club where day by day, inch by inch, he felt the wretched, mocking, green keeper's hut getting closer and closer.

He promised himself that one day he was going to hit the ball straight over the tormenting and tantalising, dark building!

On the last week before his new school and term started, Sam came home with some apparently breathtaking and exciting news as he spoke elatedly to his parents.

"I've broken… 100!"

His plump fingers waved a dirty, white card under their noses as Dorothy really didn't comprehend what he was going on about but was pleased for him; she spoke complimentarily, encouragingly and lovingly stroked his fine, dark brown hair.

"Just get me some O levels as well, Sam, will you?"

The weeks and months simply ran together, Anna returned from her sojourn abroad and had decided that Moseley was definitely far too parochial or pedestrian for her.

She informed everyone that she was off to London and after relieving the family of yet more money, gave up her job even though it was still available to her, then promptly left.

Sam was privately relieved to see her go but he saw that both his mother and father were concerned, worried and fretful and felt somewhat shamefaced or remorseful that he could not be more understanding towards his sister.

But in all honesty and truth he had always found her and his relationship with his sibling, extraordinarily difficult!

The young man still had his waits outside the *Bookies*, as he was now well aware the establishments were called, and his Dad would invariably come back clutching some tatty piece of paper or other in various, uncertain moods and tempers.

He found it hard to spot the attraction of his father's interest, addiction or, *side business,* as he sometimes liked to explain it to be, and it was something, fortunately for him, all his life he would fail to see.

The initial term at his Grammar school was now upon him and as Dorothy photographed her son in his smart, black and red uniform on the first day she was literally bursting with maternal gratification and pride.

Sam was driven, as a gesture and indulgence due to his nervousness, and as fate would have it they went past the much feared, gloomy, imposing, Comprehensive he had worked so hard to avoid.

He knew inarguably that however bad this new centre of learning could be, it could never be as awful as the dreaded institution he had just so narrowly escaped and avoided.

It was a comforting thought, but he need not have concerned himself, as Camp Hill Grammar was an excellent, well respected school and Sam settled in straight away.

The terms revolved as time went along its normal, steady if not quickening course; Dorothy was still working, Frankie still wheeling and dealing, Anna doing what Anna wanted to do, and Sam, either at school or practising at the golf club.

Even in the winter on a Saturday or Sunday, Sam would go to the club to play and hit balls on the range or the often frozen, putting green.

Occasionally when the weather was too bad Sam would be in the inner sanctum of the professional's shop where members sat around the glowing, old, heated, metal stove, sipping hot, sweet tea and listening to Len's famous, irresistible, fantastical stories.

It was Sam's favourite time and he was always entranced by his tutor's irresistible jokes, tall tales or irrepressible reminiscences.

Len undoubtedly had the gift of the gab, of communication and conversation; everyone that came into contact with him couldn't help but like, be captured by him, and be enraptured by his unique blarney.

One afternoon when the weather was particularly cold, bleak, wild and wicked outside, he sipped his steaming mug of tea, stared out of the icy, glazed and frosted window then drawled exquisitely in his spectacular fashion.

"I've played in, *The Open*...!"

There were a few members gather around and, along with Sam, listened intently and with engaged, wide eyes as Len annunciated each word as if it was Shakespearian prose.

"...The final qualifying... 72... I did in the first round, nicely placed..."

He sighed only for theatrical or dramatic effect.

"...I went out that very evening and decided to walk, Lytham... *The Open* course..."

Again there was an elongated pause as he looked around at his captivated, spellbound audience and pondered an unspoken question.

"...Do you know...*What*...?"

The members in the heated changing room were silent and completely engrossed like his young, engaged, mesmerised charge as the red glow emanating from the burning, antique stove reflected visibly in the old professional's face and rugged skin.

With his balding head and impressive, grey side-burns the physical, warmth from the raging, crackling fire made him look even more striking, distinguished and imposing than normal.

He whispered as if it was haunted Halloween at the chime of midnight, and he was telling a terrifying, ghost story.

"...Big stands... massive, enormous, huge stands... bearing down on you ... and do you know... *What...?*"

It was his favourite term or expression and his listeners breathed in, all equally tense, involved and very much in suspense.

"...I decided there and then it wasn't for me... too much *pressure*...!"

He sipped his sweet liquid once more and continued ever onwards.

"...I went out the next day, in the second round... shot another 72... quietly put my clubs in my old boot and drove away; missed the cut by 2...!"

He smiled, almost poignantly at his recollections, stroked his commanding, slivery side-burns softly, absentmindedly and finally mumbled distractedly

"...But really...I wasn't trying *too* hard!"

Nobody in that room doubted him for a single minute, as if he had told them he could have won the whole, magical, famous competition if he'd wanted to, they would have all believed him!

The man was just irrepressible, magnificent and irresistible.

Just before Sam left he pulled the wizened, old professional to one side; he questioned and spoke to him with awe and confusion in his familiar, innocent, respectful way.

"Mr Thompson…what's pressure?"

Len looked at his youthful, innocent face showing hardly a single, tell tale trace of the signs of life or aging, then laughed heartily and chuckled in ever present, good humour.

"If you carry on playing this game the way you are, Son…"

He smiled compellingly once more at him.

"…Then, you'll know soon enough!"

Sam heard the beep of his father's horn then ran out not realising at all how insightful and prophetic his tutor's words were; the sage professional was right when it came to his chosen vocation and trade, Len Thompson knew about golf!

Christmas came and as Sam's birthday was also in December as well, he was spoiled and inundated with combined gifts of everything to do with his blessed and cherished sport.

Looking around at his incredible, new, small but perfect, selection of junior clubs and boxes of balls in rows made him long for the coming spring when his practice and dedication could begin again with the change of season, and perhaps miraculously he could somehow bloom or blossom as well with it.

Inevitably, slowly, the ice melted, the flower buds started to open and eventually the commencement of the club season began; Sunday March 10th was a momentous day for Sam as it was to be his first ever, official, medal round.

The committee had decided that because of their youngest member's extraordinary enthusiasm and effort, the club was to allow him to play in the adult competitions and grant him an honorary handicap of 18, the maximum permissible for senior, competitive golf.

Sam therefore, on this particular, historic morning stepped proudly onto the 1st tee as his two playing partners allowed him the distinction of hitting first.

Tommy Harris, one of his companions for the round, spoke kindly to him but with a trace of barely disguised, teasing wit.

"Pro's, always get the honour; you go first, Sam!"

The man was a slim, 50 year old regular, playing off 14 and he winked in amusement at Bill Johnston, a rotund, red faced man, playing off 11 who was the other member of the trio.

Sam breathed in and ceremoniously bent down to place the red marked *Titleist* up on an immaculate, long, white, wooden tee.

He focussed on the ball then tried to remember everything his coach had taught him; head still, left arm straight, knees bent, slow back, turn and release to a full finish.

He swung then felt the ball connect sweetly and, to the genuine and enthusiastic applause of his colleagues, it despatched itself between the two large trees, then right into the middle and very centre of the green, beautifully mowed fairway.

Everyone smiled and was pleased apart from Sam as he was already only concentrating and thinking about his next shot; it seemed that golf was already an extremely serious business to the small boy!

The round continued apace and Sam, although inconsistent was scoring well; he came to the 18th needing a par 4 to break 90 for the first time in his young, emerging life.

Out of bounds unreasonably beckoned on the right and Sam tried to block it out of his active and agitated mind as he went through his familiar set up, routine and preparation.

Finally he made the fateful swing and shot but felt his balance go as he fell back off his uninspired, ungainly endeavour and attempt.

He jerked then looked up in frantic horror and saw his chances of a record score disappear with his ball's dramatic leap and dive over the excruciating, white stakes indicating the separation of the course from the familiar, pretty, pristine, practice ground.

Sam instinctively slammed the driver down in audible frustration then groaned loudly and very angrily.

His companions, although sympathetic, were slightly shocked at his outburst; Bill Johnston muttered firmly but kindly in self-deprecation, as he teed his own ball up.

"You'd better get used to things like that, Sam…I've been hitting it there for years!"

On this occasion however the gentle, red faced man did not and neither did the other adult in the trio, and it was left to Sam to go again with a provisional shot.

Still uncontrollably fuming and annoyed, he swung quickly then grumbled again as the annoying, miniscule, round object swung left sharply then disappeared into the trees shielding or bordering the opposite side of the fairway.

The boy's mouth was drawn tight, his face flushed with uncontrollable fury and irrational agitation as he grabbed his bag to hurry after his infuriating, divisive, little, white globe!

7 further shots later the round was completed and it was not until the young man was back in the quiet of the locker room that he finally started to recover his composure or more amiable demeanour.

He then apologised to his playing partners, who were by now changing their shoes on the rickety, wooden seating, for his tantrum, and Tommy responded to him tiredly but with great understanding and cordiality.

"That's OK, Sonny…"

He rose up and placed a large, strong fatherly arm around the boy.

"...We all get frustrated by this *ruddy* game at times!"

Sam went into the clubhouse for a drink and a sandwich and later when the course was empty and utterly deserted, he walked the 370 yards back to the 18th tee.

His small feet stood firmly on the raised ground and he hit practice shot after shot, all onto the centre of the short, colourful grass of the course and fairway; Sam, then felt empowered, soothed and satisfied at each subsequent, successful attempt.

He privately admired and congratulated himself on his determination, intensity and demonstrable will to try to put his game right.

Unfortunately for the young man, he failed to recognise the important lesson of the day's play, which had been his flawed temperament, and not understanding its importance or significance could not possibly attempt to correct it.

Frankie was waiting in the shoe room to collect him, sipping tea as usual and chatting to Len as if they had still not exhausted their endless, jovial badinage.

His son was extremely pleased to see his father; however the tall, imposing professional beside him, meaningfully raised his grey, bushy eyebrows as he teased the child as if only to remind him of his recent disaster, calamity and that his intention was to make him suffer more.

"Fell off it, did we?"

Sam looked at him embarrassed as the apparently, ungainly, disjointed man stood up then turned his large frame, effortlessly and perfectly through an imaginary shot in his normal, smooth, rhythmical manner and encouraged him by his demonstration.

"Through the ball, Sam…like this and keep your head down!"

The focus of his brief lecture nodded, promised that he would in the future and for the first time was glad to see his Dad finish his drink, so they could leave the club and the devilish, punishing, golf course behind them and go home.

To his shock and disconcertion his most favourite pastime and location was suddenly, bizarrely, unexpectedly, extremely unsettling and aggravating for him!

However the initial disappointment of his premier round and experience quickly passed into history then was soon forgotten; thus enabling Sam to continue playing and practising every second he possibly could.

But golf was a tortuously, difficult game and it was fully four months, before he stood on the 18th once more needing a 4 to break 90 again.

However on this occasion, much to his delight, he drove into the geographical middle of the fairway, placed a 7 iron onto the green and smoothly rolled the put in for a 3!

Sam signed the card excitedly and very proudly; it was the first time he had played below his handicap and was elated and ecstatic as it felt to him as though he had scored a 66!

The spring moved quickly into summer as the boy was once more overjoyed with the onset of school holidays; he just secretly hoped he would not be called upon too much to suffer and help in equal measure, with the expanding business.

Dorothy was now working and running two shops and his Dad, in between frequent stops at the *Bookies* and full days on Saturday glued to the racing, was still trading wholesale to other local customers in the small, dirty, unbearable warehouse.

Anna was now in love with, Timmy, a pencil

thin, dark-haired man with a thick, black moustache; he was English but had an Asian look about him and seemed pleasant and friendly enough.

Sam felt sure that his Mum and Dad would not have been so delighted had it not been for an unspoken suspicion that Anna may have already been pregnant!

But married they were while it rained all the grey, grimy Saturday to and from the registry office, then back to a sumptuous celebration and reception at one of the town's most opulent, exclusive and expensive hotels.

Frankie, as normal paid for everything and, although Sam never knew what the amount of the cheque he saw his father give to Timmy, the young man grinned incessantly all night as he sipped his beer at the reception and got slowly, unattractively drunk.

Sam was content to just reach the end of the long evening then finally remove his itchy, uncomfortable, dark suit; he was even happier to see Anna and her new husband driven back to London, in an exquisite, black Rolls Royce and a hopefully, self-sufficient and independent life.

They were flying out on honeymoon tomorrow from Heathrow to somewhere exotic and, it appeared to everyone that Frankie had given his daughter a splendid send off.

In all truth Sam didn't like Timmy very much, but could not help feeling a little sorry for him as the newly hitched couple drove away in the magnificent, gleaming car.

He felt the empathy of knowledge, thought only about what an unfortunate person he was, and wondered how the naïve, young husband would manage when the real Anna sprang out from behind her affable facade that she was so clearly putting on!

Then, with the day concluded and as before; it was soon just Sam and his mother and father once again.

The growing youth imaginatively felt they were a little like the three musketeers from the book he had just read; they were always there for him and he always tried to do his level best for them in return!

With Anna now married but not forgotten, Sam returned to his golf and his attention was drawn to a leaflet on the junior notice board, advertising the Warwickshire Junior Open at Ladbrook Park, Golf Club.

Sam looked at the dates and realised if he hurried he could get his application in for the

12 and unders' competition.

Fortunately for him the club secretary was still around and the boy quickly filled in the form then placed it in front of stout, and always approachable, Mister Phillips for his signature.

The plump, voluble, friendly, middle-aged man was pleased to oblige and informed Sam that he would send it off for him in that evening's post as Sam smiled and spoke warmly in appreciation

"Thank you, Sir."

He then ran off to tell his coach excitedly and enthusiastically that he was entering his first outside tournament as he knew that Len Thompson would be interested and truly pleased for him.

The starting times came through a week later and Sam saw that he was due to play early; he showed the list to his father who agreed to caddy for him on his inaugural, external competition.

Dorothy was privately concerned about Frankie leaving the business for the day but her husband explained to her in his uniquely insightful, charming but logical style.

"I can't leave him by himself...can I?"

His wife just smiled, shrugged, deferred to him as normal then worried immediately and endlessly as she always did!

On the actual day of the tournament Sam arrived in the clubhouse to see an old gentleman sitting and literally surrounded by young boys of various sizes and ages; he was extremely small, thin and wore a pair of, round, silver, bifocal glasses perched on the end of his tiny, pert nose.

He was bald, apart from manicured sideburns that were pure, snow white, and Sam thought he looked friendly and extremely distinguished.

The man was handing out pristine, gleaming cards and talking animatedly to the melee of eager, chattering competitors and Sam nervously took his place in the bustling queue to sign in.

Eventually the crowd thinned and the young boy stood directly in front of him, looked straight into his crystal, blue eyes then noticed how they glimmered and shimmered; his globes still sparkled with effusive life and he spoke brusquely as he glanced downwards.

"Name?"

The boy replied nervously.

"Sam Chester."

The man looked up then down again and the boy watched as his intricate, delicate hands extricated his card from the mountainous pile of white, hardened, starched paper, in front of him.

"Ah…under 12's…?"

His sentence was both a query and an answer; he then looked at Sam under the narrow rim of his unusual glasses then smiled as he saw the boy nod in his apparent or transparent anxiety.

"…Don't you worry, Young Man I am sure you will do yourself justice… you're off in 30 minutes with…Tim Harris and David Jones!"

Sam thanked the engaging official and went to find his father who was waiting in the bustling, energised, locker room.

They both changed shoes in silence and Sam only had time for a few practice putts before he made the short walk across the scenery and greenery to the 1st tee.

The first hole at Ladbrook Park was a long, par 5 and Sam felt his pulse quicken as his name was ceremoniously read out by the starter.

He walked determinedly on to the tee then

purposely placed his ball on a fresh, white, wooden peg; he vaguely saw the stream in the far distance and concentrated with all his will and focus on the immediate task of hitting his first shot.

He pressed his fingers around his driver's grip firmly, turned his shoulders slowly and to his relief then great delight looked up to see his ball bounding down the middle of the fairway at the completion of his rhythmical swing.

The small crowd were complimentary then chorused and echoed together in enthusiastic approval.

"Good shot!"

After his fellow competitors had driven as well, Sam proudly marched off down the centre of the course, with his enthused, admiring father pulling his trolley somehow leisurely but fervently behind him.

Frankie, being the ever competitive animal he was, had discovered that there were fourteen boys in the under 12's competition and from what he had ascertained, David Jones, Sam's playing partner, was regarded as a hot favourite.

By the 7th hole, Frankie had decided that his son was a superior player, as both in style and concentration he seemed to have the edge.

However he was secretly, extremely irritated or even frustrated to find at the end of the first 9 that Sam was 2 shots behind this prime competitor on the *net* score which was calculated with their substantial, respective handicaps removed.

David Jones was a chubby boy with dark, curly hair; he had a lazy swing that looped around his back and it contrasted profoundly with Sam's slow smooth, more functional and considered approach.

The difference on this day's play however was that David was receiving the *rub of the green* the fact highlighted prominently and distinctly at the 12th hole.

David's poorly hit tee shot ran down weakly towards the brook, running teasingly in the fairway but had the audacity to bounce across the narrow, concrete bridge to get the opposite side, rather than fall into the watery grave as it was patently far more entitled to do.

Frankie had to contain himself in his overwhelming passion and compulsion to win, although he couldn't help muttering out loudly, as if everyone else around him was deaf!

"Bit fortunate that bridge was there, David!"

His son frowned at him in embarrassment and irritation; he also realised that he had a chance to take the incredible prize of first place and was equally annoyed at his companion's unreasonable, good fortune, but knew that to comment so outrageously like his father had done, was rude and inappropriate.

Enraged though, by his opposition's latest piece of luck, Sam resolved to muster all his effort and concentration, and sure enough, as the possibility of winning loomed for the young, Mr Jones, the pressure, that Sam used to muse and wonder about, started to rear its foul, ugly head and began to have an unsettling effect on the leader.

Putts that David had been holing easily suddenly went astray and in a 3 hole spell from the 14th the chubby, young man's hold on the competition disintegrated amongst the rough and the trees allowing Sam amazingly came to the last a full 3 shots clear of his rival.

The boy's concentration was therefore absolute, his face set, determined with his manner stern; each shot up the 400 yard last hole was played with extreme care and his final putt for a gross round of 85, net 67 was greeted with rapturous applause from his electrified, spellbound and enthusiastic father.

Sam shook hands with his companions and was surprised to find that David Jones was not unduly disappointed or affected by his sudden misfortune as he spoke to him with charm, grace then abounding good spirit and humour.

"Well done, Sam....I could see from the start that I was up against it!"

His humble, modest, attitude and approach was a lesson in temperament and humility that Sam would have been well to learn, but he was too young, puerile, ecstatic and wildly excited to do so.

He sat on an old, green wooden bench near the putting green and checked his score thoroughly on his card, signed it and then handed it in to the elegant lady with striking, grey hair who was meticulously and professionally dealing with such important matters.

She stared at the figures then looked up and smiled broadly at him.

"You are in the lead, Young Man!"

Sam smiled widely and much to his boundless happiness and joy, that was how the result remained!

Frankie immediately phoned his wife in his

excitement, told her the fantastical result then informed her that they would be remaining for the presentation which was to be held in a couple of hours after all the other competitors had finally finished.

It was quite a wait but eventually the presentation procedure and ceremony began.

Sam's prize was to be awarded after the under 10's prize, where an innocuous looking child called, Paul Sandy, had walked away with the competition.

Instinctively and instantly, Sam noticed or detected a confidence combined with competitiveness in this young, slender boy as he took his award that burned within him.

However, suddenly the voice of the elderly man with the white hair, who was now handing out the prizes, called out directly, clearly and loudly.

"The winner is, Sam Chester!"

The boy immediately found himself walking to the hub of the buzzing, applauding, crowded room and being presented with a gift voucher from the self same gentleman that had given him his card earlier in the day; he congratulated him enthusiastically, warmly, with a wish and a firm, manly handshake.

"Well done, Sam, I hope this is the start of a fulfilling, County career for you."

The young boy's face was a picture of ecstasy and delight that seemed to illuminate the small bar area as he returned to his father, who was standing similarly proudly at the side of the lively room.

It seemed however as if he was the only one there to notice that his son was secretly and actually disappointed with his winning accolade of a mere, insubstantial, paper reward.

Although he had tried his best to hide the fact, Sam had truly wanted his prize to be a trophy, his first cup, just the same as the large, impressive, silver prizes being awarded to the Colts and under 18 winners!

He looked on at these older players in awe, as he did their actual scores in the low 70's, and hoped that one day he too could win a competition without the need for the use of an unnecessary, bulky handicap.

But such thoughts were for the future and both father and son returned home flushed with success as Dorothy had dinner prepared as usual for her all conquering heroes.

She listened seemingly enraptured about the events of the day and she too was soon aware of her son's, hidden disquiet in not being able to show her a glinting, gleaming cup of triumph and victory.

This however was rectified the following day when Frankie went to buy the biggest, grandest, sparkling trophy he could find, and had engraved upon it, *Warwickshire under, 12's Amateur Champion*!

He left the trophy in Sam's room on the pretext that it had not been awarded in error, but his son knew that such a pathetic and lame excuse was not true.

However he did not really care and proudly, thrillingly displayed the gleaming, glinting, silver cup in the downstairs living room as a testimony to his talent, ability, prowess and the promise of his sporting triumphs and inevitable, golfing victories to come!

Chapter 2

Autumn, then winter followed and Sam found

himself back in his familiar schoolboy routine; Camp Hill was truly an impressive place of education but the maturing, young man had to adjust to the quality of academic excellence that was now expected of him.

At his junior school he had always excelled but in truth he found that he was no longer so talented or exceptional against the cream of the cleverest boys from the local area.

He eventually settled into the middle stream and always managed to obtain reports at the end of term that were passable and favourable but definitely not outstanding.

There was certainly no clash of sports interest however, as the main school tradition was rugby and Sam quickly realised that being in the middle of a scrum with boys that were twice as big as him was definitely no fun or entertainment at all.

Sam never quite understood the attraction of the game at schoolboy level, for as soon as the biggest or fattest boy got the odd shaped ball, they would simply jog or waddle their way to the try line while all the smaller boys pretended to tackle them!

It seemed a somewhat perfunctory and wasteful passage of time!

Golf was restricted to weekends only as on holidays, evenings or any spare time, he was expected to assist in the emerging, developing business and he did so with his normal enthusiasm, diligence, combined with grudging acceptance.

He was however rewarded with a newer and fuller set of clubs on Christmas morning and although he knew he was getting too old, he gave his Mum and Dad a childish kiss each as way of a thank you.

Frankie had also ordered his son the monthly golf magazines and the boy used to spend hours devouring the tips, advice and the profiles of his heroes such as Jack Nicklaus or Lee Trevino.

Sam's time with Mr Thompson was intermittent but their relationship was intense and strong and the boy revelled in the constantly entertaining atmosphere of his company.

The old professional's stories and reminiscences were compelling and he had that divine, ethereal way of speaking that made even the same tale seem new, fresh and interesting; as he did seem to like to relate the same memory or diversion over and over again!

Sam occasionally listened, mostly privately

between them, to Len's recollections of his own youth, the small, golf club on the west coast of Ireland, the boat trip over to play the tour and his eventual settlement at Shirley Golf Club.

He even recounted how he had married his wife, Jackie who was already engaged when she had just come for a lesson but, before she even realised, she had fallen for the lilting charm that captured anyone fortunate enough to come into contact with this amazing man.

It seemed that he was, as Sam so well knew, so engaging, likeable and strangely irresistible!

Anna came up from London for Christmas day to show off her son, Simon, and although she was clearly overjoyed with her new child, Sam noticed how quickly she slipped back into gear with the family then emphasised the hardships and financial trials of her life.

Sam silently seethed to himself as he looked at her husband, Timmy, drinking scotch and looking blankly out of the window, and he mused that if she wanted a decent and prosperous life why on earth, marry a lethargic twit like him?

It was perhaps a cruel criticism but there was more than a grain of truth in his thoughts and observations.

During the festive day he listened to or endured his sister's complaints and moans endlessly then considered that in some ways both Anna alongside her listless partner were somehow deservingly and seemingly well suited.

The day of goodwill mixed with celebration eventually finished and everyone was happy; Sam, because Anna had gone back to London, his Mum and Dad because they had seen their first grandchild, and Anna and Timmy because they had returned with the obligatory, fat cheque!

The months passed and progressed and as Sam started to change from childhood to adolescence he became increasingly more informed and aware of the relationship between his parents.

His Mum was oppressed, she worked most days, came home, cleaned, cooked and then had to deal with her husband's moods which seemed directly linked to his *hobby,* as he was well aware by now, how his Dad justified and described his nefarious activities.

His father had grown ever more audacious with his betting exploits, continuing to choose to spend Saturdays in front of the television going red in the face and talking about *Doubles* and

Trebles whilst his mother constantly, always endlessly grafted, scrimped and laboured.

Frankie had even convinced himself that his gambling obsession was now a business and he always had his special, well informed contacts or connections phoning him with some vital information or other.

The irony was for Sam, that where his father was inherently lazy towards the everyday things in life, there was *no river* he wouldn't cross to place the next wager he sought or wanted that brought the flush and rush of blood he so craved and required.

Sam could see more and more how his father's actions upset his mother, but in practical terms there was nothing either of them could do given his parent's blinkered attitude to the compulsion that consumed him and his domineering nature.

Frankie was not a bad man, in many ways he was exceptionally warm and generous but he had a problem he would not face or recognise which was proving to be extremely destructive for himself and his surrounding, dependent family.

Sam came home one night from school to find his mother in tears, a *For Sale* sign in the front garden and the realisation that golf was not the most important issue in the world or even in his forming, as yet, insignificant life.

His father, as he found out, was at the bank and all their futures were in the balance as Frankie negotiated for his life and the very house that they so comfortably lived within.

Thankfully his forceful and gregarious character spilled over to his business persona as he arrived an hour later to inform them that he had re-negotiated his loans and the roof above their heads did not have to be sold after all.

His Mum and Dad had some fearful rows but, as normal, Dorothy eventually submitted or acceded to her husband's demands and ongoing, dictatorial, all powerful control.

It was not until some months afterwards that Sam was made aware that their home had in fact now been signed over to the bank as a guarantee of the family's, for him, unknown various business loans.

The feeling of economic unease that he initially experienced that day stayed with him just as it constantly and so clearly lived with his long, suffering mother.

Life seemed better for a short while, Frankie seemed to concentrate more on his business as Saturdays were temporarily more productive than simply glued to the television but, by the time the summer holidays were upon them once more, the phone calls from his informants had returned to their normal frequency and his yen and addiction was in full flow once again.

As any young boy, Sam did not dwell on things he could do nothing about and as the spring and summer golf season ensued he looked forward to it with real anticipation.

He often had regular games arranged at the golf course and most members were friendly and always interested in his progress.

However, ever more frequently, Sam often ran into the so-called *etiquette* of the club as exercised by many of the senior players, and was frequently lectured on his lowly position as a mere almost unrecognised, unimportant, junior member.

He was often told to wait whilst these older men either, continued through, or then would have to patiently stand and watch as they spent seemingly hours looking for lost balls without the common courtesy or good manners or grace to let him simply carry on ahead.

To his credit he took it all in good part and his own frustrations were relative and minor compared to the indignities suffered by his wondrous teacher who, although extremely valued and popular, was treated extremely disdainfully by so many aged and important committee members of this small, private, privileged hierarchy.

It seemed being an admired and feted professional did not get you very high up the pecking order of respect there!

Sam often watched amazed and open mouthed as some of this ruling group would wait, often irritatedly and impatiently, while Len or one of his assistants would busily try to locate their clubs from the bursting, store room at the back of the decrepit, wooden building.

"I'm off in 5 minutes, Len!"

Mr Beak the Chairman and one of the original founders of the club would often mutter to him sharply and snappily, then on production of his tatty, vintage bag he would then spend the 10 minutes inspecting whether he had gleaned full value for money out of the 50 pence a week, club cleaning service!

Sam silently marvelled at Len Thompson's inexhaustible tolerance and patience, although in the quiet, private moments they sometimes shared, he detected an undercurrent of resentment that was alien to the man's entire disposition and character.

"Bloody Committee…bloody…!"

He once spat out these rare words of anger and frustration into his boiling tea against the senior powers that had just given him a further, demeaning dressing down over some petty, puerile matter or other

"…They couldn't run a *pis…s…*"

He looked then gazed at the boy's wide, blue eyes, half way though his tirade of imminent abuse that gave vent to his feelings then quickly smiled, and immediately came to his senses.

The sun seemed to re-appear then emerge once more from behind the transient, movable, temporary, grey clouds of his scarce and infrequent temper.

"…You know what I mean, Son?"

Sam didn't really of course but he nodded anyway as the old professional returned to his normal good humour, changed the subject and mood as he made his enquiry of him.

"What's your handicap now, Sam?"

His pupil replied proudly.

"17!"

This figure was now an official and not an honorary figure as it had been to begin with; it enabled him to enter all the club competitions and he had decided to play in every one he could, just for the glorious adventure and competitive fun of doing so.

Often at the end of the day when the members had gone home and Sam was waiting for a lift, they would endlessly play together on their favourite, small loop of 3 holes around the turn.

Len had watched the progress of the boy with more than a teacher's passing interest as he took immense satisfaction and pride in seeing the free and uninhibited swing that he had so patiently but lovingly helped to create and fashion.

Late in July, after dedicated playing and practising for months, Sam came to the 12th, the last hole of the stretch of 3, 2 under par; the short hole had hardly a breath of wind or breeze blowing to disturb the serenity of the late, tranquil evening.

The boy selected a 6 iron then slowly but methodically turned and flew the ball high into the bright reds and yellows of the setting sun.

Neither the professional nor the boy could see it land behind the large bunker guarding the left hand side of the green but then heard a lone clap of appreciation from Frankie who had just appeared to collect his son and Len drawled in admiration to his young, playing partner.

"It must be close!"

Len acknowledged the boy's fantastic effort with enthusiasm and vocal encouragement.

"OK…now…. let's see if you can finish it off."

Sam knelt down over the 6 *foot* putt and tried to ignore his small audience or the fact that this was to go 3 under par for 3 holes!

In truth it was some innocuous fun and distraction on a glorious, late summer evening but to the boy it was a lot more than just that!

He kept his head perfectly still, struck the putt clearly then listened until it emphatically *clunked* into the cup as he then screamed and raised his small arms skywards in celebration to take the rapturous applause from the two, amazed, watching spectators.

"Yes…yes…Yes!"

Both father and son drove home with a glowing, burning, sense of euphoria; even late into the darkening night Sam was still replaying in his mind the feeling of incredible pleasure and gratification as that last putt miraculously went down.

His progression through the summer continued apace and he was a regular feature at all the medals and competitions that were now available to him.

He was preparing for the county tournament again and was pleased when he could put 14 against his handicap that seemed just reward for all of the continual sweat and effort he had put in.

Sam realised that he would have to enter the under 16 section of the competition as did Mr Phillips when he signed his entry form and the elder man commented on how the competition was going to be fiercer than the previous year as he counselled him wisely.

"It will be good experience for you…My Lad!"

Sam respectfully ignored his well meaning advice and warning as he had already concluded that the only further *experience* he wanted was a continuation of his previous, winning streak.

On the day of the competition the weather was poor; the sky was full with thick, sticky, dull, oppressive clouds and there was a slow, steady stream of fine rain that threatened to intensify as the day unfolded.

Sam made his acquaintance once again with the ever friendly, distinguished, Mr Earl, the small, neat looking man from the previous year and he thanked him for his initial compliment on the reduction in his handicap then listened as he addressed him further.

"I don't think you'll figure in the gross...Young Man..."

He smiled pragmatically and with the knowledge of previously witnessing so many hungry, eager boys and their unrealistic intentions or dreams of victory.

"...But I wouldn't bet against you for the net...!"

The old gentleman looked at the child's engaged and agitated face while his experienced, blue eyes twinkled with equal amusement and enthusiasm.

"...You might need a pair of flippers though..."

He chortled, glancing pointedly at the increasingly, darkening sky.

"...I think it's going to rain!"

Sam smiled at his joke and after hitting some quick, practice shots in the old net, set in a rusty, corroded, metal frame, he walked down to the 1st tee with his father once again trailing supportively but doggedly behind him.

The course this year was called Olton which Sam had not seen or played before and, as he looked up the extensive par 4, 1st hole, the sky above him turned a worryingly, dark grey then an apocalyptical black and he realised that he was in for a long day.

His first drive found the bunker on the right of the fairway, 3 further shots put him near the edge of the green and a chip then 3 putts left him marking an 8 onto his card.

Frankie looked away as Sam reactively felt the hackles on his back start to bristle and rise; he still had the red mist on the next tee causing the ball to be hooked into some bushes on the left side of the fairway on the equally long and demanding 2nd hole.

A further 8 resulted and, somewhere up the 3rd hole as the rain started to wash and fall in cold, blinding sheets, Frankie began to realise that golf, even junior golf, was not as much fun as he first thought!

To his eternal credit he still valiantly pulled the heavy trolley and watched as his son lost his young, naive game completely, being too unsure and inexperienced to cope with the atrocious, relentless, wet conditions.

Eventually they reached the locker room after the 18 interminable holes of purgatory and Sam felt close to tears.

He was tired, sodden, exhausted then also embarrassed by the huge three figure score on the saturated card in his icy fingers.

He dried himself the best he could then walked bedraggled into the main clubhouse where his fellow competitors were eating or conversing about the rigours and scores of the day.

Sam handed the soaked, crumpled, soggy paper to the small man with white hair who smiled at him most sympathetically as if he understood the boy's abashment, upset and discomfort with his performance.

"It's just a game, Son…"

He whispered to him quietly and with the empathy of having witnessed a thousand, disappointed faces long before he had even met this hopeful, young lad.

"…A hard, uncompromising game and you just have to accept that there's a lot to learn…if you want to succeed."

Frankie was behind his son, heard the sage words of the knowledgeable and well meaning official then spoke equally with real, projected authority.

"Just what I told him myself, Mr Earl..."

He purposefully took and shook the small man's hand and reacquainting himself with him from the previous year's tournament.

"...You just have to learn from your mistakes!"

The man looked at the boy's presumptuous, somewhat boorish father quizzically not being quite sure how to take his exuberant approach and busied himself with the other competitors coming back in.

Sam saw some of the boys from last year and he was relieved to hear that they had all struggled on this devilish, difficult day and his score was not so outstanding in its awfulness.

Frankie informed his son during lunch that he would pick him up later as, in all hidden truth, he was spent and fatigued; Sam therefore continued in the afternoon fighting the wind, rain, his shattered confidence and swing, by himself.

His score marginally improved from the morning and he marvelled at how anyone could play when the endless water soaked your grips, the clubs and even the towel used to dry them was drenched as well.

He changed then as he waited for his Dad to collect him he looked at the large, white, hand written scoreboard carefully being updated and itemised by a plump lady official with striking, orange hair.

He was utterly amazed to see how some of the older boys had completed scores in the mid 70's while Peter McEvoy, one of the county's young up and coming stars had actually knocked it round in the morning in level par 71.

It seemed simply incomprehensible or even impossible to Sam and he fantasised or foolishly imagined that maybe he had missed a couple of holes out on the back 9; or maybe all of them!

Sam also noticed that Paul Sandy had won the under 12's by 25 shots and in fact had beaten his own score by much the same margin.

This infuriated him and he didn't quite know why but it just did; he knew he was not yet good enough to win but he desperately wanted to and it burned his dignity and pride to be beaten so effortlessly or easily by so many.

His father arrived just as the main cup was being presented to Peter McEvoy and Sam watched in wonderment, admiration and secret envy; he too wished, craved and wanted to be presented with something so spectacular and cherished.

He left Olton Golf Club that evening suitably chastened, grounded, better informed, more realistic but strangely more committed than ever to improve and eventually succeed.

Determination was not one of his failings.

The summer faded into autumn, school resumed where the further realities of academic toil and struggle returned to fill Sam's days.

He enjoyed the Grammar School but the endless grind of books mixed with homework was never that appealing and Sam revelled in the weekends when his release and frustration could be expelled or expended on the airy, open spaces of the golf course.

He practised incessantly, on the putting green, the course and ever-naturally the range where the shed was slowly coming nearer and drawing ever closer to his full shots.

However it still remained so frustratingly and tantalisingly far from his vision and dream of the powerfully struck ball soaring then rising into the pale sky as it flew dismissively over it.

Home life was the same, his father meandering in between the continuation of his *obsession*, while his mother working incessantly and interminably both in the shops and at home.

Anna, was still moaning, although mostly now by phone, week in week out she needed money and he was aware of many arguments between his Mum and Dad about what to do for the best.

But Sam was only 13, such things were still so far beyond his control or influence and he contributed what he could unselfishly, and did anything required of him to help.

He worked at the dreaded warehouse then in the shops through the busy, trading periods and his mother noticed how the boy was beginning to make the slow, gradual metamorphosis then gradual transition to early, juvenile manhood.

He was a little stronger, a tad taller; she knew, further to his ever replacing wardrobe, that he suddenly was no longer the small boy that she had nurtured and treasured so much.

The early part of the year brought incessant wind or rain and it was not until late into March that Sam could properly return to the golf club.

He was having yet another lesson with his mentor and the wily professional immediately detected then markedly noticed the actual and physical changes in his most enthusiastic and attentive pupil.

His shots started to have a new length and power for whereas the boy always, swung and struck the ball sweetly, it was clear that he now had the formative tools in his arms and shoulders to make massive strides in his development leading possibly to the reduction of his still substantial handicap.

Len Thompson cooed silently and quietly as another 7 iron whistled cleanly off the shiny face of the club then nestled in a tight group at the small valley down the dip in the practice ground.

He drew in his breath and teasingly smiled, as his elongated arms and long fingers reached out and handed him his driver.

"Have a go with this, Son!"

Sam changed his weapon of attack and tentatively gripped the longer club; it was the one he'd always struggled with as he teed the ball up in anxiety and trepidation, not wishing to disturb the fragile confidence allied to the elegant, smooth rhythm he had just found.

He tensed his left arm, turned then felt the ball connect, unusually perfectly at the base of his swing; he immediately looked up to see the ball was sailing, pitching and flying in a pretty parabola or fashion he'd only vaguely dreamed and imagined up to now.

It landed way over the group of other balls he had hit, bounced up angrily, reared its white head until then, almost at the ultimate limits of the force and power it had been struck or given, rolled and gently hit the unreachable, dark, wooden shed!

The old professional instantly saw the joy and complete disbelief in his pupil's, amazed, energised, young face then laughed softy as he seemed to murmur his thoughts out for all to hear.

"It just show's you, Son... what you can achieve if you want to!"

Sam gasped in his own shock and incredulity at what had just happened so wonderfully but unexpectedly.

"I hit it...I actually hit it!"

In that memorable, single, solitary instant the world became a fraction smaller and nothing any longer seemed impossible.

Sam hit the shed once again before the lesson concluded and shared the joy with his father who warmly congratulated his tutor but Len refused to take any of the credit.

"I once told you, Frankie, that there was no such thing as potential in this game..."

He sighed and wiped his, ever sun kissed, lined and windswept brow.

"...But if there was... your son would have it!"

Sam was elated for days and even managed to plough through his homework with new vigour.

Dorothy was happy because her son was pleased although, in her secret, normal honesty in such matters, she could not really or truly see the delight of the cause for celebration in regards to a small, inert, white ball hitting an old greenkeeper's shed.

Sam's progress at the club was now a revelation; he broke 90 on a regular basis and his handicap quickly reduced to 13 then 12.

He had developed a friendship with most of the members, especially a cheery, silver-haired gentleman who lived locally to him, and they entered most of the doubles tournaments together.

The man would often pick him up then drop him off on the weekends and his assistance was greatly appreciated by both Frankie and

Dorothy who could not fetch and carry Sam all of the time.

The man was called, Joe Derning and he was a Polish immigrant who had come to Britain long ago, just before the Second Wold War.

Sam found that although there was almost a 50 year age gap between them it did not interfere with their relationship either on or off the golf course; they just got on extremely well.

Sam immensely enjoyed the companionship and camaraderie of his always positive and amiable partner and in his company learned about the pleasure of joint competition; it was with him that he won his first ever club competition.

In most of the other tournaments he came close as well but he was disappointed with his performance during the main day of the club championship and net prize, but he was determined as always to quickly improve.

The best player at the club was a man called, Martin Holt; his handicap was 3 and on the big day of the auspicious event, managed to go round his home course only dropping 6 shots in all.

Such ability was still well beyond the capabilities of the younger man as once more he could only applaud and be envious when the sparkling, glinting cup and trophy was awarded.

Sam's annual pilgrimage to the Warwickshire, Junior Open was imminent and he was proud to put 10 against his handicap on the entry form; he was well aware of the junior team that represented the county and it seemed far too much to hope for, that he could somehow manage be a part of it.

He felt at home however when he arrived at Edgbaston Golf Club, a pleasant, short, local parkland course and he happily saw the officials then mingled with his fellow competitors again.

Mr Earl was in his normal, seated, official position, apparently captured as ever by enthusiastic, young boys and masses of score cards, but he promptly gave Sam a meaningful, beaming smile when he saw him.

"10 handicap, Sam…well done."

He glanced at the sky together as if they both instantly recalled the previous year's event in combined amusement then some discomfort and disquiet for Sam as he teased him.

"No storm clouds today, eh!"

Sam smiled, he really liked the small, friendly administrator and was pleased to feel his enthusiasm, warmth, and good humour once more; he remembered the traumas from 12 months before then laughed in camaraderie and good spirits with him

"I hope so...no rain... *please!*"

Sam had played a practice round the previous week, knew something of the venue and he now charted his way most carefully around the tricky front 9.

He had learnt to plot a course out as each hole had been paced for distance and all the possible hazards or dangers had been marked on his small, black notebook that he carried in his back pocket.

On the 10th tee he was only 2 over par and he knew the competition was open for him to make an impression; the next 3 holes were also completed in par when suddenly Sam felt a cloying anxiety inside him that he had never previously experienced.

He was always aware of a potential, good score, the frustration and flash of almost painful anger in a mistake, but never a clawing, growing cancer of steadily building tension.

His teacher's words rang in his fuddled,

muddled head as he looked out from the 13th tee, a 150 yards carry over a large, uninviting lake, *Keep improving, Son, and you'll understand what pressure is!*

Sam tried to relax but he felt his mind struggling to ease then to only focus only upon the small, white ball; his shoulder therefore turned uncomfortably as he swung back while his hands released much too quickly.

Reflexively his pale eyes then jerkily looked up, as if in confirmation and terror of what he already knew, to see his precious ball, hooking viciously into the deep, dark blue of the previously, perfectly flat, spread of water.

He watched in genuine horror as the ripples spread out in a delicate, telltale, concentric pattern as if trying to belittle his efforts while a violent rush of raging temper and fury swelled inside him.

His shaking hand reached for another ball, before that too created mocking, pretty patterns and perfect circles in the smooth, diabolical, still, surface of the previously calm lake.

He only managed to reach the other side of the water by slicing wildly to the right and he left the tee, consumed by his fearful stupidity, banging his club loudly and sharply onto the green, unreceptive, solid, earthen floor as he did so.

A score of 12 finally, then rashly ensued causing further shots to be wasted or lost through his foul temper and temperament until eventually his round was destroyed and the real chance to impress had long since evaporated.

His father sat down with him in the lounge and attempted to be conciliatory, empathetic or understanding as he murmured his words of support, but he was also distressed at what he had witnessed and it reflected in his less than discerning, inspiring comments.

"You just needed to get over that water and lake, Sam…then you would have been OK!"

Sam listened to his ludicrous comments then looked up, stared at his father and held his tongue, realising his frustration had already got him into enough trouble today, but he could not contain a single, brief riposte.

"I wasn't actually….*trying* to hit it in the water!"

His dry, sour mouth bit down unenthusiastically into his cheese sandwich and he tried to eat but his appetite had been diminished, dulled and almost extinguished.

In all honesty he didn't have the maturity to realise that it was not the hole or the single shot that had cost him so dearly; he had experienced a small, diminutive, introduction to the sharp, prickly pressure of competition and he had simply not handled it well.

The scoreboard reflected that again, in his final year in the junior competition, Peter McEvoy, was streets ahead of his peers and contemporaries.

A level par round in the morning was followed by a score of 2 under in the afternoon and Sam was utterly in admiration and awe of him.

It put into perspective his bumbling, foolish vision of actually being in contention and the tension he had felt had all been in his weak and feeble mind; he realised that at no time at all did he ever have the faintest chance of actually winning the competition.

He also noted that Paul Sandy had reached the same handicap as he had, and once again, even though he was far younger, had performed inestimably better that him in the bright, flaming heat of challenge or battle.

Sam was also aware, Paul Sandy had also been asked to join the county, junior squad and his success, allied to his own failure, made it a tart, difficult and bitter pill for him to swallow.

Both Frankie and his son were subdued as they drove away together; Frankie had seen the gulf, the chasm of ability between his son and the leading players in the county making him leave the prestigious, golf club with a clear dose of pragmatism and reality.

At this stage of Sam's development, Frankie's goals were simple, the enjoyment and well being of his son as maturely he tried to take it all in his stride.

Sam's intention was something else, more of a dream than an ambition, a fantasy known only to the inner reaches of his mind, but surely every young boy was entitled to that!

However the growing man's disappointment did not dampen his enthusiasm for too long as, the endless beauty of sport in general and golf in particular seemed to be, that tomorrow was always another day where possibly anything could happen!

Sam therefore was sanguine, threw himself into his remaining club competitions with unremitting zeal and by the end of the year was teetering on the edges and brink of a single figure handicap.

Chapter 3

Time evolved then span, the regular, busy year had passed and it was Sam's birthday, just a few weeks before Christmas.

It meant that he was now 14 years old and, as he looked out at the thick snow falling in soft, silent, effortless motions, making the garden so incredibly, perfectly clean and white, he privately contemplated another coming year.

Could he actually and finally make the transition to single figures? It seemed many months had passed and it was still a daunting task!

He had learned already that golf was a series of stages, each seemingly and progressively more difficult and unrelenting than the last.

He could visualise himself playing off 9 or even 7 but further than that?

Beyond was the far off, difficult country of low, single figure golf and such an accomplishment seemed so incredibly distant and unachievable.

He childishly wished his life away, longing for the pale curse of winter to depart and for the return of the spring, when he could resume his burning quest for adventure and improvement.

The shops and the warehouse still commanded his time; his mother, as normal was working unrelentingly and his father driving agitatedly about giving instructions to whoever would listen.

Sam still had his waits outside the betting offices, experienced the variety of his father's moods or occasionally watched him worryingly close up as he sat with his face, blood red and his eyes bulging wide, literally hypnotised by the television, as he tried to encourage or will his latest, financial favourite home.

Or not, which was far more usual and uncomfortable for them both!

Sam hated and detested the horses, simply abhorred his father's addiction as it insidiously corrupted everything he held so precious and dear; specifically his father's normal, good temper, bright humour and especially his mother's peace of mind!

Most of all, his mother's peace of mind!

He saw the unease constantly and always in her brown, sparkling but troubled eyes; the sadness or frustration as she fought against his father's cursed *obsession* and how it seemed to continually undermine her extraordinary efforts.

His mother was a contradiction, a person of immense courage and determination, yet incapable of standing up to her husband, but there again, Sam had seen very few people that could stand up to his ever dominant and challenging father!

The festive season came and went; Anna was pregnant with her second child, moaning once more while her hopeless husband was unemployed or unemployable yet again.

Sam seemed to feel whatever small profit the business may have made in their combined labours and endeavours, continually departed with Anna and her spouse down to London.

It was unfair, but his father, as normal seemingly knew best; he explained his unique, generous perspective on their family life or obligations and informed him with incredible pathos and simplicity.

"Their need is greater, Son…we'll be OK!"

Sam as always was unconvinced by his father's logic although from his perspective it had always been and would always forever be like this; it was as if his parent failed to see the obvious even though he always insisted that he did!

Then one unforgettable night he overheard a suggestion, in discussion between his parents before he went to bed, that perhaps Anna and her husband should come to Moseley where then Frankie would take them into the business and show them how to make money!

Sam shook his head in disbelief as if he had misheard or misunderstood; even his Dad couldn't be that ludicrously, outrageously crazy!

But his father proved him wrong as he indeed was that insane and, unbelievably by March, his sister and her layabout partner had been entrenched in the small, questionable, tiny, dangerously, fiscally balanced, honey pot of the family business.

A house was bought for them and many evenings were spent around the family's electric fire listening to Frankie pontificate about how they were all going to expand his growing, business empire.

Sam, on these occasions only looked at his mother; the worry was etched in her face, her daughter's growing womb, more bills, loans, overdrafts; yet further, endless responsibility!

He felt her unspoken prayer and desire to scream, to stop, stop! Couldn't they just stop and lead an ordinary, small life.

A quiet life!

But her husband, Frankie wasn't destined for a small, insignificant existence; he had a design, always seemed to have a plan and Sam listened, almost palpably feeling the family tension, simply unsure whether his father really and truly was the business guru or genius he purported himself to be.

But he had no control and he often found separation or resolution in the calm, peace and tranquillity of the golf course; the greenery was always soothing, the walk and effort refreshing as it was often a refuge, away from any family turmoil and strife.

He was becoming larger and older; he had broadened further from the previous year and Len Thompson would watch him strike the ball with increasing authority and maturity.

Early medal scores reduced his handicap to 9, single figures for the first time; he felt proud and noticed even his fellow members looked at him with a new, sometimes grudging, respect or admiration.

Sam participated in all the club competitions,

suddenly finding that he was starting to play at a different, competitive level to his weekend opposition and general everyday members.

He moved effortlessly through most rounds, struggling only occasionally when confronting someone of an undeserved, high handicap.

Before the club championship his father warned the competition committee of his son's rapid improvement; he had been on the verge of many level par scores, but had had various, minor disasters that had prevented his handicap from being cut further.

Frankie considered that he was being thoughtful, not *boastful* as he sounded; he told the relevant members that his son's handicap should be reduced on general play but they were not moved with his bluster, entreaties or admonishments.

They were not impressed with his boasting and bragging, that was until Sam went round the 36 holes dropping only 7 shots in total!

He had won the net tournament by 10 shots and was a mere couple of shots behind the gross winner once again of Martin Holt!

The champion immediately came over to Sam as he was clearly happy and relieved to have prevailed; he was a slim, tall man, thinning on top but with a ruddy, round, happy, face and he grasped Sam's hand enthusiastically.

"Well done, Sam… what a great performance, I don't think I'll be so lucky next year."

Sam accepted his congratulation then watched the informal presentation trying not to once more covet the gleaming, silver cup that represented the main championship he wanted so badly.

But he had won the net event and the physical prize was even larger than the other trophy as if to make up for the diminished value Sam thought it represented against the more difficult competition.

Sam was now off a 6 handicap; he noticed that there were many junior competitions that he was now eligible for and he started to enter the local events that his father could drop him to relatively easily.

However this handicap he found difficult to play to and his competitive schedule yielded little success either in gross or net honours.

He started to recognise the boys that he'd seen over the previous years at the county junior events and developed a friendly banter and rivalry with them.

Paul Sandy played some of these tournaments as well intermittently; invariably he was always in the first three places and he was now off a 5 handicap, already a stroke lower than Sam's!

Privately and to be honest, he didn't much like Paul Sandy; he felt he was arrogant, superior, stand offish and worse of all he seemed a better golfer than he was!

The county junior competition was held earlier this year and on this occasion when Sam arrived he felt more like part of the bustling, energised, local golfing scene.

Mr Earl welcomed him as normal, congratulated him on his handicap improvement once again, as if it was a special annual happening, and they chatted briefly about his continuing development.

Sam sat down with some of the boys and nodded at Paul Sandy; neither of them was expected to win but there seemed always strangely an undisclosed, personal battle between them.

Peter McEvoy was too old for the competition now and his departure made all the other challengers now feel they were in with a chance to take the title.

Martin Biddle was the favourite; he was a

popular, short, sturdy youth, with a mass of curly, brown hair and stocky shoulders that seemed to propel the ball vast and incredible distances.

He was off scratch, but he was not unique in this vaunted competition.

Warwickshire had an abundance of low handicap, young, enthusiastic golfers and Sam felt privileged that his efforts had placed him in such exalted company.

Robin Hood golf course was the venue for the event and Sam's new strength and maturity enabled him to finish with two respectable, competent but unremarkable rounds.

He dropped 12 shots on the day but was thrilled to see his name in the upper echelons of the score board; he finished 12th in all and his only disappointment was that once again his nemesis had finished four places higher.

A tall youth with cropped, dark hair called, Andrew Carmen won the competition with a score of 2 over par and smiled ecstatically when he collected the gleaming, glistening, silver trophy.

Sam however was encouraged and very pleased, especially when Mr Earl informed him he was actually being considered for the county junior team.

The boy knew that this group was to represent Warwickshire in an annual junior competition between four, local counties and he desperately wanted to be part of it; to actually play for the county surely it would be a privilege and an initial, dream come true!

He received a letter about a week afterwards but his heart sank with disappointment as it informed him that he was unfortunately only to be first reserve.

The competition was to be in a fortnight and if anyone dropped out he would be called upon.

Paul Sandy was already in the team however meaning Sam tried as best he could to be understanding, pragmatic and hide his envy; he concentrated on his work, his school, his golf and tried to improve, he always tried so desperately to improve!

The call came through on the Friday before the *Four Counties* tournament was due to begin next day, that Peter Davis had called in sick and Sam was incredibly and excitingly in the Warwickshire team.

Frankie drove him the following morning to Kings Norton golf course where Sam pottered around excitedly on the putting green, killing time just waiting for his fellow county team mates to arrive.

Martin Biddle, the energetic, junior captain suddenly strode over to him and shook his hand enthusiastically and encouragingly.

"Well done, Sam…delighted you're with us… I wanted you in the team straight away!"

Sam looked directly at the youth and he could see immediately why he was so visibly popular with everyone.

Martin Biddle had a happy, slightly freckled, friendly face; he always seemed to be smiling, his good humour and enthusiasm was infectious and undoubtedly he was a perfect captain and leader for any team.

The other boys soon arrived and after the short, opening ceremony the trial and test of everyone's competitive abilities then began, as it was to be all singles matches.

Sam was to play game number 8, the last game out; he was seen as the weakest player, the other boys being older, more battle hardened and mostly off lower handicaps.

The nervous young boy had never played match play at this level before and as he watched each game tee off he felt more and more anxious and agitated.

However finally his minute and turn arrived; he shook hands purposefully with his adversary then, having the honour, proceeded to slice his ball wildly into a deep bunker on the right.

His opponent was calmer and more experienced; he quickly proceeded to be 3 up after only 5 holes while the newly blooded, Sam continued to stress or struggle.

He had never had an experience like this, as just by his nature he always wanted to win, but never quite like this!

Sam had never experienced internal fire *like this*!

3 down felt like a sharp, twisting dagger inside him and he suddenly hated his opponent, an innocuous, small, friendly boy with glasses; he then found a determination and grit inside him he never even realised he possessed.

Every shot, every single hole was now incredibly intense, his face was concentrated, thunderous and although he was not playing well he fought then battled until he eventually came back and ultimately vanquished his opponent.

He won 2 up and was applauded by his team

crowded around the final green; he felt drained, tired but elated as well and the lunch of fish and chips had never tasted so refreshingly or mouth-wateringly good to him.

His side had beaten Staffordshire, in the morning 6 to 2 and they had Worcestershire after their break.

Sam enjoyed and thrilled to the camaraderie, the heightened environment and heat of raw conflict but also he liked winning; Sam truly loved winning best of all!

His father joined him in the afternoon and watched as his son, encouraged by his morning triumph, found a rich vein of form then won comfortably by 5 and 4.

His captain congratulated him again, his team had triumphed one more and Sam went home overwhelmed with emotion as it seemed that there were simply no words to describe his boundless jubilation.

Dorothy welcomed her men home as always and instantly noticed that her son was ecstatic but strained; he looked drawn, ashen and not his normal effervescent self, causing her to question him concernedly.

"What's the matter, Sam?"

Frankie snapped at her icily and rudely.

"Leave the boy alone, Dorothy...he's had a great day, he's the hero of the team; won both his matches!"

Sam's mother bit her lip and said nothing further, fed her child and concerned herself only with his wellbeing.

She listened to his tales of victory with an interest and a false glee she did not truly feel but seeing the delight in both her husband and child let her unease lie dormant.

The following day both father and son were up early and when they reached the golf course Sam went to the practice range to hit some balls in preparation for the day.

Frankie watched the smooth slow rhythm of his son then furtively compared him to the other boys; he used his trained, keen eye for sport, talent or form and was increasingly assured and confident that his runner was indeed a special *thoroughbred*.

Sam was out last again but he did not mind, it was a position of importance as his result could, change the match, but today it would not matter.

Warwickshire had won the competition before

Sam sunk his 5 *foot* put on the 17th hole for a 2 and 1 win and his third victory.

His team-members were joyfully celebrating on sugary drinks and sandwiches and he was a vital element and piece of it; he was part of a winning team!

At the presentation ceremony shortly afterwards he collected his small, cast, bronze medal as if it were an official decoration of honour, of courage and of course of triumph!

He said his goodbyes to his compatriots as if they were now all old friends; they had tasted success together and forever after, he felt they would be allies and companions.

This was all except Paul Sandy, even in victory he was still aloof, his red hair, freckles, blue eyes and apparent innocence, belied a passion that ran deep; it was far too deep for mere friendship!

Sam was thrilled for days, his name was in the small print in the local paper and he proudly cut out the clipping and stuck it into a large, red scrapbook purchased by his father, who was sure this was just the start of his son's ongoing successes.

The experience inspired Sam to even greater efforts, more competitions, further practice resulting, by the end of the season, his handicap was unsurprisingly improved and down to 5.

His progress at his school however was less spectacular; he was not truly focussed on his educational studies and in many ways did not fully appreciate how it could shape his future.

Frankie also was not overly concerned with academia, he had done well without it and school was just an unimportant stepping stone before starting work; Sam could always be involved in the business or get a job!

In Frankie's universe and within his worldly experience it really wasn't all that important.

As normal Dorothy watched on helpless, her voice lost, strangled by the overpowering, dominant character of her husband.

She so wanted do discuss her son's future, school, university, but night after night they talked of nothing but golf, golf and of course the accursed business!

Anna had her second child during November when Sam assumed then presumed that such an important event would finish her questionable contribution to the business and workload forever!

As if he was a psychic, although in all honesty the impending fact was not that hard to see, sure enough his sister's, brief interlude in helping in the family enterprise was pretty much quickly, already extinguished.

However she now needed more bedrooms and space and Frankie had the answer; he always had the solution to every problem!

He re-financed, yet again, borrowed a little more and bought his *precious*, precocious daughter and wasteful son in law a house far bigger and more expensive that his own!

Sam was no expert on business but even he could see that Timmy was surely a revelation; each part of the business he went into lost money and in keeping with his father's, illogical, perverse judgement, the less he seemed to produce the more reward was provided for his emerging family.

The results of this disparity was that Sam's obligations to the burden of labour increased and as normal his Dad explained that he should accept how things were; how they had always been for as long as he could remember!

"We've got to help your sister; her need now with the children is so much greater!"

Sam blanched and kept silent, nothing ever seemed to change concerning his sibling, while he felt the seeds of impending disaster and catastrophe sown in those few months, as though at his immature, fragile age he had laid and thrown them about himself.

After school and during all holidays, Sam would work in the expanding empire - three shops now - or the warehouse and although he disliked the labour and obligations he gave his best endeavours, as always.

He was needed and always gave his maximum effort.

Christmas gave him a small reward, a net that his father had suspended up in the garage and hour after hour in the, cold, wet misery of the winter months Sam would hit balls into it.

Frankie had noticed that all sportsmen were incredibly fit and he encouraged, cajoled, even bullied his son to start running; Sam sometimes had a tendency to be a little chubby and Frankie knew from his *side business* and *hobby* that ultimately only the sleekest, leanest horse won the races!

So Sam started to jog, around the block at first and once he had started his father chastised him if he missed a session and he made it clear how vitally important it was; in truth, it was important to Frankie!

Sam still went to the golf club at weekends and even if he couldn't play all of the time because of the unpredictable or often appalling weather, loved to be in the environment and company of his exuberant teacher.

To his amazement and excitement one bleak day, Len asked him if he wanted to play in the *Sunningdale Foursomes*, a mixed professional and amateur event that commenced each golf season and Sam looked at him as though he was mad.

"Really... do you think I'm good enough?"

His tutor smiled and teased him.

"It's only a friendly game, Son, just a bit of fun... if your father will let you go...? It would be my pleasure and...give me a break?"

Not unexpectedly, Frankie was more than happy to give permission; he was aware that this competition contained some tour professional golfers and understood that it would be wonderful experience for the future of his boy.

His teacher sent the entry form off in February, after which time, Sam watched the time and the days pass until the end of March when the week of the tournament commenced.

Frankie dropped his son at the club early on the appropriate, grey, cloudy morning and after filling Len's antiquated, Rover car with assorted clubs, bags and shoes the intrepid travellers, departed for the southern roads leading down to Ascot, Berkshire.

Sam has never been on such a long journey and as he watched his teacher nervously negotiating the busy, occasionally narrow routes or the endless roundabouts, he wondered if his driver had either!

Len grimaced at the queues: the road works: the troubling fact that only a cone occasionally separated his vehicle from the oncoming traffic and nervously shifted the old, almost classic car through the gears continually through their expedition.

Sam noticed that instead of a normal black, plastic, gear knob Len had a silver, golf ball cover and he watched fascinated as the round, shiny object was manipulated up and down the mechanism, propelling the car forward then slowing them down as necessary.

They arrived at the course, much to Sam's relief about 11a.m and, after his tutor had signed them in, they drifted over to the practice range to hit some shots before their game at

1p.m.

Sam tried to concentrate on his preparation but was swept up in the excitement of the occasion; everywhere there were people, matches were coming up the 18th, shaking hands, winning, losing and he thought it was just an electrifying, exhilarating atmosphere.

Their match started half an hour late; a couple of games had run to extra holes and Sam bit his lip impatiently only anxious to be off and into the blazing, latent heat of battle.

He had the honour and looked at his teacher in dismay after he had hurriedly, anxiously scuttled the ball only a hundred yards left toward a mass of bushes, and Len just smiled dryly at his pupil's apologies and patent anxiety.

"There's a long way to go, Son, nay worry…relax!"

The opposition was a rotund professional from a nearby course and a tall, young amateur, with glasses and straight, fair hair who was off a 2 handicap and from the same club.

After customarily, politely shaking hands on the 1st tee, no one had spoken; it was conflict, combat, serious scratch competition, as Sam fretted, fumed and railed at being 2 down at the turn.

His tutor was playing well though, his long, wristy, rhythmical swing effortlessly guiding the ball skilfully, with experience and guile around the tree-lined fairways.

Sam was less effective, struggling to cope with both the course and the new, senior experience but the match actually turned on his efforts on the 14th hole; they were still 2 down when Sam unexpectedly held a snaking *25 foot* from way across the green.

He raised his arms in joy, his frustration released and as if undermined by the eager, young man's effort and persistence, their opponents faltered and eventually lost the game 2 and 1.

The four of them shook hands and Sam held the vast, expansive palm of his teacher warmly as he smiled and congratulated him.

"Well done, Son…you played well."

The young boy was elated and, as the gloom of evening gathered around them, he gently asked his mentor a pertinent question.

"Doesn't this mean we have to stay?"

Len responded and chuckled in response to his

obvious question.

"Aye, Son...aye, and..."

His velvet Irish brogue was in full flow.

"...If I'd a thought we were goin' to *bloomin'* win I'd have booked us into some accommodation!"

They reported back to the recorder; their next match was at 10.30a.m in the morning and they drove down the bustling, main road and soon found a small, local hotel.

Sam phoned his father with the news and after a brief chat, then a quick wash, he met Len in the dining room for dinner and told him something he already knew.

"Dad was pleased!"

The food tasted sweet to him, victory was undoubtedly, succulent and delicious; he simply revelled in both the environment, surroundings and having the gentle charm of his mentor selfishly all to himself.

Len told the boy in more detail about Ireland and his youth; his decision to come to England and about the incredibly difficult and short putt he had to hole as a teenager at a local tournament to be sure of eating that particular night.

He described what happened as only he could.

"Now that was pressure, Son, *6 foot...* left to right without a bean in my pocket!"

The innocent boy's eyes bulged and widened and he wondered in genuine amazement how could anyone hole a putt like that under those extreme circumstances?

Sam admired the man greatly, it had meant so much to him to win with Len at his side and he dreamt of success the following day but unfortunately, he was too overwhelmed, their opponents a little too good, and they ultimately surrendered 3 and 2.

Sam tried to be disappointed but, as he felt the old car take them home, he realised how much he had revelled and enjoyed the experience and the time spent with his teacher and friend, Len Thompson.

It had been extraordinary and memorable.

The older man was quiet on the return journey; secretly he was pleased to have lost, the competition was time, time was money and he had a family to support.

He looked surreptitiously at the young man who was drifting in and out of sleep intermittently, his brown hair cascading over his forehead and he mused then thought upon how he played the game so intently.

He could see the boy had ability and the desire to succeed possibly, even as a professional; but he also knew that there was a lot more to golf success than just that!

Frankie picked his son up from Len's house and thanked him for his efforts as Len smiled at him barely being able to disguise his obvious fatigue.

"It was a pleasure...he's a, Good Lad, I think he enjoyed it!"

Sam certainly had as he gushingly then endlessly told his Mum and Dad all about it; he had seen Peter Allis and countless famous, professional golfers his parents had never even heard of.

Frankie was pleased for his son and how the experience would help for his emerging future while Dorothy was just genuinely thrilled that her boy returned looking so vibrant, happy and well.

Chapter 4

Sam's golfing season now stretched before him; he had been enthused and encouraged by his adventure with Mr Thompson and subsequently applied himself with ongoing vigour and effort in his endless efforts to improve.

However he noticed ever more that a low single figure handicap was now a hard taskmaster, a slip or an error always resulted in a score above his par and he spent many fruitless months playing in all sorts of tournaments without much success whatsoever.

He could now enter both the junior and senior county competitions and although he was pleased to see all his companions, his performances were uninspiring, patchy and distinctly and disappointingly average as another junior county title evaded him on the appointed day.

Worse, was that Paul Sandy was runner up for the championship and had performed well in the senior competition; he had actually been asked to play for the county senior side!

It seemed unbelievable at his junior, tender

age!

Sam was asked to play in the *Four Counties* junior event but was again placed behind his rival in the pecking order!

Although he won all his matches and the team grasped the tournament once again, his small, delicate, bronze medal did not seem to hold the same magnetic value as the previous year.

He read golf books avidly trying any avenue to find the magic swing, tip or formula that would progress, his game, to the next level.

He was bought, Ben Hogan's famous book of the *Five Modern Fundamental's of Golf* and he read it, looked at the diagrams, the pictures but was utterly confounded and confused.

It was a description of a game he did not recognise, he understood about the grip but the section on the swing plane, the door opening and closing, the sheer scale and *feel* of it, it was beyond his comprehension or understanding.

He read the information again then looked endlessly at the diagrams; the emotive, fantastical, wonderful drawing of the turn, the position of the hands, the shoulders but even in detailed and fantastic transposed form the solution for him personally was a mystery as he eventually discarded the book in pure frustration.

The game after all was simple to Sam, straight, left arm, turn your shoulders and focus, concentrate hard, will the ball into the hole; that's what had brought him success and after all, what did Ben Hogan know anyway!

The whole year to Sam just contained cruel disappointment; tournament after tournament his small, fragile handicap was a weight around his neck, teasing him, frustrating him until his patience was worn so very fine and thin sometimes almost before he had started to play.

His lessons with his mentor were becoming equally unsatisfactory; the previous joy of hitting the elusive shed was a distant almost childish and transient memory by now.

He only wanted to fly the ball over it at this stage; shot after shot, controlled, with the ball sternly under his will and power.

Endlessly Sam looked at his inspiration and teacher with a raging, unspoken frustration as he murmured only to himself.

"Why…Why, can't I improve?"

Len however seemed to hear him, almost

physically feel his rage and yearning; he tried to smile and be casual but the child's impatience was insidious, infectious and unsettling even for him, as he tried to placate or pacify him.

"It takes time, Son... lots of time and struggle and even then..."

Sam only looked at him tortuously, weakly, needfully and spoke silently into his tumult and turmoil of a driven, difficult mind.

"Tell me the magic swing, the perfect swing, something that works all the time, repeats. Tell Me, Tell me!"

The voices, questions, complaints exploded endlessly in his brain, but he did not utter them; Len taught him to the best of his ability, of what he knew, it had always been enough, enough for him!

They walked off the practice ground one afternoon and somewhere in the environment of the old professional shop, Sam and his teacher regained their respective composure as the experienced man murmured to him evocatively.

"Sam, you're only, 15... doing well, just try to relax take it easy, it'll come to you..."

The boy sipped his tea then tried to be calm and listen as his teacher continued.

"...Golf's not everything...have some fun, do your schoolwork, anything, just don't get so uptight...it's not good for you!"

He looked at the large man sadly as if recognising his immaturity mixed with his insatiable desire and longing to improve.

"I try...but I just get so annoyed... it's..."

He patted his growing and expanding chest.

"...Like a fire here...it burns me, I get so frustrated when I put all my effort in... for nothing!"

Len Thompson laughed softly then counselled him wisely.

"But life's like that; you've got to learn to be patient and let it evolve naturally!"

Sam looked at him then nodded in full agreement and in that insightful second and instant was determined not to be annoyed, frustrated or intolerant any longer.

He resolved and promised that he would in future remain in control of himself and volatile temper but good intentions lasted until his next medal round when he left the 7th hole with an infuriating 8 after being level par after 6!

His putter then winged and flew its way along the ground where it hit a stump of a tree and broke instantly into two, useless, silver, shimmering pieces!

Dorothy increasingly had noticed Sam's changing demeanour; he was less sunny, the child with the innocent, willing, smile, was disappearing and the youth he was growing into was far too serious, or more uncomfortably for her, even surly!

She mentioned the fact to Frankie, who was dismissive of her as always.

"It's just a phase…all kids go through it."

She spoke of her concerns however although she knew she was treading on dangerous ground with her husband.

"It's the golf…it's making him depressed!"

Frankie turned on her; his eyes spiked and sparked with anger and screamed in pure, cruel, bad temper.

"You're so stupid…the boy loves his golf, he…"

He was searching for the correct descriptive

word but his own missed education during the war years had not provided him with much of an English vocabulary.

"...He ...needs it....it's just a phase, keep your silly, ridiculous opinions to yourself!"

Dorothy sat silent as her heart told her that she was indeed correct, but she also knew how much her son loved his golf; her head thought then mused, secretly and introspectively on how something you love so much could bring you so much hidden pain and aggravation?

Ironically Dorothy looked directly at her flushed and agitated husband; heard in her head the coarse, disrespectful way he had spoken to her and smiled ruefully at her own rhetorical question.

She understood exactly and perfectly how something *she* loved so incredibly brought her similar if not equal discomfort!

The year was nearly spent; Sam had reconciled himself to the fact that his handicap and golf had this season defeated him as he continued diligently with his education and general work in the business.

His family obligations to the so called, *Empire* were growing almost exponentially and this ongoing but continuous burden was a constant bind, grind and sore to him.

Anna didn't do anything apart from some occasional duties whilst Timmy worked but produced actually less; his father seemed to give lots of orders and his mother...his mother worked for simply everyone, morning, night and day!

She was an incomparable revelation and almost sainted in her unselfish and altruistic ways; she simply never took, asked or wanted anything for herself!

The shops seemed busy to him, they were always taking money, but Anna had a large house, her two children suddenly *needed* to attend private school and as Sam began to understand what pressure meant at golf, he began to sense and feel the strain of his life as well.

His mother always looked worried, there were numerous arguments in the house between his parents and his father always won; he shouted loudest, was the most stubborn and was undoubtedly King in his domain.

Frankie's *hobby* or *affliction* was also a part of everyday existence and as Sam progressed towards adulthood he made no attempt to hide his gambling compulsion; it was no addiction to Frankie, he had a system, he always had a scheme or a plan, he was in his own eyes, a winner!

Christmas came then went; another year and another shop to run and care for like some demanding, screaming, temperamental child.

This one was a full hour's drive away and Sam felt his mother's angst or raw anguish as if it was his own.

He knew full well by now the house was guaranteed to the bank and all the extra shops meant even more work for her.

His father could find the locations for trading; even agree brilliant, commercial deals on them but, like vulnerable babies, they all needed extraordinary, constant nurturing, and attention!

Frankie's analysis and answers to any question were always the same.

"Well, Anna will help!"

Sam, when he listened, tried to smile but his good humour towards his sister and brother in law, if it ever existed at all, was already a long gone, distant memory.

Sam took the bus to the golf course as much as he could but irritatingly, in the first few months of the New Year, it always seemed to be saturated and utterly water logged.

Len Thompson did not ask him to play in the Sunningdale Foursomes this year and Sam remembered the cones, so dangerously alone in the central reservation that had made his teacher so anxious, nervous and maturely understood why.

Len was needed here; he had a family and his own responsibilities and perhaps the roads to Ascot were treacherous after all!

Early in March, late one quiet, peaceful afternoon when the rain and wind had stopped and the abandoned course was neglected, the low, bright sun suddenly came out.

It reflected on the rich greenery causing the ground to glisten and shimmer; it was an intoxicating sight and Sam was magnetically drawn to the deserted practice area where the small green shed shone out to him like a glistening beacon or torch.

He was completely alone, the quietness and stillness of his surrounding was almost spiritual and he breathed in the clean, damp, warm air with zeal and relish.

Sam had brought some balls and his driver with him; he then swung the club, feeling and hearing the emotive *swish* in the vacuum of the afternoon, as he propelled the glittering shaft back and forward in perfect motion and timing.

He placed one of the balls on a new, white tee and stood back looking at the shed again; its wet roof, shining powerfully, literally glowing from the resplendent, glinting, sun's rays.

His body settled on the ball feeling the strength and power that it now contained; his arms and legs were strong from practice or running and he felt undeniably athletic and alive.

Sam followed his swing routine, straight left arm, turn, release and felt the ball explode off his club and looked up to see the small, white object clear the familiar, increasingly friendly shed and disappear into the shining, shimmering greenery beyond.

His lips drew and curled in dry satisfaction, it wasn't quite as in his dream but it was nearly as good!

He was bigger, fitter and better than he had been before and was sensing or even sure that this year things were going to be different!

From the first medal round Sam felt and saw his improvement, his shots were longer, more controlled and although he didn't break his handicap he began to feel it was within his capabilities.

The early tournaments came and went; still no breakthrough then suddenly as if in a rush in June, Sam had a sparkling three weeks of form and his handicap reduced to 3, becoming directly under the county's jurisdiction for such rare people that played golf to that level!

Sam had performed well in the junior open, coming fourth and then the senior county open where he broke into the top 10 final scores; the junior side won the *Four Counties* yet again with Sam playing number 2!

Paul Sandy's progress however was superior and more spectacular; he played number 1 for the juniors, won the junior event - the youngest ever winner - and was tied 3rd in the senior county competition!

Sam however was pleased, he had been even been asked to play for the county's senior second team and his new handicap gave him the opportunity of entering nearly all the national, senior amateur tournaments.

Leisurely he sat with his father late one night in early July with various entry forms discussing his possible, tournament schedule; he was too late for the English Amateur this year and went to discard the detailed entrance paper as his paternal parent queried him.

"When's the closing date?"

Sam looked and inspected the form closely.

"In two days…we'll never get it there in time."

His Dad smiled as if once again he could do the impossible.

"Fill it in, Sam, we'll see."

His son did as requested and gave it to his father who, to his amazement took it up to the golf club the following day for the secretary's signature; then proceeded, with his mother to drive the two hundred miles to the heart of Lincolnshire to deliver it personally to the organisers of the event.

Frankie was nothing if not resilient and resourceful.

They arrived home late, tired from their journey and trek as the man smiled at his son then spoke with boundless self-satisfaction.

"You're in…you're in the, English, Amateur Championship!"

Sam was elated and waited impatiently for the starting times to arrive when he was eventually thrilled to see his name printed in the elegant document that detailed the matches to be played.

He was to play P. Wingfield, in the 1st round and he felt his stomach wrench into a small, tight reactive knot as he anticipated the excitement of competing in such an auspicious and prestigious event.

It was hard for Sam to concentrate on his club golf or the local tournaments although he continued to compete well, but they seemed so trivial and insignificant somehow next to his forthcoming, national test to come.

However the time as always, inevitably arrived and he left with his father for the long drive to Woodhall-Spa golf club, set deep in the country heart of Lincolnshire.

The journey took them, many hours and they arrived late afternoon; Sam was due to play his initial match at 9a.m the following morning.

They booked into the best hotel - no bed and breakfast for Frankie - then went to the course; the competition had already begun and Sam looked around at all the golfing hustle and bustle in fascination and utter wonderment.

It was all so impossible and incredibly exciting!

He pulled himself together quickly however and he reflected that he wasn't there to be impressed; he was there to compete, to win and he followed a couple of the ongoing matches and paced the whole course out so he knew the distances for the following day.

He noticed when he looked on the massive score board that some of his county comrades had won their first round matches and he went to bed that night dedicated and determined to follow their example and lead.

He awoke early, was wildly excited and pressed his father slumbering in the bed beside him who's incessant snoring had kept him up intermittently; but in all truth and honesty his mind was extremely agitated and active anyway!

He shook his sleepy parent playfully.

"Come on, Dad, I need to hit some balls!"

Sam rushed breakfast and they were soon on the busy, practice range where seemingly hundreds of enthusiastic golfers were honing their abilities and talents for the coming battles ahead.

Frankie saw the pandemonium and picked up Sam's, small, red, bag, emptied the balls on to the green, peat turf and stood down, but to the side of the narrow, practice fairway as a target for his son.

Sam went through the bag professionally, starting with his wedge and progressing through to a couple of rhythmical, long drives.

The turf was perfect for golf, it was peat, spongy but firm, and happily, Sam sensed he was in form.

His father brought him his balls back in the bright, garish, practice bag, relieved to have escaped from the melee of small, white, airborne projectiles that were dangerously flying about everywhere!

Finally the enthused, young man waited excitedly by the flat, mown, 1st tee for his match to begin.

The starter was a tall, thin dapperly dressed gentleman with a large, bright rosette with the words *official* on it and he announced the game in an elegant, perfectly clear, English accent.

"On the tee, match 75… P Wingfield and S Chester!"

Sam walked confidently onto the immaculately, trimmed, driving area and shook hands with his opponent; he was middle aged, plump with grey hair that was brushed down flat.

He smiled at Sam, but the youth did not respond as he felt in all reality this was war.

The youth strangely hated his opposition, who's only purpose in being there was to be defeated as he felt his determination well and swell up somewhere deeply inside him!

Sam looked at his caddie; his father had employed an innocuous almost miniature, local man whose nickname was ironically, *Tiny*.

He *was* undoubtedly petite and small but had informed them that he had local knowledge, something that Frankie thought may come in extremely useful around the testing, parkland course.

The greens were perfect, but subtly infuriating, like sheet glass or marble, and on either side of the lush green fairways there was thick, wiry heather that was there only to consume balls and frustrate everyone playing.

However, Sam, for the first time in his life actually felt like a professional golfer in such an important event; he watched his opponent's smooth rhythm propel the ball into the middle of the fairway and then took his turn.

He balanced and watched his effort catch the bunker on the right of the fairway then grimaced; but they were off, enabling him to walk out purposefully and as confidently as he could.

His diminutive caddy and his father were following him directly and close behind as though they were his own private entourage.

When he reached his ball he found that the bunker was flat with the sand, clean and fine; his teasing, white sphere sat up well and he contacted it sweetly but then watched it disappear into yet another the bunker by the side of the green.

His opponent nestled his 9 iron, *10 feet* from the hole and Sam knew he had to, at worst, get down in 2 from the bunker.

But he liked the sand as it was so incredibly, silky smooth and felt so perfect and luxuriously good beneath his feet.

His hands expertly splashed out to *6 foot*, watched his opponent miss and then rolled his putt perfectly in for a half and clenched his fist as if he had already found the higher ground of advantage.

However the early holes were fairly even when suddenly the older man held a couple of putts and at the 9 holes turn, Sam was suddenly and smartingly, 3 down!

His pale, blue eyes stared and glared as he saw his opponent whisper something that he presumed to be disrespectful about him, to his plump, blonde wife caddying for him!

The man appeared so happy, smug and very self satisfied that he was beating his young opponent and Sam's fire of single combat blazed, roared and raged within him.

He stood on the 10th tee, his face set grim with determination, hit the green in 2 and looked at his *30 foot* putt with ferocious intensity.

In almost hypnotic concentration he held his head down, not looking at the ball's progress until it had been firmly rapped and long left the club, as his mind simply raced, *Get in*! Literally, willing it to fall.

Finally he looked up to see the divisive, small, globe disappear into the teasing, black hole and he clenched his fist once more; only 2 down!

The next hole he repeated the process, 1 down, and by the time they had reached the 17th tee, Sam was 1 up and P Wingfield was not jolly or smiling any more!

Patently he had no desire to lose to a 16 year old boy and his demeanour was inseparably similar to his young opponent's, which was pallid, determined and somewhat strained.

However the young man was flying; he shaped

his drive around the bunker, hit a wedge to *8 feet* and to his opponent's dismay, disbelief and chagrin, holed yet another put to win 2 and 1!

The man tried to be sporting and a good loser but he simply couldn't smile as he gripped Sam's, youthful hand and spoke without any trace of sincerity or warmth.

"Well done, Young Man…well done!"

Sam didn't care about propriety, he'd won and he skipped down the final fairway as if it were already a ticker tape, victory parade!

He proudly reported the result to the official recorder, and watched in indescribable pride as his name was passed forward to the next round on the huge scoreboard.

He saw some of his friends from his county then exchanged stories about, birdies or putts revealing their respective resolve under the extreme heat of conflict and competition.

Tiny his caddy was also delighted and Sam watched uncomfortably as his father handed him a £20 note; but his assistant had been undoubtedly helpful and they made arrangements for the 2nd round tomorrow as he was off at 1.30 p.m.

Sam and his father ate at the nearby hotel and unexpectedly all the officials from the English Golf Union were staying there.

They interestedly and politely congratulated Sam and his proud parent on his success and Frankie was unsurprisingly in his element

He told whom-ever asked, about his son's progress, and his opinion on golf; Frankie always had an opinion on seemingly everything and liked to continuously share it!

Sam had a close battle the next day but miraculously held a *25 foot* putt on the last to win by 1 hole and suddenly he was in the 3rd round.

The following day he was 1 down with just the long par 5 last hole to play and he had a *35 foot* putt to stay in the match; he breathed in and followed the familiar routine he had slipped into for the week.

Head down, concentrating, determined he watched the brass coloured, *Ping* putter strike the ball and then willed it, willed it with all his mental power or physical energy.

He looked up, the ball rolled perfectly following the beautifully, manicured contours of the green then remarkably and unbelievably fell into the small, round cup seemingly so far away.

Their contest went to extra holes; they were forced to interrupt the games departing from the 1st tee and Sam was very much in the spotlight and he instantly and naturally liked the feeling, although it undoubtedly made him edgy.

The starter called them to the tee and Sam had the honour.

He felt a hundred eyes watching him around the busy area near the clubhouse; a new experience that distracted him and he hit a terrible shot that dribbled a mere hundred yards up the fairway.

His opponent, an eminent, southern county player hit a powerful iron that soared into perfect position far up towards the green.

A few spectators ambled after them and Sam tried to ignore his small crowd as he weighed up his next shot of over 200 yards.

He swung determinedly, enthusiastically and saw his effort finish on the front edge of the green leaving a treacherous, difficult long putt, right to left across a slippery, sloping green.

His experienced opponent placed himself within *10 feet* of the pin and Sam tried the same ongoing drill on the closely, cut green.

He concentrated, used the strength of his spirit then watched, almost as if a mere observer in his own match, as the ball curved across the slope of the green and impossibly disappeared into the hole!

His opponent was a pleasant, blonde man with rich dark eyes who was enjoying the cut and thrust of competition but was visibly shaken by Sam's seemingly unnatural good fortune on the greens.

He missed his putt and then took off his navy, peaked cap, wiping the sweat and strain out of his curly, blonde, shining hair and smiled broadly then murmured with a trace of humour and irony in his tone.

"Well done, Sam…"

He drew his bated breath.

"… Your putting was just wizard…"

He put a long arm friendly around, Sam and squeezed him firmly.

"…*Wizard of the green!*"

He laughed happily because he had enjoyed their bout and walked back with him towards the clubhouse as if unaffected by the unfortunate outcome of the day's adventure; he was an amateur and golf was just a game to him!

His name was, Peter Heather and Sam, although somewhat bemused at his positive demeanour, could not help but admire his attitude in defeat; it was refreshing and admirable!

The man was from Surrey and before he made his long journey home shook his conqueror's hand for the second time then genuinely and sincerely wished him well.

"Best of luck, Sam!"

With that he vanished into the mass of people still wandering about and Sam incredibly was still in the ongoing war of continuation in this tournament.

The result was reported to the recorder and Sam went to look at the giant scoreboard, his name had progressed almost from one side to the other.

He was in the 5th round, the last 16; he was impossibly amongst the best 16 amateur players in the whole of the country!

Sam also noticed that Paul Sandy had

matched his success and when he spoke to his mother that evening she told him that his name was being mentioned in all of the local papers along with his troublesome, arrogant, county colleague.

They were the only representatives left from Warwickshire and the golfing, written media revelled in their youthful and seemingly heroic exploits on the course.

Frankie was in his element; the officials at the hotel fawned on him, complimenting him on his son's achievements, asking him to recall the details of the matches he had seen.

Frankie was instantly seduced, his experience and insight in such exalted company was suddenly valued as he talked and talked in his exceptional pride of his boy; he was always so extraordinarily proud of his son!

The new day dawned, the practice ground was quieter, with only the sixteen competitors left and Sam hit shots at, *Tiny* in relative peace and tranquillity of the emptying space.

His match today was against Nick Brunyard, an English International and one of the clear favourites to win along with, Mark James, who had an equally growing reputation.

Sam proudly walked, almost swaggered, onto

the tee, his opponent wiped his glasses and shook his hand; he was thin, of medium build and had a mop of neatly trimmed, sandy brown hair.

Instantly Sam hated him, he tried to hate him, but loathing each opponent just to defeat them was tiring and his youthful body was starting to feel the effort and strain.

However the young warrior focussed on just seeing the course and the ball; he only concentrated on his swing, game, his score, and played inspirationally for the first 6 holes.

He was 2 up and his opponent was reeling; then there was a short hold up on the 7th tee making Sam's mind unfortunately begin to meander then wander with the wasted time and delay.

Irrationally his imagination visualised him actually winning the competition, his name in the paper, becoming an English International and, when the match re-started once more, he was suddenly unnaturally affected and extremely nervous.

Shot after shot was then squandered, allowing his opponent to come back from his disadvantaged position and suddenly Sam was 1 down.

He searched for the fire, it was still there as he hated losing so much, but suddenly the magic formula for the *Wizard of the green* no longer worked; his putts slid by the hole and he lost 2 and 1.

Nick Brunyard shook his hand warmly, patently relieved to have won and gushed in his admiration for the younger man.

"Well done, Sam, you're going to be a great player!"

The boy, because that was still what he remained, was disappointed and trudged back disconsolately towards the clubhouse, the car and eventually home.

He shook hands with, *Tiny* who seemed as disoriented and upset as him - Sam could smell the beer on his breath - and the older, vastly experienced caddie mumbled and complained to him gruffly.

"You should have beaten him!"

Frankie gave him some money and the man cheered up; they both made their final goodbyes to the officials, then the course while Sam noticed on the board that Paul Sandy had won his match.

He'd made it into the last eight, once again his

ability and success eclipsing his own!

Then suddenly it was just Sam and his father alone and the young man mumbled like the developing juvenile he now was and spoke a partial but incontrovertible truth,

"I'm sorry Dad...I should have won, my head just went to pieces!"

Frankie smiled at him; he was fatigued as well but he had enjoyed the experience beyond measure.

"That's OK, Sam...and anyway, I only had £10 left in my pocket..."

He laughed ironically.

"...If you had beaten him then don't know how I'd have paid for tonight's accommodation!"

Sam suddenly realised how much the week had cost and felt indulged, spoiled then embarrassed in equal measure.

He was indeed tired but resolved that he would work harder in the business and shops to save for the endless, contests, events and competitions to come.

The return journey was long and arduous; Sam tried to sleep but could not and was delighted to eventually see the familiarity of Moseley and finally the warmth and comfort of his family home.

Even Dorothy had been caught up in the excitement as she listened to the stories of the competition and matches with interest.

Her son looked understandably drained and tired but he was also elated and his young face and brown eyes sparkled or literally glowed with the reflected pride of his success.

He read the reports saved from the local newspaper and for once she allowed him his victory afterglow without her normal, overly protective, motherly concerns.

Sam followed the continuing reports on the immense competition and was uncharitably and secretly pleased when Paul Sandy was knocked out in the quarter final; Nick Brunyard was also eliminated at the same stage and Mark James was the eventual winner.

Sam read the newspaper report on the final with interest, comparing his performance with their scoring; he simply wished that he could have been in the culmination of such an auspicious event but was justifiably satisfied to have played his part.

The adventure however was now concluded;

Sam was a minor celebrity at the golf club, members inquired, congratulated him but it was a temporary thing, a few brief days of flattery and interest, that was all!

The next major challenge was soon approaching; it was the British Boys' championship in Hoylake, a links course on the outskirts of Liverpool on the very edges of the Irish Sea and therefore the subsequent, possible, wild wind.

Sam was both nervous and incredibly excited; he knew that as a direct result of his performance in the English Amateur he was now on the brink of getting into the full, English Boy's team.

Amazingly he had indeed received a letter asking him to play in a trial a couple of days before the main competition started and he was aware that from this initial test the *Boy's* team was picked for the annual match against Scotland.

This was historically played the day before the main event started and to Sam it would be almost an actual further wonderful ambition and experience if he could somehow represent his country at golf.

Sam and his father arrived in Liverpool the day before the assessment and round started; they booked into a local hotel and Frankie dropped his son at the course at midday while he drove into Manchester to do some business.

Sam walked straight to the 1st tee and joined a couple of boys who were also having a practice round; he noticed immediately that the turf had that soft spring that he'd experienced at Woodhall Spa and the greens had a wonderful, slick sheen and grain of link's golf that he'd never experienced before.

The course was playable, manageable and not too long but all of the surfaces were incredibly fast and tricky.

As Sam stood on the 8th tee looking out at the endless, flowing water, sensing the wonderful, saline freshness of the breeze; he felt alive, happy and looking forward to the challenge ahead.

He finished his round early, thanked his playing partners and satisfied that he had taken all measurements and completed all preparations; he went inside the historic clubhouse to wait for his father.

There was a luncheon laid out for the competitors and after he'd had a sandwich then a drink he wandered around the atmospheric interior of the building then, in reaction to sound and noise, found himself drawn to the upstairs, elegant, darkened, snooker room.

The Scottish Boys team seemed to fill and command the small, luxurious area and Sam immediately noticed, David Robinson; he was incredibly famous and well known as he was the winner of the British Youths Championship.

Sam shrank back to the wall suddenly intimidated and in patent awe of his contemporaries and opposition.

David Robinson was broad, well built and not to be overly unkind he was very fat; but he had the reputation of hitting the ball a country mile and Sam could see immediately see why.

A couple of English boys who had achieved an automatic place already in the team were having a colourful badinage with the boisterous, *Northern Contingent* as to who was going to win the match, the competition?

They all seemed so…so spiritedly confident; Sam felt insignificant and small suddenly, out of his depth and as he drunk in the apparently boundless assurance of his fellow combatants, he immediately felt extremely uncertain and troubled.

He sat almost invisible in the corner for an hour, watching the other boys play animatedly or loudly then was relieved and pleased when his father walked in as he could thankfully escape; the atmosphere in the murky, darkened room had been weirdly nerve racking and stifling!

Sam was quiet over dinner and his restlessness then inability to sleep during the night was not due to his father's snoring; Sam felt tense, nervous, he sensed his lack of courage and suddenly doubted his ability against his peers at this level of competition.

The day, when it eventually dawned, was sunny and bright as Sam went through his normal, professional, practice routine, before attending the 1st tee in readiness for his 10a.m start.

The officials were extremely hospitable and kind but Sam had a tightness and tension in his stomach that no amount of compliments about his performance in the *English* could eliminate.

The 1st at Hoylake was a right angle dogleg; the practice ground was over a small, high moat to the right that ran the entire length of the hole, which was *out of bounds* and a very unsettling, disconcerting hazard.

His name was called and he instantly felt the glare of attention and focus upon him - unwelcomingly this time - from hundreds of officials and competitors; in his anxious mind he tried his level best to block it out, settle and to simply concentrate.

But as his body stood over the ball all he could sense was the pull of the trouble on the right, as if it was demonically magnetic, and Sam vainly endeavoured to shrug off the insidious, destructive thoughts flooding through his brain.

His arms swung while his shoulders turned and he hit the ball but felt himself fall back then watched in horror as the tiny, bright projectile sailed effortlessly and seamlessly directly onto the middle of the vast, welcoming, preparation area.

The entourage around the 1st tee went quiet and Sam felt the ignominy of reaching into his bag as, Mr Micklam, the chairman of selectors looked on disapprovingly; his bulbous, bloodshot eyes seemingly, contemptuous and disgusted by his feeble, awful effort.

Sam teed up another ball, anxious to leave the spotlight and the isolation he was under, but then hit exactly the same shot as previously; the ball went even further down the *out of bounds* than before!

Shaking in anxiety and shock he rapidly changed down to a 5 iron; he could feel his whole body shuddering in nervousness, anger and horror as he made a poor and weak contact and watched in embarrassment as the ball dribbled down the manicured fairway, finally in play!

He held his head down in shame then marched swiftly after it fighting the tears and the shame that seemed to have overpowered him.

His trembling hands then struck a further poor shot to turn the corner of the hole and a few minutes afterwards came off the green with a mortifying *cricket* score of 11 shots

The young man felt his determination rise within him as always but although he fought manfully, he could accomplish no better than 85 around the teasing links made more taxing by a rising, whipping wind that came across from the coast so visibly adjacent to the course.

As he finished he handed the card into the officials dejectedly and was surprised that they asked him to play once more in a further trial and round the following morning.

Sam had impressed everybody at the *English* and the selectors could not understand the difference in his form; they wanted a further look at him and he had another chance.

But the following day the he was worse;

somehow he kept his ball away from the *out of bounds* on his first effort from the tee but subsequently shot after shot was wasted then lost until his score mirrored the exact same number of his initial, previous attempt.

He was utterly devastated and he was forced to stay and wait for the main tournament to start then watch the England, Scotland game as a mere interested but frustrated onlooker!

Needless to say Paul Sandy had made the team on the first trial and Sam spent most of the afternoon on the hateful, practice ground and the putting green trying to ignore this vital game and fierce battle on the course that he had so desperately wanted to take his part in.

Therefore Sam longed for the tournament to start where he would display his true form, but on his opening match as he reached the turn 3 down; he realised that on this occasion there would be no comeback although he tried with all his mental and physical energies.

The tournament had undoubtedly been a baptism of fire, it devastated the confidence of the inexperienced boy and it would take him many weeks before he could come to terms with what had transpired.

Frankie was also disappointed but he'd been used to losing as he saw it as just a part of the game in the sport of life; he was pragmatic and consoled then encouraged his disappointed son once they were packed and had set off on the long drive home.

"You'll get your own back on that place, Sam... your day will come!"

Sam didn't listen, he didn't believe him, but unusually, his father's prediction on this particular occasion was to eventually prove to be surprisingly and spectacularly correct.

Chapter 5

The golfing season was winding down but the few local tournaments remaining brought no great results and again, Tom Holt won the club championship, with Sam disappointingly having a disastrous back 9 in the afternoon.

However reflection was a valuable, inestimable thing and it revealed that the season had overall been a partial success.

The boy was now ready for a full challenge at

the Amateur game of golf; only a single stroke less on his handicap needed to be shaved from his present low figure and this would give him entry to the British, Amateur Championship.

He only now needed a solitary, further reduction after this before he could amazingly play in the qualifying for the very *Open Championship* itself!

It was a time in his life for his father and Sam to plan and imagine great things; fantastical dreams of adventures, clashes then inevitable glory with fabulous victories that were barely seen but surely and enticingly just around the corner.

Winter however was soon upon them, the shops, the school, each held their horrors, pressures and obligations for the growing, maturing boy.

Sam, although struggling in some subjects, was performing reasonably well with his schooling and Dorothy was pleased to hear at the parent's evening that he was attentive and diligent.

He was predicted at least 5, O level passes that would be a step toward further learning then eventually university.

The educational disciplines were due to take

place in November and not wishing to fail, Sam concentrated all his efforts in this regard.

He knew the sciences and languages were beyond him but felt quietly confident of the other subjects.

The business seemed constantly busy and Sam worked every spare hour that came to him; he sensibly saved money each week towards the cost of his proposed, sporting schedule for the coming year.

If it were not for the fact he had to see his sister and brother in law most days, he would have been happy and relatively content.

Understandably he no longer felt or considered himself a child and it rankled that, his sibling and husband took such advantage of his parent's generous, good nature.

His mother, on top of all her other duties, also immersed herself in looking after Anna's children as her mercurial daughter was ill intermittently or even constantly; she was seemingly always in bed or at the doctors and no matter how hard the medical experts looked they could never find anything wrong with her!

Unfortunately for everyone that was just the way it was, seemingly the way Frankie had almost personally shaped it to be; Sam was truly beginning to experience and learn that life definitely and distinctly wasn't always fair.

November and the exams came with a flash; Sam sat down in the large wood panelled assembly hall with the other students then felt the clawing tension and pressure just as he did on that unforgettable 1st hole at Hoylake!

He concentrated, as one by one the tests came and went resulting, that Sam could only wait along with his classmates for the judgement on their fraught, academic endeavours.

It was soon December and the business was now his focal point, even Anna pretended to work occasionally, buying stock whilst her husband amused himself in one of the more distant outlets.

Timmy's shop was consistently and always the most disorganised and dirtiest; further to this fact, it was always the very centre of where the business lost the most money!

Sam still exercised or ran, and most evenings he would don his tracksuit after dinner and pound the dark, dimly lit streets around his home.

If he ever missed his session, his always watchful father would still sharply but briefly lecture him on being disciplined and his own personal, enormous experience of exercise and sport in general.

"I used to be captain of the cricket team…"

He would sigh in recollection of a glorious, sporting past…although only in the Local Park!

"…And was something of an exceptional, tennis player… "

His advice was always heartfelt.

"…You have to force yourself… be dedicated!"

Sam tried not to pay too much attention to his ramblings as his Dad often irritated him with his nonsense; he saw the burgeoning waistline of the stout man and sincerely doubted and mistrusted that his Dad had ever possessed a fraction of the regimentation and sporting prowess that he persistently claimed.

However out of love and respect, he always listened or pretended to and on many nights would run and exercise when he did not really feel in the mood and it made Frankie proud; his son was under his guidance and he, of course, was his expert trainer, the brilliant, master tactician.

The bustle of Christmas evaporated as did the family dinner, presents and general good cheer; the early new-year brought reality, bills and Sam saw the lines of worry visibly marked and etched in his mother's gentle but often harrowed face.

But a brown envelope arrived in February and Dorothy beamed as she read its contents; Sam had achieved 6, O level passes at a high grade and his future at the school and beyond seemed secure.

Her husband also read the results and was pleased with his son's efforts, but he placed little value on education; *he'd* succeeded without it and considered it, just vacuous froth and bubbles.

In his vast experience he'd never met a professionally educated man he'd respected; they weren't clever, they had little or no common sense and his son was going to be a professional golfer or at worst a prominent, wealthy, successful businessman, as *he* was!

Frankie pondered his son's future, considered every conceivable possible angle to come and then sagely confronted Sam one evening and asked him an impossible question.

"What do you want to do with your life, Sam?"

The growing youth looked at him blankly and spoke honestly without a trace of introspective thought.

"I'm not sure, Dad…"

Sam sat back and quietly he whispered about the only thing he considered himself to be good at.

"…I'd like to be a professional golfer…"

His voice had an uncertain edge and tone to it.

"…But that's a dream, isn't it?"

Frankie seemed to puff out his expansive form then murmured with his eternal, ever present and abounding confidence.

"It doesn't have to be, Son, if that's what *you* want then…"

Sam was held breathless.

"…We can make it happen!"

The young man was stunned for a moment, then gazed wondrously and listened intently to his father as he outlined to him, his master plan!

Sam could leave school - he was only an average student after all - he could concentrate on his golf, full time and spend all his spare time in the business where he could save money for his competitive schedule.

The naïve boy could simply not believe what he was listening to; it was so extraordinary and fantastical.

His young, immature imagination raced and rushed excitedly; *leave school, play golf*...of course that's what he wanted what a foolish question... that's exactly what he wanted!

They told Dorothy their joint decision and when he went to bed he heard an explosive, virulent argument between his parents the likes of which he'd never heard before.

His brain was so mixed up as he questioned himself over and over again; *did he want to leave school*?... of course he did, didn't he?

It was patent, obvious and clear, but as he heard his parents bicker he suddenly experienced a creeping shadow of doubt deep inside him that settled on his increasingly troubled, juvenile mind.

Dorothy insisted that her husband should discuss this matter with the school and Frankie, just and only to appease his wife, went in to speak to Mr Chumilly the headmaster of the auspicious, respected establishment a few days later.

The old, experienced gentleman and academic was well aware of Sam's sporting prowess and from his privileged, vantage point was well placed to confirm that Sam's academic achievements were indeed distinctly average.

But the salient point purposely or foolishly missed by Frankie was that just to be ordinary in this particular and exceptional school was not really average at all and, as Mr Chumilly listened to his plump, bombastic visitor, he privately was genuinely amazed that he wished to dispose of his son's educational future so casually.

But the headmaster had hundreds of boys in his institution and under his learned wing; he listened somewhat exasperated as his guest rambled on, giving his bloated, ill-informed, egotistical opinion on learning, sport and career prospects in general.

The worldly man eventually realised less than halfway through the meeting that, Mr Chester senior really only wanted to hear one opinion, his own, and past a certain point he did not feel he had the time or inclination to argue with him.

Frankie left the brief meeting and interview convinced that his assessment and opinion was correct; the headmaster had told him that, Sam was an *average* student and he put this angle or slant on the subsequent, protracted discussion with his wife.

But he never persuaded or convinced her as he never could or would win her over to the view that his way was correct.

However Frankie browbeat his partner, shouted, while the apple of her eye sat listening on the chair beside them as his future road and opportunities were decided.

Dorothy gazed, glared and stared at the innocent and almost pathetic, hopeful look on her son's face and realised she was fighting a losing battle; in the end she was simply too drained, exhausted or tired to fight any more.

She could never endure for long against her husband; it was like trying to tame the eternal wind or the waves that beat forever onto the shore and impermeable rocks with inexhaustible energy each and every day.

In the end she submitted but was indescribably unhappy; her brown eyes stared, and burned out fiercely but passionately at the two men in her life and her spirit railed then seethed in frustration and indignation.

If this choice and decision had been simply and only what her son wanted, it would have been acceptable and enough for her; however, even then, only barely or just!

But she looked at her husband, his face, pink and flushed with the excitement of this new, outrageous, unacceptable gamble with her treasured son's life then future and it infuriated her as she knew it was what *he* wanted most of all!

Dorothy had no option but to surrender and, for the first time in her life, somewhere deep within her heart she was bitter against her spouse; it was sour anger that was ground into her soul and something she could never truly confront him with, or ever truly forgive him, for what he had so casually and imprudently done.

But the die was cast and her son was due to leave school in March, ironically as the approach of the new golf season beckoned.

Sam, therefore on his final day, walked slowly to the main, school entrance; he watched the other boys bustle and bluster, lost in their carefree life and he said his previously vocal but now private, silent goodbyes.

To his friends, his teachers, the vast playing fields where school rugby and cross country had been something of a trial and a burden, and finally his education; his heart was full of mixed emotions as he realised he was saying goodbye to his education!

He was melancholy for a while but such thoughts did not last for too long; his Dad had read about a small, training school set up by, Henry Cotton, the famous former *Open Champion* and he had written to him in detail about the potential of his brilliant son.

The old master had replied and a holiday had been booked in April at Penina, in Portugal, where the feted and honoured professional held court and gave lessons.

Sam was elated, golf in the sun, with a former *Open Champion*; it was unbelievable, and he prepared his schedule for the coming year with new relish then waited with expectation and impatience for the day of their departure to the distant destination.

Sam practised every day, focussing entirely on his game; it produced instant results and by the time he left with his parents for the trip to Henry Cotton, his handicap was 2.

He now had access to all amateur tournaments and positively felt the world was his oyster.

Sam had only ever been abroad once before, and the trip from beginning to end was an experience; he was frightened by the plane, the sudden noises that he imagined were the engines failing and found it hard to settle or relax at 30,000 feet.

However he arrived safely, Portugal was hot and dusty, but not at Penina, and as Sam approached the complex in the heated, jerky taxi he marvelled as the greenery of the golf course rolled out before him in stark contrast to the arid, barrenness of the sandy, scorched, surrounding land.

They settled in quickly and within the hour, Sam with his father were striding purposely towards the golf centre anxious to make the acquaintance of Mr Cotton, whom Sam understood had in fact incredibly won three *Open* Championships!

A striking man appeared and promptly took them into his office to greet them properly; he was old, a little stooped in his gait and seemed as though he was faded by the years.

His face was clouded by unsightly, brown, age spots, but he still undeniably had an air of distinction; he was noticeably a man of experience, breeding and undoubted success.

He walked with a slight shuffle, his shoulders almost imperceptively bending forwards and Sam noticed that his hair was snow white; pure, brilliant, dazzling white and he spoke out with perfect, incredible, clear diction.

"You must be, Mr Chester…"

His aquatic blue eyes peered intensely at the nervous youth, directly by his father's side.

"...And this, Young Man must be, Sam?"

The awe struck boy had never heard English spoken like this before, it was so eloquent, clipped or precise and, as he felt the man's piercing, azure globes ever watchfully inspecting him, he shivered silently then felt understandably shy and uncomfortable.

Frankie however had no such inhibitions and he took the man's gifted, bony hand enthusiastically.

"I'm very pleased to meet you, Mr Cotton...very pleased!"

Sam watched his father move to the grand, antique desk in the old man's office and willingly provided him with some money; he always felt guilty that he was the recipient of such indulgence and extravagance but could not dwell upon it.

He distracted his guilt and focus then looked at the numerous photographs that adorned the walls of the intimate, personal room and space of the famous man's, inner sanctum.

There were black and white pictures of the *Maestro* -his current nickname in the media- in his hey day; he looked so vital, slim, dapper, smart, young and elegant in the photographs.

Sam came across an image where he was clutching a small, silver jug close to his chest and recognised of course that it was *The Open* championship trophy.

His father walked back to him then they both nodded in respect to the *Maestro* and walked out of the amazing, fascinating office; Frankie subsequently told Sam that Mr Cotton had informed him that lessons would not start until the morning due to the lateness of the hour, and he was to be on the practice area at 10a.m.

Sam found it hard to settle or sleep that night as he knew that in the coming morning he finally was going to discover the unknown, divisive secret of golf!

He was going to be educated and taught, unbelievably by, Henry Cotton, a former *Open Champion*, one of the best players that had ever lived!

Chapter 6

The walk down the practice area was short and along a twisting, dusty trail; his parents were still having a lazy breakfast and Sam breathed in the sweet, aromatic, warm air of the invigorating, sublime, Mediterranean climate.

After the oppression of the English, foul, winter weather, it was a treat indeed for the youth to be in short sleeves and to feel the early morning sun on his back.

He walked, with his bag of clubs across his sturdy shoulders, down the sandy path that led him to a sparsely tree lined, practice area where three other boys were waiting patiently for the famous man to arrive.

They were talking or hitting the occasional shot and Sam could see that the other players were all good golfers, his equals or better!

Sam had no time to introduce himself, as theatrically, Mr Cotton appeared on the top of the rise in an elegant, white, golf buggy that careered along the gravel road then stopped in a wild, dynamic explosion of gravel, dust and grit.

"Good morning, Boys,"

His beautiful, immaculate, cultured English prose rang out like a song in the gentleness of the Portuguese morning; it was countered with an unfortunately less than musical choral reply from all of his expectant pupils and entourage including his ever anxious and latest charge.

"Good morning, Mr Cotton!"

Sam was looking eagerly at the pristine, white balls piled high on the floor as he longed and wanted to desperately show then demonstrate to the experienced professional what he could do.

His chance came shortly after the *Maestro* had formally introduced himself to the young men gathered around him; they were from different parts of England and all with the aspirations or dreams of an impending and triumphant tournament career ahead of them.

It seemed, not unsurprisingly, that the much vaunted and heralded genius of Mr Cotton was a *guarantee* of success for them all!

Sam and all his compatriots took separate positions, side by side on the range and almost in unison started to fire their shots down the unhealthy and dry looking, green and yellow plain in front of them.

Sam's attempts were crisp and clean, his club

connecting sweetly off the rich texture of the heavily watered grass where they were showing off their respective talents; the *Maestro* stood behind him, watched and then passed comments that were full of praise and admiration.

"That's good, Young Man...Good!"

His words were stated calmly and factually as Sam felt his chest swell up instantly with incalculable pride.

The old professional however taught them nothing specific on the morning session and the only focal point of their golfing education centred around a couple of worn out, rubber, car tyres lying forlornly along the scrubby parts of the top practice area.

Henry Cotton showed and demonstrated how the tyre could be used as a training tool; he slammed a club into the soft, yielding edges of the rubber with his right wrist and his entourage looked on amazed as he went on to explain his reasoning and actions.

"This exercise strengthens your hands...arms and trains your muscles through the hitting area."

Sam, when given the opportunity, then launched his own club against the reactive tyre and instantly felt the pronounced recoil.

He understood the principle of what the expert had alluded to, or so he thought, as it indeed seemed an ingenious idea and instantly decided there and then to purchase a suitable round circle of hard rubber for himself, when he got home.

Frankie watched his son from the brow of the hill in a sheltered, shaded spot, loftily above the practice ground below and he felt immensely self-satisfied and fulfilled.

His son was listening intently to instruction, improving and honing his talent and the idea of this visit had been undoubtedly innovative and inspirational on his part.

He ambled slowly down as the session finished and listened as, Mr Cotton informed the small group to assemble on the starting hole of the course after lunch.

His son was so excited he could hardly eat his meal as he gossiped and rambled on incessantly.

"He told me I was hitting the ball well...really, really, well!"

His voice enthused, raved or rambled on incessantly and animatedly about the incalculable merits of the tyre until his father assured him that procuring one would not present a major problem.

Sam, in his enthusiasm, was the first to arrive on the tee and was joined shortly afterwards by the other boys and then the *Maestro* in the inevitable buggy that was always driven at startlingly frightening, breakneck speed.

Sam was the first to hit and placed his shot proficiently into the fairway; the other students then played until it was only the ex *Open Champion* to strike.

Sam then watched on in utter astonishment as the old man of nearly seventy gripped his club so delicately and lightly, turned gently and then rhythmically and elegantly swung through the ball which was dispatched on its way as if it was connected to a long, invisible piece of fine and magical string.

His swing seemed to be controlled just by his hands but even with his physical powers so shaded, jaded and diminished by the years, his confidence and authority on the golf course was still incalculable and clearly visible.

Sam suddenly could not concentrate on his own game; he watched transfixed as this *Master* gently and effortlessly teased, guided then shaped his ball over the first 9 holes.

Each shot seemed identical, each strike measured, perfect and what the man lacked in power he made up for in domination, style and grace.

As the expert eventually drove away from them to let them play the last 9 themselves leaving Sam feeling undeniably humbled and strangely confused.

He had recognised his own personal style and method in comparison to this *Master* was amateurish and clumsy; his private, golfing ability was intense, sheer effort or will and he could not truly, possibly really comprehend how this game, at any rate the competitive game, could be played so effortlessly.

He put these thoughts temporarily to the back of his mind as he continued then engaged in friendly badinage with his compatriots on the subsequent holes and learned something about them all.

Martin, a tall gangly boy from Surrey was an enthusiastic amateur off a 2 handicap; James was a small youth with ginger hair and freckles and was the son of a professional golfer from a municipal course in London.

The other member was David, a broad, incredibly strong lad from Dorset and Sam watched how each member of his foursome had their own distinctive style or method of playing.

Martin seemed stiff and awkward; James looped his back swing around his shoulders and David seemed to hit the ball vast distances with just his powerful hands but was distinctly inconsistent.

Sam felt that his own technique was superior but as the holes concluded he found it was David's, length that won the paltry few Escudos at stake.

Dorothy and Frankie had thoroughly enjoyed their day by the pool and Sam changed and dived into its cool, clear water to eradicate the heat of the round and his concerted, sweated efforts.

He was happy, contented, felt privileged as he let the warm water surround and lap against him, and thought disconcertingly about the cold, English climate and the depressing warehouse that seemed thankfully so far away.

The subsequent days flew by in a hurry, Sam would endlessly luxuriate in hitting shot after shot in the sunshine and then practice the drill on the tyre until his still, growing arms, hands or wrists, wracked and ached.

Each afternoon the *Maestro* would always join

his pupils for a few holes and Sam would endeavour to learn, ingest and absorb whatever knowledge he could from just observing him.

Henry Cotton's teaching method was unique; he did not involve himself with technique but emphasised the importance of using your hands, the ability to adjust your game on a daily basis as necessary.

He described it as *hanging your hat*, or relying on a certain anomaly in one's method that made you play well, if bending your knee or standing straighter worked, use it, rely on it until it didn't work any more.

Sam understood this strangely, as often something clicked one day in his golf that failed the next; it indeed seemed as though it was a constant, eternal battle of tinkering.

Sam tried to ask about the perfect swing, the one that could repeat always and the older, still energetic man smiled dryly and seemed vague and evasive.

He simply gestured and pointed to the arid, practice ground then spoke softly, with emotive, reflective, long experience in his tone.

"That's where I found my answer, Sam…"

His voice was hard and barren like the lifeless dirt he referred to as he carried on.

"...In the ground... the dust... practising until I taught myself how to use these properly."

He thrust out his wondrous palms and hands which were blotched and wrinkled with age and the passage of time but were still incredibly elegant; his fingers long and slim and his nails manicured so immaculately.

The old professional said little more than that as surprisingly, he was actually quite reserved; he encouraged rather than preached and suggested rather than insisted or dictated.

He believed and imparted that his understanding and secret of golf lay in the hands and attempted to instil his pupils with the thought that, if they truly had the belief and the dedication, then anything was possible!

Sam was completely involved with the experience and near the end of his holiday he hardly noticed the soldiers that seemed to have suddenly appeared in and around the hotel like blue, predatory, menacing, uniformed wolves.

Portugal was in the midst of a revolution; the new military *Junta* had commandeered the site and, Henry Cotton, former *Open Champion*, or not, was unceremoniously dispatched to the smaller hotel across the road, along with his dependants and entourage.

Sam's main concern initially was that his daily, golf routine was not interfered with but, and far more sensibly, it was with much relief to his mother that when their time arrived to depart, the passage and flight to and from the airport, was uninterrupted and unhindered

Her husband tentatively arranged for another trip the following year and Henry Cotton was happy to accommodate his son, but with regard to the trauma in this troubled country told him that he may well have to set up a new teaching base elsewhere.

It seemed that even in retirement the profession and calling of golf was never easy or straightforward even for the best and most gifted of champions!

Frankie looked on silently at the soldiers and the guns and understood that although he could solve most of life's riddles and problems, he was relieved and pleased that sorting out the Portuguese revolution was not up to him!

Some things were beyond even his powers!

They were delayed at the airport and Frankie had noticed that sitting in a quiet corner of the airport lounge was the famous, diminutive, sports broadcaster called, Harry Carpenter!

Frankie purposefully and almost intrusively walked over to him, much to Sam's embarrassment, as if he was this unknown stranger's long lost, best friend!

But that was his father's way; he felt he was everyone's companion and his confidence and impudence was never ending.

He started to talk enthusiastically to him and, at him, as Sam was dispatched to buy some coffees and he returned to find his father alongside the small man engaged in full debate.

Harry Carpenter looked different from the television, smaller and less imposing, but his large, brown glasses hid a warm, friendly face as he entertained both father and son with marvellous stories and reminiscences of the famous and mesmerising people he'd met.

Frankie, in return and Sam's, brief absence, had told the presenter all about his son, his prowess on the golf course and the distinct possibility that he might have to interview him one day!

Harry Carpenter smiled and listened; he'd met boastful, doting fathers many times but Frankie's charm and exuberance amused him then passed the time in the melee of disorganisation and confusion that was Faro airport that particular night.

Eventually the flight was called and they exhaustedly and tiredly boarded the waiting plane.

They had all had an enjoyable holiday and experience each in their own particular way; Dorothy had relaxed and lapped up the sun while Frankie had talked, confirmed the potential of his undoubtedly, talented son from an expert and then talked some more.

Sam had been educated and learned something, or he thought he'd learned something, but he wasn't quite sure what?

The tyre drill: the hands: the commitment; the effort, it was all circling and spinning in his youthful mind and as he looked out at the dark, grey clouds floating in the blackness of the night sky, like soft ghostly apparitions, he wondered what the coming season had in store.

The family settled quickly back into their respective routines, the shops were crying out for Dorothy's expertise, Frankie had numerous financial pressures and Sam concentrated on finalising all his tournament applications.

He had entered every event possible, starting with the British Amateur Championship in May; it was to be held at Hoylake and Sam shivered and shuddered when he remembered his painful, horrendous previous experience there.

He then had an ongoing schedule including, the English Amateur and various stroke-play competitions and another final attempt at the British Boy's championship in Scotland.

Sam had just passed his driving test and was provided with a bright, yellow, ford Capri; it was basic, but reliable and to the young man, was a passport to a new, expanding and exciting world.

He was still committed to his golf club and competed in all the main competitions but he started to notice a distinct change of attitude in many of the members.

His ongoing passage from boyhood to adolescence then approaching manhood, especially with regards to his developing, golfing prowess, meant some older and younger members were becoming resentful of him, and the time he spent at the golf course.

He was a constant source of complaint and gossip around the clubhouse; every one seemed to have an opinion of the young man.

"The boy should be at school...His father should leave him alone...He's ruining the course... practising out of bunkers... playing 2 balls...He's rude... loses his temper on the course!"

On and on, ad nauseam, the bile, resentment and spite continued from a small but vociferous and vocal section of the membership that surprisingly enjoyed using and occupying the bar far more than the 18 holes!

Sam's success at the club, always winning or being in contention for the competitions, was also a source of real antipathy and the complaints were relentless.

"It wasn't fair...He's playing all day...He's really a professional!"

In truth Sam was what he had always been, polite, respectful; a good hearted and good-natured youth, but he was driven to succeed and more and more often he fell foul of one or another of the committee that wished to bring him down a peg or two.

As he had learned from his faithful instructor, he tried to take it in good part, but it upset him and he felt that much of the poison came from such a tiny clique of committee members that seemed to spend an inordinate amount of time around the gossipy and insidious 19th hole.

He ignored it as best he could, taking his lead from his tutor and practiced in the far recesses of the course, well away from prying eyes that would report him for breaking the club rules regarding the playing of only one ball and practising out of bunkers etc.

As best he could he tried not to be diverted or distracted; he needed to improve, always to practice and the tyre was now a permanent feature on the range as he continued with Henry Cotton's advice to him.

The *Maestro* was writing a column for *Golf Illustrated* at the time and Sam was surprised to see a small article concerning himself and the other visiting boys in the well regarded, *Penina Patter* page.

Henry Cotton had praised him and his ability and Sam proudly pasted his words and the compliments into his scrapbook and turned over the endless, empty pages; he wanted them all so full of amazing deeds and articles recording his incredible triumphs to come.

He also read that the great man was relocating to Sotto Grande in Spain and he hoped that he would be able to visit him again.

The starting times then arrived for the British Amateur Golf Championship; Sam excitedly opened the brown envelope then flicked through the white document from the world-renowned, Royal and Ancient Golf club.

Hundreds of matches were listed, competitors from all over the globe searching for a single, elusive, but much treasured, solitary prize until eventually he found his name; he was due out on Tuesday at 9.15a.m against somebody from America called J. Pate.

Sam thought nothing more about it and busied himself over the next few weeks with his practice and his business obligations.

The Junior Open was to be played at Moor Hall Golf club before this major competition, and both Sam and Paul Sandy were hot favourites.

This was Sam's last chance to win this title as he would be too old next year therefore he was desperate to make it count and take the elusive, much valued, county crown.

Mr Earl greeted, Sam like an old friend and after their normal, yearly ritual and conversation pulled the young man to one side and murmured to him agitatedly and with unusual anticipation.

"Congratulations with your draw in the *British*, Sam…"

The young man looked at him blankly as he

continued and explained in more detail.

"J.Pate... is...Jerry Pate... he's the reigning, United States Amateur Champion!"

Sam stepped back in genuine surprise and shock.

"Really...really?"

Mr Earl nodded, his glinting, ocean blue eyes gleaming more than normal behind his small, silver, rounded, transparent glasses.

"You go and show him what we're made of in this county..."

His smile was effusive, warm, genuine, enthusiastic, and he patted the young man's ever broadening shoulders.

"...And...by the way, you're playing with, Paul Sandy today... favourites together!"

Sam had never played competitively with Paul Sandy before and that, combined with his revelation about the *British* was disconcerting, overpowering and almost overwhelming.

He related everything to his father, who looked suitably astonished and exhaled in fevered expectation.

"The United States Champion!"

His face was immediately flushed with enthusiasm and excitement, thrilled that his son, his *pedigree runner* was about to enter a new race, a new level of competition and experience!

That however was the future, today, both father and son, were determined to lay this continual nemesis and bogey of, Paul Sandy and finally beat him!

Sam had never really studied the boy before but he could now hardly avoid looking at him directly.

He was broad, well built with light brown hair and a face so full of freckles that belied the all apparent iron and steel underneath his childish façade and visage.

His eyes were icy green and as Sam shook his hand he noticed how they sparkled with cold intent; his skin was hardened sandpaper from practice but strangely also gentle and soft and he thought only of the *Maestro's* palm and fingers.

He was forced, even in close and immediate competition with this difficult adversary, to admit that there was something of definite, specific and distinct golfing quality about him!

Paul Sandy had the honour and unusually his

father was caddying; he was a professional from a course at the furthermost part of the county and he was obviously grooming his son, just as Frankie felt, he was directing Sam so masterfully.

He swung slowly, rhythmically; there was a slight twist at the apex of his swing then a controlled *whoosh* and the ball sped, expertly away into the far reaches of the fairway.

Sam ignored his opponent, the location of his ball and concentrated solely on his own game; his first shot was good, his temperament calm as he walked out into the course clearly intent and focussed on the challenge ahead.

He played to par around the first 9 holes, birdied the 10th and was 4 shots ahead of his rival by the 12th.

Then, for no real reason he hit a poor shot on the 13th hole and suddenly his round started to collapse, until by completion Paul Sandy was 1 over par and he was 4 over, 3 behind.

His opponent had an air of superiority Sam found insufferable; he had all the appearance of being relaxed and friendly but Sam could sense his real attitude and purpose.

Paul Sandy undoubtedly felt he was better than anyone else - his father was a professional - he was going to be a professional, just like him, and these minor, passing, inconsequential tournaments and opposition were just mere stepping stones in a running stream, or rungs along the tall, high ladder to success.

Sam did not eat lunch but practised on the small grounds by the putting green and was determined to turn around his deficit in the afternoon round.

He birdied 3 of the first 5 holes but, as if only to infuriate him further, his insufferable, playing partner held a *30 footer* on the 6th, drained another long putt for a par on the next and Sam's game fell apart once more!

At the finish he had the shame and indignity of not even finishing second; Paul Sandy finished level par for the day and was unnervingly 9 shots better than he was!

The victor and conqueror shook his hand firmly and smiled almost superciliously with dry humour.

"Hard luck, Sam…"

Sam felt the fire of defeat welling up then burning inside him; the boy was laughing at him as he sounded so superior and sanctimonious!

"...Maybe, next year?"

He knew this was the last time for Sam and he was being droll and somewhat sarcastic!

Sam tried to be magnanimous but the words of congratulations spoken by him stuck in his acidic throat and stayed there as he was forced to endure his eternal arch-rival receiving the shiny, gleaming, silver trophy in happy triumph.

Paul Jones came unexpectedly second and his smile lit up the room like a small glow and Sam received his own third prize with virtually no emotion at all!

What would have filled him with satisfaction and glee only a couple of years ago now only belittled, frustrated and disappointed him!

Both his father and Sam were quiet and subdued on the way home; Frankie tried to analyse why his son had failed once more but they both found it hard to accept that Paul Sandy was a better player.

He didn't necessarily swing better or putt better, he just *was* better; he seemed more in control, less frantic and achieved superior results with apparently less effort.

It was a cruel and bitter pill to swallow but all Sam could do was vow to work harder, practice more and never give up or give in!

Dorothy sensed how her son was deflated, he was visibly tired and sad; she so desperately wished that there was something to take his mind off his disappointment but he had nothing else now.

No school or college, nothing but golf and the family business; she wanted to cry in frustration but as always remained fuming or silent as there was not anything she could practically do!

She wanted her son to go into the world and socialise but Sam was shy and his outings to local discos with his old school friends seemed less successful than his golf, and he was gradually becoming insular and almost introverted.

All she could do was support him, feed him and hope that everything would somehow and eventually work out.

Sam practised over the next few days and weeks with a ferocious intensity; he broke par for the first time and his handicap was teetering on being reduced to 1!

Jerry Pate, the United States Amateur Champion was now just a week away!

A couple of days before he was due to depart for Hoylake, Sam had an attack of the *shanks*; the ball flew off the club at right angles especially when he was chipping, and he was in utter despair.

Len Thompson watched him on the practice range, shot after shot would be perfect and then suddenly this destructive, disastrous shot would reappear.

Sam banged the ground in fury and frustration; he was red faced and frightened that he was facing such a challenge with his game in apparent shambles and disarray.

His tutor had no immediate or magic cure and tried to calm then soothe him in his customary, gentle style.

"Just relax, Son…It's just a phase."

Sam watched another shot veer off perpendicularly right and slammed the unrelenting ground again and screamed in his building frustration.

"What am I doing?"

His tutor and father left him to his suffering but day after day he would concentrate and struggle to release this gremlin from his game; just as he thought he had cured the problem it would intolerably, maliciously creep back in.

It was insidious, sinister and undermining his confidence, his enjoyment and more importantly his tolerance and peace of mind.

Chapter 7

The drive to Hoylake was long but not unfamiliar; his Dad had booked them into the same hotel as the previous year but unfortunately somehow his reservation had been lost or mislaid.

Frankie asked to see the manager and charmed then persuaded the man, as only he could, who eventually asked the receptionist to vacate her room to enable them to stay.

Sam could not sleep in the same room as his father any longer as his snoring was now legendary, although Frankie insisted of course that he'd never made a noise due to his breathing in his life!

Accommodation then settled they drove to the

course; it was the day before the competition was due to start and it was heaving, packed and crowded with people.

Sam put his name down for a practice round and he had some lunch before looking out at the green fairways with hundreds of small bodies swarming over them like busy insects.

He played reasonably, only a single *shank* on the short 4th and was relieved; he did so not wish to make a fool of himself tomorrow.

He ate with his father in the hotel and as Frankie was tired, Sam drove the short distance himself back to the course and wandered over to the practice area to familiarise his mind with the surroundings, relax, contemplate and think.

He stood silently and watched some of the American Walker Cup players who were practising late into the evening.

Sam had read about the recent Walker Cup match, Great Britain and Ireland had lost narrowly to the strong American team.

He was also aware that Jerry Pate had failed in every match and been defeated by Mark James in the singles; Sam felt this was a good omen for the coming morning.

He watched the few remaining Americans on the range, the same vast area where he had so painfully and dramatically gone *out of bounds* at the *Boy's* trial.

George Burns III was hitting balls into the setting sun; the man was thickset and sturdy, with immensely strong forearms and the ground seemed to shake and the ball, literally screamed as he struck it.

So many of these players, Sam knew were destined for the pinnacle and top of the professional game, George Burns, Curtis Strange, Craig Stadler to name but a few.

In the stillness of the twilight, as the darkness melded the colours of the sky and the greenery into one; insightfully and in a small crisis of confidence he honestly wondered once more if he really had the game to compete at this heightened level.

He did not dwell too long on his insecurity as he had attitude, resolve and sheer gritty determination, to win; most of all he had the intensity of willpower and desire to win!

The day dawned, mild and fresh and Sam walked into breakfast to find his father sitting down eating with a huge grin on his plump, constantly amused, friendly face.

It transpired that one of the hotel cleaners had seen him coming out of the receptionist's bedroom, put two and two together, made five and assumed that the poor but supposedly, promiscuous girl from the front desk had entertained Frankie to a night of fetid fervour and smoking, heated passion!

The news and gossip travelled around the small hotel like wildfire and when the manager and receptionist heard they told Frankie and everyone saw the funny side of such a mistake and hilarious anecdote.

Sam laughed as well and it was a welcome release and diversion from his edgy thoughts.

He glanced at the paper and saw that one of the broad sheets had written an article on the British Amateur and predicted, Jerry Pate would win and not even be troubled until the quarter finals.

His combative nature was already up, bristling and sensing his ire and strength of mind rising already as he murmured defiantly, as if to only to steel and inspire himself.

"We'll see about that...we'll just see about that!"

The match was delayed and due off at 10.30a.m and Sam struck some practice shots on the range; the whole course was streaming and teeming with golfing life so he just hit some short wedges as there were too many people about for anything longer.

He was relieved that the dreaded *shank* was nowhere to be found and he saw also that it was now 10a.m.

He put the practice bag back in his car then meandered to the putting green where he saw his father purposefully shaking hands with Jerry Pate - he knew and recognised who he was by now - obviously and somewhat presumptuously introducing himself.

Sam had no intention of placing himself in such a polite, respectful but docile situation; to him that would have been submissive, an admission of the man's superiority and he'd decided that he would meet him on the course and the green field of combat!

A small crowd gathered around the 1st tee area and Sam walked towards it, projecting an air of confidence he did not truly feel.

Jerry Pate was waiting; he was tall and slim, with bright, short, blonde hair and his clothes were gaudy, seemingly a resplendent mass of garish, primary colours.

Sam looked through his bag to select his ball

and panicked when he realised he'd left his favourite *Penfold's* in the car; it was an obscure brand of golf ball but Sam felt comfortable with it.

Frankie went running back to the vehicle whilst Sam shook hands with his opposition but the younger, smaller competitor didn't gaze at him squarely; he had a game plan, and looking at his opponent and being amiable and friendly was simply not a part of its design.

Sam had concluded that Jerry Pate, U. S. Amateur champion or not, was only human and if he ignored him and concentrated purely on his own performance and score then he could or would not be intimidated by his celebrated adversary.

Sam's only opposition today was the course, the 18 arduous, demanding holes that had previously given him such grief and disappointment; he was determined to beat them this time!

Jerry Pate had the honour; he swung slowly and rhythmically in perfect synchronisation and the ball was dispatched expertly to the very corner of the right angled dogleg.

Frankie arrived back breathless from the car park, much to the amusement of the spectators and thrust six wrapped balls into his son's shaking hands as the starter called out in that familiar, perfect, crisp, exquisitely English diction and tone

"On the tee, Sam Chester!"

Sam quickly removed the crinkled paper from his chosen ball and without rushing, walked proudly and erectly onto the perfectly mowed tee area.

He felt the sun and the slight breeze from the ocean then inhaled in celebration of his life and silently dispensed his own sound advice under his heated and bated breath.

"*Just… play the course, Sam…just the holes…ignore the rest*!"

He bent down, teed up the small, white ball and, focussing all his energy upon it, turned and thankfully felt a firm and solid strike; he looked up to see his effort end up on the right of the fairway at the sharp, distinct angle of the dogleg.

He marched off, looking and concentrating only at the lush, green floor; he ignored the following spectators and multitude of competitors on the practice area to his right over the dreaded and wicked, raised, dark line of the devilish, *out of bounds*.

Jerry Pate played first and although Sam did not watch him swing, was relieved to see his ball finish somewhere to the left of the green.

Sam's shot was difficult, he had to thread a 3 iron into the small neck of the hole and avoid the, *out of bounds* again just those mocking few yards to the right of the fairway.

He shook his arms and tried to relax and again, only concentrating on the small, hypnotic, white sphere then turned and released; he looked up to see that he'd hit a wonderful shot that drew a little towards the flag and nestled delightfully on the front fringe of the green.

Jerry Pate chipped clumsily to *15 feet* and Sam used his golden centre shafted putter to propel the ball to *3 feet* from the hole that he was now the favourite to win.

The American missed his putt narrowly as Sam then knelt down behind his shot to read the contour and the line to the cup.

The greens were exceptionally, beautifully manicured and smooth and almost velvet to the touch; the ball rolled so silkily easily over the surface from a minimum amount of projected force.

Sam concentrated on the curved wording on his ball; lined up directly to the right hand side of the hole and released his right hand to make a perfect contact.

The tiny sphere took the *borrow* and disappeared into the innocuous, teasing, white hole as the small crowd broke into spontaneous and instant warm applause; he was 1 up!

Sam did not look at his opponent as in his head he was only level par; his battle was with the course and he had to keep focussed.

The 2nd hole was a short par 4, downwind and Sam, with the adrenaline flowing through him like tainted blood, unleashed a ferocious, wonderful drive of immense length causing a slight gasp from the incredulous crowd.

Jerry Pate caught one of the bunkers on the left of the fairway and after 2 further shots to hit the green, Sam had the luxury of 2 putts for the win and he left the second green 2 up!

The 3rd was a long par 5 and was halved in par then the famous champion took 2 shots to extricate himself from a green side bunker at the 4th that Sam amazingly won with a bogey.

Another bad shot from Jerry Pate at the 5th left Sam with a *5 foot* put to win the hole; he went through the same, protracted, precise routine and raised his fist to take the crowd's growing appreciation as the ball dived underground.

Unbelievably, Sam was 4 up and as the news filtered back to the clubhouse the crowd following the match started to increase and multiply with both spectators and competitors interested to see the possible demise of the tournament favourite.

Sam tried desperately to stick to his inspirational game plan but he felt his body tense as the realisation of his position started to tantalise and play with his mind.

Anxiously and clumsily he then hooked his drive off the 6th tee and after coming to rest against a boundary fence eventually conceded the hole to his opponent.

He glanced at Jerry Pate's smooth, swinging action at the short 7th and felt an unwelcome twinge of admiration as the man's, silky power propelled the ball within a few feet of the stick.

He was unnerved, dropped a further shot and lost another hole; he was now only 2 up and felt decidedly rattled and shaky.

The 8th hole overlooked the mouth of the estuary to the sea and as he felt the softness and freshness of the strong gusts he became set with a fierce determination; he vowed he wouldn't surrender his lead so weakly or easily.

The subsequent holes became a dog-fight, Sam wasn't playing wonderfully but the match wasn't about playing well any more, it was about guts and determination and Sam had these characteristics in abundance!

He was only 1 up coming to the par 5, 13th and he held a tricky *8 footer* to reclaim his 2 hole advantage which he still held as he stood on the 16th tee.

He was now 2 up with 3 to play, famously in golf an unpredictable and precarious position to be in!

Sam's concentration wavered and almost disappeared; he saw the clubhouse near the 16th green then watched as the multitude of spectators were pouring and streaming over to watch the spectacle of his match and he suddenly felt like he was the very centre of the universe.

His tee shot ballooned off the tee and after a further three, ungainly efforts he again was forced to concede another hole to his illustrious opponent; Sam was now on the proverbial, fated edge, being only 1 up with 2 to play.

Anything could happen!

Jerry Pate then hit a superb drive up to the 17th hole, whose green sat snugly at the boundary of the course and Sam, his game plan exploding in front of him, was impelled to watch and felt his mouth become dry with insecurity and tension.

His own shot scuttled only 100 yards off the tee and a further 2 scrappy shots only placed him on the front side of the immensely long, undulating, unfathomable, sheer surface whilst his opponent was only *10 feet* away in 2!

Sam looked at the huge crowd now thronging around the green and felt embarrassed at his collapse and inadequacy; after all his toil and effort he was mentally preparing himself to being all square with only 1 further hole to play.

Sam saw his father attending the flag in the far distance of the green and with only a cursory glance sent the ball on its long journey towards it.

He knew he'd struck the shot sweetly and watched relieved as it sped up the sharp incline towards the pin and murmured absentmindedly to himself.

"At least you've played one decent shot on this blasted hole!"

He watched the bright, rolling globe interestedly, like just another member of the audience all around him, as the ball took another sudden break along the green's contours and then, up the final hill as it slowed and, although he couldn't any longer see its movement, instinctively felt that it was close.

Then he saw his father pull the flag out in sudden panic and excitement and heard an outrageous scream and crescendo of noise as the ball dived spectacularly into the hole as if in the fulfilment, flourish, salute and ultimate end of its lengthy, incredible journey!

Sam, almost disbelieving his own spectacular, outrageous, good fortune raised his arms into the air and relished the wild applause as he slowly walked the 40 full, impossible yards to retrieve his ball.

The spectators were three or four deep around the impromptu, rowdy, amphitheatre and Sam looked directly at the pale expression on his opponents face; Jerry Pate was trying to look calm and composed but he'd been dealt a hammer-blow and Sam knew it.

As he'd seen his professional heroes do in competition on many occasions he raised his slender hands and arms and waved the excited noisy crowd quiet.

A deathly hush came over the assembled audience but to nobody's surprise the *10 foot* putt proved beyond the American champion and outrageously he was still 1 up with only 1 to play!

Sam was dormie!

He had seen *The Open* on television many times and as he looked up the short par 4, 18th he felt as though his own match had been magically transported there.

Spectators were everywhere but Sam was no longer intimidated; he had been energised and empowered by the previous hole and his tee shot was placed long and advantageously in the centre of the fairway.

His opponent achieved a similar result and Sam was left with an *80 yards* wedge to the pin on the front left hand side of the green.

He stood back and gathered his thoughts, his concentration and determination were immense as he stood over the shot trying to eliminate any self-doubts or possible traces of the debilitating *shanks* that had so recently affected this part of his game.

He kept his left side stiff; he felt the club hit the ball sweetly then raised his arms to acknowledge the gathering applause from the crowd as his ball moved inexorably closer and nearer to the hole, finishing only a mere *9 feet* away as he heard a voice from behind him gasp excitedly.

"He's done it...he's done it!"

Jerry Pate's effort ended double the distance away from his own, and it appeared that he had!

Sam saw absolutely nothing now as he walked, head down to the green; he would not allow himself to be diverted or distracted, and as Jerry Pate's effort glided past the hole, did not even notice the man remove then place his glove in his large bag as if to acknowledge his defeat.

Sam stood over his putt and tried to clear his turbulent mind, his trembling hands and this terrible, cloying dryness that had become part of him as he gritted his teeth and encouraged himself once more.

"*Come on, Sam...come on concentrate!*"

His head, mind and will drove his attention not to desert him and he sensed the crowds' silence, struck the ball and watched as it trickled to within *2 feet* of the hole.

Instinctively he then carefully marked it and again addressed himself silently as if his spirit had been suddenly placed in two separate parts of his mental and physical sides.

"*This to win the match!*"

To the American Champion's eternal credit he did not have to; he determinedly walked over to the young man, held out and shook his opponent's nervous, shaking hand.

He'd lost and did not wish his young challenger to hole the short putt to prove it!

The crowd instantly went wild with celebration and Jerry Pate relaxed as he pumped his conqueror's hand, his gaunt features illuminated by a rich, warm smile.

"Well done Sam, you deserved it!"

Sam only fully realised when he was much older, the lesson from the American title holder of dignity in defeat; the man's manner and actions that day were exemplary and worthy of a true golfing ambassador and champion as he handled the embarrassment of losing to a 17 year old boy, with immense charm, grace and style.

But such retrospective thoughts were for another day; Sam stood on the green and felt his father's arms around him as he enthused and cried out in such an outpouring of unsurpassed joy.

"You did it…did it!"

His temporary grip released him to acknowledge the remaining adulation and congratulations of the crowd as they cheered and clapped endlessly until the moment of jubilation had eventually gone and they slowly, happily, started to disperse.

There was a tremendous enthusiasm for defeating the Americans and years of painful thrashings at all levels of golf competition had left an atmosphere of barely concealed antagonism between the competing countries and their supporters.

Sam put his clubs and glove away and prepared to walk the few yards back to the clubhouse; he looked out at the course still jam-packed and busy with numerous games then finally at the final green where he'd won his famous victory.

It was only golf, the green course was still the same, only earth and grass, he was still the identical, young and unsure person but something had undoubtedly changed; something fundamental had changed!

Frankie pulled Sam's bag, hardly noticing its weight and walked to the car park to enclose it in the boot of his vehicle; he was so thrilled and excited he could hardly contain his joy.

Nick Faldo came up to him and almost threw

his arms around the chubby man in delight at what he had heard; in the communal excitement of defeating the Americans everyone was seemingly captured and caught up in Sam's victory.

Frankie was well aware of the young Faldo's, illustrious growing reputation and prowess; he was unprepared and overwhelmed at his sudden promotion to prominence as the Young Lion addressed him as a friend and an equal.

"We showed 'em…well done, Mr Chester!"

Frankie shook his hand and accepted the congratulation with unusual reserve; he was still numb with shock but in keeping with his bullish character, resolved to soon take charge of the situation.

Sam stayed around the 18th green for a few minutes; he waited for the crowds to fully dissolve and for the incredible event in his life to fade quickly into history.

He realised sensibly that ultimately it was only another match and as he looked, yet another story was being unravelled in the contest up on the 17th fairway and he needed to concentrate on tomorrow.

He walked towards the clubhouse acknowledging the handshakes and congratulations from people he hardly knew or recognised, and was pleased to enter the sanctity of the locker room where he started to change his shoes.

He noticed his father was in one of the telephone booths dialling frantically, he presumed his mother or the office or whoever?

Well his Dad always did like to talk!

A voice called him and captured his attention.

"You're, Sam Chester, aren't you?"

Sam looked up and a slim young man with ginger hair and grey eyes was looking at him curiously; he had other companions with him and Sam nodded, unsure of what they wanted as the stranger went on and spoke warmly and with real interest.

"I'm, Jim Duncan…Daily Telegraph. Wonderful performance, Sam, we'd all like to ask you a few questions, if we may?"

Sam leant back against the wall, it was both an expression of his need to relax and somehow for support as well; a sudden enclave of reporters seemed to fill the small, changing room and they formed a tight, questioning, semi circle around him as he gasped in surprise and tried to take it all in his stride.

"Sure...ask away...!"

He wiped the sweat still on his brow through his thick, brown hair and attempted to retain his composure.

"...Sure, what would you like to know?"

The reporters were polite, complimentary and extensive in their queries or interrogation; they asked about the round, how he felt, the famous putt, on and on.

Suddenly Sam heard one of the journalists at the back explode in sudden anger and cry out in exasperation.

"Can't you shut up!"

He slammed the shuttered, panelled glass door on the plump male in the telephone booth who was endlessly screaming and shouting something down the phone line.

Another reporter quickly informed him that this tubby, annoying man was in fact Sam's father and a ripple of amusement went around the small crowd as the writer who had lost his temper fell sheepishly silent then promptly returned to his notes.

After fully 20 minutes the grilling and interviews were over and, after Frankie had also fielded a few extra enquiries to glean matters from his paternal side, father and son went up to the café at the top of the clubhouse to enjoy some much needed sustenance.

As the two of them just ate as it seemed that they were both too excited to talk; Frankie was especially pleased that his premonition of revenge on Hoylake for the misfortunes the course had heaped upon his son had been proven correct.

They both remembered the cruel, bitter experience and his insightful, prophetic predictions in the car, as if it was yesterday.

Eventually the afterglow from the victory was fading and other games and results were soon being discussed; they returned to the hotel and after dinner Sam drove the short distance back to the club to confirm his starting time for tomorrow.

As he reviewed the score board he discovered that he had a bye and was in fact due to play the day after next.

He heard his name called and acknowledged a young man with spectacles carrying a small, black case who took and shook his hand and introduced himself.

"David Timpson, local BBC radio, can we have

a chat?"

Sam naturally agreed and they found a quiet corner of the clubhouse where the boy answered questions into a woolly microphone and gained a tiny, new experience in the world of media.

He answered the questions calmly and quietly until the interviewer seemed contented and pleased as he addressed him a final time.

"You'll be on the radio first thing in the morning... best of luck in your next match, Sam!"

The young man practised a few putts and watched as the sky burnt the last traces of red away to black then returned to the hotel as sadly, or happily, a memorable, unforgettable day had ended.

He knew it was now already the past but it was etched in his mind, the excitement, the struggle, the putt, the long unbelievable putt and it was now locked away forever inside him!

He slept well and was unprepared for the revelations of the morning for, as he sauntered in for breakfast, the attractive, blonde receptionist called him to her; Sam blushed unused to such female interest and walked the main desk as she whispered excitedly to him.

"I heard you on the radio this morning...you sounded great..."

Sam was genuinely surprised as if the recording he'd done the day before hadn't transpired and she turned up the volume on her small tuner and muttered to him.

"...Listen...I think you're on at 9.30a.m..."

Like magic, as they both strained their ears, the sports section soon came on the air when sure enough, his vocal talents and comments were clearly heard answering in an apparently professional way.

To Sam, if felt somewhat unreal and bizarre standing and listening to himself.

He smiled at the girl almost embarrassed but she just laughed gaily and enthused in her patent admiration for him.

"...You sounded good...really great!"

Sam thanked her shyly for her interest then walked in to join his father for breakfast somewhat unsettled and startled.

Frankie was lost behind countless newspapers that literally covered the white, linen cloth on the large table and as Sam sat opposite him he completely froze.

There on the back cover of the Sun was a photograph of his own face smiling at him with a headline above in huge, dramatic, startling emotive letters.

Cheeky Chester Stuns Champ went the bold script; Sam picked up another tabloid and stared in bemusement at the next paper.

Pate is top of the Flops, even the broadsheets continued the theme; **Young Sam Chester gives U.S. Champion a Golf Lesson**, it read in brassy, brave type!

Sam watched his father's flushed face and sat back stunned by the publicity, he'd expected a mention or even a picture, but this was national coverage and was crazy!

The whole breakfast room seemed to know and whoever had been ignorant of his son's fame, Frankie had soon informed; the middle aged man simply revelled in the notoriety of his brilliant offspring's success.

He was literally bursting with pride and although Sam had played and won the match, he realised silently and privately that it was his far-sightedness and management that had really and truly produced the audacious result!

Sam sipped his tea, tried to eat some toast but felt somewhat overwhelmed by the glowing articles about him and about this recent raw battle and challenge.

He recalled his spectacular good fortune on the 17th and in his own mind it had genuinely been only another match, where in truth he'd been exceptionably lucky.

His father, as he could see, certainly did not share his modesty and he was secretly annoyed with him for appearing to be so openly vain or even boastful.

Sam only wanted to put the victory behind him now, get it into perspective and concentrate on the next opponent.

Needing some separation he left his still buzzing parent to his breakfast and study of the fantastical papers before heading to the course that as usual was teeming with endless multitudes of busy people.

His hands grabbed his practice bag and, relieved to be by himself, used them to hit shots quietly and gently into the least occupied corner of the huge area of greenery.

Sam then went to the putting green and subsequently the score board where he was secretly pleased when he read that Paul Sandy had been eliminated in the first round.

It was the only time in his young, golfing life he had ever managed to surpass or usurp him!

However, Sam was still badgered with compliments and congratulations; he tried to be amenable or polite even though he no longer wished to talk about the adventures of the previous day.

He was due out at 10a.m the following morning and eventually left for the hotel, for a meal, a chat with his father and finally bed.

Frankie told him how the local papers at home had made such a massive spread and that they had phoned his mother and wanted to interview him again when he eventually returned.

Sam was flattered and complimented at all the attention but not really that interested; he was now focussed and concentrating only on tomorrow's, coming, single combat.

However the bout in the morning was something of an anti-climax; the wind swept in from the Irish Sea and whipped fiercely over the exposed course making playing conditions exceedingly difficult.

His opponent was overcome by Sam's sudden, illustrious and somewhat undeserved reputation and without playing well Sam won 3 and 2.

He was then due to play Simon Martin, a Scottish international in the 5th round and returned to the hotel fatigued but pleased to still be in the celebrated competition.

He spoke to one of the local, midland newspapers that had asked him to ring and he reported how he had progressed as they asked their questions and wished him continued success.

Sam aimlessly turned on the television in his room, *Sportsnight* was on and he dozed as Harry Carpenter guided the viewers through the various items on the show.

At the very end of the programme unexpectedly, the small but charismatic presenter addressed the camera directly; he related the innocuous tale of him being confronted with a proud, doting parent in Portugal when his plane had been delayed.

He told of the man's confident almost boastful enthusiasm for his son's golf and his conviction that he'd sired a champion.

Incredibly a picture of Sam then came onto the live screen and the boy gasped in disbelief as Harry Carpenter informed the world about Sam's victory over the U S champion and eventually spoke mischievously into the camera a final, teasing time.

"...It would appear that, Frankie Chester just... may be right!"

The recognisable music sounded and the programme was over and Sam knew for certain that he was suddenly, truly famous and it was the most bizarre and unreal experience of his existence up to now.

It was simply astounding and beyond belief!

His father came running and dashing into his room flushed with excitement mixed in with bemusement then questioned him.

"Did you see it?"

Sam nodded trying to act as if such an event transpired everyday and was dismissive although in truth he was more than amazed.

"Yes...yes...but come on, Dad I need to get some sleep, I've a game tomorrow!"

His father departed suitably admonished and surprisingly even in this bubble, Sam slept; he was simply tired out and exhausted!

He noticed that on the 4th day of the tournament the field had slimmed down considerably and as his pale eyes glanced at the board with the remaining competitors he observed that it still contained a rich sprinkling of upcoming stars.

Many of the American Walker cup players were still in, Nick Price from South Africa, many leading English internationals and of course himself, Sam Chester!

It made him so wonderfully proud that his golf had progressed to the level to where he could compete in such exalted company but deep down and in all truth, he still had these gnawing feelings of self-doubt.

He hid them as always with driven determination and made a blistering attack on the course over the first 6 holes to be 2 up on the vastly experienced, Simon Martin.

As with the English championship the previous year, for no apparent reason, mistakes started to creep into his game and without the good fortune he'd experienced in the previous rounds he allowed the much relieved, bespectacled, Simon Martin to turn the match around.

Sam lost 4 and 3 then took the long walk off the course tired and bitterly disappointed; the contest was there to be won and once again he'd let it slip, mainly he sensed because of what was going on in his always unstable and tortuous head!

It was as though when he needed to bring his game to a consistent, sustained, higher level of competence it proved to be beyond him both physically and mentally.

The long drive home was a mixture of exuberance for them both, at their famous victory, and Sam's personal upset and disappointment of not progressing further.

They were both pleased to see the house once more and Dorothy hugged her son lovingly when she saw him.

She noticed instantly again how weary, insipid and drained he was and even with all the excitement and success she was concerned, at his tender age, about his ability to sustain such effort or absorb such pressure and stress.

Congratulation cards were piled high; from the golf club, family abroad, friends and people that they hardly knew, even Anna came round to see her famous brother and at this stage Sam was utterly convinced that he *must* now be famous!

Reporters were due in the morning for some pictures and his sister asked if she should have her hair done as Sam looked at her as if she was mad and excused himself to bed!

He really, honestly could not understand what all the fuss was about; he'd won a single game and now he was out, he'd lost, that was the reality and end of the situation.

However the new day came, the reporters took their photographs, commiserated him on his loss and left, printing a general article in the paper the following day and mentioning that he was now one of the favourites for the county, *Courage* golf tournament, sponsored by the local brewery, in a few days time.

This was one of the county's most prestigious events and would contain all their senior stars; Sam had progressed in a week from a nobody to one of the local favourites and it was quite a leap!

If Sam had any ideas of grandeur his return and first visit to his golf club quickly dispelled them.

After heartfelt and effusive congratulations from his tutor and general compliments from the members that he passed; he suddenly felt his shoulders grabbed firmly and with feeling.

He turned around and there was, David Rubicks, one of his father's oldest friends; the man was short, chubby and wore glasses, the bifocal centres of the strong, black frames were fixed firmly on him as he spoke and addressed him.

"Don't move...I want to hear all about it, every detail... every shot....tell me exactly what happened!"

Sam, a little embarrassed and surprised at the man's, ardent enquiry sat down on one of the nearby, window seats, breathed in and as requested, started to relate the fantastical tale.

He began at the 1st hole and after recalling his drive, described to his small audience how his 3 iron second drew in the wind until it was over the flag.

Before he could continue the ebullient, Mr Rubicks butted into his reminiscence and story abruptly, forgetting instantly that he had so insistently and demandingly asked to hear it.

"Funny you should say that..."

His tone was serious and his mind was wandering.

"...Because I did the same thing at the 2nd on Sunday in the medal... mind you on the 3rd I hooked it and then... in trying to correct it on the 4th I sliced... then 3 putted!"

Sam listened politely, but in utter astonishment as the man recounted to him every shot of his obscure, forgettable, medal round and was relieved after 10 minutes when he finally finished.

He never mentioned Sam's match again and the boy learned a huge lesson that morning; the truth was that no one was honestly really that interested and like all things, his victory was transient, relevant for seemingly that day or a given, short space of time only.

Golf as he knew was a selfish game; that was at its very nature and although people were temporarily involved in his results, on a general basis they were always more far more concerned with their own success and play.

However and in all truth, Sam found it far more difficult to get the exhilaration of that day fully out of his system than he expected.

Although he had managed to place it into perspective with its implications for his immediate future, it made club golf seem tame and insignificant and he was pleased that the *Courage*, county test was only a few days away.

This further prestigious tournament would give Sam proper competition and a chance to make and affirm his ongoing quest for a place in the full county team.

On the day of the tournament, Sam was greeted at the course like an all conquering hero; he had represented Warwickshire wonderfully and they were genuinely pleased and thrilled that he had.

The officials and generously even the established stars shook his hand and told him how fantastically well he'd done!

Sam's golf on this particular day was also good and his putting sound and positive; he finished the competition in 2nd place.

It was his first senior success at medal play and he felt extremely contented and pleased with himself when he eventually collected his prize.

He was then asked to play in a 1st team county match and that evening as he relaxed and drank his tea, he felt thrilled as though his sporting career was finally moving in the right direction.

Sam's life became and was immersed in competitive golf; his handicap reduced to 1 and he felt the golfing world was his, to challenge then eventually vanquish and defeat.

He practised each and every day and

competed in endless local tournaments and county matches, all the time searching for that elusive spark that would meld his game to consistency.

Sam progressed to other tournaments but his performances were sketchy and inconsistent; a good round was followed by a bad one and trying to play well at all times under the pressure of clash or combat was proving elusive and frustrating.

As the British Boys loomed large for his last attempt, Sam recognised that although he was so well renowned for his feat in the British Amateur, his subsequent season was riddled with frustration and disappointments.

He'd been knocked out in the first round of the *English* and in the other tournaments had achieved little; regretfully he still did not have a formal title, junior or otherwise to his name and at the grand old age of 17 it worried and concerned him immensely.

He realised that leaving your name on trophies; a marker and a footprint along the road travelled, was a vital part of becoming a professional golfer and when he stared back at his own journey all he saw was a single glowing, incredibly lucky match!

He tried to analyse what was wrong but the

cause was intangible, his shots were sound and his swing seemed solid but he noticed that where he could focus and concentrate his effort at match-play, stroke play was a different *animal* altogether.

It was impossible to strain and focus throughout a 4 round competition; it required, guile and patience, consistency and most of all character and temperament.

Sam in his heart realised that his nature was undoubtedly suspect, often during a round he would feel that terrible stab and electrical flash of frustration, that seemed to then fester like a perpetual recurring sore that affected his focus and balance.

It only left him when the round had been completed and finished then, when his score was below his high standard - as it often was - he would feel disappointed and sad, only wishing for the following event when he could seek to put things right.

It was a disturbing, unhealthy cycle which was becoming more of a regular pattern and occurrence.

Depressed, was too strong a word to use, but Dorothy grieved for the sunny child she knew and, as with her own life, she felt trapped by the road chosen by Sam, but so foolishly guided by her husband.

In her perpetually ignored, humble opinion, so much energy and effort was expended for what?

Very little, as she viewed it!

A brief moment of fame and a short exposure to the intense, bright light of celebrity and success only then to always return to the pale darkness and shadows of mediocrity then struggle!

It confused and intensely saddened her but when she tried to discuss it with, Frankie he would tell her that, as with business, she really didn't understand life and golf in particular!

He informed her very sharply and acidly as to the facts of existence from his distinctive point of view.

"To succeed…you have to be prepared to suffer; Sam is very happy…I'm positive and sure of it!"

Dorothy stared at her husband icily and darkly as she rolled the words around in her concerned, troubled mind… *to succeed you have to suffer…* and she smiled wryly and poignantly!

Sometimes in life, as she knew to her endless pain and cost, you could suffer profoundly and still not succeed!

Chapter 8

Dorothy could never have stopped the steamroller that was her son's life; it was in ferocious motion, work, golf and training, an endless round of dedication and sacrifice.

Sam sometimes missed his friends who were by now at university and his social life was poor, providing little release from his ongoing effort and obligations.

Just before he was due to drive to Edinburgh for the British Boy's championship, his mother noticed that a sharp, bright rash had appeared on his arms and around his neck as Sam impatiently brushed her concern away.

"It's nothing…nothing…I've had it for a while, it flares up then disappears don't worry so."

Dorothy ran her fingers, showing the rough skin from years of her own endless work, over the boy's formerly perfect face; there were traces of the inflammation there and she could feel herself immediately start to panic.

She knew that her child was organised to go on his journey and didn't wish to unsettle him but as he drove away she rang the doctor and booked him in for an appointment.

Her mind dwelt and thought about the pressure he'd been under for so many years and although she knew her cherished boy's dreams and ambitions, she selfishly hoped for his well being that he'd be knocked out of this latest tournament, quickly!

Sam had no such thoughts about his rash, it didn't affect his golf and he settled back in his driver's seat for the long journey north.

His father could not accompany him and although he often enjoyed his company there was something exciting and refreshing about being by himself.

He had again been asked to play in the trial for the English boy's team although, Paul Sandy was an automatic choice due to his superlative performance that year in the *English* championship, where he'd reached the semi finals.

Desperately Sam wanted to represent his country and his mind meandered on him wearing the famous, bright, yellow jumper with the red English rose crest upon it.

The drive was arduous but as he reached Scotland he came to roads that wound through open, exposed wilderness full of gorse and heather; it was a wild and desolate country but there was also something wonderfully, calming and therapeutic about it that Sam liked.

He was tired when he reached his hotel; it was late, he was extremely fatigued and ate quickly then went immediately to bed.

In the morning he drove straight to Bruntsfield Golf course where he put his name on the board to play and had a chat with some of the boys that he knew.

The trials were the following morning and Sam patiently marked out the course, charting and creating the ready path that he hoped to tread the next, coming day.

Bruntsfield was a pleasant, parkland course and as with all tournaments run by the Royal and Ancient, the venue was superbly and immaculately prepared.

Sam was extremely nervous as he teed off the following morning and desperate not to repeat the disaster of the previous year; he played steadily but unspectacularly and eventually finished with a respectable 74, 3 over par.

He hoped that this, solitary, solid round would

have been enough to gain him a place on the team but when the list of chosen players was put up on the notice board his name was once again not listed upon it.

He'd yet again now been asked to come for a further trial the subsequent day and his place as an English International golfer seemed as faraway or distant as ever.

Sam practised a little into the evening and finally drove back to the hotel; he was increasingly beginning to appreciate that an endless, touring life was not all excitement or fun.

He found the time between rounds boring, the hotels to be antiseptic and impersonal which only highlighted the difference between the cut, thrust and the thrill of competition.

Sam tonight however was getting on extremely well with the young, brown-haired girl that served him his dinner; she was to quote the local vernacular, *bonny,* with deep, dancing brown eyes, a sparkling white, flashing smile and an engaging laugh.

He told her all about himself, his golf career and how he was playing nearby in the excitement of the British Boy's championship; the restaurant was not busy and Debbie listened and exchanged stories about her own life.

Sam was attracted to the girl but as always golf came first, he had an early start tomorrow and after finishing his meal, he wished the girl goodnight and thanked her for her best wishes for his success the following day.

He felt, stupidly, like a fabled knight going into battle with the favour of a young maiden and he thought, intermittently both about his attraction for the girl and his equal if not more passionate desire for the yellow sweater before falling into the separation of a deep slumber.

The following dawn was bright and still and Sam set his mind even before he'd reached the course; this was his last chance to get into the team and he would not accept any further disappointment!

He played and concentrated well and suddenly found his putting touch; the *Wizard of the green* was having a rebirth!

Sam was both thrilled and relieved with his score; it was 69 the best of the day and the boy knew he couldn't be left out now!

Sure enough his name was on the top of the sheet pinned up shortly afterwards on the small, cork, notice board and Sam was asked along with the rest of the chosen English team to attend a meeting in one of the rooms in the upper echelons of the historic, old clubhouse.

Paul Sandy was effusive with his congratulations but Sam always felt there was something vaguely patronising about the way he complimented or spoke to him.

It was as though he'd been seen to endlessly battle, but Paul Sandy had breezed into the team, what was a success to Sam was just another easy step along the road to, Paul Sandy.

Sam however was too excited and pleased to have such thoughts or feelings for long and listened intently as one of the officials gave the elite group a pep talk about the match with the old enemy to come.

Excitingly he was given some T shirts with the small emblem of a red rose of England upon it and the famous, yellow sweater also adorned with the same, wonderful motif.

He simply floated back to the hotel and gushed with enthusiasm as he told the lovely waitress, Debbie all about his success.

The restaurant however was busy and the young girl had little time to sit and chat and could only wave to him as she passed until eventually he left to return to his room.

In the morning there was a small opening ceremony between the English and Scottish boy's teams and suddenly Sam was waiting for his match to start when he would be in the latent heat of conflict and combat.

The morning games were foursomes, a form of golf not suited to Sam's game or temperament where each partner played alternate shots.

He did not like relying on anybody and unfortunately Graham Turner, his partner and himself did not gel or form a coherent team at all.

Graham Turner was a tall, thin boy with curly black hair and a slow jerky swing that propelled the ball forward in a spurt rather than a solid, firm strike or hit.

Sam just wasn't impressed with him particularly, nor the standard of his golf and in the end, his first match, so proudly representing his country, resulted in a sound beating of 5 and 4.

He therefore fretted throughout the lunch and, without the dead weight and liability of his partner, exploded onto the course in the afternoon with a mass of birdies.

He won 6 and 5; his score of 5 under par and his wonderful play would have beaten anybody in any of the matches played between the two countries!

England triumphed in the contest and the award ceremony was attended and watched by both the teams and crowds of boys waiting for the start of the tournament the following day.

The president of the English Golf Union made a short speech and commented on the high standard in all of the boy's golf; he mentioned Sam's name and congratulated him in front of all his contemporaries and peers about his historic victory in the *British*.

He then went on to also mention Paul Sandy's performance in the *English* and finished his address by wishing all the competitors the best of fortune in the coming week of competition.

Sam stood with his team mates listening and felt an immense sense of puffed out pride; out of all the competitors and boys in the country only Paul Sandy and him had been singled out for a special and most honourable mention!

He held his head high and the red rose on his chest seemed to burn into him as listened as the anthems of all the competing countries played.

The evening was soothing, balmy and gentle, he'd won his first international match and the morning brought a new prospect of glory; life seemed, temporarily perfect and divine!

Sam's young, female friend was not working that evening and he missed her smile and the opportunity to chat; he phoned home and told his father all about his adventures.

Frankie was also elated and eventually passed him on to his mother who questioned him about his rash and he answered childishly, sharply and unreasonably.

"It's…fine, Mum, don't ask…don't fuss!"

However after he put the phone down he noticed, whilst bathing that night, noticeably the coarse red and rough plague seemed to have worryingly spread.

Sam also observed how the inflammation had started to itch and feel uncomfortable but with another exploit and adventure coming up in the morning he did not wish to dwell on such unimportant or inconsequential things.

His match was not off until the afternoon and as he wandered around the busy course and clubhouse, he began to be aware of a strange and new phenomenon.

He was something of a minor celebrity; many of the competitors asked him if he was the boy that beat the US champion and looked at him with awe, admiration and respect when he confirmed that he was.

Sam remembered and recalled the previous year and the dark unnerving snooker room; David Robinson, who had now progressed to youth and senior golf, and realised how much had transpired in such an unbelievable short space of time.

His opponent in the 1st round was a small, young player of slight build and short, ginger hair; it was obvious that he was nervous and felt that he had no chance against Sam's, growing reputation.

The boy played the first 2 holes badly and as Sam had his putting touch, was soon shaking hands in defeat on the 12th having lost 7 and 6.

Sam felt his small, soft hand inside his own and his vanquished opponent congratulated him with wide, engaged, pale eyes.

"You were great, Sam…"

He spoke only in such admiration.

"…I expected you to be good but not that good!"

Sam shrugged in embarrassment; he tried to

be modest and walked away slightly overwhelmed and disconcerted at such enthusiastic and undeserved praise.

Debbie was back on duty later and Sam was pleased to see her, she sat down at his table and showed Sam a cutting from the local paper; it was detailing the boys that were favourites to win, Sam's name was high up amongst the list as she chuckled deliciously.

"They describe you as being dangerous…"

Her tone became a giggle and her dark eyes shimmered and shone in teasing amusement.

"…Are you dangerous?"

Sam read the article quickly; sure enough he was described as… *The dangerous, Sam Chester*, and he smiled at her then laughed equally mockingly in self deprecating humour.

"I suppose I must be!"

He knew for certain that lovely Debbie would have met him after her work, for a drink or a walk but he was off early; golf was his girl, and an exacting and demanding mistress come to that!

Sam won in the morning then the subsequent day and by the end of the week he was in the quarter finals.

His father was making arrangements to fly up for the final and that familiar cancer of pressure was increasing as each round and adversary was passed.

The quarter finalist's included Ian Woosnam, Brian Marchbank and of course, Paul Sandy as well as five other internationals.

Sam was drawn against Alastair Webster, a leading Scottish player, and they both looked at each other determinedly on the 1st tee.

The match was tense and very close, holes were exchanged throughout their contest resulting in them standing on the last, all square.

To his credit, Sam once more held his nerve and played a wonderful 7 iron through a swirling wind onto the putting surface, while his opponent went fatefully through the green and into trouble.

Sam had won 1 up and he was in the semi finals to be contested and played that very afternoon!

His foe was to be Brian Marchbank a local favourite who had headlined and featured constantly and continually in home papers since the day the tournament started.

He spoke to his father at his office and Frankie informed him that he'd be up for the final on the evening flight and Sam tried to calm and caution him.

"Don't jump the gun, Dad...I haven't won the Semi, yet!"

But his words might just as well have been spoken wastefully into the whistling wind as in his father's ever confident head, the match was a foregone conclusion and the flight was already booked!

Sam was nervous but strangely expectant on the 1st tee, he felt he could be victorious and was not worried or intimidated by the small but obviously partisan crowd.

He struck first, long and solidly down the fairway and after a perfectly faded 2 iron into the heart of the green, he was favourite for another flying start as his opponent was far down the fairway for 2.

Brian Marchbank pitched to *25 feet* and Sam lagged his put up for a par then watched in disbelief as his opponent perfectly, rolled the putt in and raised his arms in joy to take the delighted, enthusiastic applause of the vociferous, local, enthusiastic crowd.

Sam regrouped then set himself again, even more determined, and flew a 6 iron second shot to the next hole to only *5 feet* while his opponent struggled for a par; he had this putt for 1 up.

However his attempt stayed agonisingly on the lip and on the long par 4, 3rd, after being in a better position in the fairway, Sam just drifted a wood shot left of the green and watched it kick punishingly, then wickedly fly out of bounds.

He'd played well for 3 holes and was 1 down and after his opponent held another long put on the 4th he was 2 down and sensing that this was not going to be his day!

He struggled valiantly but the fates were against him and Sam suffered the indignity of losing by the margin of 5 and 4, his largest ever defeat in all of his junior golf.

The walk back to the clubhouse from the furthermost reaches of the course was long and lonely, and although he'd felt he tried his best, the taste of defeat so close to the final was unpalatable, acrid and bitter.

He phoned his father who listened in disbelief and their conversation was extremely short and brief each too disappointed to say or converse very much.

Sam was too tired to drive back that evening and ate silently, Debbie tried to cheer him up in her delightful if misguided way.

"It's only a golf tournament…"

She played with her long brown hair and spoke entreatingly in her soft, seductive, Scottish twang

"…And you can walk me home later if you like."

Sam smiled at her and in the dusk of evening he forgot his defeat and malaise as he walked hand in hand with the girl along the leafy lanes of the quiet, elegant suburb where the grey, stone houses sat back from the road like sculptured, chess pieces.

They arrived at Debbie's home and the girl looked at him shyly as they swapped numbers and addresses promising to keep in touch; she leaned up to him and let him kiss her, before running excitedly into the safety of her home to escape his clutches.

I mean from what the young, impressionable girl had heard and read perhaps he really was *dangerous* after all!

Sam slept tiredly and early in the morning pointed his yellow car south and breathed the clean, fresh Scottish air for the last time.

The adventure was over, the week of golf, Debbie, the seclusion of the hotel was ended and real life was waiting again for him only a few purposeful, driven hours away.

At home the celebrity life lasted literally minutes, stock was needed for the shops and Sam spent the afternoon of his return on various duties, necessities or deliveries.

It was not until the evening that he was able to sit down with his family when he could relate to them the full tale of his week and his eventual failure, dissatisfaction and demise.

Dorothy noticed that the inflammation was now clearly, concerningly visible on his face and informed her son that they were booked at the doctor's first thing in the morning.

Frankie then asked him in his patent frustration how he could have possibly lost so close to the final; his own discontent was almost still tangible and Sam looked at him curiously then explained it as best he could given his youth and inexperience.

"I was trying my best…I played well…"

His mind sought an answer and he partially found one.

"…It's just golf, Dad… sometimes that's how

it's fated and meant to be!"

Chapter 9

The doctor was concerned about the rash covering Sam and immediately referred him to a specialist as he commented sagely to Dorothy.

"It is psoriasis..."

He was unemotional but concerned nevertheless.

"...But I have never seen such a large area affected in such a young man..."

He stared, examined the markings further and questioned her.

"...Is the boy under any pressure?"

Dorothy told of her son's talent and expertise on the golf course and the carousel of effort and dedication he had chosen; it was as if she'd been wishing to reveal then release her concerns from her chest for ever as she spoke passionately.

The thin doctor sat back in his chair and listened intently then spoke calmly and with some experience.

"I'm no expert…"

He exhaled in thought then continued.

"…But psoriasis is directly related to nerves and pressure and it sounds to me like the young man has a lot on his plate…"

His dark eyes focussed kindly on the Sam and caught him with a difficult and pertinent question.

"…What do you think, My Lad?"

Sam looked at him blankly and inadvertently ran his fingers over the rough, red skin on the right hand side of his neck and cheek; this was a query he did not wish to face.

He knew exactly how the cut and thrust of his sport played with his mind; it teased, frustrated and incensed him all at the same moment, instant and tortuous time.

It demanded a lot but Sam was prepared to give it; golf was part of his destiny and future and he recognised that self-sacrifice was a price to pay for success as he replied uncertainly.

"I'm not sure…?"

He mumbled and simply wished the vicious, sinister plague away.

"…I'm just not sure!"

Dorothy told her husband immediately on his return from work then watched with amazement as he slowly worked himself into a fury and subsequent crescendo as he screamed at her in his reactive anger and wild frustration.

"Doctors…Doctors! What do they know…?"

He continued spluttering and exploding in irrational, childish ire and uncontrollable irritation.

"…Pressure, stress… we're all under stress…!"

He was simply apoplectic as he ranted and raged.

"… How do they know? The boy's happy… he's doing exactly what he chose to do!"

Sam was in the other room but he heard clearly his father's tirade and infuriation as it made him intolerably miserable.

His father was right, it was what he wanted but he caught his reflection in the mirror and looked how disfigured he appeared; he was facing a crisis and a paradox in his life and he did not know how to deal with it.

The golf season was over apart from a few, minor tournaments and the approach of the appointment with the specialist became the focus of his and his mother's life.

Things appeared normal; work was incessant and unrelenting but he had never seen his parent's relationship so strained; they had argued in the past but not like this!

The appointment with Mr Lewis, the specialist, came in early in December and the three of them were ushered, by a rounded, pretty, young nurse in a white coat, through to a wood panelled office where a slightly built, elderly man with short, grey hair strode out from his desk engagingly to greet them.

"I'm very pleased to meet you…"

He smiled happily, shaking hands with Dorothy and Frankie before turning his attention to the youth, and he then shook his hand firmly as well then continued on jovially.

"...You must be the famous, Sam!"

Mr Lewis as it transpired was an avid golfer as well, and he was well aware of the boy's notoriety; he examined him then listened dispassionately as each member of the trio told him their particular, personal version of the young man's life.

The conversation went back and forth for half an hour, Dorothy worried, Frankie dismissive, and Sam confused, until finally the man raised his small, thin delicate hands and they fell silent.

He looked at them; his coal black eyes seemed to peer intently behind his tightly lined eyelids as he murmured educated words that he knew would not please everyone.

"I wish I could tell you a simple answer..."

He sighed in the difficulty of his task and duty.

"...Sam's condition, in my professional opinion, is undoubtedly caused by the pressure of his chosen vocation..."

Dorothy visibly exhaled in satisfaction as if vindicated in her own analysis, but unfortunately for her the doctor progressed.

"...However, if this, Talented Boy gives up the

game there is no guarantee his condition will improve although the prognosis would be more favourable…"

He took a final intensive, strained, deep breath and relaxed in his rich, brown, leather chair, as if enjoying and relishing suddenly dispensing his expensive wisdom.

"…If you are asking me to tell you to do that, then I cannot… it is a choice for, Sam, it's his life…"

Dorothy and her husband were on the very edges of their seat.

"… After all what we are talking about is not clinically dangerous, it is a matter of vanity, some would say good skin is nothing more than a mere adornment or indulgence!"

Dorothy stared at him as if he was mad or clinically insane; Frankie nodded in communal wisdom and Sam simply felt upset, frightened and confused.

They prepared to leave the expert physician's rooms with a prescription for some cream and advice that suited the particular purposes of whoever wished to selectively listen then interpret what had been said.

In a nutshell it seemed that Sam was

undoubtedly affected by golf and should give it up, but that was no guarantee of a cure; he could therefore continue on, try not to worry and must avoid stress at all costs!

Loving and understanding her son, Dorothy knew that this was a conundrum and a contradiction in terms; such self control was way beyond her son's, existing, mental abilities.

Mr Lewis finally ended the meeting by congratulating, Sam on his victory over the United States Champion, Jerry Pate and wished him the best in his path and career for the future.

Dorothy sat in the car deflated and exasperated; she felt that she had just visited an asylum and as she looked at the flaring redness burning her son's face she could not believe how the idiotic, *learned man* could not see the simple facts that had been placed so obviously before him.

She wanted the best for her son, for him to give up this stupid quest for a golf career; like any mother she wanted him to find a job, go to college, to have a normal, fulfilling, happy life.

To her distress her husband drove away slowly, melodramatically deep in thought and after a suitable length of time whispered sagely.

"What an intelligent person…"

All previous references to professional people being idiots were suddenly and instantly dispelled.

"…It was a very interesting debate and discussion…"

He turned his gaze to his shivering son.

"… What do you think, Sam?"

The focus of his attention sat quietly in the back watching the trees roll past and trying to ignore his reflection in the glass; he tried to avoid looking at himself at all times as he was beginning to feel extremely self conscious and sensitive about his disfigurement.

Frankie did not allow his son to respond and badgered him in mock threat and challenge.

"Do you want to give up the game?"

Sam responded instinctively.

"No, Dad."

His mind panicked and raced; give up? What else did he have?

His future seemed inextricably linked with the game and he could not contemplate a wasted life in the shops or the awful warehouse forever unloading boxes.

Frankie smiled in satisfaction and turned to his wife and spoke with utter condescension and dryness.

"Let that be a lesson to you, Dorothy…"

He was so arrogantly, odiously contemptible and for more than a second she wondered why she married him!

"…The, Boy's happy, he wants to strive; he's just got to control himself a little more!"

Dorothy looked at her plump, smug partner and she wanted to hit him; he was either completely insensitive, stupid or both!

Only her blinkered husband could have come out of a meeting like that with such a puerile, fixed or narrow view.

As normal it was not about what she wanted for or even what Sam wanted, it was always about what he wanted and thought was right!

Frankie always made out that he knew best even when in all honesty and fact her infuriating partner simply knew nothing at all!

However for Dorothy the positives were that Sam's condition was not more serious, he had a few months off where she would work with him to try to alleviate the condition and eradicate it if it was possible.

Christmas was a subdued affair; endless work then a festive dinner at Anna's palatial home.

Timmy had been busy buying presents, he never seemed short of money and Sam was positive and sure that as usual his shop would have the biggest deficit and the worst, stock control.

Sam had given up trying to reconcile his father's logic concerning his sibling and her family, and Anna had hardly made any appearance at work owing to one form of *illness* or another.

Sam ventured out into town with some of his friends that had returned from university and marvelled at how confident they were with the opposite sex, as opposed to his own bumbling and nervousness.

He felt conspicuous by the pronounced affliction on his face and noticed how the eyes of so many girls he spoke to were drawn to it as an evil mark or a focus of unusual disfigurement or fun!

It was supposed to be a crazy and exuberant time of life when good looks, youth and wildness counted for a lot, but Sam felt lost and inadequate in this evolving, energised, mating game.

The worse his social life became the more Sam would immerse himself in his golf as this was one part of life where he felt comfortable and in partial control; in the small, insular world of golf he was something of a success.

This was another unhealthy sequence but Sam was drawn into it as a moth is drawn to a bright light; it was as though everything happened in reflex and on automatic pilot away from his ability to influence his future.

And so it was with all these confusions mixed in with contradictions at 18 years of age Sam faced the coming year, his combative schedule crammed with ever more tournaments and competitions.

Junior golf was now nothing more than history and Sam was to be tested at the highest levels of senior amateur golf; it was an exciting time but it seemed that the emerging, struggling adult had more to cope with than, just the sport.

Sam had resolved to try and control his temperament more, the fire that had won him so many matches needed to be quelled, quieted, used sparingly; he wanted to play and compete but understandably to control his psoriasis and condition as well!

The year started poorly and seemed to get worse. Sam was terribly inconsistent; one good round was followed by three poor ones and in the testing examination of stroke-play golf Sam was always found wanting.

The only point of interest was in April when his father, mother and he went down south to the West of England Championships at Saunton Sands golf course.

He made the cut and played the three days around the rugged, seaside course; Sam enjoyed the trip, the people were friendly and the views over the barren, windswept coastline were always spectacular in their unique, sandy, desolation and beauty.

Unusually Sam's mother accompanied them and stayed at a hotel that stood bravely near the edge of cliffs that gave wonderful, panoramic views of the tumbling, always rolling, Atlantic Ocean.

One evening, a guest in the hotel commented to Dorothy on Sam's noticeable problem; she kindly suggested that he visit a famous herbalist in Wales that was renowned for his expertise and cures of such conditions.

Dorothy, her normal avenues of ordinary medicine restricted to thick, white cream, was happy to grasp at any available straw and the following week the three of them were waiting in a tiny, reception room in the little village of Pontypridd.

Mr Thomas was the expert's name; he was small and gentle with deep black, straight hair and kind, brown eyes.

He was incredibly charismatic and spoke with a charming, Welsh lilt that reminded Sam somewhat of his tutor.

The man related the story of his own life threatening cancer that proved the catalyst for his initial, and understandably earnest, interest in his chosen field of herbal medicine.

Apparently he had learned his trade in Russia and Dorothy listened enthralled and enraptured.

He informed them that he had been cured and had subsequently decided to devote his life to help and educate as many people as he could with regard to this art and insightful way of natural remedies.

Frankie, as always, was sceptical but if the

man could help he was certainly willing to pay and they drove away from the sleepy village armed with bottles of Ginseng, B vitamins, Royal Jelly, alongside various other lotions, packets and books.

Sam felt like a moving, endless, ocean wave, washing helplessly from one thing to another; he reacted to other forces, without any control, almost without thinking, conscious only of his endless work and his golf!

It was hard for him to know whether he believed the herbalist, Mr Thomas or not, but the essence of his argument that, *you are what you eat*, seemed sensible and he was willing to attempt anything to try and help himself.

He was tired after the long trek home and went to bed feeling frustrated and angry that his illness and condition was the cause for such effort then further expense for his parents.

The tablets and changed way of eating henceforth became part of his everyday routine; his golf however did not improve and tournament after tournament yielded nothing of substance.

He had the occasional victory in an early round of the *British* or *English* championships but he was dispatched soon afterwards.

Sam spent his time trying to control himself, not to get too excited, not to release the demons inside him; it was all such an endless, painful, arduous continual effort!

The psoriasis improved, the roughness lessened slightly, the redness faded fractionally and Dorothy was thrilled.

She prepared all food recommended by Mr Jones and Sam tried to convince himself that liver and grilled fish with vegetables were his favourite meals.

Resolutely he tried to maintain his good humour but there were times he felt, as if a large, moody, grey, debilitating, dull cloud was permanently hanging over him.

Sam approached his golf as if it were a mountain that had to be climbed or conquered; hard work he was sure could eventually win through, provide and achieve success.

His determination for accomplishment and progress was still intense, even if it was now tempered by restraint on his volatile temper and temperament.

The tournament season had ended, he still practised day after day, relentlessly pounding golf balls towards the shed that had long ago lost the mystique and attraction it had for him as a child.

Paul Sandy had continued to improve exponentially; he was the youngest ever English international and had recently featured in almost every major, amateur tournament.

It only highlighted Sam's lack of progress or success and it hurt his self-esteem and pride deeply.

But the beauty and seductive enticement of golf was that there was always another year, another tournament, and Sam tried to be philosophical and positive.

As the family approached a further Christmas, Dorothy was exasperated and Frankie was uncontrollable; his gambling seemed to know no limits or bounds of common sense and the work and pressure upon her seemed insurmountable.

Sam's situation continually upset and frustrated her; she felt his effort and disappointment and recognised that the road chosen for him was so horribly constrained and endlessly fraught with problems.

She watched as he performed his obligations to the business and he worked relentlessly as she did; in the shops and the warehouse but as with his golf, the seemingly, eternal enterprise was ever more demanding and gave them scant security for their efforts.

How could they be protected or safe, even her limited education told her that with her daughter not working, her son in law a malingerer and her husband just being Frankie, finances were still finely balanced or honestly much, much worse.

She never knew the real position, that was her husband's domain and he never disclosed the accounts, but the responsibility, work and eternal selfless love of her family made her constantly tired.

That was her life; had she really chosen it to be like this?

It all seemed so long ago when she had a choice and, as another year dawned, she could only hope for the best; it was a poor second to really having any option, alternative or control.

In the quietness of the winter season Frankie had tried to analyse just why Sam had not made the breakthrough they had both been looking for.

He sensed the answer to Sam's performances lay in changing his teacher; Len Thompson was fine for club golfers but his son was a star and stars, like champion horses, needed top coaches and trainers.

He had met another professional in their travels called Anthony Sander during a Pro-Am event late the previous year, and had been impressed with the man's stories of his previous playing exploits with his contemporaries such as Tony Jacklin.

The man was professional at a club on the very outskirts of the county and he made arrangements for Sam to start lessons in early February.

Frankie informed Len personally of his decision before even discussing it with Sam, but the old professional just smiled and took it all in his exceedingly long stride then drawled in his amiable manner.

"If it's good for the, Boy… it's fine with me!"

No one but his wife knew how personally he felt insulted or just how childish and ignorant of golf he thought Sam's father was; he sipped his tea in the comfort and warmth of his own home one evening and looked into the smouldering fire and addressed his wife with his concealed, private thoughts.

"You can't buy a golf game, Jackie…"

He was angry and discontent; he had also

invested emotionally in the young boy he had known for so long.

"…Frankie and his son are going to learn that you just can't!"

Sam was amazed and taken aback at his father's revelation that Len had been dismissed from his teaching role; he wanted to argue but could not dispute that his performances lately were continually poor and a new *broom* as his father suggested, may help?

Frankie also told his son that he was booked to go to Sotto-Grande to visit Henry Cotton again in March and Sam had to conclude that he had no choice but to give this new change of direction a go.

Sam was taken to Anthony Sanders during the cold first week in February, the wind whistled around his ears as the chubby man with neatly combed, jet-black hair dissected his swing.

He didn't change too much on the immediate lesson as his father and his new teacher decided that more extensive amendments could be implemented after Sam's forthcoming trip to Spain.

Sam played little competitive golf prior to his departure to see the, *Maestro* and on this occasion travelled by himself.

Upon his arrival he was surprised to find that he was the only student there and Henry Cotton welcomed him like an old friend.

The Spanish complex was less imperious than Penina but Sam was impressed by the huge practice area and was anxious to loosen his muscles that had been confined by the hours of travelling.

Henry Cotton invited Sam to join him for lunch and the youth was surprised, after selecting his food, he was then asked to pay for it; the old adage that there was no such thing as a free meal certainly rang true in Spain.

But Sam began to slowly appreciate and understand that this man came from a tough school of life where nothing had ever been given or provided without a pecuniary or financial cost for him!

The *Maestro* was however extremely interested in Sam's progress and listened intently to his story about Jerry Pate and his now famous victory.

The old, experienced, golfing Master knew it was only another small step along the lengthy road of achievement and there was still much for the young man to traverse.

Sam practised briefly in the afternoon and

Henry Cotton watched him; as with the previous year, he did not attempt to teach but just to re-affirm his belief in the tyre training and the importance of self-improvement and ability to change.

Unfortunately Sam fell ill so for a couple of days stayed in bed and it was a relief when he eventually re-emerged to feel the warmth of the Mediterranean winter; always so welcomingly different and a release from the bitter coldness of England.

The *Maestro* made a fuss of him and they played then practised together over the next couple of days.

Sam enjoyed riding in the same buggy as the great man, listening to tales of competitions and adventures seemingly so long ago in a different era and age.

Henry Cotton recounted his time when he appeared in the variety theatres, performing a one-man show and Sam laughed as he recalled how he would pretend to hit a real, golf ball into the audience only to change it to a hollow, light, plastic sphere at the last minute.

The old man laughed loudly at his memories.

"They all used to cower with fright…"

His blue eyes were so full of the fading past.

"...But that's what you had to do in those days to make a living..."

Sam detected a trace and a certain air of resentment in his voice as if he recognised that in the modern time, inferior professionals were earning vast sums that in his day seemed unimaginable.

But his dissatisfaction was a mere sliver or ember of the past and the renowned old sportsman had undisputedly and undeniably lived an exceptional and rich life.

"...The thing I loved..."

His wonderful clear diction was so delicious, like crystal, icy water.

"...Was to know that wherever I went... I was the best, I liked the feeling that no-one could beat me!"

Sam listened and understood him, as he comprehended the demons and devils that plagued him during the pressure of his *Open Championship* rounds and victories.

He could relate them strangely to his own troubles, his own physical and mental problems, but recognised, as he marvelled at his aged, playing companion's eternal finesse and rhythm, that they were still barely or hardly comparable golfers.

The following day Sam practised in the morning and whilst meandering aimlessly, near the putting green fell into broken conversation with a tall, athletic, broad but lean young man, with a thick, German accent.

They agreed to play and made a small, side bet; with the language barrier, conversation was difficult, protracted and drawn out and they both concentrated on their match, each determined to win!

The man had a stiff, wide action and propelled the ball vast distances but Sam's competitive instinct rose to the challenge and he won the Pesetas on the final hole.

The combatants had no conversation at the end of the game and the following afternoon met again then agreed to do battle once more; they were both quietly focussed and concentrated to take the small, financial prize and after a tense contest, Sam came to the last hole 1 up!

The man wound himself and the English boy drew breath in awe as the ball seemed to literally disappear from sight; Sam's own shot was solid and straight but was easily 140 yards behind his opponent!

Remarkably Sam hit his wood shot onto the green and with his opposition unable to get up and down in 2 from just in front of the green the fiscal reward was again in the possession of the smaller golfer.

The blonde man however beamed a warm smile and shook Sam's hand and muttered in friendly, broken English.

"You played good…good, golf!"

Sam returned the smile and iron handshake then spoke as if realising their previous lack of verbal exchanges between them; it seemed that golf had its own special communal language and dialogue without the formal need for words!

"Thank you…I enjoyed it…"

He was suddenly aware that in the intensity and concentration of their contests that they had not formally introduced themselves.

"…My name is, Sam Chester."

The tall, muscular, man simply laughed.

"Pleased to meet you, Sam…"

He answered, trying to make himself

understood.

"...My name is, Bernhard... Bernhard Langer!"

They tried to converse but the lingual barrier was insurmountable and Sam dwelt no more upon it, other than the man had been part of an enjoyable, successful game and day.

He thought no more about it that was, until the self, same stranger lifted *The Masters* at Augusta just a few years later and went on to become one of the best European players of all time!

The week was over; Sam travelled to compete in the Spanish Amateur Championship and after successfully qualifying only made it to the second round before being defeated.

He was however invigorated, after the break from the terrible weather and spending time with the *Maestro*, it was impossible for any golfer not to feel enthused and better!

He returned to England fully ready for the Amateur tour, his father came to meet him at the airport and Sam told him all about his most recent adventure.

Frankie confirmed that he had made an appointment with his *brilliant* new teacher at the end of the following week.

Sam played a couple of medal rounds at the club over the next few days and found it increasingly hard to face, Len Thompson.

The tall, ever friendly professional sensed the young man's disquiet and unease then thoughtfully took him onto one side when the shoe changing area became quiet.

"Don't worry about me, Son..."

His voice was kind and soothing.

"...If this new professional can help you then your father's doing the right thing... the clever man learns something from everybody."

Sam looked into the man's dark green, intelligent, expressive eyes and was comforted by his words; he thought so extremely highly of him and did not want him to be upset with what was happening.

"It's my Father...," he explained weakly "...He's..."

Len waved one of his exceptionally large hands at him to silence and still his excuses.

"...Your Dad's just trying to do the best for you, Son, don't dwell on it... just... *go with the flow!*"

Sam sat back on the old, wooden bench and

listened; Len was always so approachable, cool, refreshing or relaxed and he wished he could one day, be more like him!

The morning of Sam's new lesson dawned and Sam and Frankie spent the 40 minutes driving there in complete silence.

Frankie also felt badly about taking his son from his original tutor, but he was convinced of his logic as it was obvious that Anthony Sanders had the experience to help.

After all he'd played and competed with Tony Jacklin; he was sure that this expert and experienced man would finally provide the missing link in his son's game.

Chapter 10

The home course of the new tutor was barren; the eastern wind swept across the gorse and the heather and after the initial niceties of formal introduction in the small professional's shop, the three of them trooped across to the practice area that ran directly alongside long, par 5, 1st hole.

They were all wrapped in waterproofs providing some respite from the chilling gusts and Sam started to hit shots toward a round marker far up the fairway.

Frankie watched breathlessly in the stiff, icy cold breeze; his boy seemed to be striking it well and it was only after about 20 shots that he saw the plump, rounded professional slowly start to shake his portly, thick head.

The man spoke sharply and with real, strained and stressed purpose.

"No, Sam you're not extending, keep your head still, straighten your arm through impact… NO!"

Sam was taken back he stopped his practice and tried to understand what this unknown man was trying to explain to him.

The professional aggressively took hold of his left arm and, as if it was within an actual shot or swing, then showed him the stretched and extended position he wanted him to reach.

He had to be stiffer, more pedantic with each effort, to stay down through the hitting area and reach out with this upper limb to provide the power then consistency he desired.

He turned to Frankie and sighed in agitated, clear frustration.

"There's a lot of work here…"

His voice complained as if, Sam was a mere beginner.

"…An awful lot of work!"

Sam left the practice area with his game in pieces, he watched as his father handed money to the man, *more money* he thought, feeling sick to his stomach, *always forever more money*!

Sam attacked the practice ground over the next few weeks with an intensity he'd never previously experienced.

He was determined to please his new teacher, to implement the changes that the man had felt were so vital; he had to try as it was the only way he knew to improve and make things better.

Week in week out, however hard he worked and laboured at his game, his tournament scores and performances got progressively worse, making little or no impression on the local tournament scene never mind the national stage.

Sam's psoriasis also deteriorated and throughout this period, Anthony Sander was calm, collected, arrogant, phlegmatic and pragmatic to both him and his anxious father.

"It takes time!"

He spoke encouragingly and his fleshy face and dark, closely set, black eyes were framed in an image of concern that Sam felt disingenuous and insincere.

His empathy with Sam's struggle did not prevent him from accepting whatever fiscal reward was on offer and the reasons for Sam's performance was, in his teacher's view, purely due to his formative swing.

Sam failed to qualify for almost every tournament and was knocked out early in all the major amateur events; it was suddenly late June, he'd been with his new mentor for nearly four months and was beginning to question the wisdom of his father's, rash, unilateral decision.

The last few weeks he'd been obligated to catch a train then a bus over to this isolated wilderness of a venue and his *inspirational* new teacher had not been there on more than a couple of occasions.

He had passed the lesson on to his assistant, on the basis that the younger aide had his unique system and could guide him.

The fee was still the same however and sure enough after nearly two hours travelling Sam arrived at the course one afternoon to find only the tall, spotty, junior, and as yet unqualified professional, there to insipidly welcome him.

Sam trudged dispiritedly over to the deserted practice area and went through his familiar, demoralising routine; his shots as always nowadays were weak, inconsistent and disconcertingly erratic.

He had tried everything to master, Mr Sander's technique, but with all the effort and body gymnastics he just could not understand the theory; it did not work at all.

Sam watched as another shot drifted weakly right; his left side was tense, as he'd been instructed, and he slammed the club down on the soft earth in despondency and bitter, gnawing frustration.

"This fu…!"

The tall boy looked at him blankly, as if mildly amused and continued the spiel and patter of his employer as he spluttered ever onwards.

"You have to keep working at it… Mr Sander's an authority on this method!"

Sam looked into his irritating, indented and marked, gaunt face and it reminded him of his own affliction; the raging fire that he'd been trying to control suddenly and instantly exploded inside him.

He'd beaten a US Open golf champion and there he was being taught by who? *Plug* from the comic *Beano*!

He had an inspiration as if in realisation of his lunacy; he handed the tall boy his club then confronted and challenged him.

"Show me, Andy…you show me how it's meant to be done!"

The large youth stood back as if he'd been slapped, but was trapped by the reasonable demand and then stood unsteadily and reluctantly up to the ball then addressed the small sphere nervously.

It was as if it was about to bite him painfully, and his lips muttered defensively as he readied his attempt at demonstration.

"This club's a bit light for me!"

Sam snapped at him, his tolerance and patience completely drained and exhausted.

"Just hit it…just hit the bloody thing…!"

His supposed instructor turned and made an unbalanced, ungainly swing at the little globe; his follow through had a trace of his employer's process, but the resultant shot was struck poorly, amateurish and inaccurate.

Sam exploded, his anger welling and swelling ever more inside him.

"...Again...again...do it again!"

The youth repeated, then repeated once more and Sam recognised that his *teacher* could not in fact play the game, hardly at all!

After a dozen shots he offered Sam the club back and whispered embarrassedly to him as if he had been caught out in a trick.

"Come on...we're here to help *you*!"

Sam put the iron club firmly and meaningfully into his bag and without another word walked alone, irritatedly back to the clubhouse; he paid the full lesson fee in absolute, seething silence and waited patiently for the taxi that would take him to the train station.

As he left the gravel, car park he looked for a final time at the ever-open expanse of the golf course and the practice area that had sadistically tortured him over the previous months.

Even in the warmth of the car he sensed the wind, the endless, evil, icy arctic blasts of air that seemed to beat continuously from the exposed east; he vowed that he'd never return and he never did!

Sam was learning the same lesson over and over again; everybody wanted money; money for teaching, for clubs, for advice and his naïve and impressionable father unfortunately found it difficult to discern the genuine from the deceitful!

He informed him on his return that he'd decided categorically that the experiment with the new instructor was over; he explained about the assistant teaching him but Frankie put up no argument at all, the new *stables* had indeed not been a roaring success.

The British Youths championship at Pannal, in Yorkshire was just a few weeks away; his contemporaries seemed to be developing and improving whilst he unquestionably was moving backwards.

He desperately wanted to make the *Youth's* International side but knew that he had no chance that year with his inconsistent and continual poor performances.

He found Len Thompson in his shop repairing an old wooden driver; he was patiently winding the thin, black twine skilfully at the base of the silver shaft and he looked immediately and kindly at the young man.

He had watched the boy grow up from that very first lesson and had an enormous affection for him; he recognised his change in nature, the cruel redness that disfigured him and his endless, eternal struggle to find his way forward.

His blue eyes still had the warmth and sparkle of youth that he'd first noticed but the sport had undeniably pressed then burdened him with its seductive and enticing promise.

It was an elixir he'd briefly tasted himself and he knew that it was an intoxicating and irresistible thing; the promise of fame and glory was there for the taking, but somehow available only for the very special and favoured few.

There were times in recent months that he'd wished Sam had not taken his formative steps into the game's magical wonders, but what was done, was done and Len knew that there was no point dwelling on the past or what was unchangeable.

He sensed the seemingly perpetual, Young Man, wanted to speak and he made it ever easy for him to do so.

"What is it, Son…tell me?"

His voice was as rich and emotive as ever and Sam shuffled his feet in embarrassment as if he was still the identical child that had come to him all those years ago.

"My lessons haven't been very successful…"

He whispered in his cloying abashment and discomfort,

"… I was wondering if you…"

Len did not give the boy time to finish; he'd felt snubbed by Frankie but he had no desire to put any more pressure on his charge.

"Let me finish this…"

He was understanding and delightful as always.

"…And we'll go out then hit a few shots…see what we can do!"

Len had seen over the recent months Sam's new swing and it had not impressed him, not one iota or a single jot!

He finished his binding then leisurely walked with him out to the range and allowed him to hit only three shots before he began to chuckle and then laughed mockingly, very gently and softly.

"*What's this?*"

He teased him, and moved his own club as if to imitate his pupil's weak, cumbersome effort.

Sam looked on amazed at the demonstrated, contorted position; the manufactured extension through the ball and the general lack of grace or rhythm and he shrugged and smiled sadly although he felt like crying.

"I don't know…I just don't know."

They both laughed together and that sudden release of tension immediately broke the small but significant gulf that still undoubtedly existed between them!

Sam instantly remembered that it was still just a game; finally he discarded all of his recent tutor's advice and, within a dozen shots, had recaptured the essence of the freedom of movement he'd learnt so joyously as a boy.

He revelled in the comfort and return of his motion and even though the shots weren't perfect, he felt a certain control and familiarity that had not been there for seemingly such a long, long time.

By the end of the brief session, Sam was

relieved and thanked Len sincerely for his patience, understanding and help.

As they walked the short distance back to the shop, Sam asked him what he owed him for the lesson but the tall, craggy man put his extensive arm gently around the boy's shoulder then just let it rest there very tenderly and lightly.

"There's no charge, Son, no charge at all!"

Sam felt as if a burden or a huge weight had been lifted from him as over the next few days he practised and recovered much of the style combined with rhythm that he'd so unfairly and casually discarded.

He still felt that it was insufficient for the very top level of competition but at least he now felt he'd again got something to work with.

He drove to Pannal with some hope; the journey was arduous and long and as normal, his father accompanied him.

The incident with the tutor had been the first time that Sam had ever directly gone against what he'd thought were his father's wishes, but Frankie had taken it in his stride.

This was only a minor mishap along the way, his confidence in his son's, or his own ability was immense, and he knew that it was only a matter of time until they broke through the golfing barriers once again, as they had at Hoylake!

They booked into a large bed and breakfast that overlooked a local park and drove to the course for a practice round; Sam was playing well and they both left feeling positive about the coming, trial and competition the following day.

As they left Sam saw the afternoon *Youth's* International matches starting, Paul Sandy - of course - was in the team and Sam watched them enviously and uncharitably, with a trace of bitterness.

He wanted and craved the mauve, *Youth's* jumper just as desperately as he'd wanted the yellow, *Boy's* jumper he'd worn with such pride for the junior team.

They spent the afternoon at the hotel, Frankie relaxed in his room and Sam walked aimlessly around the small park opposite, or the quaint, nearby town.

As he returned to the hotel he almost ran into an attractive, young girl with bright, green eyes and long, curly, jet-black hair; she smiled broadly and held out her hand.

"I'm Dianne...this is my Dad's place, you're here for the golf aren't you?"

Sam was a little flustered but tried not to show it as he stumbled and muttered,

"Yes...but I can't do any more practice today... I'm just killing time... I've been over to the park."

The girl was, bubbly and effervescent.

"Have you seen the indoor gardens?"

Sam was instantly very aware of her beauty, youth and friendliness but self consciously felt the unattractive, rough redness on his face burn him like an open wound.

He shook his head stupidly.

"No, I didn't even know there was an indoor garden!"

Dianne wore a brightly coloured, flowered dress then quickly offered to show and escort him as, to his delight, in the late, warm and humid afternoon, she chatted happily while they found the large, old building then conservatory that beautifully housed the blooming, hidden gardens and shrubs.

Sam started to relax with her; she did not seem

to notice the disfiguring marks on his face, or his shyness and he listened enraptured as she told him about herself and her studies at the local university.

In return, Sam recounted his adventures in his small, insular world of golf and she listened wide-eyed as he recalled the memorable days at Liverpool, the ensuing media interest and then verbally poked and teased him.

"You're famous!"

She smiled, her dark hair had fallen over her sparkling eyes and they looked at him playfully above her small, pretty nose; Sam didn't know if she was being serious or not and he shrugged embarrassedly and retorted with real sarcasm.

"Yeah...I'm a real *celebrity!*"

They both laughed and continued to interact then stroll lazily around the scenic gardens and it was idyllic.

Too soon for Sam, their dalliance was concluded, Dianne had university obligations that evening and, much as Sam loved his father, he found himself looking at him devouring steak and chips and wishing that he could replace him with his gorgeous, delightful companion from earlier in the day.

All such thoughts however were dispelled early on the following morning; Sam's starting time was 9a.m and he was on the practice area at 7.45a.m. hitting shots through the soft mist of the emerging, bright, summer morning.

Sam looked around and as always he was fascinated by the hustle and bustle, the crowds and the possible, emerging, golfing greats; Nick Faldo, David Robinson and Paul Sandy to name but three, were ever conspicuous and present.

The reporter's caravan was busy watching these potential stars, as were the selectors, who mingled with the chosen team players and watched from a close distance, the awesome, aspiring talent on show.

They held real power over their young charges so desperate to qualify for the international teams.

But such high honours were already irrelevant this year for Sam, and as his name was called to begin his round, he set his cap, cleared his mind and concentrated only on the immediate task ahead.

He played steadily for the first 7 holes and was level par but suddenly at the turn his round fell apart resulting, as he stood on the 18th, which was a short par 4 that fell dramatically to an upturned green, he was 5 over par.

The hole was reachable to a good shot and after hitting his drive into the bunker on the right of the green Sam managed to get up and down in 2 for a birdie and a 76.

The early scores showed that Pannal, playing short and easy with the hard fairways and receptive greens, was taking a hammering with a succession of low scores and Sam knew that, but for an exceptional performance tomorrow, he was set for yet another missed cut.

Father and son had no desire to hang around the course therefore, after a brief sandwich they *retired hurt* to the sanctity of their nearby hotel.

Sam showered and feeling tired from the efforts of earlier in the day rested in his room.

He emerged about 4 p.m feeling better if not still disappointed, and his despondent thought processes analysing his round, were interrupted by a familiar, sweet voice.

"Not so good, hey?"

He looked to see and it was, Dianne that had enquired of him; she looked bright and fresh as always and Sam's melancholy mood lifted instantaneously as he laughed softly.

"Not such a *celebrity*, after my round, today!"

They walked over to the park together and Sam told her all about his event whilst the young girl pretended that she understood or was vaguely the least bit interested.

She invited him to a barbecue held by the university a little way out of the town and as he was not due out to play until midday tomorrow he readily agreed.

Frankie was happy to dine by himself and Sam excitedly met her in the lobby at 7.30p.m as they had previously arranged.

He felt himself extremely attracted to the girl; Diane still did not seem to look at, or notice his disfiguring psoriasis and, as they drove along the elegant, historic streets of Harrogate, he thought about the numerous girls that had always gazed at his face in mock horror or wickedly pointed in ignorant amusement.

When he had tried to chat or talk to them, he'd always felt conscious about his condition and it had made him feel inadequate, shy then awkward around, often immature, young women.

But with, Dianne he was natural, relaxed and

happy; Sam relished her company and the ever-expanding greenery of the glorious countryside as they drove out into it.

They soon reached their destination, an open field where seemingly hundreds of young people were busy enjoying themselves.

Sam couldn't help but introspectively wonder briefly how his life would have been at university; the social and educational development that he'd never experienced or had.

But such matters were incidental and past now; Dianne introduced him to her friends and Sam drank wine, ate from the barbecue then sat on the dry, parched grass breathing in the wonders of the fading light over the high, rolling, Yorkshire hills.

They drifted and diffused slowly into gathering darkness through the dying radiance of the setting sun that shed shadows and bright orange light in seemingly equal proportions.

Dianne took Sam's hand as they eventually strolled away from the crowds, laughing together as they twisted and twined in between the trees until they settled comfortably and privately under a large, leafy, elm and admired the waning view together.

They looked out far to the horizon and the simple beauty that had been provided was, as if for them alone.

Dianne nestled in Sam's arms and they kissed then, as the shadows lengthened and the warm summer evening enclosed then engulfed them, Sam learned that there was far more to life than golf alone!

Eventually they returned to the hotel in silence, both lost in their own personal, private thoughts, kissed goodnight and Sam retired to his bed, his mind still tingling from the wonderment of the evening.

It was all indelibly imprinted on his mind as it was somewhere perfect to return to when things were not so rosy.

Dianne was nowhere to be seen in the morning but as he drove towards the course his thought process returned to golf; always to golf!

As he'd expected, the scoring had averaged just over par and as he walked up the first fairway he knew that a substantially good score was required and needed.

After 9 holes he'd in fact dropped another shot and he knew that the long drive back in disappointment while his father would pedantically and infuriatingly analyse his mistakes, was beckoning.

He thought about Dianne, their wonderful evening together and stared at the short 10th determinedly; he wasn't ready to go home yet and was going to fight not to!

A long putt snaked into the hole across the green for a birdie and as if inspired, Sam shortly looked down onto the 18th hole 4 under par for the back 9.

He drove the 18th green where after 2 further putts signed the card for a 68 and smiled in satisfaction; he'd made the cut, his first ever at senior or youth's level.

He saw Dianne after dinner and they walked again around the quiet, luxurious greenery then revelled in the natural flash of colour opposite them.

Sam read instantly that there was to be no repeat of the previous evening; it had been precious and memorable to them but they were both moving in different directions.

Surprisingly, he was not upset or disappointed, he valued Dianne's companionship and directness as they talked and held hands in friendship; it was as if their loving experience and intimacy of the previous evening had been just a brief moment in time.

Then with 2 rounds on the Sunday, the British Youths Championship at Pannal was completed; Sam played well finishing 15th but a full, 14 shots behind the eventual winner, Nick Faldo.

Dianne was not about when Sam left the hotel early on the Sunday morning and although they promised to keep in touch they somehow never did.

As if in summation of Sam's existence and golfing year, when at Christmas, he looked back upon his sporting efforts in the swiftly passing, recent, few months the only crumb of pleasure or comfort came far, far from the golf course on a warm, radiant, dying summer evening under a huge, leafy tree amongst the colourful, spectacular, secluded hills of Harrogate!

Chapter 11

The fact that Sam was not a teenager any longer seemed to catch him by surprise as if it was something unexpected or a bit of a shock.

He was 20, still to most, a young man but as he sat in the lounge of his parent's house and looked at the rain falling in relentless, and apparently, evil energy on the abandoned, neglected garden he tried to take stock of his life.

His golfing ambitions were still alive inside him but a growing, nagging realisation was beginning to shape itself; perhaps in all honesty he just was not good enough?

So many people had warned both him and his father, cautioned them about the uncomfortably huge failure rate of aspiring, professional golfers and such insight was beginning to seem well founded and an unpalatable reality suddenly.

Sam had discussed it briefly with his Dad but he was the eternal, paternal optimist, and his view was that if he didn't make it, then there was always the business!

The Business, it was a source of ever increasing burden to Sam; he was leant upon to carry the load of endless amounts of the work and to take ever more onerous responsibility.

He was not however allowed to involve himself

with the financial affairs of the firm; that was strictly his father's domain and he guarded its secrets furtively and jealously.

The emerging man did on one occasion see a statement that showed the business had an overdraft of over £150,000.00 but when he questioned his parent he flushed pink then dismissed it as a mistake.

As the rain continued to make puddles of broken light on the cracked paving slabs of the patio, Sam realised that his options, as his mother had predicted many years ago, were now limited.

He was nearly grown but somehow he was still a little boy; he felt the power and dominant authority of his father at all times and did not know how to break away from it.

It seemed that the routine of endless labour and struggle on the golf course was his destiny; it had been a path chosen by him, or was it?

His life seemed as if it was constantly a paradox and conundrum that he could not reconcile in his mind no matter how hard he tried.

As normal when there was no answer, Sam's only conclusion was to try harder, work more intensely and improve to the point where his dream of a professional, tour career became a reality.

And so the era of, *just another year* began and Sam attacked the early season's tournaments with a passion and a vengeance.

He had partial success at local level, a good round here or an impressive result or match there.

Sam achieved a handicap of scratch and he was well known in the amateur golfing world and treated deferentially by all the club golfers he came into contact with.

Apart from the committee members and the small, vitriolic enclave at the bar, of course!

However as Sam realised in his frank and candid assessment of his abilities, when it came to competing at the highest stroke-play level, his game did not seem to have the quality or consistency required.

Tournament after tournament he would either miss the cut or scrape in by an odd shot; he was knocked out early in the *English* and *British* championships and was increasingly deflated or disappointed by his lack of skill, ability and constant, poor performances.

Paul Sandy was already an established international, representing his country at all levels and in comparison, Sam's only progression was to just merit a lowly, occasional place on the exclusive, Warwickshire county team.

In all of his disappointment however his dedication and effort didn't waver; he still trained, watched what he ate, went to bed early before every tournament, and tried every possible, conceivable way of improving his game and results.

There was much written about the, *square to square* method which although Sam didn't really understand it, was explained to him as limiting the amount of moving parts in the swing.

Therefore he tried to incorporate this into his own game, becoming stiffer and more measured or exact, anything to try and become more consistent, but the results forever seemed the same, seemingly one step forward and two, then even three, back!

Sam drove to Northumberland towards the end of the season to compete in the North of England Youths Championship expecting nothing but unusually, finding a rich vein of form.

The course was hard and running fast and as Sam was driving and putting exceptionally, he found himself vying, then tying, for the lead on the first day and in fact a stroke clear after two rounds of 68 and 70.

His caddy was a small, energetic, enthused 10 year old boy called, Jamie; he was petite and small for his age, slim with dark hair, freckles, a vibrant, cheery personality and a huge, infectious smile that almost shone out from ear to ear.

He was the son of the local professional and somehow he instilled a confidence and sense of fun in his employer that Sam enjoyed and relished.

Paul Sandy was competing but he was 8 shots behind him after the 2 rounds as Jamie, after watching him swing, commented seriously and mischievously to him.

"You're much better than he is, Sam, winning this tournament's going to be *easy*!"

In spite of him being amused, Sam was however understandably nervous and anxious but tried not to fret or let the demons in his mind, disturb and unsettle him.

After the end of the 2nd round he spent the afternoon prior to the final Sunday in a darkened cinema and simply wondered just how he would cope with the pressure on the last day.

His morning round of 70 showed that thankfully he could manage and at 2 under par he was actually tied for the lead going into the afternoon, final round.

Unbelievably Sam started with 3 birdies in the ultimate hurdle and test, and was 5 under after 9; after that it was a question of hanging on, feeling his swing getting ever tighter over the last few, demanding and tortuous holes.

The 16th was the ultimate examination, the narrow fairway had *out of bounds* on the left and thick bushes on the right and Sam felt his whole body, physically shaking as he stood on the tee.

He steered a 5 iron down the fairway, then played a 6 iron to the right of the green, determined to stay away from the boundaries of the course that were waiting ever eagerly to punish and destroy him, as they so often had on previous courses before.

He chipped to *2 feet* and raised his arms in triumph as he held the short putt for a par; he knew he'd done it!

The fact that he dropped 2 shots on the final 2

holes was incidental and his wonderful, effervescent, young caddy, Jamie, threw his small arms around him excitedly at the end in joyous celebration.

Sam had won his first ever national tournament by an amazing 2 clear shots from a field full of the finest youth, golfers in the country!

He checked his card and handed it in to the recorder in a daze; he was elated, thrilled, his contemporaries were coming to him and congratulating him and it was a powerful, sensational, ecstatic feeling.

Tired and with some disorientation he changed, bought himself a soft drink then sat back on a large, soft, comfy, restful chair in the bustling lounge to await the prize giving ceremony.

The seat was slightly set back and a group of young men were busy chatting and gossiping not realising Sam could clearly overhear every word their conversation.

One of his competitors suddenly spoke enquiringly.

"Who won?"

Another voice replied.

"Sam Chester,"

Sam recognised it as belonging to a popular and mouthy member of the youth's international side.

"Yeah..."

A voice laughed acidly, cruelly and sarcastically.

"...*Scarface* won!"

Sam inhaled in distress, revulsion and trauma as he recognised the voice immediately; it was Paul Sandy's!

The words hit Sam like a speeding bullet causing him to shrink back into the seat as the whole table erupted into laughter as another boy viciously joined in their crude, vicious banter and badinage.

"He's an Ugly, Bastard..."

Then a further crass voice joined in.

"...Why doesn't he get some large pieces of sticking plaster or something....just cover it up, *Man*!"

The whole table erupted into hysterical, juvenile, sick, mocking laughter and suddenly without thinking Sam felt himself thrusting up angrily out of his chair and in barely restrained wrath and fury addressed them all.

As the boys saw him they immediately hushed and there followed a guilty, deathly quiet.

"I'm pleased you all think it's so funny…"

His voice was infuriated and cold as he stormed at them.

"…Because I don't!"

He felt the redness on his face burning him, but it was his pride and the lack of real confidence in his appearance, that truly demoralised, stung, belittled and hurt him.

Ironically even in his moment of fantastical triumph, life's realities seemed everlastingly there to taunt and persecute him.

Instinctively he wanted to cry but he would not give the ignorant boys who had insulted and meanly teased him so sadistically, the satisfaction of any further evidence of how their words had so deeply wounded and upset him.

To his credit he regrouped and found the strength of character he did not know he possessed and received the huge, beautiful, silver trophy with a smile and a speech that expressed his genuine appreciation for his small, effervescent, inspiring assistant.

"Local knowledge…"

Sam stated and smiled directly at Jamie, his tiny but special caddie and the thronging mass of well wishing people gathered all around him appreciated his sentiment.

"…Was instrumental to my success!"

The speech and his generous, humble manner were well and truly welcomed and Sam received warm applause from the crowd thronged into the restricted but lively clubhouse.

He felt better, as though he'd met a challenge but survived and was surprised to see Paul Sandy blocking his way as he struggled with the enormous trophy he was carrying out to his car.

Sam's lifelong adversary looked at him unhappily; it was the first time he had ever had seen him lacking his normal, insufferable, supercilious confidence.

"I'm sorry, Sam…"

He spoke then whispered in his regret and embarrassment.

"....It was a ridiculous and stupid thing to say...I'm sorry... well done on the victory."

Sam was feeling magnanimous; he'd just beaten him!

"Don't worry about it, Paul..."

His lips were twisted into a forced smile.

"...It's forgotten!"

And it was by his rival, but not by Sam as it was something he always remembered; as he started the long journey back home, in all the flush and excitement of his success or achievement there was a distinct, painful hint or dose of sourness and sadness mixed in with his joy.

The trophy sat proudly on the shelf at Sam's house; it dwarfed the hundreds of smaller, meaningless awards that Sam had won or medals for endless, local or club tournaments.

The tall cup meant and represented different things to the three people that lived there; to Dorothy it only represented a mere, shiny bauble to her son's wasted life, to Frankie it was a monument to his own management skills and his son's talent, and to Sam it was a tantalising glimpse into what was possible and achievable.

For the first time, when he had been tested at the highest level of stroke play he'd been equal to the challenge; he'd won a 4 round national tournament and perhaps his dream was possible after all.

On that slender success Sam reached 21 years of age, another year had departed and surely, the coming one would provide the final breakthrough into the highest echelons of the Amateur game.

Sam, with his victory in the Northern Youths felt assured of a place in the Youth's International side; no player who had ever won such a famous, prestigious tournament had not subsequently then gained access to the team.

He only needed to continue his progress, his improvement and in his final year as a youth he would take his place within the side and then another important step along his career path.

The winter was long and arduous, frustrating Sam's ambition to play; he longed for the grey clouds and cold winds to dissipate and the gentleness of spring to take charge of the elements.

His spirit and disposition was more positive than it had ever been and Sam's initial, poor performances did not undermine him.

However a disastrous 85 in the Warwickshire Amateur, then a pair of 80's in the area championship was more concerning as this was followed by another missed cut in the English Stroke Play competition.

Sam was desperate and practised harder then trained with ever further intensity; he concentrated fanatically but watched in horror as his psoriasis got worse and his life seemed to almost fall apart.

The *British* and the *English* championships went by with equally horrible results and Sam's only point of interest was to play in *The Open* qualifying for the first time.

As a scratch golfer he went straight through to the final stage which was to be two rounds held at Hillside, just down the road from Hoylake.

Sam played with, Mark James who had just turned professional; the young, ambitious man was renowned for being quiet, almost to the point of rudeness when he competed, and seemed to be extremely separated from his playing partners for the day.

Sure enough for the entire two rounds, Mark James hardly said a word as he carved out a 69 and 70 with a simply immaculate and wonderful golf and putting display to win the right to go forward into the main event by 3 clear shots.

Sam played neatly and consistently but could score no better than 79 and 80; the void in sporting class between himself and Mark James seemed so immense and vast, both in striking combined with of course, the intricate and subtle craft of scoring.

Sam then drove home cheerless and disappointed, he had enjoyed the experience of accompanying such a talent but it only seemed to further reinforce the growing realisation that his abilities once more did not stretch to the highest, golfing level.

The Open was being hosted at Lytham St Anne's, Sam had a playing badge that entitled him to free access to the competition and a couple of days before the tournament began, Sam went for a day out.

He travelled to the course by train that dropped him off at the picturesque, local station from where he walked the short distance to the course.

He arrived just as Jack Nicklaus and Tom Weiskopf were walking to the 1st tee; an eager, engaged, small crowd had gathered and Sam watched as Nicklaus teed the ball up in his familiar manner that he had seen so often on the television.

It seemed strange to see this legend of a man in flesh and blood or real life, but there he was and as he swung at the ball, Sam literally and physically held his breath.

The club seemed to explode into the ball like a whip, the sound was a sharp crack and the ball disappeared into the stratospheric blue of the clear, seaside sky.

Weiskopf repeated the process and then Sam walked quietly behind them to the small green on the long, tight, par 3 where both balls nestled close to the pin.

The two famous sportsmen exchanged friendly banter about the pair of shoes in the professional's shop, that was their bet, and Sam watched, marvelled then admired their respective mastery of the devilish game that he had tried so hard to understand and command.

He followed the match to the 12th hole before he then proceeded over to the practice range where a line of established and rising stars were busily engaged in honing their talents.

Sam was fascinated by the varying styles and tried to spot the common link between them that enabled them all to play so well.

It was however beyond his ability or experience to understand or pick up such an insightful thing and he could only stand back and admire, as Peter Thompson, a five times *Open* winner, hit the ball rhythmically and effortlessly into the light but stiff, coastal breeze.

Sam also noticed Gary Player had just arrived on the open arena and, quickly, before anyone else could block his view; he stood behind him then was struck at how small and slight the man, dressed immaculately in black, was close up.

Even his caddy was famous, who was a tall, black American with a big hat and an even larger personality; he deposited the clean, white balls in front of his employer before walking down the range in readiness to receive them.

Gary Player stretched then slowly went through his full repertoire and the full range of clubs; many of the shots landed perfectly for his lofty caddy to catch after a single bounce but occasionally, to the shock of his small audience, a sudden *shank* would appear.

Sam could not believe that one of the *Big Three*, stars could actually *shank* but watched as the little, celebrated sportsman toyed with his swing as if trying to analyse what the problem was.

The day was solitary but enjoyable and on the

train journey home Sam tried to think about what he had learned.

Not a lot he concluded; the only thing he knew for sure that with a *shank* in his swing, Gary Player had absolutely no chance at all to win *The Open*!

The fact that the man did turn out to win that *Open* at Lytham, hitting his famous reverse shot at the final hole seemed to sum up Sam's lack of knowledge and understanding of the game.

He could play well, to a fashion, compete with an intensity matched by few of his contemporaries; Sam could even win in certain circumstances but in truth, there was far too much effort and not enough guile in his golfing ability and questionable skill.

The remainder of the season was filled with inconsistency or frustration and the Youth's international place Sam coveted so much, was not to be realised.

In spite of his victory in the *Northern Youths* the previous season, his subsequent form and results had made inclusion for him in the team, an unfortunate but understandable impossibility.

He in fact missed the cut in the *British Youths*

then struggled to 20th place in the previously successful *Northern Youths* event for him, and suddenly the year end was upon him once again and Sam's junior and youth career was at an end.

The realities of his position were unpalatable but whereas Sam worried and fussed, Frankie was far more ambivalent.

His boy was fine there was always next year and anyway his son was a good worker, almost invaluable, there was certainly no need to adjust or change things.

The world according to Frankie was simple and always reflected from his peculiar, selfish viewpoint; he would never recognise the quandary his son was in or the turmoil of uncertainty that continually swept through him like a constant, restless, turbulent storm.

It seemed to Sam that all he could do was continue, keep grafting, keep trying and that is what he did.

But effort without success bred profound changes in the developing man and in his quieter moments he was introspectively forced to recognise the surliness and hardness that had developed in his personality.

During his first round that following year at the

West of England tournament he slighted then ignored an engaging, friendly, old man that had made his and his father's acquaintance on a previous visit.

Sam was on the 3rd hole, deep in concentration as the grey-haired gentleman, wrapped up well against the wicked, early season wind, asked politely how he and his father were.

Before Sam realised what he was doing he railed and turned on the man as if he had struck him.

"Can't you see I'm concentrating…?"

His words were incredibly and undeservingly aggressive, then as if correcting himself he continued his reply.

"…Yeah, we're fine, fine…fine!"

Putting his head down to avoid any further distraction he walked quickly away leaving the gentle, kindly person nonplussed and bemused as to what he had done to upset him so badly.

Sam's round again was disappointing and, in the silence and loneliness of his hotel room, Sam thought about his actions on the day, his rudeness and he was truly ashamed.

He always regretted never having the chance

to apologise to the polite and kind stranger as he missed the cut the next day, and it set the tone for another fruitless, exasperating year.

The area championship was *the* major local competition, it took in all the top national and midland counties players; it was always staged at Little Aston golf club and Sam's experience was typical.

He managed to qualify for the last day and he reached the 10th hole in the 3rd round in contention at only 1 over par for the tournament.

The hole was a long par 4 that meandered through, thick woods bordering each side of the fairway and Sam tried to block out of his mind that he'd *shanked* his shot into the trees from the centre of the fairway the previous round.

Sure enough his tee shot split the central, closely cut track and, after trying to compose himself, he prepared to shape the ball into the small green in the far distant corner.

He swung and then watched in instant, heated fury as the ball went at right angles from his club then disappeared into the greenest, deepest and thickest part of the wood.

Desperately he managed his reaction and his

instant, intense, spiking annoyance; he always tried so hard to control himself, to keep the plague and disfigurement on his face from getting any worse!

Somehow he found the ball and accepted an 8 then fought the remainder of the round and by the time he'd reached the same hole in the afternoon final round he'd recovered some of the shots he'd lost.

He was on the centre of the fairway once more; again trying to eliminate the previous round's disasters from his mind, and focussing only on the arduous 180 yard shot ahead of him.

Sam kept his head still, his left arm straight and concentrated desperately on trying to extend through the shot.

His arms swung then instantly felt the ball veer off the club at right angles once more before disappearing despairingly into the blackness of the murderous forest of gently swaying, seemingly mocking trees!

He walked silently, unnaturally calmly towards the darkness; entered through the rough barks, his shoulders hunched and his eyes almost drugged, glassy and glazed.

He squinted as he focussed and tried to spot his ball amongst the gloom and mass of foliage then, suddenly in turning, sharply struck his head on a low, heavy branch.

It was as if an explosion had gone off in his bursting brain; he screamed in fury emitting a deep, animalistic howl of frustration that had been locked up inside him seemingly for an eternity.

Without realising he smashed the 5 iron in his hand against the nearest tree snapping it instantly and ranted at the top of his voice as if the living but inert wood, could hear his pain and anguish.

In temper his feet marched quickly back towards the fairway with tears welling in his eyes, and muttered viciously.

"Ball's lost!"

Sam's playing partners looked at him with incredulity, it was as if the young man had lost his mind and in some ways they were correct.

He smashed another shot towards the green but hardly bothered to look or try with each effort that took him only slightly nearer the final hole, and hopefully some peace and respite.

He finished the round at 15 over par for the tournament, shook hands weakly with his bemused and shocked playing companions then slumped into the car as his father eventually, slowly drove him home.

Frankie, who had all the answers, had none; he had nothing to say, his son had acted disgracefully but Frankie understood the frustration; it was a rage and helplessness that mirrored his own!

How could his trained and cleverly schooled *thoroughbred* have turned into a nag right before his eyes?

Sam, his confidence and patience or tolerance destroyed, had little enthusiasm for the remainder of the season, and just went through the motions.

Tournament after tournament repeated, all with minimal success and he truly began to hate the game that he had relished and loved so much.

Sam also seemed to have lost his reasoning powers for at the year end he was so caught up in his routine of work and golf that *one more year*, just to see, was almost mandatory.

The break from golf, due to the weather, was some relief, but he still lived at home, continually had to suffer the unfairness of the family wage structure and still had to endure and listen to his demanding, dictatorial, paternal parent.

According to his knowledgeable, brilliant father it was just another step along the way, another stumble, but Sam felt low, depressed and completely without any hope or direction.

Sam's social life was of little comfort, wine bars and clubs, but his affliction was no help to him finding much solace there.

His contemporaries and friends were finishing various degrees or starting careers and as Sam sipped his wine and watched the bustle of another wasted evening he wondered forlornly whatever should he do for the best?

Chapter 12

The next golfing merry-go-round commenced as the last had finished; poor or average scores and abject failure in every major, local or national tournament.

Sam had enjoyed the brief respite over the winter period but it was not enough relaxation or separation to match the deluge of further frustration and disappointment soon heaped upon him once more when the competitive circuit began again in earnest.

Naturally he tried; he practised harder and harder to no purpose or avail until late one lonely, soft, tranquil and perfect summer evening towards the end of the season when there was no one else on the deserted course.

He was back on the familiar, practice area; beating balls once more toward the old, green shed that seemed to be almost a teasing, old friend and companion to him by now.

His mind concentrated then endlessly tried to find the missing link, straining each sinew or part of his being, but every few shots he'd *shank* the ball right and could only watch as the ball went scuttling off, as if to torment, infuriate and endlessly frustrate him.

Purposefully he gathered himself and started over, then again, until his whole body was soaking wet with sticky perspiration from his endless exertions.

There was another swing but sickeningly he felt the evil sensation of a further right-angled contact as something inside him just mentally shattered then snapped completely.

He dropped emotionally, even theatrically to

his knees then beat the silver instrument of his suffering in his hands childishly, pathetically and rhythmically into the turf.

The tears that he'd held for so long inside flooded out and, he sensed the still wind suddenly swirl, covering him with irritating specs of grass, belittling or confusing his senses ever more.

His head was bent in torture while his eyes filled with emerging water and he sobbed as if from his very soul itself; his tears were of self pity and of humiliating capitulation, combined with debilitating, insufferable defeat.

Sam had lost, he could take no more and finally, bitterly he accepted for certain that he could not continue or carry on; the dream that he'd cherished for so long was over!

He'd never, ever be good enough to be a tour professional, be *Open Champion*; it was just a stupid, idiotic, boyhood, puerile, empty, vacuous, ridiculous fantasy!

He looked up at the empty course, the lush greenery, the darkening sky then the shed and somehow it seemed as if they were all laughing and mocking him.

It was as if they were privileged in observing, watching, sharing and witnessing his ultimate calamity then ultimate, dramatic, temperamental surrender and failure!

Finally he had reached the point where he could tolerate and suffer no more; it was beyond his ability to endure any longer!

Sam reached home tired and despondent; he did not discuss anything with his father but the following morning withdrew from the last two major tournaments that involved any travelling.

He toyed with not playing in the last, local competition but decided that he'd just treat the event and rounds as some fun or entertainment; he didn't want to give golf up altogether, as yet!

Frankie did not comment at the realisation that Sam had pulled out from the last national events but was surprised on the night before the next important, nearby test he was dressing to go out to town and cautioned him concernedly.

"Big match tomorrow, Son, you need to go to bed early!"

His offspring was no longer a child; he stood and listened to his father still forever hectoring him like a baby then spoke coolly.

"Dad… I'm 23… I'll make my own decisions!"

Frankie shrugged as if his boy was about to throw away something precious and Sam ignored him as he ran swiftly to the sound of a car horn outside.

It was his best friend, David from junior school and the two of them drove into the bright nightlife together; his companion studied in Lancaster and had started work as an estate agent after completing a surveyor's course.

He was in town to visit his parents and as they drank wine, David told Sam some of the secrets of the trade and sowed the merest germ of an idea in the young man's mind.

His closest confidante was clever and smart; he was also blonde, slim and good looking, enabling the two of them to soon have a bevy of the best looking girls gathered around their table, sharing the evening.

They had a wonderful fun, carefree time; Sam took a taxi home finally stumbling happily into bed, weary and drunk at 5 a.m. in the cool, dark morning.

He felt himself roused, disapprovingly by his father at 7a.m. and, almost on automatic pilot, showered, dressed but did not eat before Frankie drove him unhappily, given his demonstrably, unsteady state, to Handsworth golf club where the local competition was to be held.

Sam sat in the clubhouse, drank coffee but did not so much as put a single club in his hand before he was standing on the 1st tee, waiting to hit his first shot over a *150 yard* carry of water.

His name was called and he teed up the ball increasingly feeling so disoriented but trying desperately not to be sick or keel over!

He shaped up to hit the shot then suddenly realised that he was rocking ever so slightly and wondered why there seemed to be disturbingly two white balls on the tee instead of the normal one!

Given what he had ingested last evening he was undeniably, unusually hung over as he laughed inwardly and understood that it was definitely not ideal preparation for sport!

He was however, committed and after re-focussing, swung then watched, almost completely separated and detached, as the little, bright sphere dribbled horribly off the tee before splashing so easily into the dark, murky liquid of the welcoming lake!

He wanted to giggle, but he was too disengaged for that and took another ball, another swing then he looked up with relief as his second attempt somehow managed to find solid ground on the far side of the still rippling and disturbed water.

Sam saw the disgust on his Dad's face, but he didn't care; he knew that at this tournament some of the members ran a book where you could place a bet to odds, and he also knew for certain that his father had backed his favourite horse and pony!

Of all the things that irritated, Sam; that he loathed and hated about his pushy parent, this was definitely and distinctly number one!

He knew that he'd secretly gambled and wagered on his golf privately and publicly many times and no matter how he'd asked, begged and protested his feeling about such matters, his father paid no heed.

It was yet a further pressure Sam felt he could do without and he would feel no responsibility today for him foolishly, losing his money!

After 5 holes Sam was still dizzy and 6 over par; Frankie had left him abruptly after 3 holes then walked briskly off the course in utter contempt and disgust at his son's inexplicable, casual attitude and approach.

One of the *bookmakers* for the day saw him leaving and out of curiosity asked him where he was going; he responded sharply with terrible, impatience, ire and anger as he stormed out and on his way.

"Rubbish like that I can watch anywhere!"

Sam, now all alone, looked down the 6th fairway and felt how incredibly uncomfortable his swing always was; it was not just the hangover but it was all the strain and effort he'd put in over so much endless, interminable, constant, time.

His swing was tense, unnatural and with his head still befuddled, on a beautiful, late summer's morning he looked down the long, green track ahead of him then had a radical and inspirational thought; he was going to swing and play in a way that felt comfortable just to him!

He flexed the club in his hands and felt the motion of it back and forwards; he had a practice swing then released all the tension that had been instilled with all the perpetual, eternal years of practice.

His hands swayed, moved the club naturally back and through the ball trying to sense the rhythm and, after a few minutes with his playing partners looking at him curiously and strangely, he ultimately, patiently then eventually addressed the ball again.

He relaxed, felt his hands, and in a fluid motion despatched the ball sweetly and perfectly down the fairway.

Shot after shot repeated effortlessly, rhythmically and almost mystically until he was heading up the 16th fairway in the afternoon round, level par for the day and amazingly 2 shots in the lead!

His 2nd shot found the bunker, his only poor shot since his sole spectator had departed and as he looked up his beloved but impossibly infuriating father was ironically, standing silently, just by the green!

However this time Sam did not get anxious but just smiled to himself; the irony of the situation was not lost upon him and, ignoring his small audience, he simply got down in 2 from the bunker.

He then birdied the short 17th then held out from *5 feet* at the last for a par and his first senior, tournament victory by 4 shots!

Sam was delighted, but not as much as his father who wasted little time collecting his winnings from the club members fronting as temporary *bookies* for the day.

The man, he had spoken then complained to previously and earlier in the day smiled as his plump, disbelieving, but extremely satisfied customer counted out his money, and mocked and he teased him as he did so.

"Rubbish like that…eh?"

Frankie just shrugged without recalling exactly what he had said in haste and temper; he had been right after all and now the winning team of *him and his boy* could head for bigger and better things!

Sam changed into his shirt and tie and after a short wait took the applause from the small crowd as he accepted the beautiful, silver cup and some cut glass that he knew would look wonderful and perfect on his mother's dining table.

He drove home with his father in silence holding the trophy in his hands and he looked at the bright, shiny object and the list of the many famous, past winners inscribed on it.

The day had yielded many things, both in his golf swing but also something much, more revealing and profound.

Winning, he realised was in truth something of an anticlimax and, as he gazed at the sparkling, glinting prize grasped in his cool fingers, he pondered and wondered if he had truly worked and laboured so hard all of his life just for this?

It was a time and pivotal moment of awareness and discovery; a day when the boy finally started to grow up!

Sam had various county matches or general, local competitions and with each further round and match he began to learn and build on the unexpected discoveries he had made.

His only focus on playing now was his rhythm; he'd always felt that his back swing had become forced and somewhat manufactured and he sensed that if he turned and opened his shoulders further he could swing through more easily.

The fundamental thought process was to only do what felt relaxed and natural; Sam wanted to enjoy his golf and all the years of professional tuition, endless golf magazines and tips were instantly dropped from his game in a cold, insightful, reflective instant!

The other major amendment and change for Sam was to realise that his desire to reach the highest echelons of the game had evaporated and disappeared like so much heated steam; he had decided absolutely that he wanted a more normal life!

Over the coming weeks and months, as the

winter routine of Sam's family business obligations took hold, the enlightened, young man realised that the warehouse combined with the shops were also not where he wanted to devote the rest of his time and future.

He still wanted to play his sport, but as a hobby for some pleasure and entertainment; it was still a part of him but the endless travelling, commitment and pressure was to be a thing of the past!

The sad truth and understanding came upon him that really his golf game had been all smoke and mirrors; Sam's unquestionable ability had only, in reality and all, harsh truth, definitely and undoubtedly only *flattered to deceive*!

A glamorous victory or an occasional, good round could not disguise a distinct lack of prolonged or sustainable achievement at the highest level of competition and against the most talented opposition.

His attempts and efforts into the world of professional sport were patently unsuccessful and in fact had been an undoubted burden and a strain to him all of his life!

It was a dreary, grey day in February when he'd finally worked out a plan of action and he sat in the quietness of the family lounge and confronted his unprepared parents with his decisions.

Sam looked at his father and whispered softly to him words that he knew he did not wish to hear.

"I'm not playing the Amateur tour anymore."

Frankie, not believing a word, just smiled at him knowingly.

"Sure, Son... whatever you want... it's your choice, your mum and I only want you to be happy..."

Sam's father, who had aged rapidly with the increasing weight of the business over recent years continued ever onwards.

"...You can help in the business and I'll increase your wag..."

Sam butted in abruptly, almost rudely!

"I don't want to work in the business any longer either..."

He stuttered and stumbled though his thoughts but he needed to speak out loudly what had been on his mind for so long.

"...I'm fed up with it... with Anna's rubbish, Timmy's laziness... it's only the three of us that do any work at all... it's unfair and unreasonable and ..."

He sighed as if struggling to express himself; this was incredibly difficult for him to say.

"...I'm not doing it anymore...!"

Frankie started to bubble and boil, his face reddening with every passing second; Dorothy inhaled then held her breath in shock, almost disbelieving that her son was actually expressing her very own, buried, hidden feelings and sentiments.

"...I work in the business..."

Sam continued bravely but honestly.

"...I'm a director but I don't know what's going on; you never let me see the figures, the statements, all I know is that we're always under pressure...and..."

He explained everything as best he could.

"... I need a future, Dad...I need a future!"

Frankie in all his life had never been confronted or challenged like this; he did not respond maturely or well then spoke rashly, with bitterness and palpable anger.

"You ungrateful little... "

Frankie was lost for words and… he was never lost for words!

Sam however was unfazed; he had pondered and suffered for far too long to be distracted from his decision by his father's theatrics, machinations and tantrums.

All his existence he had been under his parental thumb and rule; it had been seemingly forever and Sam knew that he had to somehow find the courage and strength get out.

There was no going back on his decision; it was set in stone and he spoke and poured the setting concrete!

"I want to start my own business, David's given me an idea about developing some derelict houses and I'm setting up my own property company!"

His father gazed and looked at him as if he was completely mad or insane; he tried to maintain his grip or control in the only way remaining and open to him.

"And where are you going to get the money for this…"

His legendary temper literally blew up like a bottled up volcano suddenly exploding and erupting in burning, heated lava.

"...I'm not going to finance..."

Sam had thought it through already.

"I'm not asking you to, Dad; I've not thought that far ahead but I'll find it somewhere... I need to do this for... *me*!"

His father frothed then seethed in his obvious distress, anger and ineffectual frustration.

"Do what you want... do what you *fucking* want!"

He then rose up and literally stormed from the room, out of the front door and careered down the path in a demonstrable hail and expressive volley of stones.

Sam had never heard his father swear before, ever, it was a shock but, as the intensity and vibration of his departure faded, he was left only with the despair and calmness of his mother.

His pale eyes looked at her as if he'd not previously noticed the lines or grey hair that had seemed to have suddenly appeared; she'd become old before his eyes and somehow he'd not noticed.

He suddenly felt callow, ungrateful, callous and selfish as if it was only his own problems he'd considered and he went quiet suddenly as his mother spoke to him sadly, soothingly but in empathetic, tolerant comprehension of his thoughts and actions.

"Sam, I understand... I know that you need your independence, but... your Dad's always only done what he thought was for the best..."

The emerging man nodded; he acknowledged that to be true but he also knew that in itself was not a good enough excuse for the situation to continue on and on any further.

His mother's gentle voice went on and softened as she addressed her precious boy.

"...I've a little money saved...I'm going to give it to you to start your business, but... there's something you have to do for me."

Sam looked at her admiringly, in all his life his mother had always been a rock, quiet sometimes and often unspoken, but always selflessly there for him, for all her family; he truly loved her with all his heart.

"Yes, Mum...tell me...What?"

She sat beside him and took his hand and squeezed it firmly.

"You can't leave the business completely..."

Her brown eyes seemed so pained, weakened and fatigued.

"... I can't do it all and... your Dad..."

She looked at her son, the evil, demonic redness on his body burnt into her own consciousness and suddenly her malaise and upset almost completely overwhelmed her.

"...You know... your Dad!"

Sam saw the trace and imminent formation of a tear appearing in her soft, earthy, troubled eyes that had suffered so much unnecessary hardship and his resolve relaxed, just a little.

He accepted immediately that he could never desert his mother.

"Yes, Mum... I know him well...very, very well!"

And so Sam's new life was agreed, in pain and compromise; Frankie needed his son's energy in the business just to keep going, and Sam started to turn his mind to finding houses and finance for his new idea, enterprise and his own way forward.

Slowly, Sam started to discover the horrendous secrets hidden in the business; the overdrafts were colossal, money was owed everywhere and, as the obligation of Sam's golfing ambitions declined, he was saddled with new pressures and responsibility.

His sister's needs were vast, her house, cars, private schools all came from the family enterprise but when he broached the possibility with his father that these needed to be reduced it became another battle or argument; something that seemed to be happening more and more regularly and frequently between them.

He found a derelict property in need of development, raised some money on the back of his mother's loan to him and set to work; endless effort but he sincerely hoped that it would prove to be more meaningful and productive labour.

In the main business, privately he marvelled at how his father had kept the finances of the company continuing as he knew, given the guarantees the bank held on his parent's house that he would now have to do the same.

Golf suddenly became a release, a distraction, a pleasure and more frequently, as the early, summer days approached, Sam's enjoyment was to just play 9 holes by himself after work into the murky darkness of the warm evenings.

Has had found that once he had removed the tension and expectation from his shoulders, he started to discern things about the game that he'd never previously realised; his swing was changing, almost by itself, from tense and regimented to relaxed, graceful and rhythmical.

Sam suddenly started to strike the ball with an assurance he'd never experienced before; there were gremlins and problems but his golf was his own and undoubtedly he was on the formative steps of a personal journey into the sport, and an inspired, educational voyage of discovery.

Determinedly he ignored all magazines, lessons, even with his much loved tutor; Sam's golf was his personal responsibility and he often recalled Henry Cotton's words, told, recounted and made to him those many years ago.

"Champion's are formed in the cruel earth, on the practice grounds, by the beads of their own effort and sweat!"

Sam though, no longer viewed his golf as sweat; the heavy, wieldy, unmanageable weight of ambition had been removed, enabling him to swing freely and without any of his former inhibitions.

He chose not to play in any of the early, major, national tournaments; he had no desire to travel as both his family business and his first, private, personal development in his own enterprise, were keeping him focussed, pressured and busy.

He played the occasional, county match; normally right at the end of the pecking order, but 36 holes on a Sunday with his county friends he found a pleasure rather than an obligation.

He entered the county championship with no thoughts other than a day's release from the grind of commerce.

Peter McEvoy was playing round his own course, Copt Heath, and both he and Paul Sandy, in what was probably his final year as an amateur, were competing and expected to win easily.

Sam, had no aspirations at all; simply none!

However, he played as if he had been awoken and released from a golfing nightmare and was utterly serene and fluid all day; he did not dwell on his bad shots or become over confident on his many good ones.

With 5 holes to go, he was 2 ahead and surprisingly felt absolutely no pressure; all he focussed on was a full turn and a rhythmical swing and he picked up 2 further birdies to win the competition by 4 full shots.

At the prize presentation there was a full turnout, Mr Earl, the undersized, distinguished gentleman with snow white sideburns that he'd first met as a young boy led the applause, as Sam went to collect his prize; the not so *Young Man* was a popular winner!

In an instant, Sam was elevated to a status within the county that even his victory over Jerry Pate had not achieved; he had won against the best over 36 holes stroke play and it was definitely *not a flash in the pan*!

His father had walked the last 9 holes with him and as they drove home he tried to subtly resurrect the prospects and thoughts of Sam's golfing career.

Frankie had been surprised at his son's resoluteness, his ability to stand up to him and his ongoing confirmation that he would now do all things, golfing and otherwise his own way.

The thrill of victory however did nothing to change Sam's mind or new approach though; he almost visibly or physically felt that his ambition had actually, utterly and completely vanished.

He now enjoyed his golf and his victory, as it was undoubtedly sweet, but he realised that it was transient, almost unimportant and it would not put bread on the table.

He was starting to have a sense of proportion that was previously beyond him as he had no wish to live any longer in the narrow, selfish world of sporting glory and achievement he once inhabited.

The initial house development was a success; Sam had split the building into four flats and had little trouble letting them.

He used the property as collateral and started on a new venture; he comprehended that rectifying the family business was a task beyond him and it frightened him to realise the bank could take everything away at any vulnerable, unguarded moment.

This drove him to work almost as much as the golf had done, but it was a different type of pressure, something tangible and real and he coped with it the best he could.

Sam's psoriasis started to improve, the redness on his face began to fade and suddenly with a small, but flourishing property business of his own, he sensed and actually felt like a success.

It gave him the confidence to begin to enjoy his life; girls that had always been such a mystery and frustration to him were suddenly available and, as his second house became ready for occupation, Sam took on one of the flats for himself and moved out of the family home.

It was the next progression to adulthood and his parents accepted his options, opinion then ultimately respected his decision.

His mother missed him but she was content that finally he was beginning to have a life; he was making good choices and it pleased her.

Sam started to slowly lead the existence he'd missed as a teenager; girls, parties and travel to share time with his friends in different parts of the country and unusually his days were enjoyable and good for him

Chapter 13

Sam's golf was now a revelation; he hardly practised at all yet when he competed, he often played astoundingly well.

Over the subsequent years he won the Midland, Area Championship, twice, numerous local tournaments and on his occasional foray into the national tournaments, that did not involve too much travelling, he had spectacular success that resulted in him nearly winning the *English* stroke play and match play championships.

With Paul Sandy having turned professional, and even with Warwickshire still boasting of the talents of Peter McEvoy, Sam often played number 1 for the county team; it was an honour he relished and he was instrumental in helping the side reach the national finals on more than one occasion.

He was in fact a reserve for the full, English International side and it was indeed a compliment, gesture and a tribute to his ability considering his limited tournament schedule.

Sam, however still practised and played hardly at all yet, he now had the ability to pick up his clubs, almost cold, and compete at the highest, possible level of amateur golf.

An example of his talent was demonstrated one Sunday when Warwickshire were due to compete against Lincolnshire and their feted and leading player, was the new, recent, British Amateur Champion, Peter Parkin.

Sam, holding the top position for Warwickshire by merit, was due to play against him and he considerately rang his father to ask if he wanted to come along and watch.

They were still close but the power and authority had shifted to the junior man and in some ways it suited both of them more, and Frankie was pleased to *allow* his son to have the reins and dominion.

He always had to put his own slant on things, but Sam could accept this, and tried not to argue with him more than he had to!

The match was off at 1p.m and a small crowd had gathered around the 1st tee; Sam tried to loosen up his dormant body still stiff from a full week of work and no practice at all.

He attempted to be smooth and rhythmical but after 6 holes he was 4 down and Peter Perkins was chatting busily to his father and the local newspaper reporter, demonstrating somewhat irritatingly, for his playing opponent, his bumptious and somewhat overbearing personality.

The young assertive *Lion* was certain and confident of his victory, Sam's former or lost reputation meant nothing to him; he was the best golfer in the country after all, and he mentioned to the scribe with him, that he sensed for sure that his scalp for the day was probably, Warwickshire's *Kamikaze* man!

In other words Sam was just a token offering or sacrifice for him to beat because he was so wonderfully skilled and exceptionally good and no one playing that day in any side could defeat him!

On the 7th tee, Sam's flesh suddenly crawled as he looked and stared at the cocky, gangly youth with thick, curly, dark hair and a supercilious smile; a sudden fire that he'd not experienced for many years stirred, welled up and flared up inside him.

He stretched his muscles, concentrated sharply on his timing and shape and proceeded to reel off 7 birdies in the next 9 holes!

Peter Parkin was incredibly now 3 down and the smug, superior, self satisfied smile that had been so apparent and visible earlier on was nowhere to be seen.

He wasn't chatting to the reporter anymore, or Sam's father; he was trying desperately to ward off an embarrassing defeat.

To the young man's credit he birdied the 16th and 17th but, when Sam laid his chip shot dead on the long par 4, 18th the British Amateur Champion had lost, 1 down!

The story made headlines in the morning local papers and unfortunately, to Peter Parkin's abashment, the words *Kamikaze Man* were mentioned; in truth Sam had given the best and most notable player in the country a *4 hole* start, and still won!

Sam's swing was now formed in his mind, he understood certain fundamentals that enabled him to play well with little or no effort and in all that period of success at no time did the seduction or temptation of professional golf bite him again.

He was enjoying his life, the family burden was still an enormous pressure but, as his own business developed, Sam could afford to buy a small, sports car and for a few years became more involved in chasing girls.

A local playboy would have been an exaggeration, but he did catch a few of the young ladies he went running after; the point was he had some frivolity, fun and a life!

Golf slowly became less and less important; Sam would only venture to his golf club either in the evening or once a year to win the annual scratch championship!

He had become something of a hate figure at the club; the members resented him not competing in the competitions as an ordinary member, and begrudged him winning the prestige tournament so easily and the small prize that went with it.

Sam had no patience however for them or, ordinary golf in general; somewhere in all his previous, endless drive and practice for larger competitions the desire and patience to win the monthly medal had disappeared along with the craving for a professional career.

The years were starting to roll away and Sam was turning 30; he watched as many of his former adversaries tried to make the grade in the professional golfing world, with varying degrees of success but with most falling by the wayside.

He again started to question his own position in the universe; he longed for a family of his own, his own solid, growing future and, as with his golf, the appeal of a life full of vacuous, empty pleasure was not appealing to him.

However his life changed forever one evening when he was visiting his friend, David in Lancaster.

A beautiful girl was standing or leaning lightly at the busy bar they were visiting and instantly Sam was drawn towards her.

This female vision had large, warm, brown eyes, coal black hair and bronzed skin; she also had a broad smile with an apparent spirit and zest for life that Sam found utterly irresistible.

He was no longer shy and after initially introducing himself found that he was soon captivated by her.

The girl was named Tahnee, her skin and sultry looks inherited from her Spanish mother and, from that very first night they met, it was as if they had always been together.

Therefore his trips to Lancaster became more and more frequent until, only 6 months after they had met they announced their engagement, and set the wedding day for the spring of the following year.

Sam was happier than he had ever been, golf, apart from the occasional game, was forgotten and he only concerned himself with the forthcoming wedding and his business obligations.

The family organisation was forever a major trial and problem for him; he had reconciled and modernised what he could but it was an old fashioned trade, unable to be adapted to the modern world and could not cope with the financial abuse the family had heaped upon it over such a tortuous, long period of time.

Frankie still endlessly pursued his *hobby*; in all the years Sam knew him he'd never referred to his addiction as anything other than a harmless distraction.

His sister and brother in law continued to do virtually nothing and Sam realised that with the overdrafts and creditors still enormous, the day of reckoning was not far away.

But nothing could dampen his spirit or his wedding day, the sun shone, their family and friends cheered and as Sam kissed his delectable bride, his own skin was as clean, clear and healthy as his new wife's.

Dorothy cried profusely and unashamedly; it was as if in spite of all the adversity, her son had found his own way and it filled her soul and heart with endless pleasure and joy.

They honeymooned in Majorca, a wonderful, carefree fortnight where they spent the days lounging in the hot Mediterranean sun and Tahnee's skin, darkened to a luxurious, rich, velvet brown.

Their nights were full of love, tenderness and passion and Sam brought her back to his hometown where they settled happily in their serviceable and pretty new house.

Fantastically the love and joy they shared was soon cemented by the news that Tahnee was pregnant and Sam's cup of happiness was literally full to overflowing.

The call came through at 6a.m the following

Tuesday, Sam's father had died in his sleep; the constant strain and pressure had taken its toll and as if in a nightmare, Sam was soon standing forlornly in the cemetery.

As he stood over the newly dug grave his mind thought about all the things they had shared together; the golf journeys they had taken, the eternal battles, trials, plans, the destructive business, endless struggle and the eventual, bitter arguments!

The stark memories of so much incredible joy and the pain came flowing then flooding into his mind like an explosion of pressured water suddenly released from a huge dam of emotion.

So much of the time it was if they had been as one; Sam could strangely not bring himself to weep but as the wooden coffin was lowered into the arresting, brown earth he made his peace with his father.

He knew that for all his Dad's faults, he would never again have his love or strength to guide him or distract him and it pained and cut him sorely, deeply and decisively.

In that instant he loved him eternally for what he had given him and forgave him for what he could not!

He understood and recognised that his deceased parent had not been a perfect man but without doubt had always done, and tried to do, what he thought and believed was best for him.

Sam stayed long after the other mourners had departed and gone; he wandered slowly and aimlessly around the graveyard staring at the carved stones that seemed such inadequate and paltry monuments left to the unknown stories of so many forgotten lives.

It took him a long time to actually cry, but eventually he did and felt better; finally with his head bowed and lowered, he stood in front of his father's, black headstone and read his Dad's name so clearly inscribed on the newly engraved, gleaming surface.

In so many ways they had been inseparable and bound together through all the good and the bad; he had always loved him completely and dearly and with all of his heart in spite of everything!

The subsequent months were surreal as Sam tried to keep himself distracted and busy at work; he expected to see his father everywhere and he made every effort to support his mother who was simply overcome and overwrought with incredible, debilitating grief.

That was the strange thing about Frankie, that whether you loved or loathed him you could not ignore him; he had been a larger than life character and he left an open, enormous, gaping, huge, chasm and void behind him.

In so many ways he'd given Dorothy a hard life, full of work and suffering but he'd always provided love and incredibly energy and spirit.

She wept every night for the man she knew and the boy she had met and fallen in love with when she had been a mere schoolgirl; but he had been taken from her, and it grieved her more than she could bear, cope, deal with or simply endure.

The sadness lingered; the days became weeks, the weeks turned into months and the depressing, black clouds only lifted when Tahnee gave birth to a beautiful, precious new life.

The boy's name was Oliver; he had his mother's skin and exquisite hazel eyes that even on his very first day of life shone through instantly with vitality and intelligence.

He lifted the spirits of all who saw him and, in this perfect, small bundle, Dorothy found the strength to somehow find the courage to look towards the future rather than live and dwell only in, and upon the past.

Sam kept the business going and the family supported for a further year and then the realities or pressures of the overdrafts, lease renewals, taxes and the futility of the family outmoded business finally tipped over, poured and fell tumbling down on top of him.

The bank had given him an ultimatum to repay the huge debts or they would foreclose and Sam had very few choices or options open or available to him.

The bankruptcy was a tawdry, messy affair; Sam tried to arrange for a partial payment to be made to the creditors but by the time the *carpetbaggers* and the insolvency practitioners, who were acting for the institution, had finished, there was nothing of value left.

Fortunately Sam's property business was separate and he was able to secure a deal for his mother's house and retain the lease for the well placed, market shop that Frankie and Dorothy had started their business from all those many years before.

The vitriol Sam received from his sister and brother in law was to be expected, after being provided for, protected and cushioned for so many years they would now have to work for themselves.

It was an understandably traumatic, daunting

and frightening thought and actuality for them!

After the liquidation was completed Sam had his final family meeting; there had always been family business gatherings as long as he could remember.

These were events where his father would hector and dispense his eternal, *genius* and worldly wisdom but as Sam looked at the distraught faces of his sister, Timmy and his mother he was genuinely pleased that this was to be the very last.

Sam had made the decisions and he solemnly told the assembled trio that his own precious small family of three were going to move to Lancaster; he could not stay here any longer now.

What was left of the business, namely the market shop, he was giving to Anna along with some stock he'd been able to bribe the assessor to put on one side to give them a start.

His mother had a small pension and he'd cleared the mortgage on the house so, with a little help from him she would be relatively comfortable and be able to manage.

Everyone was in tears but Sam now had his own family, more people that depended on him and he needed to get away, to be released from Anna's family's, financial obligations that had burdened and shackled him for so eternally long.

His sister and Timmy departed, shell shocked by life suddenly rearing up and biting them; Sam had done the best he could for them, and the shop was a good living if they worked - as his mother and father had done forever - as a close team.

He had looked however at Timmy's, drawn face - a cigarette still dangling unattractively and pathetically out of his mouth as he left - and realised this could never happen; in that very instant he doubted whether their marriage could stand the financial disruption and turbulence now placed upon it!

His mother was tearful; her face lined with the stress and worry of her new and lonely existence.

Her hair had an abundance of grey but her brown eyes were still alive and soft and she smiled at her son gently and spoke in a whisper.

"You've always had to look after everybody, Son!"

Sam put and placed his arm gently around his

shaking mother's shoulders and hugged her warmly.

"Like you, Mum…just like you!"

They both instantly and instinctively thought about, Frankie and they laughed together almost as one; it was as if his memory had suddenly infused them with spirit once more, just like the energy that had always been in him, and it helped Dorothy gather herself together.

"It's right that you're going away, Sam…"

Her words were loving and heartfelt.

"…You've got a wonderful family… they deserve a fresh start…"

She sighed in her tumble but jumble of sad and happy emotions.

"… You deserve a new beginning… don't worry about me… I'll be fine… and I'll come and see you, Tahnee and Oliver all the time!"

He knew how difficult his leaving would be for her but as always, she had been, brave, strong and resolute for her family, for him!

He drew her to him and as always they were together and inseparable.

"Thanks Mum…it will be, OK….it will!"

Sam went home that night to the glow and comfort of his wife; she too had been shocked and upset by the recent, financial disasters but they had discussed the problems and reached a decision.

Lancaster was the right move for them; she wanted to be near her family and Moseley had nothing to offer if financial security could not be provided.

Sam loved his wife for her common sense, compassion and fortitude as much as he did for her sensitivity and beauty.

She had not balked at selling all of Sam's own properties here to ease the pain of the liquidation and secure a home for his mother as she summed their sacrifice up in a few, short words to him that evening.

"We've got the future, Sam… it's a bitter, but small price to pay… to let go of the past."

She was correct but it was still painful for him to see the successful, developing, property business he'd created decimated and his own immediate family's security threatened.

Over the course of the next few weeks Sam and his family spent most weekends in

Lancaster.

They stayed with Tahnee's father, Harold and her brother Peter - her mother had died many years ago.

They house hunted and eventually Sam found, by chance, a small, inexpensive, dilapidated house; it was more than a little run down and its tiny garden, ironically for Sam, backed onto the local, golf course.

They both loved it, Sam because it was a good deal and he could develop it, and Tahnee, because it was comfortable, snug and homely; just right for the three of them.

Chapter 14

The family house in the Midlands was sold, the new one purchased and they spent many weeks with his in-laws, Harold and Peter whilst their new property was improved.

Sam tied up his local, business affairs and after a few months all the contracts for his investments there had been signed, with the financial ties to his familiar, home town finally broken.

One last thing remained for him to do and as he drove up to the golf club he let his mind drift back to his first lesson all those years ago.

He idled up the long drive then saw, as normal, Len Thompson was in his treasured, familiar position on the practice ground passing on his experience as only he could.

It was as if nothing had changed where in reality the whole universe and been turned and thrown upside down.

His fingers and feet drove slowly, inching his car along and his eyes looked hard at the tall man in the distance whose shoulders seemed more hunched over than he remembered and his hair, what there was, even whiter and thinner.

But he could see he remained vital, still enthusiastic about a game that's appeal Sam seemed almost to have forgotten.

He had written his resignation to the club years ago; they were fed up with him and he was sick of them.

The final straw for both sides had been when

he'd won the club championship for the umpteenth time on his annual visit and received a letter from the chairman virtually and ridiculously accusing him of insulting everybody but the green-keeper!

Golf had become irrelevant to him and on receipt of this ludicrous correspondence from the senior, committee man he submitted his resignation by return.

It was sad in some ways for them to part, but in truth it was inevitable and he had passed gaining any enjoyment or pleasure from club golf, many, distant years ago.

Sam sat on the evocative, wooden bench in Len's old workshop; even after all this time it hadn't changed at all and he loved its unique, cosy and special atmosphere.

His pale eyes gazed out of the window towards the shed, the famous, inspirational shed and watched as Len and his lesson were gathering the balls like busy, misshapen *Lowry* figures in the distance.

He walked out to the back of the 12th hole and remembered his first birdie; he could see himself, the child that he had been, raising his hand in triumph as the small crowd of Len and his Dad applauded.

He felt like weeping and crying, but there was no point as undeniably they were happy memories; it was only the subsequent, desperate struggle of ambition that had soured them.

When he returned to the ancient, black and white, wooden building, his former teacher was sitting on the bench sipping his *brew* and a hot, steaming mug of sweet tea was waiting for his favourite pupil.

"How are you, Sam…?"

Len drawled at him; his exquisite, Irish twang and accent, still deliciously expressive.

"…You've grown a bit, Son!"

Sam sipped his boiling drink and smiled at him in acknowledgement; it was true he had put on weight, but he was joyous and contented and it showed in his demeanour and unfortunately also around his waist as he joked with him.

"I can hit the ball a long way now, Len!"

The old professional's eyes tinted, pale green and then narrowed, displaying an unusual melancholy and seriousness.

"I'm sorry about your Dad, Sam…he…"

His normally quick mind was searching for the correct, expressive word until he found it and the smile returned to his face as he recalled him so clearly in his mind's eye.

"...He was a *character*, Son...Frankie...was certainly a character!"

Sam felt his throat go dry; just being here made it seem as if his father would unexpectedly walk in at any given moment and start talking endlessly, and he struggled to answer.

"That he was, Len...he sure was..."

The now, fully grown man, who suddenly still distinctly felt like a child in this environment, cleared his throat and tried to change the subject; it was too difficult to think about his deceased parent, particularly here and he changed the subject.

"You know I'm moving north, Len...?"

The wizened teacher nodded, Sam noticed that his face was more fatigued, lined and leathery that he'd remembered it to be.

"...Well, I've come to say goodbye and to thank you for all your help over the years."

The old giant raised his massive, incredible

hands then shook and waved them in good humour and mild embarrassment.

"Don't be silly, Son..."

He chastised and spoke about the past playfully.

"...It was always a pleasure... but you know... you took things too seriously for your own good."

Sam smiled; he had come to terms with his golfing memories, legacy and experiences, or so he thought!

"I know, Len, but that's history now; I'm happy... married with a small boy, Oliver..."

He gasped with more than a trace of the pride that once filled and bloated his own, loving father.

"... Len, you should see him, he's something incredible and special!"

The professional had two daughters of his own and he looked kindly at the thrilled, doting, new parent in front of him.

He had matured from the innocent boy he once knew and was genuinely delighted that he looked so happy, energised and untroubled.

His face was clear, handsome and unblemished which pleased and contented the aged, golf instructor greatly.

"Aye, Son…"

To tease him a final time however was just too irresistible.

"….And…Are you going to let him play golf?"

Sam's answer was instinctive and joking.

"Over my dead body…!"

He laughed but then shrugged in thought and ambivalence.

"…Who knows, Len… if he wants?"

The green globes of the still, enormous Goliath focussed on him seriously a final time and asked him a probing, difficult question.

"And you, Sam…are you going to play any more? You were always good but… "

Len breathed in slowly and purposefully as if choosing his words very meaningfully, gingerly and carefully.

"…In these last few years, I've never seen anyone strike a ball so well with so little work…"

His fingers intertwined with themselves as they sometimes tended to do when he was distracted.

"... And I mean *anyone*, Son!"

Sam looked at the imperious, irrepressible, lofty, elderly man and somehow realised that he strangely loved him in his own way; he knew that his mentor just paid him an enormous compliment and he thought for a lengthy moment before replying.

"Len, I've lost the heart for it...did quite a while ago...!"

He sat back tiredly suddenly as if in contemplation of all his former eternal work, sweat and labour.

"... It seems so unimportant now, with Tahnee, Oliver..."

He laughed suddenly as if to break the mood.

"... Does anyone really care if you're a good golfer?"

Len looked surprisingly wounded but his face was still soft and, as always, so friendly; he smiled warmly with a chuckle but his answer was more than an aside or a meaningless joke.

"I do, Son... *I do!*"

They chatted and Sam was truly pleased that he had made the effort to come and say his ultimate farewell to his eternal, memorable friend and of course the golf club.

Despite the last few tenuous, strained years of his membership it had undoubtedly held rich memories; his time there had been interesting, exciting and wonderful for him in his childhood, and his emerging, formative years.

In so many ways, Sam had grown up on these grounds and ever familiar holes; there were endless fond thoughts and reminiscences everywhere as he looked and simply walked around.

As he drove away for the last time he mused and realised that if he had to pick out what he'd valued the most in his sporting career, it had been his time spent with, Len Thompson at Shirley golf club.

His expressive warmth, humility and ever present charm stayed with him just as his father's wild drive and ambition did; he thought that perhaps on reflection if he'd been a little more like his enigmatic tutor, he just might have made it after all!

Sam immediately enjoyed his life in Lancaster;

it felt like it actually and truly belonged to him.

The house was soon finished and he loved to work with his hands, painting and improving the place; skills that he'd gleaned from the assorted professional tradesmen that he always employed.

He started on new projects and although he was not rich he began to acquire a financial independence that he relished.

So many years chasing money endlessly round and round made him value assets and security.

Sam loved his house, his new home, his wife but most of all, Sam loved his young boy; he adored and cherished his son with a passion that was impossibly hard to explain to anyone who was not a devoted father.

From the first moment he had taken his own flesh and blood into his arms he had felt their unbreakable bond; he'd enjoyed bathing him, changing him, taking him for walks around the park, reading to him and making sure he was settled before putting him to bed each night.

He tried not to smother the child; Sam wanted him to be strong and independent but was always there for him and fiercely proud of his precious, perfect son.

Oliver grew up incredibly quickly from an infant with rich, hazel eyes, to a toddler and then, to an impossibly, beautiful little man.

Beautiful would normally not be used to describe a boy but that was exactly what the little mite was.

His body was lean and lithe and his maternal parent had let his brown hair grow long as it framed then adorned his clear, almost feminine face and perfect complexion.

The child had a wonderful, engaging, endearing smile and sunny nature - like his mother's - and his outrageously long eyelashes made him the centre of attention whenever women of any age were about.

Sam tried not to be too proud on Oliver's first day of school but when he saw him dressed immaculately in his smart, grey and red uniform his chest jumped, pumped out and swelled with joy, and he tried to hide the growing, forming lump in his throat.

He drove him the short distance to his small, local, private, educational beginning each morning and picked him up exactly at 3.30p.m with a tiny treat of a bag of his favourite sweets.

The events in many ways were mundane or

insignificant but Sam enjoyed every, single, delightful second with him.

Stupidly, he would feel excited as he waited with the other parents for the school bell to mark the end of the day but, as Oliver came out, the boy always flashed him a beaming smile of welcome that simply seemed to illuminate him and explain why he felt the way he did.

They would often drive to the park and walk aimlessly about, chewing jelly sweets and admiring all the animals in the innovative farm and petting area.

Sam felt that this was the best time of his life; his work was successful without the pressure or rewards of big business, and his family life was as near perfect as he could ever have hoped.

He was always jovial and satisfied, happy except for just a few days a year; this being namely, when the *Masters* were shown on television in March and the *British Open* in July.

His body would sit glued, almost hypnotised to his seat trying to reconcile how so many of the people he had played against and competed with on level terms were now *Open* and *Masters* champions.

Ian Woosnam, Jerry Pate, Bernard Langer, Nick Faldo and Paul Sandy; his name rankled with Sam most of all!

Paul Sandy had won a *British Open* a few years ago: holing a wonderful putt on the last at Carnoustie to win by a single shot.

Sam didn't quite know how he felt about such a fact, as he wasn't jealous of the money or the fame; he valued what he had too much for those petty desires, but for those few days a year he felt the hidden fire of frustration that took him back to his childhood and youth.

Such discontentment lasted only until the tournament was finished and then his normal, more salient, regular routine resumed.

Sam's clubs and trophies were still gathering dust in the garage and he never got the urge to play or compete again, much to the amazement of anyone that knew of his previous, golfing reputation and prowess.

The now, aging man would often smile at their well-meaning enquiries.

"Why don't you play? Join a club? Play for fun?"

Nobody would understand, could possibly read his mind or feel his past; how could they?

He could never just play this game for simply fun. Ever!

When Sam watched golf he now viewed it with the eyes of an expert; he understood the fundamentals of the golf swing completely and would know instantly from any professional's action or rhythm if they were on form or not.

He often laughed at much of the analysis from so many of the so-called golfing specialists and commentators and he would think about some of his previous advisers, who could hardly hit their hats!

His mind also considered more and more about the Ben Hogan book he had so casually discarded as a boy.

He now understood what the arc and the swing plane were and wondered how it had taken him so much exertion and toil to comprehend and learn what had been written.

Sam always loved the incredibly detailed, wonderful, pencilled sketch of Hogan's back swing; the game was there for all to see if only you had the eye to see and the insightful mind to grasp it.

In truth however, he understood it was not that simple; golf was a game of *feel* and it could not be simply transcribed; it was ironic to Sam that he now fully grasped a profession and a craft that he no longer had any desire to practice.

That was however the way events in his life had unfolded and Sam had no complaints anymore; how could he, as he was so infinitely comfortable and content?

But occasionally, sometimes, somewhere, deep within his soul something buried and hidden, like a skeleton or a private secret that just shook, rattled and ran so deeply within his psyche, disturbed him.

It was perhaps just a shadow or a ghost of the past but he always brushed it off his shoulders and just ignored it!

On the odd occasion when it was late evening, the quiet emptiness of the golf course at the bottom of the garden called to him, and he would grab a rusty 6 iron and a handful of old, marked balls and sneak silently onto the empty grounds like a naughty schoolboy breaking the rules.

In the twilight, with only the birds and soft breeze for company, Sam would have a couple of practice swings and then proceed to hit some shots; most endeavours and efforts connecting sweetly or perfectly, as if he'd been playing each and every day.

Sam wasn't impressed or surprised, he knew what he was capable of but his was a talent that demanded time, commitment and selfishness to bring it fully to bear.

After a dozen such attempts he would purposefully pick up the balls then gratefully and lovingly return home to his family.

However his hands hit the divisive, little spheres he had no desire to turn back the clock; he was happy, lucky and knew it to be an undoubtedly true fact and, that counted for a lot!

Sam's Midland family had survived in their own ways; Anna and Timmy had lasted less that a year running the shop, it had been then been sold and an amicable divorce followed soon after.

His sister had found someone new and surprisingly, the separation from her husband and the ending of her reliance on the family business eventually made her resourceful and happy.

She would often travel with their Mum up to visit and Sam was pleased that after all these years, he had finally and truly found some semblance of a relationship with her.

As a father himself now, he perhaps had more

tolerance, insight and understood that just possibly the way he had always perceived his sister, had not been entirely all her fault.

Sam was nearing 40; he was now becoming well rounded, but his hair remained full and thick and he sensed and felt that he still had the energy and spirit of a teenager.

His existence seemed set, regimented, contented and safe, but life sometimes had a way... a delicious even dangerous way of surprising you, and the middle-aged man was in for a huge, enormous shock!

Chapter 15

Oliver was now 9 years old, wiry, independent and bright as a button; he was also sensitive and could pick up on the smallest and most apparently insignificant detail.

He knew that his Dad and him, shared something special; his mind just assumed that perhaps it was how all fathers and sons felt, but as long as he could remember he had always been together.

They were tight and closely knit like the butter or jam on his toast in the morning, and often he could sense his father's moods, thoughts and emotions almost before he spoke.

He knew he *got* and comprehended his male parent completely; his Dad was straightforward, funny, dependable, anxious, contradictory and a bit of a fusspot.

The only thing Oliver couldn't understand were his father's emotional swings when golf came on the television; he noticed it casually at first when he'd been 5 and each subsequent year he'd watch as his parent would just sit morosely and intently staring at the television.

Oliver could not see the appeal of the game, it seemed so silly; the people dressed strangely and brightly and everything seemed to take endlessly and forever.

He watched the competition with him however because in some unusual way his Dad actually seemed to like it, and he soon became familiar with the scoring system, etiquette and mostly all of the leading players.

This year had been the same, his father strangely irritated and quick tempered until this strange, sprawling theatre called *The Open* had finished and then as if by magic, he would return to normal.

Oliver asked him if he'd ever played and he just grunted and did not answer him; it was a permanent puzzle to the young boy and, as he abhorred mysteries he could not solve, he vowed that one day he would find out the answer to this particular riddle.

The long, summer months were coming to an end and Oliver had been given the unenviable task of cleaning the garage; throwing out all the junk that had accumulated over the years.

The instruction had come from his disciplinarian of a Mother who was out somewhere with his father and he knew full well that he'd better do a proper job, or else!

Box after box of rubbish was thrown into a small skip specially provided, and to the boy's amazement and surprise he suddenly came across a huge, white, funny looking bag.

He then undid a long, silver zip and there, inside the leather feeling, square container was to his incredulous disbelief a full and complete set of golf clubs.

Oliver quickly moved a nearby, dusty box to get a closer look at the previously hidden, silver sticks and it fell out of his hands spilling the contents all over the mucky, grey, painted, garage floor.

The boy gasped in surprise as a virtual treasure-trove of stained but noticeably, silver cups and medals glinted up at him in the murky, dull, dank light.

He picked some of them up, handling them so carefully and gingerly as he read the written inscriptions in fascination.

Midland Golf champion, English champion, Warwickshire Champion; an enormous selection of endless fantastical, tokens and trophies.

Oliver breathed in, startled and almost stunned; life seldom surprised him, but his Dad was a golf champion and he'd never, ever guessed, gleaned, realised or known!

He was about to put the silverware back into the box when he noticed a thick, red book almost hidden under the remaining *treasure* inside the cardboard container.

His slender, fine fingers extracted it and wiped off the layer of dust that had lain upon it for many years and carefully he opened it, so as not to damage the brittle paper.

To his further astonishment, on the first page he turned to, there was his father, as a young man, smiling at him holding up in his hands a large, handsome, trophy!

The book was extensively full of newspaper articles and, given that his parents would both be away for at least a couple of hours, the boy quickly put the gleaming awards back in the box and busily finished the rest of the work in the garage.

Once satisfied that the space was tidied to his mother's, high standards and satisfaction, he then took the intriguing book into the kitchen where he laid it on the table.

Purposefully he poured himself a transparent, tall glass of orange juice and after downing the liquid in a single, thirsty swig opened the heavy, red cover, ceremoniously exposing the very first section of information and written articles enclosed within it.

The boy's bright eyes widened with every leaf of the volume turned; he recognised his Dad, of course, but he also saw so many of famous names that he'd seen from the television, all top professionals!

This was simply unbelievable.

His father had beaten them all and in an instant

he understood his former moods when watching golf, no wonder he was upset; *he should have been there, winning the prizes, on television, his Dad*!

He read every word, savoured each written story or article and then reached the end where only blank pages stared up at him!

The empty spaces were somehow infuriating as if indicative of stories not yet written; he wanted there to be more, somehow he stupidly craved and desperately needed there to be more than this!

He hid the ruby plunder in his bedroom, deep inside his schoolbooks where no one ever looked; this book was his special secret now, his personal, private piece of treasure.

The young, impressionable boy sat on his bed and thought extensively, as he had a tendency to do and there, as the late, summer sun streamed in through the open window like celestial light, an exquisite germ of an idea appeared in his fertile mind like impossible, divine, fantastical magic itself.

He recognised instantly that it was just a silly dream or fantasy; but it was such a simple, exquisite and pure thought that only a childlike, innocent 9 year old boy could have conceived.

Therefore, Oliver embraced his lunatic fancy and brainwave; simply relished it, then was captivated and completely enthralled by his inspirational quest and unique vision.

Sam Chester, *his father* was going to win the *British Open* and he was going to help him to do it!

Somehow!

Concocting the initial idea was easy but as he heard his parent's car come up the drive and path Oliver realised that putting it into practice would not be so straight forward or simple.

However the boy was wise beyond his years and he realised what an arbitrary and obstinate person his Dad was; he'd seen at first hand his mother so often tell him to complete or attempt something, and he would always then do the direct opposite!

At first anyway, then he would normally relent and comply with his Mum's direction; she always knew how to handle him!

Oliver also knew instinctively that if he simply told him his naïve dream straight off he would just laugh at him; he needed a plan, a design that involved his father picking up a golf club once again, apparently of his own choosing.

He was subdued and quiet over dinner therefore and his Mum and Dad questioned if he was feeling all right.

He gazed at his father guiltlessly; his brain still working and turning over in precocious thought.

"I'm fine…"

He mumbled and complained.

"…Just tired from all that work… and those boxes!"

Sam looked at him; smiled at his lovely face and could not help but tease and torture him a little more.

"When I was your age, Oliver…"

He spoke with mock affliction and pain.

"…I was unloading vans that seemed to stretch…"

His clever and mischievous son did not let him finish and chipped in then completed the sentence he had heard so many times before.

"…Forever, with 10 million boxes on and…"

He was so droll and cheeky for such a small child!

"...You unloaded all by yourself!"

Indeed, Oliver had heard this tall tale incessantly and perhaps, in his head, more times than there were the imaginary boxes on the van!

Sam looked at his son, unsure whether to be annoyed or not at his sarcasm and spirit, but he just laughed; he could never ever be really upset or angry with him.

His wife then joined in, as if in league with their creation.

"You do go on, Sam...change your script a bit!"

He knew better than to argue with the two of them together and was pleased that Oliver had brightened up; he always revelled and loved the camaraderie they all had at mealtimes.

It was as the boy was finishing his ice cream that he had a sudden further brainwave and, after slowly licking his spoon clean between each mouth-full and thinking through the implications of every one of his intended actions, the quest for *The British Open* truly began.

He looked then stared at his father; he was lost in discussion with his mother about school or holidays and he politely interrupted them.

"Excuse me, Dad…"

He ensured that his most innocent, cute look was on his face; he could always deliver it to order.

"…Can I ask you a question…?"

Sam was always suspicious when his son was too polite and focussed his pale, blue searching eyes on him; they still retained both a youthfulness and intelligence that had always stayed with him.

Oliver was well prepared for his intrusive stare; he'd played this game before but not quite like this and looked sensibly past his azure gaze.

"…You said that I could choose to play a sport and you'll get me some coaching… didn't you?"

Sam nodded in some surprise at his sudden interest in anything but football and Manchester United.

"Yes Oliver, sport is important, I would like you to do something well, it will be character building for you…"

He sat back in his chair as pompously as he had spoken then shook himself urgently; he had a sudden unsettling sensation of him being his own father!

"… What do you want to play, Son? Tennis, football, Cricket…go Hors…"

The boy sucked his spoon a final time as if relishing what he was about to say then whispered so deliciously and coolly.

"I want to learn to play golf, Dad…I want to play golf…!"

Sam sat back in his chair as if he'd been slapped in the face and he was genuinely puzzled and shocked; he had not expected this and his expression raised the question of where this sudden, crazy thought and desire had sprung from.

Oliver explained as if understanding his father's thought processes; which he always did.

"…It's watching it on the television…"

He felt as if he was on stage at the school play but this time he was acting out the main part as he continued ever-onwards.

"…It's made me curious and I want to see if I can hit it!"

Sam still could not believe what he was

hearing as he countered and questioned him.

"But you hate the game; I know you think everyone looks funny and you believe it to be slow and boring!"

His child just shrugged aimlessly.

"I want to see…"

He was surprisingly insistent, much to Sam's bemusement.

"…I just want to find out…if I can hit it…!"

Tahnee cleared away the plates and Sam sipped his tea and continued to listen confusedly to his son; he would not purposely break his word or a promise he had made to him under any circumstance.

"…You can get me some lessons with the professional at the club next door can't you? I won't have far to go!"

Sam nodded, digesting this revelation and, picking his words very tentatively and carefully, spoke softly to the boy.

"Oliver…"

His own mind was racing in surprising energy and he made what he thought would be an unexpected suggestion to him.

"...Oliver...your Dad used to be a good golfer and... if you do want to play... well I was hoping you'd let me show and teach you, myself?"

His child's hazel eyes purposefully widened with mock surprise; in that split second he sensed it was an absolute crime that he never got the leading role recently in the production of *Oliver* at his school as he undoubtedly had the talent to pretend, and the name, naturally!

He smiled to himself; this was all going so well and he was about to ripple his proud father's still waters further as he sweetly mumbled and murmured to him.

"Don't be silly, Dad..."

He scolded him childishly and with perfect, comic timing.

"...I want to be taught properly... by a *proper* teacher... a professional teacher...not you!"

Sam felt his hackles rise instantly, his son had insulted him and he'd *not* even realised it!

"I am a proper golfer, Oliver...!"

He spoke to him sternly and with a growing, building irritation.

"...I used to be one of the best golfers in the country. I won my county cha..."

Oliver looked at his mother blankly who was trying her best to suppress a dry, hidden smile on her plump, open, pretty lips.

She absolutely loved it when her husband got mad as the rage somehow brought the fire out in him once more; his confidence and spark that had waned a little over the years with their cautious, safe and enclosed way of life was somehow momentarily relit and rekindled.

Oliver turned the hidden screw on his father's vanity; more than he could ever have truly realised in his genuine naivety and innocence.

"This is another story about the boxes, Mum, isn't it?"

They both laughed simultaneously and Sam's voice suddenly roused and raised in voluble resentment and frustration.

"Oliver..."

He was agitated and strangely irked; he had not had that sensation for years apart from very occasional spats with his wife, who could also have her moments!

"....I'm telling you the truth..."

He inhaled in sudden fire and barely repressed ego.

"... I'm far superior both as a golfer and a teacher to any of the local professionals around here!"

The small boy felt like laughing out loud; his father had fallen straight into the trap he'd set for him and he closed the pen and gate expertly.

"Prove it then, Dad..."

He challenged and provoked him at the same time.

"...You prove it and... I'll let you save your money and you can teach me yourself!"

Sam stared in irritation and fury at his annoying, too clever by half, Little Man, and words were out of his mouth before he realised the lunacy of his actions and reactions

"How?"

Oliver spoke the words he had been forming all night in his scheming, Machiavellian head.

"Play the professional at the local, golf club..."

He drew in his breath and took his sweet time, just for effect.

".... if you can beat him as you say, *then*... I'll let *you* show me!"

Again Sam's response came instantly and without reflection; his son had annoyed him and he was going to teach him a lesson once and for all!

Well he presumed he was anyway!

"Done...!"

He spoke as if he was concluding a major business deal!

"...I'll arrange it tomorrow...the match will be a week on Saturday, then you'll see!"

Oliver just secretly smiled inside his imaginative, lovely head, kissed his parents goodnight and went upstairs to do his homework but surreptitiously read the large, amazing, red scrapbook once more.

Sam sensed that he was unusually flustered and flushed; he went outside for a short walk into the fresh air to cool off.

He sauntered along the sandy path at the rear of his house then peered over to the darkened, golf course and a rush of unusual adrenaline and expectation that he'd not felt for nearly a decade instantly surged through his veins.

There was a match again and, in spite of himself, the sleeping competitor inside him strangely looked forward to it.

When he returned home an hour later, Oliver was asleep and his wife had poured a small scotch that was by his chair; she laughed at him as he sat heavily on the comfortable soft, beige armchair that was in desperate need of a re-cover.

"Sam..."

She smiled and whispered to him warmly and with some hilarity.

"...You know sometimes I listen to you and Oliver and can't work out who's the bigger *Kid*!"

Sam sipped his drink and as the liquid gently burned the back of his throat he smiled at her dryly in some acknowledgment of her precise observation and intimation; she was right, his blessed wife was nearly always right!

Oliver meanwhile was wrapped up in his duvet planning his next course of devious, devilish actions; his Dad was just so wonderfully predictable and he pondered, contemplated and wondered for a moment if he really could beat the professional as he had said?

Chapter 16

Sam kept his promise the following day and drove slowly round with his son to the golf shop of the adjacent course where he'd looked out, secretly trespassed and walked upon so often.

Daniel Sharp was the name of the professional and he listened to Sam's challenge with amusement and interest; he was a tall, broad, young man, about 26 years old with wavy, blonde hair and a friendly smile.

He never heard of Sam or his exploits many years ago and assumed that this was some sort of joke between father and son.

Taking his opportunity as Oliver was looking around his shop; he took the older man to one side and spoke to him seriously.

"Do you want me to let you win?"

Sam's eyes narrowed in understanding but some annoyance and irritation nevertheless as well.

"Daniel…"

His tone was foolishly and irrationally strained.

"…I've learnt in life that money talks so I'll have a little side bet with you… "

He sighed and continued sharply.

"…If you lose… your £40 fee will be lost as well, but if you win I'll double it…"

He stopped and breathed in a final time as if to make his point.

"… Now, do you still want to play? "

The confident, young professional just smiled contentedly.

"10a.m. Saturday… Mr Chester…"

He still thought of this match only as a joke and muttered mockingly.

"…And by the way…"

Sam turned and looked at him as if awaiting further information.

"…Bring your wallet!"

Sam laughed at the man's character; he had awareness and personality and he liked him.

"Call me, Sam, Daniel…"

He smiled broadly and happily.

"...My wallet and I... will see you on, Saturday."

The episode with the young professional demonstrated one thing for certain, that no one remembered his past glories.

This was a new era and however good he had been or he thought he was; it would only be the result of this match that would count!

That seemed true of golf or even life itself, Sam concluded, no matter what you achieved it seemed you were only as good as your last round or performance!

Sam had a few days before the forthcoming contest and although he meant to practice he was busy and preoccupied with the development progress of one of his houses.

Apart from a few, quick swings late into one evening, snatched furtively on the shadowy golf course, on Saturday as agreed, Sam stood on the initial teeing area at Standing Golf Club hardly having touched a club or played a single round of golf for over 10 long, productive and busy years.

The 1st hole was a short, par 4 and Oliver was pulling his father's, not insubstantial bag on a trolley, and watching on with genuine absorption and interest.

He had diligently, recently cleaned the whole set of the silver clubs, under his mother's more experienced direction, and they had a thin veneer of brightness due to Oliver's determined attempts to remove the marks of passing time and shades of rust on them.

Daniel struck first; a solid hit that finished just before the green and then Sam stepped up to his ball and stood over it feeling completely and absolutely disoriented.

He tried to swing smoothly but the shot went weakly to the right and easy par 4 secured a victory at the 1st for his opponent.

Simple pars did the same at the 2nd 4th and 5th holes and by the time they had reached the 10th tee the young professional was 5 up and feeling embarrassed about the bet suggested and offered by his obviously ill prepared and patently amateur opponent.

He could see that Sam had a decent golf swing and perhaps had played before at some stage but today he just couldn't seem to connect with the ball at all; to put it politely he was simply awful!

As they stood together the tall man spoke

quietly to Sam, out of Oliver's earshot, as he did not wish to embarrass him further in front of his son who he was obviously trying to impress with his questionable sporting prowess.

"I'm happy with just the fee, Sam!"

His whispered words were kind, considerate and thoughtful under the evolving circumstances.

"...I don't want double!"

Sam was incredibly incensed and although he recognised that this thoughtful, young man was trying to be empathetic, he felt patronised and demeaned; it utterly infuriated him as he almost spat back at him in his frustrated riposte.

"...Another separate £40 on the back 9...on top of the double bet..."

He was angry and it showed as he muttered darkly.

"...And you try and win!"

Daniel saw the fire of passion raging in the plump, middle-aged stranger's, blue eyes as he smiled then nodded; if that's what this misguided and delusional man wanted then he'd take his money!

He was a professional after all; of course he would!

Oliver observed the match in silence, disbelief and disappointment; all his life his father had never lied to him but he was being hammered and humiliated by someone that he'd told him he could beat easily!

The dream was fading faster than running water from an open tap; maybe his Dad was not a golf champion after all or perhaps he was simply just too ancient and old?

Sam was however, absolutely furious and incensed with himself; he was determined to keep cool in front of the child but it burned him that his body would not respond as his mind instructed it.

He acknowledged the difficulty of expecting to compete well after not playing at all for so much time, but he still felt a fraud in front of his boy and it awoke the dormant, snoozing, competitive tiger inside of him.

He holed from *20 feet* on the 10th for a win and suddenly found his rhythm as if it was a close, missing friend coming back home to him.

Shot after shot found the centre of the club and at each of the incoming holes he was putting for a birdie.

Daniel, after initially being surprised at his unexpected reversal of fortune, tried to fight back and as they came up the last hole, he was still 1 up on the main challenge having lost the side bet on the back 9 on the 14th hole.

Sam could manage no better than a par and he watched as his young adversary holed from *6 feet* for a half on the hole, and a victory on the overall match 1 up.

The professional walked over to him and shook him firmly by the hand, "Sam, Sam...I can't believe you haven't played for over 10 years..."

He was raving and enthused with what he had witnessed.

"...Your back 9 was simply fantastic... the best I've ever seen... "

He shook his head in genuine admiration and amazement.

"...*Ever*...it was just unbelievable...fantastic...!"

Sam reached into his pocket as they left the green and withdrew his wallet; he handed the man four, crisp £10 notes but his opponent tried his best to refuse them.

"...It wasn't fair, Sam..."

He was embarrassed to win like this.

"…You just needed to warm up, there's no way I can beat you. You're too good…."

He shook his blonde hair and sighed as if measuring his own performance against what he had just seen.

"…Much, much too good!"

Sam however was insistent.

"A bet's a bet… Daniel!"

The young man reluctantly took the money as finally Sam turned to his son and stroked his soft, brown hair; he could see he was weary and tired from his day's exertions.

"You've been a Good Lad, Oliver, you've walked round without a murmur of complaint, now…"

He muttered words to him that made him distinctly uncomfortable.

"…Go with, Daniel and book your lessons as I promised!"

Sam felt almost physically sick as he saw his son walk into the door of the professional's shop; he'd tried his best but he'd failed, again!

He railed and cursed to himself under his breath in his infuriation and frustration; golf always seemed to confound and defeat him one way or the other.

"*This, bloody game....this bloody game!*"

Oliver was tired but elated at his father's sudden form, with each shot on the back 9 he could sense that his inspired, crazy, insane proposition and juvenile fantasy was maybe still possible and not so ludicrous after all!

Obviously his father *was* far superior to the local professional and if he could play like that with just a solitary day's practice, then maybe…?

He appeared from inside the shop shortly afterwards chewing the chocolate bar that Daniel had given him and he scampered jauntily over to his waiting parent who snapped at him sharply in barely concealed irritation.

"When's your first lesson, Oliver?"

His child bit off a huge, dark, brown piece of confectionary and let it dissolve slowly on his tongue, relishing his Dad's, patent exasperation and mouth-watering discomfort.

He put his free hand into his father's fingers and ambled leisurely with him back to the car park and mumbled as he kicked his toes against the gravel just because he wanted to.

"I've decided, Dad... that I'm..."

He munched and noisily swallowed the rest of the sweet treat and then carefully, pedantically threw the wrapper into the bin just to relish and stretch his little bit of punishment out for his parent a little further.

"... Going to let you show me after all..."

He continued ever more gaily.

"...You were right; you are better than, Daniel and I want to be taught by the very best!"

Sam squeezed his son's hand in ludicrous, humble appreciation of his decision and sensed a rush of his own childish glee, satisfaction and elation run through his body like buzzing electricity.

His young son had made him feel more pleasure and achievement in this meaningless, unimportant defeat than bizarrely all his previous, tournament victories combined, had been able to do.

He had wanted to teach him so badly!

They drove home quietly and happily, both

drained by the day's energetic endeavours; Sam promised him that next week they would go onto the practice range and he would start to educate and instruct him how to play this difficult game.

Oliver sucked and savoured the last remnants of the cocoa and sugar in his mouth and relaxed into the easy softness of the car's comfortable seats.

"Yes, Dad…that will be great…"

He seemed to laugh and smile at the same time.

"…I'll look forward to it!"

Secretly he marvelled in his head how this initial adventure and experiment had gone far better than he could have hoped for.

The seeds of his father's renaissance had been sown and next week it was time for the next and perhaps the most important stage of his ingenious, master plan!

Chapter 17

Daniel had given Sam his consent to use the practice area at the local golf club and the following Saturday morning, as promised, Oliver and his father excitedly drove the short distance to the quiet, colourful range.

Sam had cut down one of his old clubs, it was an 8 iron and was from the same antiquated set he had used as a teenager when he'd confronted and beaten the U.S champion at Hoylake.

The morning was delightfully bright and clear and as they walked onto the lengthy patch of greenery, Sam breathed in the sharp, fresh air of the new day deeply; somehow it felt good and great just to be alive.

He released the golf balls from the bursting, black, practice bag and couldn't help but be transported back to his own childhood and that very first day with Len Thompson.

But Oliver wasn't him and he certainly wasn't his irresistible, incorrigible former instructor as he placed the small club in his son's hands then gently, softly encouraged him.

"Just relax, Oliver,"

He stood quietly behind and guided him back

and forward through an imaginary shot then, when he felt he was ready, placed the small, white ball in front of him and tried not to admire his smart, blue trousers and white shirt too much.

He was undoubtedly such an adorable and handsome boy.

Oliver swung gainfully at the ball but missed it completely and over the next half an hour Sam tried everything to show him how to make that initial connection with the devilish, tiny, bright globe.

The boy was calm and patient however, never once roused to the type of frustration so inherent in his father's nature and eventually connected with the ball then cheered himself in happy mockery, as it trickled tamely along the emerald, shaven floor.

Sam held his head firmly, just as his had been restricted on his first lesson and to his surprise, Oliver made a sweet hit and Sam felt the thrill of seeing his son's first, airborne shot.

However the boy looked tired and sat down to open the drink that his mother had sent with him and his large, pure, hazel globes found his father as his pink lips murmured to him

"You hit a few, Dad…"

He mumbled almost as an aside, simply ever so quietly and innocently.

"…Show me how it's done….*please!*"

Sam had brought a couple of his own clubs with him and selected a 5 iron; he saw no harm in simply demonstrating what he had been trying to teach him.

He stood over the ball and settled, then turned his shoulders to show his son the correct angle, shape and specific plane of the golf swing and spoke as he did so.

"You always need to be in this position, Oliver; on the inside, then you can release the club head naturally."

Oliver looked at him blankly as if he was talking Russian or Chinese.

"Show me Dad…just you show me…then I will understand… *please*…. show me!"

Sam set his stocky body, markedly over the ball again, turned his head and muttered intently to his child.

"I'm aiming at that marker post, Oliver."

His upper body turned and he hit the ball perfectly to within a few feet of the far, distant point then selected another ball and again it flew exactly as the initial shot had done.

Before he'd realised he'd hit a dozen shots all of which had landed within a circular pattern of close proximity only a mere few inches away from each other; Oliver was entranced, enthused and pressed him.

"Can you hit one that goes like this...?"

He gestured almost like a tiny, sprat swimming, with his small, delicate hands a motion from left to right.

Sam reflexively, instinctively selected another ball, picked his club up fractionally on the back swing turn and watched as it started just left of the marker post and faded back.

"And like this..."

Oliver's fishy mind and fingers were now swimming and moving in the opposite direction and without thinking, Sam placed another ball, flattened his swing a little and rolled his wrists early enabling the ball to land right of the target and draw back to drop inches away from it.

Oliver was astounded and definitely enjoying himself.

"That club must be easy..."

The child took such bliss and delight torturing his father.

"…What about this big one with the funny shape on the end."

His slender wrists then took the huge, cumbersome, lengthy club from the ground and intentionally handed his Dad what he knew was the driver.

He then stood back and watched in utter disbelief as his father rhythmically drew the club back and, with a sound like a sharp crack of a gun, dispatched the ball seemingly past the end of the practise area.

"Dad…"

The boy whispered in genuine surprise and admiration.

"…You're just fantastic at this!"

Sam suddenly realised that the morning had developed, from a lesson for his son to…he wasn't quite certain at this early stage of the day!

What he was sure about was that even *he* had been surprised by the obvious power and control he still had over the game.

He looked at his son and the boy's eyes were literally glistening with mischief and excitement; Sam understood the child just as well as his boy knew him and playfully, he suddenly snatched the orange juice with the accompanying straw from his hands.

"Oliver…"

He tried to give him his most searching stare, but lately he felt this old, familiar tactic was making little difference or impression on his smart and unsettlingly clever child.

"…What are you up to?"

Oliver went quiet suddenly and tried to look guiltless and above suspicion but his father already had the feel and taste of something rather unusual.

"Nothing, Dad, I just wanted to play golf."

Sam put his arm around his lad and, passing the orange juice back, sat down on the short, dry, summer grass close beside him; he then bent down and whispered directly in his delicate ear.

"Oliver, I'm not as daft as I look, tell me…what is it you are up to?"

The boy looked at his shoes, shabby old

trainers obviously in need of a good clean; he'd been trapped as well in the spider's web of his little scheme and this was the moment of truth where he had no option but to share his reverie and surreal dream.

He recognised that he could only take this idea and inspiration so far by himself and he confessed his secret quietly to him.

Sam sat and listened as his youngster slowly revealed and expounded on his thoughts; had he not already been sitting it would simply have knocked him off his feet with what his son let slip and disclosed.

"I found a book, Dad…"

His young clear, crystal eyes ignored the man beside him and looked out only to the far, bright horizon.

"…Of you being famous, winning all those golf tournaments; defeating all those men that are now on the television…"

Sam looked at him utterly astounded and amazed, but was stunned to silence and said nothing at all as Oliver continued.

"…I see you watch the golf on the television, Dad, people that you beat when you were young… and I was sure that you could still beat them...."

He waved his arm expressively towards the balls, crowded and gathered together in the distance.

"...Look how you hit, Dad... nobody could play better than you...and... with a bit of practice...?"

Sam smiled at his son and spoke dryly and with acid sarcasm.

"And what do you think I should do with my unique, *skill and talent*, Oliver, just pick up my clubs and go and win *The Open*?"

The boy looked up at him, his sparkling eyes wide with admiration for his father's brilliant, incredible anticipation and insight; this was going to be easier than he thought!

"That's right, Dad, that's exactly right... pick up your clubs and go win *The Open*...and..."

He was smiling but not jesting...not joking at all; not for a minute!

"...I'll go with you!"

Sam let his head fall backwards and simply roared with laughter; he bent down and kissed his boy gently on the top of his, silken, soft brown hair and chuckled in delight with him.

"Oliver… I do love you…!"

He stared into the horizon also at the same mystery object somewhere at the fullest extent of their combined panorama and vision then murmured expressively.

"…Only a loving son could believe his father could just pick up his clubs, walk onto the 1st tee and win *The Open*!"

His son brushed his father's arm off him in anger, frustration and annoyance; even though he was small, naive and young his Dad's patronising tone upset him.

"I'm not saying to just walk onto the 1st tee…"

He exploded in a real and unexpected fire and fury that caught his father off guard and totally unaware.

"…Look at what you've done in two days golf, look and see how fantastically well you play…"

His watery, hazel eyes and flushed face portrayed only a resolute and undeniable conviction and passion.

"… I believe in you; you can do it…don't ask me how but… I just know you can!"

Sam suddenly stared at the tears, the zeal and fervour visible in his child's expression and stopped mocking him or what he had said.

His pale eyes gazed out more closely onto the busy, golf course where the members were jousting in the monthly medal.

"It's just not that simple, Son…"

He whispered gently, almost to himself.

"…You just can't just come from obscurity, nowhere and win *The British Open*… "

He sighed tiredly and almost moaned.

"…It's impossible!"

He attempted to put his thick arm back around his son as if to end the matter but the boy shrugged him off testily then berated him pointedly and fiercely.

"What do you tell me…?"

He spoke to him icily and coldly.

"…What?"

Sam looked down at his old, now, off-white, golf shoes; he knew he'd been trapped by his own beliefs and expressions that he had tried to instil in him.

"To try your best and…if you try your best and fail then you've nothing to be ashamed of…"

He whispered the words as if he did not believe them anymore.

"…But I tried my best, Oliver… a long time ago and…"

There was despondency and self pity in his tone.

"…My best wasn't good enough!"

The boy just looked straight at him, inside him, and did not let go of his train of thought; he was as tenacious as a hungry, famished dog with a meaty, juicy bone!

"I don't believe you, Dad, I look in your eyes and I don't believe you!"

Sam went quiet, his boy was too unnaturally perceptive for his own good and he was correct; at the point that Sam could actually play the game exceptionally he'd already misplaced his interest and lost the genuine desire to compete!

But such thoughts were personal and not to be shown or revealed to a child; even his adorable but suddenly difficult offspring!

He was the adult, the parent and decidedly, Sam brought this insane discussion to a swift conclusion.

"I can't explain it all to you now, Oliver, it's too complicated; my day for such dreams is gone... long gone!"

Sam watched as his son bit his bottom lip; he always did that when he was uncomfortable or upset.

The lesson was instantly over and they walked up the empty, jade, mown range in silence, collecting all the balls that they'd hit together.

Sam marvelled privately at how close his grouping of 5 irons had been, he felt that he could hit any shot, any shot at all; but such a fact was unimportant or incidental and all he thought to himself was, *so what... so bloody what*!

Instantly he felt a sudden rage inside him as his son had just opened a chapter of his life that he'd thought forgotten; how could he understand all his wasted years and the unbearable pain he went through?

In spite of himself Sam recalled his son's words, *win the British Open*, but it was ludicrous, impossible!

Why? Why was it impossible!

It was as if he was a crazy boy himself once more and he started to battle and argue privately within his perturbed, disturbed head; was it crazy only because he *thought* it was insane and impossible?

Or was it actually...so ridiculous...just as a theory?

He'd always been a fighter but how could he take on such a daunting challenge; he'd always failed at the highest level and he couldn't subject himself to disaster and disappointment once again.

The questions and answers plagued him as he drove home; was the fear of collapse and failure so deep within him that he could not bring himself to even contemplate it, or even try?

His son had made him re-examine himself, to look in the dark, locked away recesses of his mind and find the recollections of his past; he did not feel comfortable with or admire what he found there.

Tahnee immediately noticed the rare but palpable tension between her two men, over dinner.

Oliver was very quiet and not his normal, bubbly character at all and her husband had a stress inside him she had not seen since the business problems some years ago.

She tried to break the icy mood and spoke only of the day and what she thought were positive things.

"How was the golf?

Her child spoke with an apparent, obvious note of deep insincerity.

"*Fine!*"

She tried to gloss over his patent, acerbic response and continued as if everything was normal.

"Will you be going next week?"

Tahnee could tell by the piercing and unbroken silence that such an eventuality did not seem likely.

She had learned that some things were best left to pass over and quietly ignored the festering sore for a couple of days; but Sam's mood just worsened as he became sullen, introverted and went seemingly to a far away place somewhere insular and within himself.

Eventually she realised that the matter would have to be faced and after Oliver had gone to bed that evening, she fixed her husband a small scotch, turned off the television and sat next to him in the quietness and warmth of their front, living room.

She passed him the bronzed liquid in the shiny, cut glass that caught the glow of the natural fire burning in their grate, and gently coaxed and questioned him.

"What is it Sam? You and Oliver have been upset, *off* and really strange the last few days?"

Sam sipped his drink and tried to pretend he had not noticed but he had of course; since Oliver had made his insane proposition it was as if a hundred firecrackers were continually igniting and exploding in his mixed up brain.

"It's nothing!"

The maturing woman and mother looked at her husband as her brown eyes suddenly sparked and dangerously burned into his.

"Sam, you're the worst liar I've ever seen, now enough…! Tell me…!"

Her voice was increasingly angry, forceful and insistent.

"...You tell me...now!

Sam looked at his drink and meaningfully, rotated the crystal glass absent-mindedly as if simply to watch the delicious colours, change shape and hue!

"Oliver pretended to want to play golf... just to get me to challenge the professional..."

He looked as perplexed as he sounded then just went wittering on.

"...On the practice ground on, Saturday... he ended up conning me into hitting most of the shots."

Tahnee looked at him as if he was truly as mad and insane as he appeared.

"*Yes*? So?"

Sam smiled at her dryly and in abashment.

"He told me that he'd had a dream..."

He sipped his drink for courage and he whispered then complained sullenly and indignantly.

"...That I was going to win *The British Open*... he got upset when I told him it was impossible."

His wife took his hand a squeezed it in

understanding.

"The boy found your scrapbook, Sam..."

She always knew exactly what was going on under her roof no matter how her men tried to hide and keep their secrets.

"...I found it mixed in with his school books... it's only understandable that he should think his father could be a champion."

Sam spoke as if suddenly he was the child once more.

"He doesn't believe me when I tell him it's impossible..."

His bright, blue spheres immediately paled to shame and sadness.

"...He thinks I'm a quitter!"

Tahnee looked deeply at her husband and his anxious eyes revealed the real reason he was upset.

Year after year she had observed him watching *The Open* or *Masters*, glued static, almost part of the chair in which he sat, as he looked on almost mentally transporting himself to the course.

Experience had taught her how obstinate and

contrary he was, always telling her he would not do something before eventually complying with her wishes; that was Sam and she accepted and understood him.

Tahnee therefore trod the path she knew so well, as she mumbled in apparent agreement.

"Of course you can't win…"

Her voice was intentionally condescending and patronising.

"…It is ridiculous…*of course!*"

Sam looked at her in anguish as his face so obviously burned with hurt pride then indignation and her lips formed a teasing, mocking smile; she could manipulate and capture him so easily!

"…*Well, is it or not?*"

Her husband instantly returned to his immature, moody, quiet place until his wife lost her temper and railed at him.

"…Sam you're impossible, I know you… you still think you can win; all the child has done is pose to you a question you've probably asked yourself a hundred times…"

She was like a raging typhoon or a whistling,

irresistible whirlwind; unmanageable, irrepressible and devastating all at the same time!

"...Maybe it is impossible but at least if you tried then you could watch the television in peace..."

Her voice came down slightly from a hurricane to a large storm.

"... Is it impossible Sam? Only you know..."

Then just a breeze.

"... Are you really as good as you always think you are?"

Her husband's words in reply were still those of an adolescent.

"Tahnee you don't understand... I've got the business and commitments and..."

Tahnee turned up the heat on her middle-aged partner, her long, sleek back hair twirled and span round revealing her face flushed with passion, and her darkened eyes shining with real irritation.

Sam, even in his trauma and confusion, was still endlessly captivated by her beauty and energy as she blazed.

"Excuses...!"

Tahnee wailed and swirled once more.

"...*Excuses*...!"

Her vitriol changed to a new attack of veiled sarcasm and wit.

"...Do you actually, really think the boys on site can't manage without your *flair* with a paintbrush for a few months?"

Sam went to defend himself but she spoke before he could even exhale through his dry, open mouth.

"...And before you say it, we've got enough money to last... for a while anyway...!"

Tahnee watched him fidgeting, uncomfortably and twisted the knife a little further into his apparently humourless ribs.

"...Oh yes..."

She continued apparently innocently.

"... There *is* a big problem... if you decide to have a go..."

Sam looked at her enquiringly, suspiciously, before she gave him the punch line?

"...Who's going to pick up, Oliver from school?"

Sam looked at her angrily and he felt like hitting her... and hugging her at the same time; she always managed to ridicule him when he was being so obtuse and pedantic but his love was so...utterly infuriating!

"You don't understand..."

He was unsteady and drained the last dregs of the scotch before rising to his feet as if he had somewhere else to go!

"...You just don't *understand*!"

His feet stormed out of the room, grabbed his coat and slammed the front door behind him, stepping gratefully out into the welcoming, enclosing, darkness of the evening where at least he could escape, think and more importantly, hide!

Still consumed with anger he walked down behind the house, through the trees and ambled around the edge of the golf course that was gently illuminated by the houses that backed on to it.

His wife's lecture was intense and vivid in his mind, belittling his reasons but as she had alluded to, his feeble, pathetic explanations were mere excuses, just as she had said!

He'd blamed his son for having the same dream that had always possessed him, and as he sat on a large grass mound overlooking the darkened 8th green he felt overwhelmingly despotic, tyrannical and guilty.

Sam realised his real fear was further humiliation, to try once again only to be disappointed or frustrated; golf had been such a cruel mistress and eventually a bitter, divisive game to him.

Still in turmoil he wandered around for an hour then arrived home to find his glass had been re-filled and his wonderful wife patiently, caringly waiting for him, and he muttered sheepishly to her.

"I'm sorry, Tahnee…"

He felt like such a fraud.

"…You were right, it's not, Oliver it's me… I'm scared and frightened of failing again."

Tahnee patted the couch seat beside her and Sam sat down and felt his partner snuggle up closely to him.

"Sam, you're being so silly…"

Her tone was warm, compassionate and comforting, like a metaphorical blanket to cuddle and nestle into when you felt downcast; he sensed his partner's heat and engaged in her tender wisdom.

"...I'm not sure what happened when you were younger... you've never told me, but things are different now... you're not the same person you were as a boy...!"

Sam stroked her hair and listened to her.

"...How can you fail, no one could really expect you to win..."

She laughed in the irony of her insight.

"... Except you! And that's the problem, you're always so hard on yourself, treat it as a bit of fun..."

Sam sat in silence feeling the liquid and his wife's body, fuelling and feeding his soul.

"...Sam you're not an old man but sometimes you think like one; make it an adventure, for you and Oliver, if you fail... you'll win anyway... because you'll have tried to fulfil his dream..."

Her clever eyes saw everything.

"...And your own...!"

Tahnee raised her jumper a little to expose her soft, brown belly and gently placed her husband's hand on it.

"...Sam I want you to try with every ounce of your body and spirit because you won't have time after this next *Open* finishes!"

Sam felt her soft skin and understood instantly and excitedly her true, wonderful meaning.

"Are you sure?"

His wife nodded in glorious affirmation.

"The baby's due in July, Sam...so use the time... have your journey and exploits... follow, Oliver's dream..."

She laughed suddenly, the tempest had subsided and the glorious sun had come out and returned.

"...You'll still be my champion whether you win the *bloomin' Open* or not!"

They kissed and the decision was made; the gauntlet had been thrown down and the challenge now accepted and met.

Sam, in his heart was unsure but Tahnee was not; she knew in her intuitive mind that her husband had never got this devilish game of golf honestly out of his system and it was undoubtedly dulling and snuffing out part of his spirit.

She understood that really he wanted to prove himself again, taste the fire of competition that he missed so much; he needed it, somehow strangely they both needed it!

Oliver had been trying to sleep he'd been upset the past few days and it had affected his peace of mind; he hated it when he argued with his Dad as it was as if he was somehow falling out with himself.

But his father had demeaned him, made him feel like a baby; well he understood that he was a just a boy but his original and initial idea seemed so clever, straightforward and simple.

Then when he saw his father play; he was incredible and how could anybody be better than that?

Why did he not want to try? He was so stupid and he hated him, but he loved him and that was the cruellest part; he adored and loved him with all of his heart and soul.

He heard the door creak then squinted and looked; the rounded shadow at the door was his annoying parent.

"Come in Dad," he whispered, "I'm not asleep."

Sam inched into the darkened, inky room and sat on the bed next to his resting child who spoke to him apologetically.

"I'm sorry, Dad…"

His tone was weary and regretful.

"…I'm just being stupid, I just saw the articles and…"

Sam stroked his boy's hair; it was always so incredibly, tactile, smooth, luxurious and soft.

"No, Son… it's not stupid to have an idea, a dream…"

He sighed and lightly pressed his cranium as if to just absentmindedly play with its rigidity.

"… It was me… I…was afraid."

Oliver looked at him not understanding a word of what he was saying. "Of what, Dad?"

Sam laughed acidly and dryly.

"Of trying, Son…of trying and not achieving…"

He laughed defensively.

"… I know, I know what I've always told you, but…"

Oliver was magnanimous; he recognised that he was indeed just an innocent after all and there was much he did not comprehend.

"It's OK, Dad I don't mind; we can start golf again this coming Saturday and I'll hit all the shots."

Sam theatrically shook his head as if it was he who had got the part of *Oliver* that his son so coveted in the famous, school production.

"I can't, Son!"

He whispered quietly and he smiled delightedly as he saw his boy's face drop a little in disappointment; it was about time he did his own delectable bit of teasing with his duplicitous, Little Man who replied in sudden panic.

"Why, Dad…?"

His voice was so delightfully desperate and Sam had his own sense of timing as well; and not just on the golf course!

"…Why?"

Sam inhaled and deliciously picked his moment.

"Because…"

He grabbed his son's hair in a little bunch squeezing it gently and tenderly causing him to wince just a little.

"Because, *me and my manager*, are going into training, aren't we, Son?" Oliver looked intensely at his wonderful parent and understood instantly what he meant and the familiar, tantalising game of pretend they always liked to play with each other.

His lithe body leaned up and determinedly hugged Sam's thick neck eagerly and excitedly.

"Yes, Dad…we're going to do it…"

He kissed him on his plump cheek and lay back down in his covers finally to rest; arguing with his favourite man was always exhausting.

"…Yes, we're going to win *The Open!*"

The young boy had softly whispered and murmured his last sentence before he went to dreamland, or was he already there?

Chapter 18

Sam had set his alarm for 6.30a.m and cut off the shrill sound instantly to ensure not to disturb the peaceful slumber of his wife.

He found his old tracksuit and felt how the trousers strained against his burgeoning waistline; he was going to have to lose some weight, to get fit and running was a good place to start.

He had always enjoyed the early morning and as autumn had not yet taken its grip, Sam ran along the leafy lane then onto the open expanse of the golf course.

After a couple of long, punishing holes the soft sounds of the bird's dawn chorus were drowned out by him gasping for breath; he'd never realised that he was so out of condition!

He slowed his pace, walked then ran and walked again and completed a 3-mile circuit before he arrived back at the house some 40 arduous minutes later.

He showered and met his son on the landing who smiled at him mischievously and patted his stomach that was even more bulbous and bloated from all of his effort and exercise.

"This has got to go, Dad!"

They sat down to breakfast together, the quietness of the small kitchen only disturbed by the ping of the toaster and the salivating rustle of milk and cereal.

The small boy munched and queried him at the same time.

"What's the plan then, Dad?"

Sam took a swig of tea and a large bite of his hot bread then shared his own scheme with his new *Boss*; it seemed that undoubtedly Oliver was his manager now!

"I'll have to join the golf club, get a handicap and then get down to 1 or scratch by next March…"

He spoke as if it was easy but he knew that it was not.

"…Only then can we send for the entry forms from the Royal and Ancient Golf Club"

Oliver seemed surprised.

"That's a lot, just to enter, Dad"

His interested eyes stared at him curiously.

"…And who are the Royal and *who-ever?*"

Sam continued eating; the aerobic effort had given him an appetite.

"They are the people that run golf and *The Open*... they're located in Scotland, Oliver, at St Andrews the home of golf. In fact that's where *The Open* is being held next year!"

The boy smiled in anticipation.

"I've never been to Scotland, Dad, What's it like?"

Sam remembered his boyhood as if it was yesterday.

"It's a rugged place, Oliver, but it has some wonderful scenery. St Andrews is located on the coast... and you play most of the time overlooking the sea."

The boy finished his early morning meal.

"I want to see it, Dad. I want to go!"

Sam smiled at his son; his energy and endless enthusiasm for life was always infectious.

"We'll see, Oliver, let's just take one thing at a time."

Sam dropped his son at school and, after visiting his building site, drove to the local, golf club and spoke to Daniel at the professional's shop.

He told him the difficulty of gaining a membership at the sought after course but Sam noticed him go and speak to an elderly gentleman with thinning, brown hair and the man then came purposefully, even quickly over and spoke to him.

"Jerry Pate…?"

He chuckled and laughed.

"…Jerry Pate, you're the chap that beat, Jerry Pate at Hoylake aren't you?"

Sam smiled at the man and noticed that he was far more portly than him as he answered; he also had a big, beaming smile on his reddened face, no doubt from a little over indulgence from the drink at the 19th bar!

"I thought no one remembered that anymore!"

The man snorted expressively.

"Not likely…I remember it like yesterday, on *Sportsnight* with that Coleman fellow, it was fabulous!"

Sam recalled the same, unforgettable moment and his father coming in excitedly to share it with him.

"It was a long time ago…"

He felt more serious suddenly; his golfing past and history always disturbed and unsettled him.

"…I'm gratified that you remember, Sir … now, can you get me in?"

The old stranger looked at him seriously.

"We've a 5 year waiting list, My Lad…"

Sam sensed his face fall in disappointment; then he noticed that his grey eyes start to twinkle and it reminded him of the teasing game he and Oliver always performed together.

"…Put your application form in and I'll have you a membership by the weekend… "

He chuckled confidently.

"…I do have a certain pull!"

He held out his hand and Sam shook it warmly and gratefully.

"My name is, John Miles, Sam… I'm the Secretary here… I'm pleased to meet you."

Sam was relieved and delighted at his exceptional friendliness and help and responded appropriately.

"Sam, Sam Chester…thank you for your help….it means a lot."

The rotund man turned to leave; then focussed on him and an expression of curiosity came on his rounded and puffed out red face.

"May I ask…Why are you taking the game up again after all these years?"

He smiled at him, almost embarrassed with the truth.

"John, if I told you, you wouldn't believe me!"

Sam was elated, both with the ease that he'd managed to gain a membership and in a curious way that the amiable, old gentleman knew his name; it gave him the weird sensation that perhaps he'd not been completely forgotten after all.

Daniel told him it was fine for him to continue to use the practice ground and Sam gave him all of his old clubs and asked the professional to re-grip and polish them.

He retained a single club for his temporary use today, a 7 iron, and walked to the range to begin his regime of rehabilitation with this exacting game.

His routine was simple; stretching his body trying to regain suppleness lost in years of not playing and to concentrate only on training his swing to keep in perfect plane.

Sam was amazed at how well he could hit the ball, he felt solid, powerful and by the end of the session was shaping the ball easily left and right at will.

He then gave this club to Daniel to refurbish along with the rest and went back to work.

As he drove he thought about the futility of his previous argument with his wife about not having the time; the truth was that his comments were indeed a pretext and an excuse, as he had already conceded to himself and exactly as she had said.

It was obvious that he was more aware and experienced; Sam now understood golf practice had to be focussed and specific and he did not need to work or suffer all day.

Sam knew exactly what he was doing in his sporting preparation!

He'd spent countless years on entirely the wrong things and he could devote himself now fully to his new challenge and commitment without harming his small, development business at all!

Amazingly he still was there each day to pick up his son from school and the boy would ask him about his golf and if he was making inroads into his game and sufficient progress?

At weekends Oliver would go with him to the course and the inevitable training ground; he would sit quietly behind him as shot after shot was dispatched with seemingly, minimal effort.

In the evening Sam would slip onto the golf course and play a loop of 4 holes that led him back to his house again and slowly he began to regain his feel for the short game that was so obviously missing in his recent match against the professional.

After a month of running and practise, Sam was leaner and fitter and his muscles were beginning to loosen to the point where he felt ready to tackle a formal, medal round.

Mr Jones the secretary had given him a starting handicap of 5 and Sam put his name on the board for the October, Sunday medal.

As he stood on the 1st tee with his companions, wrapped up against the chill wind, Sam felt anxious and smiled to himself at the irony of such an amazing fact.

He was nervous about a medal?

Inwardly he was amused but in all honesty he was not really concerned with regards to the prize on offer but more about now testing his ability, a card in his hand and a score that counted!

He knew full well that you could not hide or pretend when each shot was added and weighed.

Sam played rhythmically and well, his fellow members and companions were dazzled by his shot-making ability, they had never seen the game played in such a manner.

But the course was extremely gruelling, in the wet, barren, testing, early winter and a few mistakes left him with a 77, 6 over par for the morning's effort.

It was a creditable score on the day but when Sam related it to the mountain he'd set himself to climb, it seemed mundane, ordinary and grossly inadequate.

Oliver to his credit had caddied in silence; he had a single-mindedness and tenacity that had surprised his father but he was exhausted and almost frozen at the end of their round.

His hands were numb and his delicate lips, chilled blue, but he would not come into the clubhouse for a hot chocolate until the clubs were cleaned and stored.

Sam murmured to him apologetically on the way home.

"Not so good today, Son!"

Oliver stared at him angrily and spoke with a maturity far beyond his father's.

"You played wonderfully, Dad, it was cold and wet; you played well...there's plenty of time."

Sam listened and in their small world of developing, shared golf experiences his son was already more than a child!

He was right though in one way, he had played encouragingly and positively, but he was also wrong as well; there really and honestly wasn't plenty of time available to them at all!

November was also sodden and cold and Sam's progress was masked by the constant battle and fight against the elements.

Oliver however was steadfast and resolute in support of his father; he was with him at each weekend, practice session and would walk and watch quietly when he played.

Sam offered on numerous occasions a club or some balls for him to hit but he would shake his head gently, firmly; he was there for his parent to improve and would not let him be distracted.

The daily run for Sam, he found increasingly less attractive than its original novelty value, but laboriously through cold, wind or rain each day he would traverse the 4 miles around the golf course.

It gave him time to think and he wondered how Len Thompson was, if in fact he was still alive and, as his blood flowed and heart pounded he thought about the past and the future together.

In spite of the weather and the struggle, Sam had enjoyed the last few months and as he had realised it had not really interfered with his business at all.

As his wife had mentioned he was often more of a hindrance than help with the skilled work on site anyway and Sam enjoyed the focus of actually having a task and a challenge with something he genuinely excelled at.

He had also enjoyed and revelled in the time spent with Oliver, they had always been close but he felt in this endeavour as if he had a partner and a supporter as well as a son; it often inspired him through the freezing darkness of the early, bleak mornings.

Sam felt the crispness of the ground beneath his feet, it was late December, the day before Christmas; the ground, in the quietness of the early morning had a light, white sprinkling of frost and the day was perfect, still, clear and bright.

He could see his breath drawn out of him like smoke as he forced himself hard up the hill on the 6th fairway; he had noticed his stomach reducing and a gradual return of strength and energy he had not known since his youth.

He arrived back at his kitchen feeling jaded but invigorated as well; Oliver was sitting at their small, wooden, table waiting for him and he smiled and tortured him at the same time.

"Well…how did it go?"

Sam sat on the old, hand made stool then cupped some tea in his hands, it felt warm and comforting and he stared at his son whose hair was dishevelled; he had a crazy, luminous Pokémon character vibrantly displayed on the front of his pyjamas.

"Good, Oliver… can't you see I'm getting fitter?"

He patted his stomach and Oliver remembered the paunch that had been there seemingly but a few weeks ago.

"What about tomorrow, Dad?"

Sam eyed his son incredulously.

"Oliver... it's Christmas... everyone needs a day off!"

The boy purposely walked over to the toaster and slipped two pieces of bread inside.

"Not you, Dad...you've mentioned that we've not got the time!"

Sam had to smile at his young taskmaster, because like his mother he was tending to be always correct.

"OK, OK...a run tomorrow as well..."

He groaned in mock terror.

"...I'll do it... now what's Father Christmas bringing for you this year?"

Oliver looked at his parent as if he were foolish and mad.

"*Please,* Dad, I'm getting whatever you've bought me..."

He looked up at his father and a wicked, sly glint came into his eyes.

"...Maybe that new bike that's so cleverly

hidden in the garage…!"

He giggled and placed two, perfectly buttered pieces of toast before his hungry man.

"…You know, Dad…I'm not a child anymore!"

Sam looked at his son, his body wiry and lithe, sprouting taller, seemingly every day and nodded acceptingly and sagely.

"I know you're not, Son… but I forget sometimes!"

Chapter 19

Christmas was a happy time, Dorothy, Anna, her family and the new man in her life came for dinner and everyone was relaxed, ebullient, friendly and good humoured.

Tahnee was showing a little from her pregnancy and it was the focus of much discussion and speculation.

Dorothy noticed a small change in her son as

he was more genial than she had ever seen him; he looked fit, strong and a warm smile was never far from his face.

He was so similar now in nature to the boy she had nurtured and it made her proud and very pleased for him.

There was something else as well however, an intangible sense of a secret or a change but, she spotted it anyway, and after dinner she gently confronted him in the kitchen.

"You look different, Sam…"

She smiled at his energy and joy.

"…You're all lit up, is it the baby?"

Sam gazed at her; his mother had aged, her hair was increasingly grey and her movements were slower and more laboured as each year passed.

"Yes, Mum…its wonderful news."

His lips told her the white lie of omission, as he did not feel he could reveal about the golf or the adventure that Oliver and he were set upon.

His maternal parent would have worried and not understood and she had lived through too much of his previous struggle already.

However Dorothy knew her son and saw that there was undoubtedly something else hidden, but kept her own counsel.

In so many ways, Sam was like her but there was also that recognisable touch of devilment from Frankie in his genetic make-up as well.

She smiled and mused that perhaps that was part of what made her love him so much!

January and February went raining then flowing by in a watery rush, Sam was playing well but could not fight the interminable weather; he knew he'd have to get down to 1 handicap by the end of May or this mercurial, fanciful dream would be a non starter.

The Saturday morning for the March medal however was fine with no wind and a just a faint trace of sunshine that gave the promise of a fair spring just around the corner.

Sam was relaxed and swung well; he rarely hit a poor shot and although he still struggled on the marked, uneven, rutted greens he managed a 71, level par for the day.

He was a minor celebrity at the club, no one knew the true purpose of his renewed interest in golf and many would have laughed at the absurdity of it in any case if they had known the reason.

His dedication to the sport was intense, detailed, protracted and precise but bizarrely and amusingly, not dissimilar to the average member's, who took the game very seriously as well.

However every player at the club by now, was aware of the sublime way he played the game; it was truly extraordinary to witness.

Sam's handicap was cut to 3.8 and, in the *Mid-Week* medal a few days later, he went round in 70 and his handicap was reduced to 3.4 a playing handicap of 3.

Sam realised that given the time constraints placed upon him he would have to compete in a couple of external tournaments both, for competitive experience, and further opportunities to reduce his handicap to the desired and required level.

Every other weekend he therefore played in 36 hole, outside events, always with Oliver faithfully pulling his substantial bag on a trolley and, by the end of April, he had won a few local, minor competitions and his handicap was now 1.9, a playing handicap of 2.

Sam knew that although he had done well he

had less than a month to make the final push to enable him to enter for *The Open* and, with this at the forefront of his mind, he entered for the Lancaster, County Championship.

It was being held at West Manchester, Golf Club and as Sam arrived he marvelled at how little had altered since he had played on the county scene in Warwickshire all that time ago.

The bustle and excitement had not changed but the competitors had, and Sam felt old when he looked at all the eager, energetic, fresh faces practising and preparing for the trial and test ahead.

He was there only for a single, selfish purpose and, as he looked at so many young men and boys so tense and full of hopes and expectation, he could not help but feel something of an imposter!

Sam thought about their combined, juvenile aspirations in this game and how the successes and failures in all of these events and competitions would affect them in the future.

Professional golf was there but for the token, special few and as he knew only too well, there were many and innumerable, pitfalls and uncountable casualties along the way.

Sam had played a practice round the previous week and had marked the course out, as with his junior, golfing days; he knew how far he hit each club and played steadily in the morning to finish in level par.

His handicap was now 1.5, a fraction from where he needed to be and, lost in the concentration of achieving a further reduction in the afternoon, he completed the round 2 below par.

He was working out contentedly that he was now off an official playing handicap of 1 when a cheery, jovial, burly gentleman approached him and warmly shook his hand.

Sam and Oliver, in the excitement of achieving their initial, larger goal had failed to notice that he had actually won the tournament by an impressive 5 shots.

Oliver clapped excitedly as Sam collected the sparkling, silver cup and listened as his father politely and expertly thanked all the people that had worked hard to make it a successful day.

The boy was impressed that his Dad seemed such an accomplished speaker and he didn't realise that, just as the basic format of the contest had not altered over the years, neither had the speeches and Sam had made many in a similar vein throughout his golfing career.

After all the well meaning and congratulatory words were concluded, Sam sought out the amiable man he'd met earlier in the day; he realised that he was the County President and Sam asked him silently if he could have a private word with him.

The man's name was Trevor East; he was indeed stout, with a large belly and a pink, tinged face, flushed with the demonstrable results of too much alcohol; seemingly the sport and the spirit were eternally an enticing and addictive combination.

Sam chose his words carefully, realising the delicacy of his intended subject for discussion; but it was something that needed to be said if he was to avoid the problems he'd experienced in the past.

He murmured carefully as he began to talk.

"Mr East...There is a favour I need to ask you..."

The man smiled at his new champion and gestured with his puffy hands for him to continue.

"...I am privileged to have won the County Championship but, I would ask you not to select me for any county team matches..."

Sam watched a sudden irritation and hardness, appear around the corners of the man's eyes; he'd just been told that his new Champion did not want to play for him, but undaunted, Sam continued as respectfully and cautiously as he could.

"...It's a young man's game, Mr East...I've had my time, I don't want to take a place from one of the youngsters."

Sam noticed the man's eyes suddenly; they were an unusual and intricate mixture of hazel, green and brown and they suddenly looked at him curiously then he whispered in unexpected recall.

"Jerry Pate..."

He whistled in sudden memory and recall.

"...Jerry Pate? That's where I knew your name from! You're the boy that beat the US champion all those years ago, aren't you...?"

Sam nodded, embarrassed at the label and tag that still hung onto him for so long like an out of date sale sign; the man's features relaxed and he smiled suddenly.

"...I remember that so well...!"

He shook his head from side to side then

gazed eventually and invasively right through him.

"....Sam... normally I would be very aggrieved if a Champion of mine did not want to play for us but, if you can give me a reason I can understand, then..."

His focus was direct and intense and Sam understood that he was not a man to be trifled with or lied to.

"... I will accept your wishes and not be upset...."

The pair of uniquely coloured spheres narrowed once again and they stared intently into Sam's clear, blue ones.

"...And please don't give me that *bullshit* about, not wishing some young chap to miss out... there's a reason you played today and I would like you to do me the courtesy of telling me what it is?"

Sam had been trapped by the President's, intuition and intelligence and he thought about trying to vainly defend his original story but decided against it.

He leaned forward accepting that he would have to eventually reveal to someone along the way his plans, and spoke in hushed tones to the large man opposite him, almost silently in his ear.

"You'll laugh…"

He was embarrassed to admit his intended mission but he felt that he was honour bound to reveal the truth.

"…It sounds ridiculous even to me!"

The man stayed still, calm and patient.

"Go on, uncover yourself …and let me be the judge of that."

Sam pointed with a single finger to his son, Oliver, standing in the far corner of the room proudly holding and protecting his father's large, glistening trophy.

"My son had a dream, Mr East, and I suppose I stupidly but happily fell into it…"

Sam caught his breath and continued.

"…He imagined that I could pick up my clubs and go and win the *British Open Championship*…and I needed to play today to reduce my handicap to finally enable me to enter!"

Sam looked at the senior administrator waiting for him to laugh but he didn't; he did not part his lips or find it funny at all and replied in all sincerity.

"That's a wonderful dream, Sam...a divine quest..."

He smiled suddenly and chuckled.

"...Even worth *wounding* an old soldier like me for!"

Sam was pleased with his understanding and the lack of mockery in his response and apologised once again.

"So I hope you will not be too irritated with me, Mr East."

The chubby man markedly relaxed and laughed openly.

"Only... if you *don't* win it..."

He shook his large head once more.

"...I remember you now, Sam, you were one of the best juniors this country ever produced; you're one of the few people that could compete at that level from cold...so who knows?"

He shook hands enthusiastically with him and the two of them walked over to where Oliver was sitting and the President took his small fingers in his huge palm and spoke to him effusively and genially.

"Your Dad's quite a fellow, Oliver,"

The man's chubby hands almost jealously touched the silver cup that the child kept watching, guarding and holding as if it would disappear suddenly or he would drop and damage the precious metal.

It seemed so valuable to him in all its wonder, lustre and sparkle.

The boy looked up at him then beamed a rich, white, irresistible smile and spoke with such clarity, incredible innocence and a certain amount of boastfulness.

"I know, and…he's going to win *The Open Championship* as well…did he tell you?"

The man emitted a huge laugh that made his belly wobble expressively.

"Yes, Son…he did actually…so I know of your little scheme and plan…!"

He was extremely entertained and uplifted by them both; this was quite a story and tale to tell later around the bar.

"…Yes, I know all about it; your Dad told me…"

He leant his expansive frame over the small lad and whispered teasingly but quietly in his waiting ear.

"...But don't tell everyone, *it's a secret!*"

Father and son left the club on a mountain peak and a high; Oliver because his father had won and Sam, because he'd achieved his handicap reduction without upsetting anyone from the county!

He really liked the President, he was a *wise old bird* and he'd been surprised once again that so many people still remembered that amazing day in Hoylake all those lifetimes ago!

Chapter 20

The letter arrived a few days later; it was in a large, innocuous, brown envelope with the lettering *The Royal and Ancient Golf Club* on the top, right hand corner.

Sam did not unwrap it but waited until he picked his son up from school then ceremoniously handed it to him and the boy looked at it as though it contained a cheque for a million pounds and gasped in agitation.

"We'll open it after dinner, Dad... and fill it in together!"

Tahnee had never seen her son eat so eagerly or quickly; she could almost feel the electricity and tension between them and had enjoyed watching the growing excitement provided by her two men's, energetic, lunatic, endeavour, adventure and imminent expedition.

Oliver was always happy anyway but he was now enthused with a spirit she'd never seen before and Sam was transformed, slim, fit, vital and living his life to the full.

As she watched the two of them walk into the lounge with the precious, brown envelope still unopened she was so pleased that she had cajoled and bullied her husband out of his mental retreat.

Tahnee knew that even if he was eliminated at the first hurdle, in some ways he and they had already won; her man had found something of himself once more that he had undoubtedly lost.

Sam opened the enclosed, dark covering gingerly and withdrew the immaculate, large, white form; he then passed it to Oliver who examined it carefully as if it was a religious scroll

The Royal and Ancient's inscription was again on the top of the first page and there in stark letters it stated boldly, *The British Open Championship Entry Form.*

They spent the next couple of hours methodically and meticulously filling in, the blank, empty spaces.

Sam was pleased to be able to put scratch next to the enquiry regarding his playing status at his home club.

His latest medal round had reduced his handicap yet further and he felt a small sense of pride and achievement, given the limited time that had been available to him, to officially play golf once again without the need of any advantage at all.

Oliver enquired about the part of the form that was for applicants with exemptions and Sam explained to him that this was for past winners, the leading players and various others of the high, golfing achievers and the boy was impressed with such an idea.

"It would be so great…if you could send off the entry form and just play!"

Sam smiled at him, it would be, but the truth was that there were thousands of golfers of the highest calibre that would soon be competing fiercely for the limited, few places that were available.

The first competitive tournament would be regional, with less than a dozen places from nearly 200 competitors.

If he succeeded in this, initial stage then he would have to travel to Scotland for a further 36 holes, pre-qualifying over a local course where the available slots for an *Open* starting time were even less.

But worrying about that was for another day; they finished the form, Sam wrote out the cheque for the entry fee and pulled two tumblers of cut glass from the side cabinet.

He poured himself a small whisky and after a brief visit to the kitchen poured some orange juice into Oliver's, shiny, translucent, expensive, drinking container.

Theatrically he clinked glasses with the boy and made a toast, vow and promise between them.

"To our success, Oliver!"

As if in keeping with the spirit of the moment,

and as though he was suddenly old before his time, the boy returned the slight movement firmly, nearly shattering the fine crystal as he did so.

"To us, Dad, let's do it!"

They ambled rather than walked the half-mile down to the post box together and Oliver slipped his small hand in his father's on the way back; he was wildly agitated and fuelled with incredible energy and expectation.

Sam gripped his son's warm, slender fingers and held them firmly in his and he sensed the life blood there; but he also felt something else as his heart was beating, pounding in his own chest and he knew suddenly it was too late to turn back now!

The relentless, golf routine was the same every day, but even more focussed as he continued to train and practice; he had groomed his swing, using every ounce of his experience not to make the same mistakes as he did in his youth.

He focussed on rhythm and swing shape; surety over his swing would mean control over himself and his game, it sounded logical and simple but it was not.

Golf was an application where mere fractions

of distraction or change could result in a bad shot and Sam had learned not to panic when this happened, but try to return to the basic fundamentals.

He knew he was good but he also sensed that there was something else in his game that was always hidden that he had never been able to find, or tap into.

It was a force waiting, as yet to be discovered, almost ethereal and just a feeling, but at the level of competition he was about to engage in, Sam recognised and knew that to reach the pinnacle and goal that he had set himself he would need that intangible, final refinement to his skill.

An acknowledgement card of Sam's entry came a few days later and, as the middle of June approached, another brown envelope dropped through their door.

It was the starting times for the first qualifying competition and Sam excitedly found his name amongst the array of competitors.

He was due off at 10.15a.m on the 25th June at Middleton Golf Club just a few, close miles from where they lived.

Sam practised with a new intensity but suddenly could not relieve himself of this constant, emerging tension each time he thought about the forthcoming process of simply getting through.

Even though he had played so well in recent months and he knew his game was at a different level from when he'd last competed in this prestigious event, he was increasingly beginning to be plagued by his insecurity.

Disturbing, unsettling doubts and reservations flooded his both conscious and unconscious mind about how could he even think about winning *The Open* and who was he really kidding?

The questions of uncertainty and lack of confidence burned him and for the first time, Tahnee saw her husband unsettled and sensed some of the demons that used to torment him so badly.

Having tried and failed so many times before he was fearful and frightened; it was hard for even Sam to understand why because no one really could expect him to win or succeed even at the initial stage.

But that was no matter, and his clever wife had put her delicate, definitive finger on the problem months ago; Sam knew that there was one person that did expect it.

That was Sam himself and bizarrely, this was the greatest contradiction and the heaviest, tightest pressure of all!

The morning of the pre-qualifying saw clear, blue skies dispersed with occasional wispy clouds indicating that it would hopefully be pleasant and mild all day.

Tahnee tried to help her husband the only way she knew how and hugged him supportively and lovingly as he prepared to leave.

"Just be cool, Love, It's only a bit of fun!"

Sam tried to hide his grimace at his reflexive reaction to her words and smiled then murmured to himself ironically.

"*Yes, a bit of fun?*"

He exhaled to try and release the cloying, clawing sensation in his chest and stomach; suddenly it really and truly felt as if it was like going back 20 long years.

Father and son drove to their local, home course round the corner and Sam hit some practice shots to loosen up.

Immediately Sam sensed what a state of nerves he was in and hit more poor connections in that session than all his previous preparation and recent, carded rounds combined.

He was still agitated as they drove to Middleton Golf Club and after signing in, he stepped onto the putting green to try and somehow calm himself down.

The club was very crowded and Sam could literally feel the tension where ridiculously, people's lives were hanging on the outcome of a single round of golf.

It seemed absurd and insane but he knew that it was the agonising truth by just participating at such a level in this most competitive of sports!

40 minutes of just rolling putts on the smooth green did not soothe him and, as he walked to the 1st tee with Oliver pulling his bag, he felt like there were 1,000 busy ants and spiders crawling inside his newly, flat stomach and inflated chest.

Sam shook hands with his playing partners, both young boys with the look of intensity about them that reminded him of his former self before he jumped when his name was called to hit first.

He tried to relax but his body felt elsewhere, separated from his mind and his drive quickly disappeared into a bunker on the far, right hand side of the fairway.

Oliver watched his father with growing apprehension as he had never seen him so wound up; he didn't know how to help him so, as with his previous visits to the golf course, he kept silent and very quiet.

He then looked on in further horror as his parent's immaculate, golf game fell apart; he'd never observed him swing so erratically or deflect so many bad shots and he suffered in silence until the 8th hole by which time Sam was 6 over par and in absolute pieces.

The 9th was a long par 5 that dog legged right to left and Sam hit a shabby drive that ran closely alongside the bordering, dense trees and settled, luckily just on the fairway.

As they walked down, Oliver saw that they would have to wait for the game in front to leave the green so he instinctively and purposefully called his father into the inner edge of the little forest.

Sam walked to him still in his disorientation as his son, out of hearing range to everyone else, initially asked him to stand still then suddenly, as if he had become his mother in full, wrathful flow, turned, snarled and berated him in unexpected but irascible then growing fury.

"What is the matter with you...?"

Oliver's small lips verbally lashed and railed into him and his tenacious, unprepared comments even caught him by utter surprise; he had not thought about or prepared such a speech, it just happened, almost by instinct or accident!

"...You're performing like an...*Idiot*... you can play better than this with one hand..."

He did not give his father either the respect, time or the grace to respond then hissed and cruelly cursed him.

"...Get real, you're quitting without trying, something that you hate...now shape up... it's only a *fucking* game!"

With that he turned on his heels, walked angrily and markedly back to the fairway leaving his father shivering and dithering even more.

Sam had never heard his son swear before and it shocked him to his very soul and spiritual centre; but his boy was right and Sam felt increasingly panicky, guilty then bewildered.

His squinting eyes looked forlornly into the dark, dense woods and, reaching out, as if only to support his unstable, unsteady form, touched the coarse bark of the nearest, biggest tree with his trembling fingers and open hands.

He then inspected and stared absentmindedly at the form of the protective covering and sensed it was old and gnarled like he felt, with a thick, abrasive, hard shell.

Sam suddenly then dramatically pressed both of his palms firmly onto the ancient wood and felt its solid, static roughness and veiled life.

He closed his eyes and inadvertently released himself from the world he had previously inhabited for a second, or was it a lifetime?

In his heart and mind he intentionally and preposterously imagined that he was actually releasing and transferring all his years of insecurity and fear into that inert but breathing, sturdy, living, still object.

Sam sensed a sudden electrical charge surge through his body and skilled hands then flow directly into the old bark of the immovable, enormous trunk and incredibly, when his eyes re-opened he felt different, better, calmer and weirdly composed.

He shook himself, breathed in deeply and, when his head was fully settled, walked back out into the sunshine, stroked Oliver's, soft, brown head then smoothly swung his shoulders and arms.

In his sudden relaxation, his mind felt the swing plane he knew so much about; he had nothing to fear, nothing to lose and he felt his whole being begin to immediately bear down, concentrate and focus.

Expertly his released hands then drew his 3 wood around the trees to *20 feet* from the pin and held a raking put across the green for an eagle 3.

He walked onto the next tee becalmed, serene and determined; he was beginning to play well, exceptionally well!

By the time he'd reached the last hole he was now only 2 over par and sensed that he needed a further birdie to be sure of qualifying.

The last hole was a short par 4, 340 yards and Sam's drive was placed centrally on the fairway, leaving only a short wedge.

Skilfully he pitched to *5 feet* and bent down behind the ball; he saw his son's anxious face and placed his hand onto the warm grass as a final conduit to release whatever remaining nerves he had left.

His head was motionless, his body stood perfectly still over the ball as his mind focussed; he felt the sweet connection of topspin and then looked up to see the small, white sphere take the gentle left to right break and disappear into the darkness of the cup.

His fist went forward instinctively, reactively and he muttered.

"Yes…yes…yes!"

He desperately wanted this dream to continue; it seemed that all of his indecisiveness and uncertainty had gone in a mercurial, electrical wisp of will and he wanted to qualify, *badly*!

Sam handed his card into the recorders and went with his son to have some lunch; he was pleased but recognised that without Oliver's rude lecture he would not have succeeded and in all truth he was perplexed as he wasn't quite sure what to say to him.

He returned into the safety of his familiar, fatherly role and, as they munched sandwiches, drank tea and lemonade, Sam looked at the boy sternly as if to make his point to him.

However in some ways, he just was not quite sure exactly what observation or concerns he wanted or needed to make?

"Oliver you helped me today, Son…"

He tried to sound in charge but he knew he

was not, as he patently and verbally wandered and meandered on.

"...You brought me out of myself and I'd like to thank you..."

He did not allow his child to answer.

"...But...but..."

He continued but without his normal, parental swagger or authority.

"...I do not want to hear you swear again. Do you understand?"

Oliver nodded, noting his father's sharp tone but then Sam groaned in anticipation of a cutting riposte as he saw that familiar mischief and twinkle in his hazel eyes.

"I promise, Dad..."

He laughed, completely unabashed or ashamed at his previous, outrageous, disrespectful outburst.

"...As long as you promise not to play like a complete and *Utter Twit* for no good reason...!"

Sam leant over to him, kissed his forehead and the little boy's face flushed and lit up pink in shyness then devilment as if just to punish and plague him some more.

"...A player and his caddy shake hands, Dad... when they reach a deal or a decision..."

It seemed he was always scolding him.

"...They don't kiss!"

Oliver held out his delicate palm and Sam grabbed it manfully.

"It's a deal, Son... I'll do my level best to never give you cause to swear at me again!"

It seemed a strange agreement but somehow in the space of those few hours, the scalding rebuke, lecture and the mystical, miraculous, ancient bark of an old tree, Sam knew that he would never again let the seeds of doubt and insecurity in his ability disturb him, in the selfsame way they had done for all of his playing life.

Within a few hours they knew for certain that he had qualified, and as the final competitors came in it was established that Sam's score of 71 had made the cut off by a mere, single stroke.

Had he missed the putt on the last hole, as he had predicted and assumed, he would have been eliminated and the adventure would have been concluded and ended there and then.

They both drove home pleased and it suddenly dawned on Sam that the two of them would have to prepare and then leave for Scotland first thing in the morning.

Somehow he had not anticipated the reality of the travel, as if he'd never honestly believed or expected to pass this first hurdle, but he had, and both father and son were equally excited and ecstatic.

Sam's qualifying course for *The Open* was Ladyburn and Sam reckoned that if they drove up early in the morning he would have time for a single practice round before the further examination began on Sunday.

He knew that there was little or no time to think or fret between the ensuing rounds and it was purely because of the volume of competitors; there seemed no other alternative given the vying and trying amount of players and participants other than this brutal, harrowing, swift, culling process!

Tahnee could tell by the warm, flushed look on her men's faces that the day had been a success and Sam was surprised when he walked into the lounge and his mother was seated there.

His wife, most obviously, was due to give birth any day and her belly was rounded and plump as if ready to imminently explode in new life.

It suddenly dawned on Sam that his treasured partner needed him and, as if she read his mind, Tahnee spoke softly to him.

"I knew you'd qualify…I could just feel it… I asked your mum to come and stay with me… she'll be there when I need her… when the baby comes!"

Sam responded in overwhelming guilt.

"But I can withdraw…"

He was floundering again as if suddenly pathetically searching for an excuse and way out not to continue and see through what he had started.

"I can… "

His wife placed her hand over his mouth and his unneeded, unnecessary, empathetic words.

"I don't wish you to hold my hand, Sam, I'll be fine…"

She smiled and seemed to ignite the room with her patience, confidence, fervour and emotion.

"…You and Oliver go and finish what you've begun; I'm so very proud of you both."

Sam formally welcomed his mother and sat down with his animated, excited son to eat as they were hungry; Dorothy served them a meal then over the sweet, scolded him lovingly and gently.

"I knew you had a secret, Sam, I could see it in your eyes!"

He shrugged in acknowledgement of his deception.

"It just happened, Mum…"

He pointed accusingly and maliciously to the young man attacking his pudding and ice cream mercilessly.

"…It's his fault…!"

Oliver looked up and smiled, only too pleased and delighted to accept responsibility for this inspirational pursuit and venture they were embarked upon.

Dorothy watched the little mite; he was so happy, keyed up and she looked at her own boy, now grown to manhood.

She thought about the past and Sam observed her as she did so; her brown eyes seemed a little duller and a tad more apprehensive than he recently remembered.

"...You don't have to worry, Mum..."

He soothed her concerns as best he could.

"...I'm not the person I used to be... I'll be..."

He gazed admiringly at his child.

"...We'll be fine!"

Dorothy sat next to her grandson and put her increasingly frail arm around him.

"You take care of my son, Oliver."

She whispered to him with a mock severity as the child licked up the last trace of ice cream and beamed at her.

"Don't you worry, Grandma..."

He was having such a good time already.

"...We'll be great... just great!"

Sam put his son to bed and then, with a little help from Tahnee, packed clothes for both of them for the coming days as she asked him a query in all innocence.

"How long will you be there for?"

Sam looked as if the question surprised him and he meaningfully talked through his mental processes.

"Qualifying is Sunday and Monday then *The Open* starts on Thursday and finishes on Sunday."

Tahnee replied practically.

"So you need clothes for a week!"

Sam was unnerved once more and spoke quietly.

"Well that's *if* we qualify... its not easy."

She laughed and joked with him.

"Of course it's *easy... easy-peasy...* for my men, let's think positive. I'll give you enough for a week although..."

Her eyes were gleaming, shimmering brown as if she also had also been captured by the surreal experience and dream.

"...If you do... make it to the last day... you might have to do a little laundry!"

The cases were placed next to Sam's clubs and shoes in readiness for the early morning trip and, with everything now in place, Sam snuggled next to his wife in their large, comfortable bed as she spoke softly to him.

"I love you, Sam."

In response he just placed his hand tenderly and gently on her wonderful, pronounced bulge then mused gleefully and contentedly on what the future held in store for them.

Sam slept soundly as if he was unusually no longer worried about the competition ahead; the demons of doubt were amazingly lost and gone and he knew that the removal of such uncertainty, more than anything else, would enable him to do his best.

That is all he'd ever wanted; to play with a clear mind and purpose in order to give of his very best efforts and abilities.

The alarm bleeped sharply at 6a.m and Sam rose silently so as not to disturb his dormant companion and upon leaving his room he was welcomed by his son already showered and dressed.

"Come on Dad...," he chattered excitedly, "we've got to go!"

Dorothy was up as well and, as if it was a habit she found too hard to break, had arisen to make sure her son and grandson were well fed and fussed over before their lengthy journey.

Sam kissed his sleeping wife, tenderly and

lightly a final time as she slumbered then, without any further prevarication, loaded up the blue, estate car and, with his son perched eagerly on the front edge of the passenger seat, drove determinedly away.

He was pleased his mother was there, Tahnee would be fine, there was nothing for him to concern himself with, except... only the small matter of the challenge ahead.

Oliver as he had previously mentioned had never been to Scotland and he gazed out of the window and watched as within hours the busy metropolis he knew changed to vast open expanses of hills and heather.

Sam remembered the roads and the views and it reminded him of how much he always liked the country; the people who were warm and welcoming and the occasional, spectacular isolation or bleakness was just as fascinating or atmospheric as he remembered.

They were soon off the main motorways and on the minor roads leading to Ladyburn and then St Andrews.

Sam knew that all the main hotels would be busy and he decided to try and find a small bed and breakfast before going to the club, anywhere within 10 miles of their golfing venue would be fine.

Sure enough as they passed through one of the many, insignificant villages Sam saw a small sign for *rooms to let* and drove up a rutted access road to a quaint farmhouse.

A tiny woman answered the door; she had white hair and ruddy, red cheeks that seemed to be aflame and she asked him curtly and frankly.

"Can ah help ye…?"

Sam explained that he was with his son to play in *The Open* golf and enquired about any available lodgings.

The woman directed her attention specifically at Oliver.

"…He's a Bonny Wee Lad, isn't he…?"

Her face turned delightfully congenial and friendly.

"…Well, we are busy, but…"

She continued to stared at the young man, who intelligently returned the compliment and attention with one of his own, most special, dazzling and disarming smiles,

"…We canny throw ye onto the street, can we?"

The allotted space was small but clean and Mrs Mackay showed them the twin-bedded room that suited their needs perfectly.

Sam was pleased that the accommodation problem had been sorted out so easily and he wondered if the lady would have been as accommodating without his small *bairn*.

He had already realised that in some strange way the boy was like a touchstone and good things just seemed to happen around him; he somehow had that unique way and he was inexplicably... *inspirational*!

Mrs Mackay informed them that dinner was at 7p.m and Sam assured her that the two of them would always try to be punctual.

Sam followed his old map to the course and on arriving at the already crowded club, parked amidst the array of vehicles in a special area reserved for competitors.

He unpacked his clubs and walked with Oliver to the Royal and Ancient reception caravan and registered his arrival.

He was due off at 12a.m in the qualifying round tomorrow and he walked to the 1st tee where a large, white board with starting times for today was displayed.

Sam noticed that there was a game out in an hour with only two players and he put his name in the 1.30p.m tee time available block and space with the unknown duo.

They were both hungry and used the hour to have lunch in the clubhouse where Sam casually looked at the list of some of the competitors, many whom had travelled especially from overseas to compete.

He recognised some well-known professionals who had now to suffer the ignominy of the qualifying lottery along with the rest of the other unknowns, journeymen or hopefuls.

As he had learned so many times, old reputation or past performances meant nothing; it was always the day and the score ahead that mattered and counted.

Sam knew that there were many, top players who would not compete in *The Open* because of this humiliating and testing competition for available places and he understood for certain, that no one enjoyed the white, bare-knuckled, qualifying ride.

But Sam was resolved to, and after meeting his playing colleagues for the afternoon round he quietly marked the course out in readiness for tomorrow's examination.

He recognised that he was agitated and anxious but increasingly and reassuringly he felt that it was nerves from anticipation rather than any uncomfortable, previous tension born from uncertainty.

He knew distinctly the difference between the two things and Oliver walked calmly behind him pleased and relieved that his Dad seemed far more relaxed and confident.

Privately he was already a little overwhelmed by the size and intensity of the tournament and was beginning to realise that his dream, crafted in pure imagination and ignorance, was somewhat different and incalculably more intimidating in real life.

The lad was exhausted when he arrived back at the boarding house and had a hot bath while his father used the mobile phone to ring home.

Tahnee answered and Sam was pleased to hear her bright tone on the end of the line as she gushed excitedly.

"Hi...everything's fine. How are you getting on...?"

Sam briefly told her about the journey, the bed and breakfast, Mrs Mackay and she giggled.

"...It sounds like fun!"

They talked a little longer about nothing and then the ceremonial dinner-gong sounded with a clatter and Sam quickly washed his hands before entering the cosy, dining room with his son.

Oliver did not much like the fresh fish that Mrs Mackay had made him but revelled in the largest, freshest chips he'd ever seen, and he ate them with relish as he did the apple pie for dessert.

Sam noticed that they were the only guests seated and he made enquiries of the elderly woman as she cleared away the plates and she informed him about her business.

"Oh…ah've ma' regulars coming fur *The Open* and Ah didna want nabody else, but… you and yir Wee Laddie…"

She laughed shyly and strangely as if she was a young girl.

"… Well ye looked like ye needed somewhere nice."

Sam nodded gratefully.

"That's very kind of you…Oliver and I appreciate your hospitality, it was a lovely meal."

The old lady blushed; her face even more scarlet than normal and she chided and scolded him.

"Get away wi ye…or Ah'll charge ye both double!"

They had tea in the lounge, Oliver helped himself to some of the delicious shortbreads and at 9.30p.m they bade their goodnights to Mrs Mackay and wearily went to their room.

They lay side by side in the two single beds and Oliver looked out of the open window at the clear, summer, night sky and whispered decisively.

"I like Scotland…it's…"

He searched his gentle, intelligent mind for the right descriptive word and when he found it he spoke out like a prayer.

"…It's friendly…it's very *friendly*."

Sam looked over at him and the boy's eyes were literally closing with understandable fatigue after their extensive, exhausting day.

His own focus was caught by the stars twinkling and shimmering so sharply and brightly in the spectacular darkening sky and he stroked his son's perfect cheek as he drifted into a deep and restful separation from their reality.

"We'll see how friendly Scotland is tomorrow, Son...we'll find out then just how *friendly* it is!"

Chapter 21

Sam woke to the bright, shrill sounds of birds twittering outside his window, as he looked through the glass he could just see the coast far in the distance; the day was clear but Sam could tell by the distinct motion and sway of the trees that the wind was already up.

It was only 7.30a.m and he decided to let his son sleep whilst he walked out of the side door and down the old, access road that was so pitted and strewn with gravel or stone.

He shook himself then breathed in the fresh air, purposefully holding out his hands and saw that they were easy, still and calm; he felt happy, loved the fact that his son was with him and was ready for the examination ahead, more prepared than he had ever been.

It was quiet and peaceful where they were staying; he leaned on an old, but sturdy, wooden gate then watched, as the some of the cattle in the nearby field seemed to return his intrusive stare with bulbous, brown, interested eyes.

"Dad..."

Sam turned around and saw, Oliver, half dressed come running down to join him and he picked him up in his arms and placed him on the top of the wooden closure letting his legs dangle down just above the field as he gazed around him.

He was noticeably getting heavier than he used to be; a few short months ago he could lift him so effortlessly and readily.

"...It's a bit windy!"

Oliver observed and gestured to the bushes that were straining to one side and Sam looked as well then replied meaningfully.

"Yes, it's going to be interesting, Oliver... very demanding today!"

They ate breakfast leisurely and by 10.30a.m they were at the course and on the immense, practice range where seemingly hundreds of competitors were toning and refining their skills.

Sam selected some of the balls that were readily available to the competitors and gently swung at a few short, iron shots to try to feel his shape and limber up.

He hit only a couple of longer efforts; he could sense his position and rhythm, knowing that any further practice in this melee would not be of any purpose or practical use.

He signed in, received his card and spent the remaining minutes adjusting to the pace of the practice, putting green.

The courses for a championship like this were always immaculate and Sam noticed how fast and sheer the green's surfaces were after a close cut and shave from the mowers early that morning.

He was also attentive as to how the wind was whipping into the flags, flying bravely above the clubhouse; a pennant of sharp, telling colour seemingly for every country that had sent a competitor.

Sam waited by the 1st tee for his name to be called, a minute late incurred a penalty and he was taking no chances that such a misfortune would happen to him.

He knew from past experience that in a pressure cooker like this no one wanted to make a foolish error or could afford to throw a single shot away

Sam was second to play; he was drawn with a small, oriental golfer dressed inscrutably in black and an earnest, aspiring, young Englishman who had just turned professional.

The youth hit first, he had a wristy swing that seemed looped and unbalanced but the ball ended long and straight down the fairway.

Sam felt the tension in his chest and he swung his shoulders languidly to loosen himself; he looked at his son waiting quietly by his bag and remembered his vow or promise and of course the magical, ethereal, gnarled tree that had helped him previously.

He shook any tension remaining out of himself, made a perfect angle in his swing and listened to the cry of, "*Good shot, Dad,*" from his caddy, and undoubtedly they were off!

The course was playing short but extremely tricky; the ball bounded both on the hardened fairways and the greens that seemed unreceptive to anything other than the most perfectly hit or crafted shot.

The wind was also a factor, teasing and frustrating all the competitors with club selection and how it would affect the flight of the ball on the many holes where the trees intermittently blocked, deflected and diverted its powerful or subtle force.

Sam gained a birdie in the first 6 holes then dropped a couple of shots in the next 6.

It was an interminable day of patience, guile and skill and Sam tried to keep himself composed, concentrating only on his swing, rhythm and shape, rather than his score.

Time after time he held a testing putt to make par and after finally seeing another *10 foot* putt fall agonisingly into the cup on the last he was well satisfied with an even par score of 70.

Oliver congratulated him quickly and enthusiastically.

"Well done, Dad… you were great, I bet you're leading!"

They handed in the scorecard grabbed an unappetising sandwich from the busy, food tent and placed themselves in front of an enormous, white scoreboard where a small, dark almost indistinguishable figure, wrapped up against the wicked wind, was writing down the scores with a thick black, marker pen.

Oliver looked at a lone score where the number 64 was and turned to his father in disbelief.

"That must be a mistake Dad, isn't it?"

Sam digested the information on the board and realised that for the 7 places available to progress into the main tournament itself, 10 people were already ahead of him, even after a 70 on this testing and most difficult day's golf.

He placed his arm around his son and led him off the course and out of the stiff breeze, smiling at the enormity of the task he had set himself.

"That's no mistake, Oliver, this is *The Open*... this *is* the *British Open*....there are some very good players here!"

Oliver was silent on the drive back to their lodgings, still thinking about that leading, incredible score; Sam had toyed with the prospect of driving to St Andrews to look at the spectacle but he did not sense that he wanted or needed to be distracted.

He still believed in his chances of qualification, confident now, given his proficiency on the course today; however Sam sensed once again he was going to have to find that extra spark that was gifted only to the rarest and most privileged players.

Sam again recognised that he had to somehow climb up to that next level of proficiency and excellence; he comprehended without doubt, that he needed to discover that missing link in his golfing character and ability, very soon!

Mrs Mackay was pleased to see them and was thrilled to hear Sam's accomplished, competitive score that gave him a chance of progressing and twittered to them as she handed them both fresh towels.

"We'll be seeing ye on the *telly* afore ye know!"

Sam helped Oliver wash his hair and as the boy brushed the soap from his eyes he spluttered at him forcefully.

"I am not eating that fish, Dad, no way!"

Sam ignored him and after they were dry they took it in turns to speak to Oliver's mother and Grandma who were happy and pleased that their two men had been relatively successful.

Tahnee told Sam that she was still fit to burst but the dam was still intact and as yet to break or bring forth its new creation.

They went down to dinner, with Oliver watching the door to the kitchen tentatively; Mrs Mackay appeared with a big piece of fresh sole for Sam in one hand and then an arm that she hid teasingly behind her back with her other secret meal.

Oliver's face dropped and, as if she had enjoyed her joke and ability to create tension, the small, chuckling woman produced the plate from behind her with the largest serving of beans on toast that Oliver had ever seen.

The boy screamed excitedly in delight.

"You're the best cook ever, Mrs Mackay!"

He even had the effrontery to ask for some tomato sauce and the delightful woman placed the red bottle on the table for her *Wee Man* and scolded him in good humour.

"Ach you, *Sassenachs*...what are ye like!"

Oliver relished his simple, comforting food as it strangely reminded him of his mother; the fresh air and the exercise gave him a hearty appetite and Sam was pleased to see his face glowing and healthy from his undoubted exertions.

In the last few weeks the boy had grown substantially and Sam saw that he was beginning to have a wiry energy and power that complimented his fertile and strong mind.

They went to bed early and Sam set his phone for a 6a.m call; he was due on the tee at 8.30a.m for his last test beyond which lay failure, or the actual true, raw and real *Open* itself.

It was quite a thought but he wisely did not dwell upon it for too long.

Sam was up before the buzz of the alarm sounded and immediately woke Oliver from his snooze.

They dressed and were surprised to find. Mrs Mackay in the kitchen with a small table laid and the toast browning happily under her old grill as she smiled then laughed at them.

"I coudn'a see ye going oot withoot a good breakfast, ma Boys!"

She chattered jovially and Sam was incredibly appreciative of all her efforts and endeavours on their behalves; she was an incredibly, likeable and accommodating person.

They finished their eggs quickly and Sam turned quietly to the kind woman when his son was ensconced in the car.

"I'll be back early afternoon…but…"

He sighed realistically.

"...We may have to say goodbye if I don't play well!"

The old woman looked at him and her small, green eyes shone like, glistening, dazzling emeralds.

"After yon hearty breakfast, *Laddie*..."

She scolded him gently.

"...Ah will indeed be expecting ye, and the Bairn to qualify...and after aw...!"

She chuckled once more.

"...Ah need the rent!"

Sam smiled at her; she was thoughtful, funny and simply delightful.

"I will certainly be trying my level best... Mrs Mackay, you can be sure and certain of that!"

The roads were quiet in the early light and Sam was pleased that the morning was far more benign than yesterday.

There was still a noticeable current of air as demonstrated by the slight angle of few, tall trees that they passed, but the sky was clear blue and the sparse clouds seemed lost somewhere in the stratosphere.

After parking they saw that the course, as usual, was intense and busy; competitors had started as early as 7.15a.m and Sam unpacked his clubs and went through the normal routine of signing in.

They walked to the practice range and Sam, in keeping with his previous sessions on the packed area, hit the minimum of shots just to soften his muscles and undo any kinks in his action.

He was quiet and calm; the previous tensions and histrionics were of days gone by and he knew that any repetition would cause failure before he'd hardly begun or started.

He stroked a few putts on the shaved grass noticing how there was a light sprinkling of dew slowing the greens, before the coming wind and the warmth dried them.

At this level, golf was often about subtle changes in the conditions, your own swing or purely mental control; there was always something to watch, be aware of and guard against.

Sam tried to reach inside himself, he knew that he'd have to once more try to find something extra; something he'd never discovered before, this was his final chance and he wanted to excel.

He was paired with the same partners as the previous day, when the young man had collapsed to a 79 and the inscrutable, oriental gentlemen in black, with a simple swing, negotiated his way around in only 1 more shot than he'd finished with.

There was little or no discussion throughout the playing of the course; it was not that anyone was rude but there was just too much at stake for false hilarity, camaraderie or chatter.

Sam played 2nd again and as his name was called he stopped momentarily then closed his eyes; he mentally released any nerves he had and tried to focus only on his swing plane and the slow, excruciating examination that lay ahead of him.

He teed the ball up and was pleased to feel genuinely relaxed; he breathed in, turned then released the club back into the ball and watched as it flighted perfectly through the pale, bright sky then landed into the very centre of the fairway.

The young professional then hooked his drive into the trees and Sam strode out up the silver fairway while Oliver walked, directly behind him, trying to put his feet in the indentations his father had made in the prettily decorated and coated, wet grass.

Sam played well; his concentration was insular and undisturbed and he was able to focus his considerable energies into striking each shot precisely.

He naturally understood that he needed not to get too excited at his good shots nor too distressed at any setbacks but, as he holed from *15 feet* on the 16th green he was 3 under par and on the very precarious edge and verge of qualifying.

The realisation suddenly started to permeate his intended fortress of a mind and it immediately started to react, weaken and wander; *he was actually going to qualify, to play in The Open*!

The disturbing words and thoughts started to reverberate inside his delicately balanced brain and, as he stood on the par 3, 17th he felt the rush of spiders and butterflies suddenly awaken in disconcerting action and agitation.

His swing was suddenly forced, out of the groove he'd been in all day, and the ball landed in the front, left hand bunker!

Anxiously his hands then splashed out weakly to *10 feet* and he watched as his putt fell left and short of the hole; he was now 2 under with only the long par 4, 435 yards 18th hole to negotiate.

Sam knew he still had a good chance, a 4, down the last would do it for sure and he tried again to release the increasing, distracting tension from inside him.

Just relax, he told himself, *keep your shape...* but he frustratingly could no longer control or release his frantic mind and 2 scrappy shots left him short of the green in the light rough; he sensed once more that he needed to get down in 2 to qualify!

Sam roused himself and he felt the power of his will, concentration and determination inside him that he'd known all his life.

Bravely, he hit a wonderful pitch over the bunker and watched as it ran out to just *4 feet* from the hole.

His diaphragm drew back in tightness and he muttered and murmured under his bated, heated breath, "*This to qualify!*"

Oliver watched with his heart noticeably pounding and, although he did not know the other scores, like his father, he understood and knew this next shot was vital.

He listened to the stressful sounds of his body and felt an unreal agitation and anxiety inside him that was unfamiliar; it began to dawn on him in realisation that there was a little more to actually winning *The Open* than he had ever conceived or imagined!

Sam's pure blue eyes looked at his son and saw immediately that he was nervous for him; his playing partners had finished, both failing to qualify, and finally all that stood between Sam and the continuation of a combined dream was 4 measly, tantalising, teasing and tortuous feet of distance.

He knelt down behind the ball and tried to gauge the speed and the *borrow*; the greens had become so fast and the ground seemed to tilt fractionally to the right.

He placed his old, pewter, *Ping* putter behind the devilish, white globe and tried to shut out the myriad of thoughts and twisting emotions that were rushing and raging in his swirling brain.

Just left lip, he told himself and felt his hands were sweaty and trembling almost imperceptibly; to the small, assembled gallery he looked composed but Sam was not, he was absolutely not composed at all!

He stepped away from the ball and heard the assembled audience as the spectators exhaled almost as one audible gasp.

Everyone seemed to know what was at stake;

this putt for a coveted place in *The Open*!

Sam gathered himself again, tried to shut out the world around him and forced himself to try and fully concentrate on this final shot.

He drew the club back, still trying to adjust his instinctive, destructive, mental patterns and released the small gleaming sphere on its short, vital journey almost before he realised that he had done so.

Quickly and jerkily he jumped up to see the ball start straight at the hole, take the break and then hit the left edge of the cup before diabolically spinning out with a divisive, slight increase in speed!

He'd missed! Missed it…missed it…and he was out!

Sam tried not to let his face betray his turmoil and disappointment; he knew 1 under par would not be good enough; the dream had ended and he walked off the green and placed his arm gently around his son in way of an apology.

"I'm sorry, Oliver…"

He murmured bitterly at his painful inadequacy once more.

"...I lost my mind on the last 2 holes, Son; you can swear at me again if you want!"

His child once more surprised him as he always did, and he responded with a rich, warm, dry grimace.

"Never mind, Dad..."

His lips developed into a sly grin and then unexpectedly, a seemingly, knowing, emerging, seductive smile.

"...Maybe we're not dead, yet...!"

They walked to the recorder and his father was leader in the clubhouse at 1 under, for the 2 rounds.

Sam looked at the board and there were so many people to come in that he felt sure would beat his score, only seven had to succeed and improve on his total to remove and eliminate him.

Oliver's clear, hazel eyes however intently gazed, stared and looked out towards the nearby sea and the blue horizon.

"...I think the wind's going to get up a bit this afternoon, Dad..."

His youthful features were concentrated, as if

he was a gifted prophet or fortune teller with the spiritual ability to see the future.

"…We've still got a chance, don't give up!"

The time was 1.30p.m and freakishly, almost as they sat down for lunch in the refreshment and hospitality area, Sam noticed that his son was immediately being proved correct.

The flags above the clubhouse were beginning to twist, wail and ruffle once more as if in answer to his son's thoughts and perhaps silent, unspoken prayer.

There was suddenly and markedly a developing breeze that occasionally seemed to spring up around these coastal courses as if by will, and it howled and moaned, doing its best to help them.

The two of them sat and watched nervously and patiently as one by one the other competitors eventually finished their respective rounds.

Occasionally someone would hole a wonderful putt on the last but, by and large, the field was falling victim to the wind, weather and their combined, selfish ambitions that made them all naturally anxious, edgy and therefore unable to give of their true best.

The last trio arrived at the 18th and Sam realised that only 6 players had scored lower than he had.

It all depended on whether a tall, American professional, in a massive, grey, Stetson hat could hole from *25 feet* for a birdie and Sam actually, physically held his breath until the putt slipped mercifully by on the left hand side of the hole.

Unbelievably both they and their quest were still alive and he was in a play off with five others; five hopes and ambitions to play sudden death for the single, solitary, lonely, place!

The day was drawing to a close and the light was quickly fading; a striking, strident official announced the remaining competitors to be on the 1st tee in 10 minutes.

It was sudden death for the one remaining spot!

Sam used the time to shake the muscles that had become cold from the waiting and the previous forays into the tiny gale; he picked up a couple of stray balls and made his mind focus specifically on his swing and plane once more.

Psychologically he felt strange; he was relieved

but almost angry that his mind had betrayed him at the end of his round today with its fragility.

It was infuriating that he had slipped mentally once more but sensationally he had got a reprieve and he vowed his weakness and instability in his head was not going to happen again!

The same lesson it seemed had to be re-taught over and over; he had to learn and learn quickly, at this level your unguarded thoughts and insecurities could and would destroy your chance.

Sam therefore knew that incredibly he had fatefully been given another, final opportunity and he steeled his unreliable mind; whoever was in this play-off, he was going to be sure to win it!

His blue eyes didn't even look at his other four opponents standing on the 1st tee; he only focussed inside himself and, as his body stood over the ball, his soul was calm, icy calm!

The 1st hole was 395 yards and Sam hit two perfect shots into the now easing gusts to be in the centre and middle of the green.

The pressure proved too much for three of this final group, scoring 5 or more and Sam left the closely manicured surface with a perfectly executed par; then there was only him and the tall American with the magnificent Stetson still in the race for the remaining *golden ticket!*

The 2nd hole was 185 yards par 3; the breeze was blowing from the right and the sun was sinking almost directly behind the flag.

Even in his cocoon of concentration Sam had a sensation of déjà-vu; the sun, the short par 3!

It was the 12th at Shirley golf club having just played the loop with Len Thompson and his father was waiting reliably and patiently beside the green to take him home!

Sam focussed and used this thought as an inspiration; he was with people he loved and, fully relaxed, then sent his effort high into the fading light allowing the 6 iron to drift into the gently fluttering pin with the ever reducing wind.

"Good shot, Dad,"

Oliver had gasped and blurted out in his apprehension and admiration for the well executed shot and they both instantly heard spontaneous clapping and applause from around the heavily bunkered, green.

Sam tried not to let his mind race ahead as he

watched the slow, stiff method of his opponent reach the left-hand side of the green in less spectacular fashion.

As they approached, Sam inadvertently looked for his father as his mind was still mentally at Shirley; he snapped back to reality and realised miraculously that his ball was perched incredibly, right on the very edge of the hole.

The American raised his hat as if to signify acknowledgement of a wonderful shot and permission for Sam to tap the ball in for a 2.

The man was *35 feet* away and Sam watched his son turn in unbearable tension and stare once more out to the horizon or the sea line as it was being swallowed up by the gathering gloom.

The boy just couldn't look!

Sam however could and had to; he watched the lofty professional, ever-aware of what could happen in this cruellest of games.

Sure enough the man struck the putt beautifully, it rolled along the green's contours and it swung with the break as if the hole was about to irresistibly take and gather it gratefully.

But then it stopped, dead centre, only inches short; the late evening and moisture had made the shaved grass fractionally slower and, as if in recognition of Sam's thoughts of the morning, the subtleties had worked to his advantage and he was through!

The small gallery applauded, the tall American raised his hat, smiled in sad acceptance and shook hands; Oliver threw his arms around his father's neck and squealed excitedly like a crazy monkey.

"Well done, Dad. Well done! What a shot... the best, best, best...the best shot ever!"

Before he left the course, Sam had a brief conversation with a senior official who gave him a special pass for entry into the St Andrew's, competitors car park and a tiny, silver badge to signify that he was now officially, a competitor in *The Open* properly.

Sam looked at this glistening, innocuous object and token with real honour and pride; the elderly man, as if reading his thoughts, spoke to him gently.

"It looks like that badge means a lot to you, My Lad!"

Sam held the small, silver, diminutive, glinting treasure up to the light and admired it with undisguised, true glee, achievement and gratification in his whispered reply.

"I suppose it does, Sir…"

He smiled to himself in seeming disbelief of his incredible, positive luck once again.

"…It's a pass to *The Open Championship*…I'm actually going to play…of course it does…it represents a hell of a lot!"

Chapter 22

Sam drove back to their retreat as the gloom finally gave way to darkness and he noticed how the traffic heading towards St Andrews was undoubtedly and steadily increasing.

He knew that he now had two days for practice and preparation for the tournament proper and he understandably pondered and wondered at how he would actually cope.

Up to now he had, to a certain extent, been able to draw on past experiences but he'd never competed in a *British Open* before; at the pinnacle, peak and the highest summit of golf and it was inarguably an enticing but daunting thought.

When they arrived back at Mrs Mackay's the elderly woman was in a state of mock anxiety.

"Ach…"

Her tone was tantalising and warm.

"…An'…Ah thought ye'd gone and left the country… withoot ye payin' yer bill?"

Oliver butted in then answered and chastised her as if unusually, in his enthusiasm and fervour, he did not recognise her endless cheek and good humour which was so similar to his own.

"No…my Dad's qualified… he did it… we're in *The Open!*"

Sam smiled at her in understanding; he recognised and knew that for some unknown reason she had been nervous and expectant for them both and watched as she endlessly hid her caring nature with her wry, dry comments.

"An Ah suppose ye'll be moving tae a big fancy hotel noo that ye're so high, mighty and successful?"

Sam laughed; he was in an effervescent good

and happy mood and it showed all over him.

"No, Mrs Mackay...if you've got the room we'd love to stay with you and... "

It was time he introduced his own poking brand of fun.

"... Oliver loves your expert cooking!"

Her face was masked in smiles and delight as she turned back toward her domain and dominion of the kitchen.

"Well off ye both go and get yerselves...changed an we'll see what we've got tonight!"

Sam ran his child a bath and as the boy soaked and relaxed he picked up the mobile, rang home and his mother immediately answered; Sam could tell instinctively by her excited tone that something had happened, "Congratulations, Son,"

Her voice trembled then sparkled at the same time down the distant, quiet, empty line that separated them.

"You're a Dad again; Tahnee's had a healthy, wonderful boy. They're both fine doing well..."

She was breathless in her agitation and

excitement.

"…You are not to worry they're just…"

Sam waited and hung on her every word and then she saved the very best one until last.

"…Perfect…!"

Sam sat down on the bed as if all his energy had been taken and stolen from him and he heard his mother respond to his silence.

"…Are you OK, Sam? We all want to know how you got on."

Their own success that day seemed to pale to the amazing, revelation and miraculous news from his aged parent.

"We qualified, Mum; we got through to, *The Open*…"

He was still unhinged and so unbalanced.

"… Oliver's so made up."

His mother's tone had a sudden investigative edge to it.

"And you, Son?"

He smiled as if she could see him but then spoke to her honestly, knowing always she could read him like a book just from his inflection or her innate, sixth sense.

"I'm excited Mum... it's been an unbelievable day and now this..."

Instinctively he felt himself welling up with emotion, sent his love to his recuperating wife and new baby, forming a vague excuse to end the phone call, as he was somewhat taken aback, overwrought and utterly shaken.

Still in disconcertion he dressed, walked quickly downstairs and out of the front door where the darkness and crisp, fresh air enveloped him; it seemed to mercifully wrap him in a temporary blanket of inky calm.

Sam walked a few paces into the night's, shadowy privacy then quietly and silently released his feelings and cried with only the bright, clear, silver, gleaming moon to watch him do so.

He wept tears of joy for his new son who he had not yet met, for his father who had inspired him at the play off and, for the completely, unbelievable, unforgettable experience of the day.

Somehow he had been mentally prepared for a challenge or a small adventure but, there in the night's hush and tranquillity, the day's realities truly hit him and he was emotionally overwhelmed.

He took a few minutes to recover, but he did so and when he re-entered the house his son was seated at the neatly, prepared table where a white, linen tablecloth was covered with smart, shiny cutlery, plates and huge basket of the freshest, home baked bread.

Sam excused himself washed his hands and then sat next to his son to prepare for their feast; they both had tomato soup and Sam, a steak for his main course whilst his son had eggs, sausages, chips and, of course, baked beans!

Oliver's enjoyment and compliments to Mrs Mackay on her cooking knew no bounds and he ate the meal ravenously.

When they were both satisfied, Sam played with his cup of tea by twisting it and looked at his son leaning back on his rickety wooden chair, his still, flat stomach full to bursting.

"Oliver…"

He whispered the subsequent words carefully and cautiously as if not quite sure how his son would react to the news that there was another man in the family.

"...I've got something to tell you..."

The boy looked at him tiredly, sleepily and his father carried on whilst he had his fading attention.

"...Your Mum's had the baby; you've got a little brother."

Oliver listened but it was as if his capacity to absorb any further information or cope with any more tension or exultation had been removed from what had gone by in the last few hours; he reacted as if his father had been telling him the time.

"That's nice, Dad...is Mum, OK?"

Sam nodded reassuringly.

"Yes Oliver, your Mum's fine."

Mrs Mackay had finished in the kitchen, overheard their conversation and asked him for confirmation of what she had gleaned.

"Is that right? Have ye a new... Wee Bairn?"

Sam nodded proudly and invited the woman to join them.

"Yes, she had a boy... last night... my mother's with her."

She mumbled and seemed lost in her own world and past experiences for a second.

"Och that's fur the best…"

Her familiar chuckle was never far away.

"…You men are nae help when there's a new wee yin aboot… but hearty congratulations anyhow…"

She took her short breath and continued.

"…When Ah had ma first, ma Archie wis away; he wis a soldier ye know…?"

She rose, opened a drawer and produced a faded black and white photograph of an impressive, thin man with protruding ears, dressed in an immaculate, grey uniform.

Her voice was soft and pained somehow.

"…He wis a handsome man…"

The energy in her drained a little as she went on.

"…Died eight years back an with the bairns, long gone…."

She went quiet as if uncharacteristically melancholy suddenly, then quickly re-gathered her good humour.

"...Ye're a Lucky, Man... tae have so much new life around ye...!"

He nodded in agreement and Mrs Mackay made them both some more tea and then proceeded to chat happily about her past, her family and how she ran the small hotel for something to do.

Sam had already surmised that the hotel was not really a business venture and Mrs Mackay was extremely picky and particular at whom she let stay with her.

She informed them that her new guests were coming tomorrow for *The Open* and her five rooms would be full for the rest of the week and queried him as she went on.

"...Ah presume ye'll be here until Saturday night?"

Sam thought to himself about another cut and whether he could actually make it to the last two days?

He simply smiled at the agreeable, friendly woman and shrugged.

"We'll see, Mrs Mackay... We'll see....I will be trying with all my energy!"

Sam could see his son's eyes were rapidly

closing and he made his apologies then led his child up to rest; they hurriedly washed then put on pyjamas and slipped thankfully into the welcome softness and warmth of the beds.

"Dad…"

Oliver yawned and tried to form his words but his eyes were so heavy.

"…You were great today… I was so very proud of you!"

Sam smiled inwardly as it was praise indeed from his difficult, demanding, exceptional son and manager; his lips whispered in reply.

"Thanks, Oliver…that's a lovely thing to say."

The boy continued, almost asleep while still talking.

"By the way…"

His mind was always so active.

"…What's my brother's name?"

Before he could reply Oliver had finally succumbed to the taxing exertions of the day, fell asleep and Sam suddenly realised he did not know the answer to his question.

What was his son to be called? He had

discussed so many names with Tahnee but had not agreed and somewhere in-between Mark, Luke, James and Troy, he too fell unconscious.

He slept fitfully as images formed in his brain while he span and turned uncomfortably; a large, stone, imposing, ancient, grey building centred his thoughts, drawing him inextricably towards it like an irresistible, powerful magnet.

He was not sure if it was a dream or a nightmare!

It was many hours before he realised it was the old, historic, clubhouse at St Andrews just up the road; Sam then awoke with a start, the famous building still clear in his mind.

He dozed and recalled that he had played there once many years ago, in the British Amateur and had lost in the 4th round to Steve Pate who was now a leading American Tour player.

Initially he had not warmed to the place at first but as he sat up inside his bed stretching the night out of him he remembered his previous battles and experiences there.

His mind recalled sitting on the rear bank behind the 18th green as a small, chubby, flamboyant American with a strange, jerky swing holed a huge putt across the green to win his match.

The venue undoubtedly had a special atmosphere; history seemed to eke and pour out of every brick, stone and blade of grass and he realised that he was understandably anxious but looking forward to seeing it again.

The weather was thankfully fine and bright and, after a leisurely breakfast, they bade a temporary farewell to Mrs Mackay and headed off on the road to their prestigious setting and destination.

Oliver was quiet and commented on the extraordinary amount of cars heading in the same direction; he was genuinely surprised that so many people seemed interested in golf.

The road started to twist and narrow, the traffic was slower and more intense then suddenly they were in the town of St Andrews itself and Sam followed the final yellow sign saying *Open golf*.

He remembered the back of the clubhouse, the large car park and the panoramic view out into the bay.

Along with all the participants, he was stopped at the security barrier and casually showed them his competitor's badge as if he'd been through this privileged procedure before.

However undeniably this was a new, wild experience, one he'd only fantasised about all his life and as he was waved into the crowded car park, he felt his body fantastically jump and pump with pure adrenaline and excitement.

He picked up the mobile and rang his mother but there was no reply and Sam assumed that she was at the hospital.

In a way he felt bad about not being there with them, but he knew he would have been no practical help and he had all his life ahead of him to devote and give to his new son.

Oliver swept him out of his daydream as he noisily unpacked the clubs from the rear of the car.

"Come on, Dad," he chastised him, as always, "let's go!"

They walked along the concrete and gravel until they reached the large building at the front and Sam guided them into the large caravan with Officials and Competitors marked upon it.

Many men in jackets and large, red rosettes were waiting, working and welcomed Sam warmly as another valuable competitor; they asked him to be seated and showed him the available starting times for this day and then tomorrow.

Sam was told that he would be out at 8.15a.m on the Thursday and 2.00p.m on the Friday.

This was traditional, an early and late start either day enabling the weather and the conditions to, hopefully even out fairly, for all of the participants.

Sam's spot for playing today was in 45 minutes with two players he'd never heard of and after thanking the officials for their courtesy, walked with his child along a dark, makeshift tunnel of scaffolding, boarding and wires towards the 1st tee.

When they appeared from the man-made gloom he felt instantly that he had just stepped out into an enormous, huge, Roman Coliseum.

The stands that had somehow been shielded and hidden from them in the car park suddenly towered over him; they were on all sides surrounding the 18th green and the 1st tee alongside it.

He heard a voluble gasp from his son behind him and recalled Len Thompson's words, spoken passionately, decades ago, around the comfort of the old burning and glowing stove.

"The stands... the massive stands... bearing down on you...!"

His body turned and he saw the look of wonder on the boy's face as he gawped up in shock and disbelief.

"...Dad, Dad... they're so... big!"

Sam smiled at the child and purveyed the empty rows of seating that he knew by Thursday would be bristling and crammed with spectators.

"They sure are, Oliver, but we'll cope, won't we?"

Oliver smiled and regained his good humour but kept watching the large structures as if they were waiting to suddenly leap and pounce on him at any given, sudden second.

They sat patiently by the 1st tee as each match played off and Sam walked to the nearby refreshment area to buy them some sandwiches, chocolate and drinks.

Oliver waited by himself, mesmerised by the spectacle laid on before him; it was as though he had walked into a surreal, impossible, maniacal, mesmerising and magic world.

Everywhere people were busy, outlandishly

dressed golfers starting or finishing their rounds, men with smart, dark jackets and fantastically bright rosettes running about like scampering, industrious ants.

There were endless tents and structures, and all around the mayhem, stretching seemingly forever in the distance, the quietness and beauty of the sea and shoreline.

It was an enigma and contradiction and although the child did not know the meaning of such words, he could feel and sense the wonder of it all in every fibre of his being!

He had never seen anything like it in his young, impressionable life and before he realised, his father was back beside him, thrusting a drink and some food in his hand as he gasped at him.

"It's so fantastically cool, Dad…"

He whispered quietly as if anyone could even have heard him in all the commotion, then noisily pulling the plastic wrapping off the sandwich and evoking severe glances of displeasure from the four men teeing off.

"…It's just unbelievable!"

Sam could only drink in the landscape and agree; they were at the centre of the golfing universe for the next few days and it was difficult for even him to take in the scale and size of this Major competition.

Eventually their starting time came and Sam shook hands with his two playing partners, both qualifiers and patently young, ambitious, energetic, determined, dedicated professionals.

He loosened his muscles, stiff from the travel and waiting, and after his compatriots had hit, smoothly dispatched a 2 iron into the centre of the large green expanse of fairway before him.

They were about to leave the tee when a clipped German voice called to them with a pointed enquiry.

"Do you mind if I join with you?"

Sam turned around and saw the tall, slim figure with short, blonde, curly hair that had made the request and he recognised him instantly.

"Certainly!"

He had replied without looking for confirmation from his playing companions; the man was Bernhard Langer, for him to accompany them would be a welcomed privilege and he would never have been refused or denied by any of them.

The new member of their foursome played promptly and dispatched his iron shot competently down the fairway to join the other white spheres now waiting in the distance.

There was little conversation between them all, each person marking and grasping the *feel* of the course and trying to get accustomed to the immense, endless and unpredictably undulating greens.

Sam had not remembered the contours being so subtle and he noticed also how impossibly quick and fast they were.

The forecast for the next few days was dry and fine and Sam knew that this could only make the course ever more hard and bumpy; he would need a lot of tolerance and patience if he was to do well.

Bernhard Langer was lost in his course management, each hole was painstakingly paced and inspected and he spent endless time in serious conversation with his caddy, trying to guess precisely where the pins would be.

Sam observed how the man's dark eyes would occasionally stray to him then he looked away but, as they were walking up the 16th, he unfamiliarly walked beside him and then spoke uncertainly.

"I know you from somewhere…"

He murmured purposefully and practically in his familiar accent.

"…There is something about your golf, your demeanour, but I cannot remember *ver* we met?"

Sam smiled at him, he noticed his eyes were cold, and almost black with the same devilment and intensity as his own and he could not resist teasing him just a little.

"I'll play you for 200 pesetas over the last 3 holes."

The man listened and Sam could see his mind churning over vast tracts of memory until finally, he formed the cheeky smile Sam had seen on the television so many times.

"Sam…"

He laughed suddenly of a recollection so long ago.

"…You're, Sam… I played you in Sotto Grande!"

Sam hit his second shot to within *5 feet* of the hole and prodded him with the stick of reminiscence.

"And you lost…come on… let's see you get your money back!"

The German smiled then concentrated and put his own second to a similar distance and they both left the hole with a 3!

They spent the next few holes chatting about Henry Cotton, who had unfortunately died some years back, how Sam had given up the game and the 18th hole in their match over 20 years ago when Bernhard had hit that, spectacular, enormous drive.

Sam also tentatively asked him about his notorious missed putt at the Ryder cup and he saw the famous, German's features harden a fraction; it was obviously one subject not for discussion.

Bernhard holed from *10 feet* at the last for a victory by a shot and made a mock gesture of triumph, holding his arm up in a victory pose as Sam laughed and smiled.

"I've no pesetas…but on the modern exchange rate I guess it works out to about £1.50."

Sam handed him two coins and the man smiled and gave them to Oliver who had pulled his trolley quietly as usual.

"It vas good to meet you, Oliver…"

He ruffled the boy's, smooth but windswept hair.

"…I hope your father does vell!"

Oliver pocketed the coins and looked up at him in wonder but without ever losing his unbending and abounding confidence in his Dad.

"Thank you…I'm sure he will."

Sam shook hands warmly with his old companion and adversary and went through the pleasantries with his other playing partners as well.

At this stage, before the tournament officially began, all contestants were equal, stars and laymen alike; just competitors and names, equitable and the same, in their endless quest for eternal glory and success.

As they made their way off the green, Oliver noticed that a small, burly official with short, grey side burns and a shiny, balding head, had taken his father to one side.

Oliver saw that his parent was becoming unusually agitated then incensed and after five minutes the bulky man turned sharply and insistently on his heels; the discussion was obviously concluded but patently not to his

Dad's pleasure or satisfaction.

To his concern he saw the life blood drain out of Sam's normally, healthy face and as he watched him he sat down on the bank by the 18th green and held his head forlornly in his hands.

Oliver rushed to him and spoke in his reflexive tension and anxiety.

"What is it Dad? What did the man want?"

Sam looked pathetically up from his weakened, seated position.

"Oliver…"

The flat of his hand patted the green floor by his side and his son sat closely and nervously on the dry grass.

"…Oliver, they've told me…"

Sam gathered himself and the boy could see that he was extremely, troubled and upset.

"…They've told me that trolleys can't be used for *The Open* and that … that you're too young to be allowed to carry a bag…"

He caught his breath and tried not to break down in front of his spectacular and precious child.

"…You can't caddy for me!"

Oliver tried to catch his breath as his brain swam then span and twisted all together in panic; *how was this possible? He had to caddy, they'd come so far, it was so unfair!*

Sam looked at the ground, the hallowed turf and whimpered as if he was a whipped and beaten dog and he revealed his darkest thoughts in a heart wrenching statement.

"I'm thinking of withdrawing, Oliver…it's not going to be any fun without you…this is not what I signed up for…I won't go on without you!"

Sam gave his son a £5 note, told him to go and get a drink as he needed some time to be alone and to sit and think about what on earth he was now going to do?

Chapter 23

Oliver took the money then walked slowly back through the confusing maze of scaffolding and tunnels before he found himself outside the imposing, main entrance to the clubhouse once more.

Being small and seemingly innocuous, he walked unnoticed inside and after a few yards then a couple of turns, he was in a corridor where large, intricate paintings of golfers from the distant, forgotten past seemed to stare down at him disapprovingly.

He read the dates, *Open Champions* all of them, were standing proudly in all their majesty, some from over a hundred years ago and a wild, all engulfing rage built up inside him; what this *Royal and Ancient... Whatever,* were doing to his father and him just wasn't tolerable or reasonable at all!

Ridiculously, childishly and bizarrely Oliver wanted to see his Dad on that wall as a famous champion and they were stopping them achieving that!

He wandered slowly along and eventually found himself outside a shiny door that had *Secretary* written on it in large, elegant, gold scripted letters and he knocked lightly, turned the handle then presumptuously walked directly inside.

A large, rotund man was sitting at a gleaming, polished, wooden desk and he lowered his small, thin, silver, oblong glasses until they perched on the end of his not insubstantial nose; he stared at him then spoke sharply in the agitation of being unwelcomingly disturbed.

"Yes, Young Man…?"

His tone was severe and intimidating.

"…What do you want, I'm very busy?"

Oliver was not to be undermined or moved and spoke to him in determination, purity and his natural innocence.

"Is this your *Open*?"

The man was instantly caught off guard by the impertinence of the question and thought for a moment before replying, which he then did as precisely as he could.

"I am the *Secretary*, I help to run the competition… no one owns *The Open,* My Lad!"

The intimation in his voice was still hard, stern and exacting, but the boy completely ignored the man's attempt to unsettle him and, totally uninvited, sat meaningfully in the beautiful, burgundy, high-backed chair directly opposite his desk as if he had something to say.

And he did!

He settled into the supple, leather seat uncomfortably; then absentmindedly then aimlessly played with the shiny brass buttons that decorated the arm rests before he drew in his anxious breath and tried to think.

His hazel eyes focussed and shone out in blind defiance towards the impressive man facing him.

He observed clearly that that he was a substantial figure; his face was chubby with seemingly two chins, his hair was thin and his oblong glasses somehow reminded him of a schoolteacher.

But intuitively the boy saw something else as well, a trace and promise of warmth and softness around his eyes and mouth as well and it somehow gave him the strength and courage to speak out.

"You've told my Dad that I can't caddy for him…"

His words were almost spat out in his fierce anger and resentment.

"… It's not fair!"

The man sat back in his seat of power as if

stunned by a physical blow and placed his pen directly upon the table; suddenly this remarkable boy had his full attention.

"You're, Sam Chester's lad, aren't you?"

Oliver nodded in confirmation and prepared his mind to discuss and debate as confidently as he could with him.

"My name is, Oliver."

The bulky man stared at him as if measuring his worth.

"You and your Dad have done very well."

Oliver ignored his courtesy, intended compliment and obvious attempt to change the subject.

"You can't stop me caddying, Sir, you just can't!"

The subject of the boy's complaint and malaise looked immediately uneasy and uncomfortable at having to face this precocious, ferocious, agitated, innocent child.

"Oliver…"

He sensibly tried to take the safe, high ground of responsibility.

"…These are the rules; no one of your age has ever caddied in *The Open* and we do not allow trolleys…"

His impressive stomach moved back and forward like a large swell of the ocean as he thought out loud.

"…You'd have to carry the bag… it wouldn't look good!"

Oliver suddenly became the boy he was and not the negotiator he tried to appear to be, and began to panic and plead with him.

"But I will carry the bag, Sir…look… I'm big enough…"

He stood up immediately out of the ornate chair, to his full impressive but diminutive height and flexed his small, wiry frame as if he was a tiny weight lifter or gymnast.

"…I can do it… please, Sir."

The young man was desperately trying to retain control of himself and not to cry, whilst this learned and experienced man sat back in his seat feeling increasingly distressed, awkward and ill at ease.

"Oliver, rules are rules, Son…I can't let you caddy!"

The boy felt his hackles and temper rise and his eyes moisten ever more with rich, untapped, previously constrained emotion.

"You don't understand…"

He begged and tried to convince him passionately.

"…You don't understand… my Dad needs me…"

The man went to speak but the boy continued and the tears starting to slide, glide and fall onto his soft, easy, angelic face.

"…You don't understand, Sir… my Dad's going to win… and I know… he can't do it without me…!"

He was mentally and verbally prostrate before him.

"… My Dad needs me… *please* we've come so far."

The Secretary tried to stop him.

"Oliver…Oliver…"

The older man mumbled and muttered but then sat quietly; he was suddenly upset and troubled just like the boy and let him continue as he listened somehow spellbound and in mercurial fascination.

"Maybe you don't understand, Sir…"

Oliver gushed desperately, sitting weakly back down on the luxurious seat as his legs felt watery and began to buckle.

"…My Dad's a great golfer; he going to be the first amateur to win *The Open* since…"

The man finished his sentence for him.

"…Bobby Jones!"

This stranger seemed to laugh at him and it spiked and riled Oliver even more as he began to lose his mind then berated him as if he had the right to do such an audacious thing!

"How can *you* understand…?"

The boy railed, insultingly at him.

"…You've never been that good and had that sort of opportunity so… how could *you* understand!"

The man immediately couldn't help himself; he smiled inwardly and not wishing to show that he was amused and actually not upset by his small guest's rude outburst, turned his face away from him, then walked towards the window that overlooked the busy mayhem just outside.

The secretary's name was Michael Bonallack, probably the greatest amateur golfer of all time and, unseen to the child, he now actually slyly grinned to himself at the boy's impudence and formidable spirit.

An amateur winning *The Open*? In all of the innumerable *English* and *British* titles he had won, he'd never captured *The Open*!

He remembered that one brief moment at Muirfield when he'd been in contention; for those few holes on the back 9 he actually had a chance to win but his moment for eternal glory and fame had evaporated like drops of soft rain on his skin.

The disappointment and question had never left him; was it the pressure that caused the end of his rare opportunity?

He only assumed that maybe, simply, he was just not that good, but it was in his grasp for an instant then, like a spectre, ghost or fine, intricate, uncatchable sand, the privileged moment had disappeared and slipped through his blessed hands.

The singular, unforgettable hour to fully test him had gone, never ever to return at the same elevated level of competition.

He stared intensely out at the scene unfolding before him and privately knew how the memory still, even now, haunted and upset him.

His mind acknowledged, recognised and secretly knew that there was hardly a day went by when he did not examine or reproach himself for his failure and to eternally and somewhat childishly long for that incredible, fateful chance to go back and try to win once more.

Eventually he finished his introspection and reconnoitre of the preparations for battle outside and slowly, then heavily, sat back at his desk and stared at this bewitching, young man before him.

"So your Dad's going to win is he?"

He was teasing him but Oliver saw no humour; he was convinced in the justice of his case, his unswerving faith in his father and the fabulous cause they were embarked upon.

Oliver quickly wiped the remaining tears from his eyes in his discomfort and embarrassment at crying, but he could not disguise his true zeal and feelings as they were red with obvious anxiety and emotion.

"Yes, I promise…"

He whispered firmly and sincerely as if he somehow could deliver on his absurd pledge as he leant over towards the man's desk and whispered to him as if it was a secret.

"...I dreamt it...dreamt he would win *The Open*... it was me that persuaded him to play again, I know he can do it!"

He was adamant in his belief and his enthusiasm was somehow infectious; Michael Bonallack drew in his cavernous breath and finally spoke seriously to him.

"I knew your Dad as a boy, Oliver; he was always a good golfer but..."

His smile was dry but now full of conviviality.

"... I don't know he is a good as you say he is?"

The boy just continued to beg and plead without shame or pride and his small voice but incalculable character, roused and lifted up in one final heartfelt, emotive plea

"He needs me, Sir... *please* don't split us up...*Please!*"

In reaction to his words the man picked up the nearby phone and asked for a...Mr Carter to join him immediately, and then addressed the small boy gently.

"Please wait outside, Oliver."

In trepidation the child walked out of the room sensing his impending defeat and disappointment; he sat back helplessly in the hallway and further studied the imposing, even astounding, ancient sporting figures on the walls once again.

The golfers looked strange; funny clothes, hats, clubs but the pictures had a certain distinct and pleasing quality about them and Oliver found them interesting and strangely appealing.

The same man that had spoken to his father came bustling down the corridor; he ignored the small boy completely and, looking very self-important, knocked then went into the *Secretary's* office.

Oliver waited and returned his eyes to the paintings; he realised that they were of real people, probably all dead now and his imagination began to wonder what this competition, so large and sprawling, was like all those endless years and decades ago.

The door opened abruptly allowing the bald headed man spoke to him gruffly with a noticeable sense of irritation and even frustration in his tone.

"The Secretary will see you now!"

He then sped and marched off down the corridor, gently shaking his shiny, reflective, bald head as he did so.

Oliver walked into the room extremely nervously and sat once more on the elegant chair; he held his breath, kept quiet then patiently waited for the man to stop writing and look up at him.

Ultimately he did so and Oliver saw that his eyes were, blue, gentle, comforting and kind.

"Oliver..."

He smiled and laughed together.

"...You've given me something of a teasing riddle and a dilemma...My Lad!"

Oliver kept utterly still, hardly daring to murmur or breathe and listened attentively.

"...Normally, I would never sanction or allow your request..."

Oliver felt himself welling up again and the man sensed it immediately and swiftly carried on.

"...*But*...there are always exceptions and...for

what you and your father have achieved up to now… I am going to make an exception for you…"

He settled into his chair far more comfortably now in response to his fresh and inspirational decision.

"… I know just by you speaking to me that you will have the strength and courage to carry the bag and not let the competition down."

Oliver beamed him a disbelieving, massive smile.

"I won't let you down, Sir."

The man felt himself finally, fully relax.

"I feel confident about that, Oliver…"

He passed him a note across the desk; Oliver saw it had writing scribbled elegantly in sharp, black ink on the white intricate, *Royal and Ancient* letter heading.

"…This is a warrant confirming your official status as *The Open's* youngest, ever caddy…"

His azure eyes twinkled and shone,

"… Congratulations, Young Man, you've just made history!"

Oliver eyed the letter with a certain, nervous pride; placed it into his delicate fingers and tried to read the intricate, elaborate jumble of letters and words.

"Thank you, Sir…"

He was still trying to contain the hopes and emotions that were shimmering and shining in his eyes.

"…Thank you so much."

The Secretary pushed his glasses back up in front of his eyes then addressed the boy brusquely once more as if casually dismissing him.

"Now run along, Oliver… to your Dad and let me get on with my job…"

He flashed him a beaming smile.

"… I've a lot to do you know!"

The experienced golfer and administrator waited until the child had risen and fully departed and then, completely distracted from his original task, walked back over to the window and mused as he looked outside at his domain.

He asked himself why he gave the boy this

special permission and dispensation? Was it just because he was so devastatingly, irrepressibly polite or cute?

Undoubtedly the young man had pulled at his paternal and emotional side, there was no question of that, but there was something else, something deeper that had ultimately convinced, swayed and persuaded him.

He looked and stared as he saw the child run toward his father and he suddenly realised why he succumbed to the boy's request; the child had simply told him of his wonderful, simple dream!

His father, a relatively, innocuous, unknown, amateur golfer was going to win *The Open*; it was ridiculous, preposterous, but that is, as he well knew, what dreams were truly meant to be!

It had been an exactly similar aspiration and vision of ambition that had inspired him when he was a boy, then a man, and now, how could he in all conscience, stand in the way of such a dramatic and spectacular, idea and fantasy!

He chuckled, shook his head and returned to his desk and tried once more to concentrate; there was still so much for him to prepare and do, for the following, coming days!

Oliver went running over excitedly to his miserable parent and saw that he had not moved at all in the hour he had been gone; he spoke absentmindedly as he saw him.

"Hi, Oliver…did you have some food, Son… sit down I've got something to tell you!"

Oliver tried to argue or interrupt him.

"But, Dad…I…"

Sam was insistent and persistent, ignored and hardly noticed that his child was literally glowing in energy.

"Quiet, Oliver…"

He felt his temper start to rise as if he needed to blame someone for this disaster and quandary he was in

"…I don't need any of your cleverness…if this tournament doesn't want you then they can manage without me as well…"

Sam felt drained and almost ill as he spoke; so much effort for nothing once again!

"… I am going to withdraw!"

Oliver tried to bring him out of his despair and misery.

"But, Dad…Dad!"

Sam was somewhere lost in his former world of anger, resentment and frustration; he knew the place very well from his past and was unhappily returning to reacquaint himself with a visit once more.

"Do not try to stop me, Son…"

Sam was stern, acrid and sour.

"…I've made my mind up!"

Oliver could hardly break though his father's, negative, mental barrier.

"Dad…Dad…Dad…!"

He pushed and waved the scrap of paper below his father's nose but he ignored it, still lost in his all consuming self pity and depression.

"I'm going to the recorder's office, Oliver; we'll go back to Mrs Mackay's, get our stuff and go see your brother… I don't need this cra…"

He stopped and caught his mood and irritability just in time as he did not wish to swear in front of his child.

"…I'm too old for this petty rubbish anymore!"

He made to get up and Oliver, in utter exasperation and desperation, suddenly jumped on him, firmly trapping his thick legs and even thicker head to the floor.

"Read this, Dad..."

He screamed at him...

"... For God's sake...*Read it*!"

Sam suddenly realised that his son was showing him a small piece of paper with the familiar, *Royal and Ancient* letter heading on; he took it from him and started to read it, then re-read it over and over as if to then try and absorb what the document said.

He stared at the words and saw the signature on the bottom of the paper then finally looked at his boy in utter incredulity and amazement.

"How did you do this...?"

He was genuinely perplexed and astounded.

"...They never change their minds!"

Oliver smiled at him as though he was a genius suddenly and the famous, fictitious cat that had the cream.

"It's a secret, Dad, but the man I spoke to was very kind... he just seemed to like and understand me... us!"

Sam glared at his outrageous son with mock severity.

"Oliver...tell me, please!"

The boy stared and looked out towards the 1st green in the near distance and shrugged calmly then whispered quietly.

"I told him that you were going to win *The Open* and..."

His wonderful face seemed to emit light like a beacon.

"...And you couldn't do it without me!"

Sam laughed at the audacity and ignorant, unbridled confidence of his boy; he leant over to him and kissed his delightful head.

"That part is definitely the truth, Oliver... I know for sure I wouldn't even have got this far without you...!"

Sam's attention was drawn to his large, golf club holder, perched on his trolley and thought out loud.

"...I need to buy a smaller one...we'll carry it jointly and together around the course, Oliver!"

His son's proud, earthy eyes confronted him and burned into his, challengingly.

"We will not, Dad, I can carry the bag; that's the deal I made with the Secretary…"

He emphasised his point.

"…I am your official caddy… read the letter!"

Sam looked at his son with not only his love, but, his respect and boundless admiration for the child's, incredible, indomitable character and spirit.

He guided him towards the professional's shop, as they definitely needed to buy a more manageable piece of equipment for Oliver to bear; there was no point discussing it any further!

They chose a smart, black one with a thick, padded, shoulder strap; the boy slung it on his shoulder and it seemed bigger than he was, but he carried it, erectly and manfully and he looked irresistibly more engaging and adorable than ever!

However, Sam had found the emotionally wrenching experience of the afternoon, tiring, and he realised that he needed to get away and re-gather his thoughts.

They loaded the car and Sam decided to drive to Ladyburn, his qualifying course, and hit some meaningful, practice shots in relative peace, quiet and obscurity.

It was daunting enough to see match after match of the world's best golfers, but the incident with his son had pushed him into deciding that he needed a temporary separation and release from this fishbowl of *The Open*.

As he drove away from the crowds and the bustle, he thought about how he would react to playing in the competition, in front of a worldwide television audience?

It was a disturbing and salutary thought!

Ladyburn, as he thought, was deserted; the professional agreed to let him use the facilities and with *The Open* circus just a few miles away Sam enjoyed the silence of the late, warm, summer, Scottish evening and hit his shots towards the bright radiance of the setting sun.

Sam had now been playing intensive golf for weeks and the competition had fine-tuned his game to a level he'd never before experienced.

His timing and balance were exceptional and as the practice ground grooved his method still further; he felt confident as he struck each shot perfectly, concentrating still only on his shape and rhythm.

Sam knew however that, as actual competition was different *The Open* was different again, and it would test his ability and patience to the very edge and limit of his talent!

He was not and would not be misled by his competence and expertise on the grounds of preparation.

Sam checked his phone, locked away in the glove compartment of the car; there were two missed calls from home and he pressed the dial button and a familiar warm voice spoke to him happily.

"Hi, Daddy…how are my Boys?"

Sam was thrilled to hear his wife's voice, home safe and well, and after telling each other about their respective adventures he handed the phone to Oliver who spoke to her excitedly.

"Hi, Mum…how's…*What's his name*?"

Tahnee laughed at her audacious son.

"He's fine, Oliver… handsome like you, but not so cheeky, yet!"

Oliver rambled on and then passed the phone back to his father and he muttered his concerns to her.

"Tahnee, we need to decide on the little man's name!"

Her voice seemed to send a smile down the line.

"We will, Sam...tomorrow; now go and have some rest because we'll be looking for you on the television on Thursday!"

With blown kisses the phone went dead and Sam suddenly felt a long way from his family; he drove in silence trying to picture in his mind the description of his new son given to him by his wife.

Instinctively he longed to see him but he would soon enough; his mother and wife could manage better without him at the moment.

He laughed to himself, visualising Tahnee berating him for getting in the way and he felt better, as his immediate concern was commencing on Thursday; the rest of his ordinary, normal life was under control and would have to wait a small while.

Mrs Mackay had made a sumptuous feast for them once again but her small farmhouse was busy and the old woman had little time for tittle-tattle or gossip, although Sam wanted to tell the story about Oliver's inspirational daring and brilliance today.

The dining room was crowded with people who had come to watch the imminent, golfing spectacle and Sam noticed how relaxed and at home the guests were.

As he had worked out, they were treated as friends rather than customers and the atmosphere within the house was always, extremely genial, warm, jovial and constantly friendly.

Sam and Oliver bade goodnight early to their host as they were exhausted and had little energy, time or inclination to enter much interaction or badinage with the other guests.

They washed and settled down quietly for the night; Sam relaxed and watched the sky through the window as the bright, late, evening light, slowly faded to grey then black.

He was due to play at 9.30a.m.in the morning and knew he did not need to worry about an alarm call given his son's increasing propensity for early mornings.

He was always up and awake around 6.30a.m recently and as Sam watched him sleeping so softly, tired from his exertions of the day, he wondered how the boy would manage lugging his shiny new bag?

The coming days would undoubtedly and indubitably be a stern test for them both.

Chapter 24

They arrived at the course an hour before they were due off for their final practice round; the drive had been a struggle through the volume of traffic and Sam was pleased to eventually reach the competitor's car park.

He placed his clubs carefully in his new carrying bag and did not put in his waterproofs, given the apparent brightness of the day, to save as much weight as possible.

Immediately he went to pick it up but, Oliver's small hand took it from him and he pulled it onto his right shoulder without so much as a thought or the blink of an eye.

"Come on Dad, let's practice."

They walked to the putting area and tried to find an unoccupied space or slot amongst the vast array of golfers preparing; there were so many, familiar, famous faces, experienced tour professionals and …of course, Sam!

He felt strange, not necessarily intimidated, but it was hard to explain or for him to rationalise how he was being affected.

Sam therefore dropped some balls and concentrated his thoughts only on trying to come to terms with the slick, slippery surface of the greens.

They were superb, rich and textured, in such a way that a perfectly struck putt, hit with topspin would roll endlessly true and straight.

Sam figured that the shaved grass on the actual course would be faster; he knew that if the sun shone and the wind blew they would become tricky and, given that St Andrews was relatively short anyway, putting would be a major factor to scoring on the tumbling, massive greens.

Sam's playing companions for the day were pretty much unknown; a chubby, unheralded, American professional and a broad-shouldered Scottish player from Turnberry who had the thickest accent that Sam had ever heard.

The American was quiet, concentrating only on his game and the course, and the Scotsman was overly gregarious and chatty.

Sam had little time for conversation as he was trying to drink in as much of the actual playing arena, sensation and atmosphere as he could; he sorely understood that he could not afford to be intimidated or distracted tomorrow.

It was difficult however to ignore the famous faces, *Open Champions*, appearing seemingly on every green and hole; Sam truly felt as if he and Oliver were in some sort of fantasy world and any minute they would be waking up from a reverie.

The course had been built on quite a narrow strip of land and it seemed that competitors were virtually bumping into each other in the congestion and constriction where occasionally one immense, shiny, close cut area was remarkably used for two different flags and the conclusion of two separate holes.

That was part of the novelty, charm and lure of St Andrews; it was just distinct and different to playing golf anywhere else.

Real life raised its head on the 10th tee however when they were at the furthest point away from the clubhouse; from nowhere the clouds gathered and the rain started to fall then pour, in continual, blinding, devastating, vicious, wild sheets.

Oliver opened the side pocket of the bag to look for his father's waterproofs and umbrella but found the space empty; he instantly knew what he'd done and chastised him ferociously.

"Dad...you've taken them out to save weight, now just look at the mess we're in!"

Sam looked as the water cascaded from his son's matted hair and protectively put on him his cap that covered almost his whole head and chuckled as the rain simply bucketed down from it like a tiny stream and waterfall.

"I know, Oliver, I know..."

He spoke sheepishly and apologetically.

"...I won't tomorrow, I promise...don't shout...let's just get in!"

The 9 holes then became a test of endurance for them, Sam, despite his son's protestations insisted on carrying the bag at least some of the way to help him.

They eventually arrived on the 18th green, cold, wet, dishevelled and having forgotten something of the divine majesty of *The Open* in the insufferable experience of the torrential downpour.

Sam checked his starting time once again for tomorrow, leaving nothing to chance; he was off early as he knew, 8.15a.m, and once this was reconfirmed, walked quickly with his son and reached the sanctity then refuge of the car.

As they drove back to the boarding house they removed most of their clothes and Oliver was pleased to feel the reviving breath of the heater, as the car became as warm as toast.

The traffic was all going the opposite way to them and after an initial delay they promptly reached their welcoming home from home.

Mrs Mackay saw them and after taking their clothes for washing, handed them large, fresh, fluffy white towels for bathing the day out from their sodden skin and told them what they had both already worked out.

"The weather kin be wicked up here, *Laddie!*"

After an hour they were dry and refreshed and Oliver was tucking into some late lunch while Sam rested and cupped a large mug of sweet tea in his palms.

Oliver looked outside through the stained, wooden, kitchen window and noticed how blue the reappearing sky was once again, and he proffered a question.

"Do you want to go back, Dad?"

Sam shook his head as he did not wish to return; he had to admit privately to himself that something about being in the middle of such an event made him feel strangely off balance and uncomfortable.

It was exciting, in some ways, beyond even his highest expectations, but he undoubtedly felt out of his depth; all those famous faces, the hustle, bustle and the monumental, imposing stands!

Len Thompson's words of, *bearing down on you,* forever seemed to echo, unsettle and confuse his already fraught mind

"No, Oliver...we'll drive to Ladyburn...a little later and practice quietly..."

He sighed as if expressing his disconcertion.

"...There's too much going on there to concentrate!"

The young boy knew what he meant; he'd never seen anything with so much life and fantastical, relentless, pulsating energy.

The golf and caddying was enough in itself, but

the surrounding grounds seemed to go on forever meaning he was dog-tired after struggling through the rainstorm and softly commented in agreement.

"That's a good idea, Dad."

He threw himself on the soft, single, leather chair in the lounge and tried to find the cartoon channel on the television to ease and turn off his fatigued and racing head.

Mrs Mackay sat next to, Sam on the large, tweed settee and smiled then murmured easily in her rich, local twang.

"He's such a Bonny Lad, Sam…such a Bonny *Bairn*!"

Sam smiled at her and looked at the back of his son's concentrated head; his long, brown, silky hair gently falling over the rim at the back of the angled chair.

"He is… Mrs Mackay and he's growing so fast that sometimes I need to be reminded that he's still a *Bairn*… as you say!"

In a strange way the woman had put Sam's unease and insecurities into context; he already had what was undeniably important, in his wife and wonderful family.

Truly he had paid his dues to the sport and did belong at *The Open*; he accepted and knew that he had earned his pass and shiny, silver medal many times over.

He belonged to wherever he wanted to be, and as normal, it was the unguarded thoughts in his flowing, overheated brain that constantly made Sam have these misgivings and constantly question himself.

Undoubtedly he knew he could play as well as most, if not all of the professionals, and with his son beside him he had an added, imperious advantage; seemingly a secret weapon!

Suddenly he felt better and peculiarly infused with more confidence; the last few weeks had been a whirlwind and he knew that it was only normal that he was struggling to settle and adapt.

Anyone would battle and toil to absorb so much adjustment and unexpected excitement so quickly.

But *The Open* was tomorrow, the time had gone and Sam had to find a level of self-belief that had previously been beyond him; he knew without a shadow of doubt he would need to make such a discovery and find this hidden prize to ultimately carry him through and produce his best.

They drove down to Ladyburn after an early dinner and walked onto the familiar, empty, practice area.

It was Sam's favourite time of day as, after the rainstorm, the air was fresh and clear and the ground and trees seemed to sparkle with a fine coating of crystal water.

It was like the magical evening all those years ago when he'd first hit a single, fantastical shot way over the shed as a boy.

It was a luxurious and memorable recollection and as he started to run through his routine he could feel that his game was better honed and more refined than it had ever been.

Each effort was hit crisply and his plane was perfect; he could shape any shot almost at will and was grateful that he could start the most important round of his life tomorrow feeling that he had prepared as well as he could.

Oliver whistled quietly as Sam came to the end of his regime and ritual.

"Dad that was just awesome…"

His eyes were shining in genuine admiration.

"….Can anyone play better than that?"

Sam laughed and told him sagely what he knew for sure.

"Oliver, plenty of people can hit the ball but it's producing it on the day that counts; that's the real and acid test!"

This was the undoubted truth and it heralded an internal, unspoken, unanswerable, teasing question; could he actually bring his best golf to the fore in the full glare of such a pressurised competition?

It seemed that tomorrow was the final stage of his personal voyage of discovery; the last and ultimate trial of his skill, playing abilities and all levels of the management of both his conscious and subconscious thoughts.

He was never capable before but he would not have to wait much longer to find out if he now had the steel needed to successfully pass such an ultimate and searching assessment of his capabilities!

They spent some time practising chipping and experimenting with a variety of bunker shots; Sam's mind wandered as normal, and he thought about the infamous *Hell Bunker* on the 17th hole!

He put his practice ball against the lip of the high side of the sandy grave and, opening the blade determinedly, picked the club up sharply then tried to get the ball to rise steeply and vertically.

He had seen so many players get themselves into trouble on this hole and he wanted to be sure he had the technique to deal with any, and every eventuality.

His hands worked until he was satisfied and upon reaching the car he removed his phone from the glove compartment and rang his home number; Tahnee answered, her voice clearly, happy and audible in the confines and quiet of the car.

"Hi…how are we doing?"

Sam told her about the rainstorm and she then conversed excitedly with Oliver; the boy informed her that he was fine before his father forcefully grabbed the phone back then spoke to his wife earnestly and in some agitation once again.

"Well what are we calling, *What's his name*?"

She teased him; it seemed that it was a family tradition and trait to torment each other!

"Well…"

The suspense was tortuous and divine at the

same time for her.

"...If it's all right with you we're going to call him *Frankie*... Frankie Chester."

Sam felt a large lump in his throat and his eyes start to moisten as he mumbled his words.

"That's wonderful, Tahnee...*Little Frankie*..."

He tried to catch his mind and breath... at the same time.

"...Well let's hope he's not as much trouble as the other one!"

He heard his wife laugh in mixed, happy and sad reminiscences.

"I don't think that would be possible, Sam...now you and Oliver get a good night's sleep, we're expecting the best from you tomorrow!"

After a couple of kisses, the phone went dead and Sam flicked the static car into life and motion.

His head simply felt like it would explode in joy and excitement as he looked at his son sitting patiently on the passenger seat and smiled at him joyously.

"*What's his name* is called, Frankie...after your

grandfather!"

Oliver looked at him wide eyed in wonder as *What's his name*, was suddenly a living person; he had a real brother and it was suddenly hard for him to instantaneously take it in or believe.

He was silent for a while then asked a pertinent but difficult question.

"What was my Grandpa like, Dad?"

On the short drive back to the boarding house Sam explained and revealed to him about his own impossible and irrepressible father, but not everything!

He told him about the warehouse, a little about the business and the vans until Oliver smiled at him then chipped his words accusingly at him.

"I always thought they were a joke?"

Sam laughed and shivered equally.

"Those vans were definitely not a joke…they went on forever!"

Sam told him a little about the adventures he'd had with his own father and Oliver listened spellbound as Sam recounted the events with Jerry Pate at Hoylake.

He'd read about it in the red book but somehow hearing it first hand from the person right beside him that had actually experienced the adventure made it come alive; the young boy then realised that somehow his Dad had actually managed before he came along.

Up to a fashion and point that was, anyway!

Sam enjoyed and revelled in their conversation; he was elated at the news from his wife and it was comforting for him to talk with his son about his much loved and missed father.

Hardly a day went by when he did not think about his late parent but he rarely talked about him and he found the experience and fact that he had, helpful and strangely therapeutic.

He wondered what he would have made of this new escapade, he'd have loved it, revelled in it, but Sam also knew that he could never have achieved it with his involvement.

That was the relationship they'd always had, *flattered to deceive*, it was a terrible indictment of so much effort and Sam knew that whatever transpired in the next few days, his partnership with his own boy was stronger, built on more solid ground, and of greater substance.

Sam thought about his relationship with Oliver

and realised that the biggest and fundamental difference in their relationship or interaction was relatively simple to explain.

Unfortunately, with his own father, all he could ever remember was the pressure, duty and endless work, with the occasionally wild, sometimes joyous and happy experience thrown in, but with his son all he could recall was fun!

It somehow made everything different; lightness of being or enjoyment made existence more worthwhile and seemed to make everything, even the most inconceivable, absurd or unbelievable things, appear tangible, possible and achievable.

They were both fatigued when they reached the small guesthouse and after bathing and eating they slipped into their respective beds and settled down for the night.

Oliver yawned, feeling the imminent approach of the unpredictable but amazing, coming morning.

"How do you feel, Dad? Are you nervous?"

Sam lay back on the soft, giving, comfortable pillow and tried to work out if he actually was.

"I don't think so, Son…"

He sighed and began to settle down.

"...But don't start swearing at me if I am tomorrow."

Oliver laughed deliciously and with real purpose.

"You know I will, Dad... you just know I will!"

Sam smiled, watched his son drift into a restful sleep and surprisingly, given that his mind was full of the new baby, eternal thoughts of his father and *The Open* in the new dawn, he also fell into a tired slumber, far away from the waking world.

Normally he would drift into his secret, personal land of imagination and fantastical thoughts but on this particular, special night however, he did not have any visions at all; there was little point!

His dream was now real life and it was due to start on the 1st tee at St Andrews at 8.15a.m in the morning!

Chapter 25

Oliver awoke first; he saw the bright, early dawn outside and shook his father anxiously.

"Dad, Dad, wake up we're going to be late!"

Sam rubbed his eyes and looked at the clock; it was 5.30a.m and he mumbled tiredly and dryly.

"For what, Oliver? The first light…?"

He smiled at his son's, flushed and vibrant expression, so full of excitement and enthusiasm.

"…Today's the day Oliver, hey?"

Oliver nodded, washed his face, brushed his teeth and put on the clothes Sam had laid out for him the previous evening.

They were both ready within a few minutes and Sam was strangely unsurprised to find, Mrs Mackay waiting for them in the kitchen with fresh eggs sizzling on her old stove.

Somehow he expected no less of her.

Sam had grown extremely fond of the old woman and vowed, whatever the outcome of his golf adventure, he would keep in touch and perhaps have a holiday with the whole family next year.

Thanks to her good nature and motherly instinct, when they left at 6.30a.m exactly, both Sam and Oliver were relaxed, well fed and as prepared for the day as possible.

Incredibly, the roads were already busy and Sam tried not to show, emit or take out the tension he felt, on the traffic all around him.

They did not reach the sanctity of the player's car park until 7.15a.m and, after signing in and collecting his card, they walked over to the extensive, enormous, practice area.

Sam had not been on the player's, dedicated warm up zone before and he tried not to be intimidated; there seemed to be an endless row of early starters pounding shots towards the gentle blue and white motions of the incoming, ocean waves.

Sam recognised so many of them and just stared as if he was mere a spectator; it was truly a bizarre, disquieting and surreal experience to simply see so many famous faces.

Oliver picked up a small bucket of gleaming balls and jerked his father back to reality.

"Remember, Dad…"

He spoke sternly and seriously; this was not

just another morning or game to him, it was far more serious than that!

"…We've come too far for you to start daydreaming!"

Sam stared at him and instantly understood that what he had said was no joke; he took the basket from his hands and walked to the furthest point of the practice ground, as far away from the gathering spectators as he could be.

He selected a ball then swung and, to his disconcertion, the ball sliced wildly to the right; the next shot hooked left and as he went to make another frantic effort he saw Oliver's, trainer covered, small foot completely squashing the appointed, annoying, little, white sphere into the ground preventing him from attacking it.

Sam leant back jerkily and looked anxiously at his son standing below him who could see he was already incredibly wound up; his child troublingly observed his patent anxiety then hissed correctively and determinedly at him.

"Dad, I do not want to swear today…!"

His eyes were cold, set, and showed colours of mixed hazel and earthy brown.

"...Relax you're better than all these people, relax...*please!*"

Sam felt the boy's soul enter and permeate his own as if it was not part of him already!

He breathed the fresh, brackish air and let the soft breeze fan him and laughed as his stress seemed to mercifully dissolve until he suddenly felt easier and better.

"You always seem to know what to say, Son...sorry, it is a bit much to take in... don't worry, I'm OK."

Sam cleared his mind properly and he focussed on his swing, his shape and plane then ultimately focussed on the ball that Oliver had now released from under his toe.

He turned in rhythm, felt the familiar, sweet contact that he'd perfected as his body began to relax before his mind gradually followed; his game was ready and he would not let himself down this time.

Sam tried his best to ignore the tumult around him, everywhere there were huge, lively crowds, television cameras and so many professional golfers all giving endless interviews.

The playing course and greenery was actually

and unexpectedly some retreat for Sam; the spectators were thankfully not allowed behind the ropes and he appreciated the freedom and separation as it gave him some valuable time and space to settle and adjust.

His fingers threw some balls on the putting green and he practised his stroke around the only hole not being used; the surface was simply magnificent, manicured, immaculately prepared and Sam couldn't help but feel incredibly privileged to just be there.

The large, white clock on the clubhouse facade moved effortlessly around, match after match walked ponderously, steadfastly down the perfect fairway until suddenly it was Sam, standing on the 1st tee shaking hands with his playing companions of the day.

Specifically these were a thin, Oriental man, who was a leading money winner on the Asian tour and a small, balding, Scottish professional who had survived the same qualifying ordeal at Ladyburn as he had.

Sam, after the formalities of introduction paid little attention to them; he had to concentrate, get himself in the correct and intent, pure frame of mind.

The Oriental man swung first and dispatched the ball and a cultured English voice announced clearly in distinct and perfect diction.

"On the tee…Sam Chester."

Sam felt his mind race and his pulse quicken; he went to select the 3 iron from his bag and, as he, too swiftly, pulled it from its refuge, he felt his son's hand hold his down gently but purposefully and whisper to him.

"Dad, I'm nervous too…"

Sam turned and found the cool but, calm, smooth eyes of his child.

"…We'll be all right, just think and focus… on me!"

He squeezed his father's, eager hand and Sam inhaled the fresh, sharp breeze once more then breathed it in, along with his son's sound advice; in his head he was at home playing the course at the bottom of his garden and Oliver was caddying beside him!

He was halfway down the fairway after hitting a perfect shot before he'd realised that *The Open* had begun in earnest for them both!

Sam hit a crisp wedge shot to *15 feet* and two putts gave him a par and he walked off the green feeling relief and the slightest twinge of confidence.

As if it was a surprise and a something of a revelation he started to realise that it was just golf, a mere sport, something he'd played and excelled at all his life.

Two good shots at the 2nd yielded another par as Sam started to settle into a rhythm; his swing and his shape was polished, each shot was dispatched sweetly and as he turned into the back 9 he was level par and beginning to enjoy himself.

Sam was pleased to find that whilst he was on the golf course he was able to shut most, if not all of *The Open's* distractions out of his mind.

The gallery was behind the barriers and the television cameras were hardly interested in him as everywhere all around him there were Champions past and present.

His observant eyes only had to glance at the leader-boards, dotted around the course, to realise that there were many, leading professionals in bright red figures already and the world was not watching his match at all!

Sam's exemplary golf was unsurpassed by his playing partners who were complimentary and impressed by his skill and ability; he seemed to hit every fairway and find the centre of each of the massive, rolling greens always near to the devilishly placed, pin positions.

The notorious, road hole was negotiated with a safe, bogey 5 - Sam 3 putting from the front edge - and the shot dropped, was rescued on the last hole when he holed his first real putt of the day from *12 feet* and took the applause from the sparse, early crowd almost shyly, as if he was undeserving of such laudable praise.

Sam was round in level par 72 and, after he had checked his score and signed the Scottish professional's card, he proudly handed his own into the recorders who were huddled in the caravan at the back of the clubhouse.

Sam was pleased; he put the clubs away and walked with Oliver into one of the enormous, refreshment tents where they bought some sandwiches and drinks as Oliver raised a question.

"What do you think will qualify, Dad?"

The boy looked up at the gargantuan scoreboard towering high above him; one of the Americans was already 6 under and there were literally crowds of names huddled together just behind him.

Sam bit into his sandwich; he was relieved and pleased he hadn't disgraced himself and that, above him qualifying, had been his overriding and major concern.

"1 under, maybe…"

His mouth moved in mastication and his brain ticked over in thought creating a more meaningful response.

"…We still have a chance… if I play well tomorrow."

Oliver said nothing but just continued to eat and the only impact the two of them had made on the day was some mild interest in Oliver lugging Sam's bag around with regard to him being *The Open's* youngest ever caddy.

One of the local papers even took his picture and Sam promised his son he would look out for it in the newsagents tomorrow to put in the empty pages of the scrap book.

After the small meal, Sam wanted to go; he had coped and managed reasonably with the pressure of the day up to now but he was still uneasy in the madness and organised pandemonium that was everywhere, as it was so disconcerting and all consuming for him!

As they walked back to the car, Sam saw that Tiger Woods had started his round and was already 2 under after 3 holes; the course was playing easy with the greens surprisingly receptive and watered and Sam knew that the top professionals would all be scoring well.

Sam practised a little again at Ladyburn before finally leaving for the boarding house and his game was simply divine and exceptional.

He was balanced, rhythmical and precise and yet he knew in spite of that, he had only succeeded in a level par score when his opponents were simply burning up the course in the favourable conditions.

They returned to Mrs Mackay's at 7p.m and after bathing, they sat in the dining room where Sam started to converse with some of the guests who had visited their venue and the location of their test that day.

Sam told them his score with satisfaction and an elderly, thin man with silky, white hair congratulated him in voluble, good spirits.

"You must be proud to play in such a tournament…"

Sam agreed and listened as the aged, wiry stranger told him all about Tiger Wood's round; he had followed him for 9 holes and was raving about the legendary man's length and style.

"…He's the greatest player that's ever been…"

His mouth and piercing voice was gushing then giving in praise.

"…He was 5 under and I'd swear he hardly broke sweat!"

Oliver who had been very subdued and quiet throughout the day suddenly muttered to the man sharply as if in correction or analysis of his spoken, general, sporting knowledge.

"My Dad's better than, Tiger Woods…"

His face was fixed and firm and there was not even a vague trace of any humour in its youthful features.

"…He's going to beat them all."

The old man chuckled then smiled and looked at him kindly but his voice replied condescendingly; he did not realise that when it came to golf Oliver was not a child!

"Of course he is, *Sonny*, of course he is!"

Sam looked at his son and saw his face instantly redden then flush in reactive, spiky anger and he stared at him hard, instructing him silently to hold his tongue.

They ate the rest of the meal in relative silence and, after both speaking briefly to Tahnee, watched the television for a while.

There were brief *Open* golf, highlights of the day at 11p.m, none of which included Sam's meaningless contribution, and the duo retired to bed late in the evening; they were not due out until around 2.00p.m the following day and the morning held no pressure of time for them.

However Sam could not sleep, although he had been pleased with his round as he had undeniably played very well, somehow he felt flat, discontented and dissatisfied.

Further to this, Oliver had been so hushed and unusually muted as if he'd been disapproving or even disappointed with his efforts and subsequent, initial result as well.

He fell asleep eventually and awoke to the sound of wind rustling through the bushes outside the window.

They had a late breakfast and Sam again chose to warm up at Ladyburn rather than face the crowds, intensity, cloying claustrophobia, and nerve wracking spectacle of *The Open* practice area.

They arrived at the course at 12.30p.m and, after the normal formalities of signing in, Sam wandered aimlessly onto the putting green in readiness for his second round.

He constantly looked all around him and found very gradually and slowly he was beginning to adjust to this amazing, intimidating but sparkling carnival of golf.

The stands were only steel and boards, his opponents only flesh and blood and the crowds, television and media? Well they were not in any way there to see him!

He could relax and enjoy the experience with his son; as he studied the scoreboard crammed with fabulous names he seriously doubted if he would actually even be able to make the cut.

He'd done well, that was the main thing, he'd tried and who could really have expected him to achieve any more than he had already?

His name was called at 2.03p.m precisely and, as he'd done the day before, he hit a perfectly executed shot into the heart and middle of the 1st fairway.

Sam noticed that the wind that had been so strong in the early morning had faded a little, and he sensed and understood that he would have the advantage of the best of the playing conditions this particular afternoon.

He was extraordinarily, unusually relaxed all of a sudden and played sublimely; every shot clipped and precise with each swing shape pure or perfect.

He combined a couple of tortuous, short, missed putts with an occasional longer more successful effort and, after dropping another shot on the 17th, arrived at the 18th tee, 1 under par.

Sam had monitored the scoreboards all day and was aware that the conditions in the morning had raised the qualifying score slightly; he needed a birdie down the last to be sure of making the *36 hole* cut and getting in.

He hit a powerful, long drive 40 yards from the green and as his feet walked over the famous *Swilkan Burn* bridge, he pondered and wondered if this was to be his final hole of the tournament?

Again strangely, he was no longer nervous and he settled over his ball then pitched to *6 feet* confidently, in a pure, simple motion of timing and rhythm.

Finally, he crouched behind the putt unsure if the ball was going to move on the grain and after his partners had finished, he bent down once again directly over this vital shot.

He tried to settle, kept his body still and initially felt a sweet contact but looked up quickly to see the forever annoying, spherical object, break right, spin around the hole, resting tantalisingly and diabolically above ground.

He looked at his son but the boy's focus was elsewhere and, after tapping in, Sam completed the cards and handed his into the recorders.

As he expected there seemed to be endless amounts of players who had scored better than him and he placed his arm around his child's shoulders as if to comfort and console him.

"Never mind, Oliver… we did our best."

The boy shrugged his thin shoulders in transparent, reflexive temper and apparent annoyance.

"There's the 10 shot rule…"

His words were angry and spoken aggressively.

"…Let's wait and see what happens to the leader!"

Sam looked again at the scores and realised that his son was once again correct; Tom Janners a new, youthful, American name and rising star was 12 under and was now on the 16th hole.

He was leading by 3 and if he slipped up at all Sam would qualify!

They both sat on the parched, grass bank behind the green and watched the drama unfolding before them on an enormous television screen by the side of the stands.

The golfing centre of their attentions negotiated the 16th in par and Oliver breathed in nervous frustration as he hit a perfect drive down the treacherous 17th hole.

His second was a 6 or 7 iron that seemed to start at the pin then, as if captured and gathered by a sudden gust of the demonic, local wind, disappeared and dramatically plugged into the dreaded and terrifying, *Hell Bunker*!

Oliver watched as if transfixed; Tom Jenner's first effort only succeeded in raising the ball out of its indentation and his next two attempts hit the beautiful but towering, sadistic layers of peat forming the bunker bank then rolled quietly but infuriatingly back to his feet.

He then escaped onto the road with his next shot and after scrabbling eventually onto the green, he left the hole with a 9 and a face that matched the darkening, thunderous skies above him.

Oliver's hand formed into the fighting gesture of a fist.

"We're in…we're in!"

The final matches were concluded with the boy proven correct and Sam was given a time with the early starters and so called *dawn chorus* on the 3rd day and round.

He was due out at 7.15a.m and as Sam looked down the list, freshly pinned to the player's notice board, he had to blink twice in disbelief; he was out with Paul Sandy his nemesis from his junior days!

Sam was content but Oliver walked off the course privately seething; he had watched in increasing frustration his father play wonderfully and score ordinarily if not in all honesty, poorly.

The boy tried to be fair and dispassionate but as he watched the skill and the style of all the other competitors he knew truly and without prejudice, his Dad was indeed better than anyone he had yet seen.

He looked at the scores on the boards and compared them to his father's and tried to work out why he was so far behind when he had played so exquisitely well.

The dropped shot on the 17th and the missed put on the 18th seemed to bring with it a dramatic realisation; his Dad almost and actually wanted to fail as perhaps he honestly and truly didn't suppose or believe he could go any further.

Oliver was mad, furious and as he watched his parent smug with satisfaction after qualifying purely on the strength on Mr Jenner's disaster, he tried his best to keep his feelings just to himself.

He did still accept and recognise that he was, but a child, after all!

The two of them sat in silence in the car as his father phoned his mother excitedly, almost congratulating himself and revelling in his *wondrous* achievement on qualifying.

The boy spoke to her briefly and pretended to be interested as she mentioned that she thought she had seen them vaguely and very briefly on television somewhere walking up one of the holes before she blew a kiss then rang off.

Oliver's intelligent eyes watched in irritation as Sam smiled and his flushed lips whistled softly as he turned to innocently ask him if they should go to Ladyburn in the very early morning to practice?

Suddenly something inside the young man's little mind, violently exploded and snapped like a dry, brittle twig.

"What for...?"

His irascibility and anger was out and released, like a crazy, wild animal running riot and utterly out of control.

"...So we can play with no one watching? So we can hide from the crowds and the cameras...?

The words were deeply sarcastic, caustic and bitter.

"...What for...what for...?"

Sam was stunned to silence but the cork of his son's emotional bottle had been removed and popped, allowing the child's frustrations to simply pour and literally flood out onto the self satisfied, easy plains of his father's life and recent tepid and pale achievement.

"...You act as if you've done... *so very well...* "

He was *droll* and trembling in real fury.

"...I've watched all of these professionals and you're miles better than any of them...!"

Oliver could not look at him at all.

"… And I'm not saying that because I'm a, *sweet, cute, little boy…*!"

He spat furiously in a mock, sarcastic voice as if to impersonate all the endless people that had teased him over that last few days and he muttered with diabolical insight.

"…You didn't want to qualify… you wanted to be safe, comfortable… **Invisible**…!"

He was a whirlwind and there was nowhere for Sam to shelter as the tempest raged ever onward around him.

"…You've actually played fantastic… at the biggest tournament in the world and nobody…*bloody well noticed…*!"

His voice began to falter and his eyes glazed over but spoke his heart at what he felt, and had suffered and witnessed.

"…You scored badly because you were uncomfortable with really trying… going beyond …"

He was endlessly frustrated and exasperated.

"…I don't know the words, Dad…you did what you always tell me *not* to do…not to be half hearted….try with all your soul and mind as…you always say to me…but…"

Sam listened and his son's words, *his* actual former words, were scathing, scalding and burning him.

"...*You* didn't...*you* didn't at all!"

Oliver felt the tears well up in his eyes and he stared glassy eyed out of the window and whispered a final, injurious time.

"I believe in you Dad, but..."

He bit his tongue and lip as if he had gone too far and exhaled before he entered a cocoon of sullen silence.

"...But... it's like you don't believe in yourself!"

Sam was utterly shaken and completely stunned; he just drove on without a sound in shock and trauma not knowing how to react or reply; he went to speak and make a meaningful response but he realised that he had absolutely nothing at all to say.

His son's words revolved in his always struggling, turbulent mind; had he wanted and succeeded in being *invisible* at the biggest tournament in the world whilst playing the best golf of his life?

Had he; was that true?

Why had he preferred to drive to Ladyburn to practice?

He'd felt uncomfortable, out of place at *The Open*....that was why!

Why had he not scored better?

The answer was difficult to face but he knew precisely what it was.

He had been and felt *safe* at level par he could appear to have done well without really committing himself; the truth of his child's words, spoken in such heated anger and infuriation hit home, unsettled and upset him to his very spiritual centre and soul.

Oliver was right, in some strange way he was more contented with not qualifying; he was scared of the intensive glare of the spotlight and the true, sore, painful exposure and full test of his golfing ability.

It was true; his son knew him better than he understood himself and what he had picked up on and alluded to, was indeed factual or spot on.

Sam withdrew inside himself as he felt a charlatan; he had realised after the 2nd qualifying that he needed to find something extra inside himself to propel him to that next level of golf experience and excellence, but maybe in truth it was beyond him.

Flatter to deceive, the words always bounced around his head and tortured him forever; maybe it was always to be, how his golfing life was permanently meant to be for him.

He'd appeared to go further with his son than he'd achieved by himself but Oliver was correct; it was tasteless, insufficient, insipid, bland and simply not enough.

Suddenly what they had accomplished was not adequate for them both!

Sam and Oliver had still not spoken further, even after reaching the boarding house and after changing they sat around Mrs Mackay's table in cold, stony silence.

From his vantage point of the far table the aged man from the previous night jovially asked how they had fared today and Sam informed him that they had just made the cut as he then replied pointedly and jovially.

"Tiger's, 10 under…"

The stranger gazed teasingly and what he thought was amusingly at Oliver, and Sam watched his son's, soft eyes blaze ever more furiously.

"...Do you still think your Dad's going to win?"

Sam focussed his full attention on him and his own, blue spheres had an icy steel and coldness that he'd long forgotten.

"No, Sir..."

His tone was acid and frozen and his words enunciated clearly, meaningfully and frostily.

"...His, *Dad* thinks he's going to win...!"

He provided his most searching, disconcerting stare.

"...Is there anything wrong with that?"

The man caught the chill and tension in Sam's voice and withdrew hastily.

"No, I'm sure you're right, Sir..."

His focus returned to his meal and he quickly finished and ended the already tenuous conversation.

"...Best of luck to you!"

Oliver stared up at his father and Sam sensed the trace of a smile on his fraught, tight lips, he winked at his son and the boy responded in kind; they were a team again and Sam was tremendously relieved.

As they lay in bed that night Sam spoke softly to him about the incident in the car for the first time.

"You were right, Oliver…what you said…all of it…"

He sighed in his own private, inner turmoil.

"…Somehow I have not committed myself fully; but it is hard to give everything you've got…"

Sam recognised that facing his insecurities and eternal demons to attempt, conquer and beat them was so tortuous and difficult for him.

"….I don't know if I can do it."

Oliver snuggled into his pillow and sighed tiredly.

"Dad I just want you to give it your best shot, you played so fantastically well today…"

He shook himself as if to release any rare and hidden discontentment he had remaining from his young, slender body.

"… I know you've done well, to a point… but…you're so *bloody good*… please…just chill…give yourself a chance!"

Sam nestled into the softness of the mattress and his busy head thought fleetingly about

Paul Sandy and the early morning appointment.

"I'll try Oliver, I promise…I've listened to what you've told me…and I agree…. I'll try my very best."

Oliver was already asleep and Sam slumbered lightly, the obligation to be up early played on his subconscious as he awoke with a start; he looked at the clock, it was 5.15a.m and already time to move.

His spectacular son was still dormant and Sam looked out of the window and drunk in the amazing beauty of the early morning.

The sky was clear and bright and there was a trace of red on the far horizon that seemed to illuminate the ocean, casting a full, heavenly blended mixture of intensely bright and dark colours.

He sensed movement beside him and looked down as his child gazed out with him and purposefully rubbed his eyes.

"It's beautiful, Dad, just beautiful…"

He smiled in positivity and engagement.

"….Let's make this a perfect day."

Sam ruffled his boy's matted hair and they quickly washed and changed before quietly walking downstairs so not to wake the sleeping house.

"Good morning, Sam and Oliver…"

Mrs Mackay had spoken sharply from the dining room causing them both to jump; she laughed at their surprise in seeing her.

"…Ye dinda' think Ah'd forget mah two favourite guests…?"

Her voice, as always, was so amused and energetic.

"…Especially on such an important day, now ye both sit yerselves down…"

Sam was truly amazed at the woman; her energy and good humour seemed boundless and as normal she fed and dispatched them from the house as if they were her own family.

Sam tried to express his appreciation but the old woman just waved him aside in her normal self deprecating way as she joked endlessly.

"…Ah kin charge ye double fur early mornings!"

It was 6a.m when they left the house and, given the unusually empty roads, 6.15a.m when they arrived at the course.

They signed in promptly and Sam walked over to the practice range taking the most prominent spot he could find as if to make a point to himself, as he then warmed up expertly by going through his full compliment of clubs.

He felt vital and alive, his swing was grooved and balanced and, as his final practice drive soared towards a far distant marker, he knew that his game was ultimately honed and toned to perfection.

Oliver was yet to change his shoes and whilst his father practised on the putting green he ran into the clubhouse then into the locker room where his crumpled note from the Secretary still provided him access.

He sat on the wooden bench and started to slip on his shoes, unnoticed to the two men just opposite and to the side of him who started conversing acerbically and somewhat loudly.

One of the men wore a black, *Titliest* peak cap and the other man had mousy brown hair and the most intense, piercing, green eyes he had ever witnessed or seen.

The stranger in the hat mumbled casually to his companion.

"Who are you playing with, Paul?"

The man answered softly and with a more than a trace of nasty sarcasm

"Sam Chester...we used to call him *Scabby, Sam*..."

He laughed maliciously and cruelly.

"...In our amateur days!"

The man enquired but Oliver could tell he was not really interested.

"Is he still an amateur?"

The man with the wicked, evil eyes shrugged.

"I suppose so... he never could cut it at the top level..."

His lips formed a warped, dry grin.

"...He must have missed a few holes out to get this far; his nerves normally would have given up by now..."

He rose up and stretched his arms out high above him as if to try to loosen his muscles.

"...I always had the old *Indian Sign* over him, but..."

He sighed dramatically and spitefully.

"... I suppose I'll have to be nice and pretend to reminisce fondly about old times!"

The man in the dark hat shook his head in a theatrical display of empathy and concern for him.

"Poor you, Paul..."

The two of them were so incredibly crude, rude and patronising as they commented disrespectfully and sarcastically on his father as if in one spiteful mind.

"...Out with the *no-hopers!*"

The man with the malevolent eyes moved his shoulders up and down a final time as if in recognition of the day's obligation; Oliver shrunk back and secretly watched him leave then felt his whole body shaking with virulent fire, indignation and anger.

He realised the man was Paul Sandy as he recognised him from the television; instinctively he wanted to tell his father what he'd said but knew it would only distract him.

They'd show him; the pompous pig!

Oliver joined his Dad shortly afterwards and

Sam thought he detected something in his son's flushed and emotionally charged face but when he enquired, Oliver just murmured calmly and coolly.

"No, Dad I'm fine…"

With some effort he smiled happily, simply to try and ensure he would settle his father ever more.

"….Just a bit nervous!"

Sam stroked his arm reassuringly and rolled another 6 *foot* putt perfectly off the smooth, metal face of his club and into the hole.

"I'll try not to let you down, Oliver, I promise."

They were waiting on the 1st tee when Paul Sandy walked on, and he falsely and insincerely marched over to Sam then exaggeratedly and vigorously shook his hand.

"Hello, Sam, lovely to see you again, how are you?"

Sam replied happily and introduced his *manager* and precious child to him.

"I'm fine…this is my son, Oliver, Paul…he's my caddy."

His former, arch-rival looked down at the little

boy; *how quaint*, his devious, duplicitous, colourful gaze seemed to say and Oliver shook the hand he offered weakly so not to make a fuss.

Paul Sandy then continued his routine of twisting and stretching his seemingly unbalanced body and muttered as he did so.

"You've done exceptionally well, Sam to qualify… to get this far…well done…"

He murmured on, lost in his own supercilious, bloated ego as he continued.

"….Irrespective of what happens today you are to be congratulated."

Sam looked at him coldly and understood the underlying message in his remark; that he had no right to be there, he had never been good enough to match him or any of these talented, tour professionals

His blue eyes hardened and he looked directly at the concentration and determination etched in his son's face and it further strengthened his mind, head and more importantly his heart.

He was good enough, he was confident, primed and ready; this was his moment and time, and no petty, demeaning or shabby, mental trick or game from an old adversary was going to influence or divert his prime purpose and quest.

Not any more!

Chapter 26

"On the tee, Sam Chester..."

The familiar announcement came and Sam walked determinedly to the centre of the specified, unseen line between the two, white markers either side of the manicured surface and surveyed the beautiful, green course stretching out scenically before him.

He bent down and delicately placed his ball on a short, white, tee peg, then stood behind his intended shot and swung his arms then shoulders, balancing the club gently and easily in his fingers.

Sam closed his eyes almost involuntarily and reached deep down inside himself; he was going to discover that missing, final piece of the jigsaw needed to compete at this level and he was going to find it, today!

He looked at his hands, they were still, calm and they had a softness and quality that reminded him of the old *Maestro*; Sam understood he somehow had to control his thoughts and emotions but he knew that was no mean task.

The starter looked in his direction as if to encourage him to play but Sam stood up to the ball and tried to simply imagine that his mind and body were in perfect harmony.

Suddenly and almost miraculously it became clear to him; he had to play the round in his formerly, mixed-up head; his swing shape dictated the shot, his normally unreliable mind controlled his swing.

It was…simple and easy!

He settled then focussed his brain, solely and purely on his plane shape and rhythm; he swung, felt a wonderful strike and looked up to see the ball soaring far down the centre of the distant fairway.

Sam then hardly noticed his opponent's hit as he walked down the middle of the greenery and the already bustling course.

He withdrew further and almost completely

inside himself as his world became only the white ball, each separate shot then subsequent hole; his mind of course, controlling every shape and precise rhythm of the swing and timing needed or required.

Everything that had previously and always been a distraction suddenly became out of focus; the stands, pressure or spectators were just blurs of colour or sensation and even the constant noise, just a low hum.

His second shot pitched *10 feet* behind the pin and because of the perfect contact and early morning moisture, drew back to *4 feet*.

Sam waited for Paul Sandy to make a safe par then crouched down behind the ball; he could see the line clearly, just left lip, and as he stood over his stroke, had a strange, eerie, almost ethereal sensation of raw confidence surging through his body.

The ball rolled then span perfectly into the cup and Sam did not even hear the applause from the emerging, thronging, early morning spectators; he was already thinking about his next drive from the teeing area nearby.

Sam played two perfect shots on the 2nd and a *10 foot* putt, gave him another birdie; he gained safe pars on the next 2 holes and at the long 5th he hit a towering 3 iron to *15 feet*.

The putt was struck firmly and Sam watched as it hugged the contours of the green and, as if responding to just his will alone, disappeared into the hole for an eagle 3!

On the 6th tee, he was still composed and unnaturally, completely calm; safe within his own mental world he was not aware or even conscious of his rapid climb up the leader board.

He picked up a further 2 birdies at the 8th and 9th and he turned at 6 under par for the day; all he could think about was the coming hole, the next shot and was wholly oblivious to any distractions.

Sam drove the 10th for another birdie, found the centre of the 11th for a par and turned for home at the 12th, 7 under par.

Oliver walked with him silently and almost disbelievingly; he was enraptured and captivated by his father's play and, the bag pressing onto his delicate shoulders felt like a feather with the surge of the adrenaline pulsating around his fired blood infusing him with strength.

For the first time in his young life he truly began to get anxious and nervous as if initially sensing and comprehending the level and wonderment of his Dad's performance.

Given his father's sensitive temperament, Oliver tried to ensure that his face did not portray his tentative emotions, but as Sam Chester's name was raised near the top on each of the huge scoreboards it was difficult for him to ignore or take in his short, youthful stride.

But the boy need not have worried, as Sam strolled down the 12th, he was still deep in his own world and the course strangely and mysteriously seemed to be part of him.

His feet appeared to draw self belief, reassurance and energy from the soft, luxurious, grass surface; it held him, steadied him as if he was merely a boat on a perfectly still lake, centred and calm.

Sam gained his par at the next 2 holes then a wonderful drive and a 3 wood set up yet another birdie on the long 14th and Oliver muttered silently under his heated, shortened breath as the putt went down.

"8 under...8 under!"

The 15th yielded another par and after a superb threaded iron through the bunkers at the 16th, the pitch almost went into the hole and Sam looked out over the corner on the 17th, 9 under par!

Sam was still absolutely, mentally separated from his spectacular play and he placed his drive over the corner of the road hole perfectly with just a trace of fade.

His 7 iron found the right corner of the green with 2 putts giving him a par; sanctuary and safety from the assorted perils of the troublesome and dangerous hole that was always waiting maliciously, like a large, evil spider, with a pretty, sticky web to attract and punish the unwary fly!

Oliver had noticed that since the 8th, the crowds around their game were becoming enormous as the television cameras seemed to be fixed on them and were literally, everywhere.

He was amazed that his father did not notice; the roars for a birdie from the crowd were acknowledged with no more than a slight smile and wave and he seemed so confident and assured.

It was just not like him at all!

As Sam hit another huge drive up the short 18th he clearly saw that his Dad's blue eyes were withdrawn and glacially, crystal cold.

In all truth, Sam knew he was doing well but he was completely nerveless and desensitised; as he stood over his short pitch up the *Valley of Sin* leading to the 18th green he still mentally only pictured his shape and perfect rhythm.

As if in response to the way Sam had imagined the shot in his mind, the ball checked into the slope, slowed and with only just enough energy, reached the top of the rise then settled a mere few inches from the cup at the culmination and completion of the round.

The crowds were still forming in the huge stands - Sam's game had been one of the first out - and as he tapped the ball in for another final birdie the spectators applauded and he suddenly saw his name standing proudly at the top of the leader board high above him.

He had gone around in 62, 10 under par for the day and 11 under par for the tournament; he was leading, and he looked at the scoreboard again and seemed to wake up from some sort of unreal, mystical trance.

Sam Chester's name was at the top, *his name*; he was impossibly leading *The British Open*!

Sam raised his arm for the first time that day and with the round safely over and finished, afforded himself the luxury of acknowledging the warm, spontaneous, loud applause from all around the 18th green.

Slowly the world began to come back into focus and colour as he handed Paul Sandy his card for a modest 74 then signed it; in return his playing companion quietly checked Sam's 62 and placed his scrawled signature at the bottom.

He whispered limply and meekly without a trace of generosity, pleasure or sincerity.

"Well done...good score...well done, Sam!"

They handed the cards into the officials in the caravan where Sam was congratulated and asked urgently to attend the press room where the world's media were waiting to hear about his amazing performance and feat of golf.

It appeared that he was suddenly big news.

Oliver slipped quietly into the changing room to remove his golf shoes and there in front of him was, Paul Sandy, his green eyes, pale, dull and defeated and his shoulder's sunk and shallow.

The boy could not help or prevent himself speaking; the conversation of the early morning still rattled and stung his mind and his innate sense of decency and fair play.

"Let me tell you something, Mr Sandy..."

His tone was quiet but pointed and barbed as the man looked up at him shocked and in some confusion.

"...My Dad's a better player and a better person than you'll ever be..."

He finished his sentence in a flash of petulant anger and annoyance with this horrible, self absorbed grown up.

"...And by the way..."

His hazel eyes were wild and fearless.

"....He never missed any holes out in the qualifying...!"

Paul Sandy looked up at him at if he'd been slapped and he immediately realised that the boy must have overheard his earlier conversation; he was understandably mortified and ashamed so remaining muted and silent as his verbal thrashing concluded.

"...My Dad's a winner, whether he wins or not, in future..."

He rose up in a flourish with his shoes changed and ready to leave.

"...Keep your lousy, miserable opinions to yourself!"

He stormed off with his small body tense, as if he was about to go into battle, just as his father walked into the changing room; Sam had caught the very end of his son's conversation and he saw his past, all achieving, conquering opponent, as if for the very first time that day.

The man looked tired, old and defeated; he'd won an *Open* many moons ago, had some success but his childless marriage had failed and, as with the unpredictable and capricious nature of the game of golf, it had given him a little but extracted a lot.

In that moment he felt strangely sorry for him; Sam had his sons and the future...and Paul Sandy?

He had his fading glory and little else but the monotony of an unyielding and unfeeling, golf circus where he would try forever to recapture some fleeting, but lost talent.

It was like some sporting hell and damnation; a golfing purgatory from which there seemed no escape and, in that instant, Sam was thankful that he had followed his own path a long time ago and taken control and direction of his life.

He changed his shoes, put his arm gently around his son and guided and led him out of the locker room.

"Come on, Oliver..."

He whispered respectfully as if for the people no longer in the world of the living.

"... Let's leave, Mr Sandy alone, I think he's had more than enough for one morning!"

There was a short walk towards the large, white, press tent and as Sam passed throngs of competitors and spectators he was literally and physically overwhelmed with handshakes and congratulations.

It was only just past 1p.m and the leaders from the previous day were yet to go out.

Oliver looked out to sparkling sea and the far horizon where there was a faint appearance and trace of a grey cloud and his apparent gift of prediction came to the fore once again.

"I think the good conditions are going to turn this afternoon, Dad...I can feel it..."

He smiled and laughed gleefully as if he actually knew what *schadenfreude* meant; but he instinctively understood and sensed the rest of the field were about to endure then suffer the turn in the weather.

"...It's a good job you played this morning!"

As if in response to his son's premonition, Sam noticed the flags that had been so tranquil and still high above them on the poles, start to gently unfurl; they were beginning to easily twist and flutter in the gathering, quickening air.

He began to realise that if the wind did start to truly blow, the late starters would be at a serious disadvantage.

Sam was guided through an open leaf in the tent by one of the officials, a tall, lean man with wispy hair on the sides of his unusually, egg shaped, bald dome of a head.

Like all the organisers he was polite, efficient and proudly wore a bright red rosette; he led them up a small flight of steps and out onto a raised, wooden rostrum where they sat on the small, comfortable chairs provided for the use of the players in contention or the news.

Sam looked out in front of him and held his breath; there were row after row of reporters with cameras facing him and although he expected an interview, he immediately realised this was not to be the gentle grilling he had once received at Hoylake.

Oliver shuffled in his seat next to him and Sam heard his son whistle in disbelief quietly under his breath as he whispered.

"Blimey, Dad...there's so many people in here!"

Sam had no time to enter a discussion with his boy, an arm was raised and the buzz of conversation immediately died down; a friendly voice seemed to float out of a sea of faces and bright lights.

"Well done, Sam..."

He was slightly taken aback when the whole room reflexively clapped and applauded and sat wedged into his seat in a daze as the noise resonated then faded allowing the stranger to continue on.

"...Justin Harris, Times Sport; this must be quite a shock for you...leading *The Open*?"

Sam breathed in, gathering his thoughts as he did so, and then replied quietly.

"It is, Sir...I just had one of those days."

Another voice rang out.

"Dennis Timms, The Sun... you're the man, or should I say, the boy that beat Jerry Pate at Hoylake all those years ago...?"

Sam nodded; he was surprised that it took a full two questions before his only previous international feat was recalled and listened as the questioner carried on jokingly.

"Where've you been?"

There was a ripple of amusement that went around the assembled audience and Sam sensed that they were genuinely pleased for him; this was quite an unexpected story as he well realised, and he slowly started to smile and relax.

They were excited and engaged for him; on his side and instinctively he could tell as he responded engagingly.

"I've been busy having a life... getting married, two children, in fact my wife gave birth to a son only a couple of days ago."

He saw the man scribble down something and then start talking urgently into a mobile phone and another voice called out.

"Take us through the round, Sam!"

Sam patiently recalled his score, hole by hole and talked through each and every shot in whatever detail was required until the reporters were happy that they had captured the precise information, emotion and essence of his remarkable round and result.

"Will you turn professional?"

Sam shook his head slowly to the query as he had not even contemplated such a huge step and responded thoughtfully.

"I don't think so…that was never my intention."

A slim man with curly, black hair stood up and raised his pen.

"Derek Lawrenson, Daily Mail… what *was* your intention when you entered Sam, I understand that until recently, you haven't played for *years*?"

Sam went to answer but then heard the distinct and gentle voice of his son cut into the room like a knife through proverbial butter.

"Because *I* asked him to…"

Oliver spoke loudly but innocently to a suddenly enrapt and immediately silent audience.

"…I found his old scrap book and… dreamt he could win *The Open*….told him he would!"

The room exploded into a crescendo of questions and the official raised his large hands for decorum.

"Please Gentlemen, one at a time!"

Oliver suddenly took centre stage; he confirmed that he was the youngest ever, official caddy, recalled his fantastical idea then quest for his father's glory and, after overcoming his initial nervousness at being in the spotlight, soon had the hardened, press pack eating out of his slender, delicate hands.

He responded to the obvious question with blind confidence.

"Yes, of course his father was going to win!"

Another more pointed query came.

"What about, *Tiger*?"

Then a further voice called out and Sam placed his arm around the boy as if realising that it was a little early to celebrate and there was a certain amount of joviality, disbelief or even amusement developing in this spontaneous interrogation.

"We'll see, Gentlemen…"

Sam addressed them all politely and brightly.

"…But please allow my Son…and me… to enjoy the dream for the day….please!"

Eventually the inquisition receded and after innumerable posed photographs of father and son for every conceivable newspaper, they were allowed to retreat back towards the relative privacy and obscurity of the clubhouse.

Sam placed the clubs into the boot of the car and watched as the competitors continued to march relentlessly onwards off the 1st tee and finish down on the 18th green.

The sparse, grey clouds had by now multiplied many fold and hovered menacingly over the course; the numerous, bright flags were now wailing and beating ever more visibly to the wind coming ferociously and fiercely off the sea.

Sam walked back towards the clubhouse; they were hungry and the refreshment tent was calling out to them but a pretty girl with cropped blonde hair stopped them and spoke entreatingly.

"Diana James…BBC, would you come and give us an interview?"

Sam shook his head respectfully.

"I wanted to get my son something to eat."

The eager, insistent girl waved his excuse away frivolously and dismissively.

"We'll take care of that, Mr Chester, follow me."

Sam and Oliver were led through a small, green tunnel of scaffolding and canvas and into the central core and heart of the television centre.

The attractive, blonde, young lady gave instruction to another assistant and almost instantly a tray of tea, orange juice and sandwiches appeared as if by magic.

Sam poured himself a drink then took a bite out of an appetising cheese and tomato treat; he was still ravenously eating when a door opened and a familiar face appeared and the man attached to it, extended his chubby hand in genuine delight.

"Peter Alliss…"

He whispered emotively and warmly.

"…And may I say what a pleasure it was to watch your round today, My Lad…a terrific performance…!"

Sam nearly choked on his mouthful of delicious food and the dark-haired commentator waved his wrists at him disarmingly and patiently.

"…Finish off…then come upstairs and let's have a little, *private* chat for the public…"

The famous presenter walked up to, Oliver,

shook his hand and smiled equally engagingly.

"...And we want to see you as well, Young Man, naturally!"

Oliver munched his lunch as if undaunted or unfazed by the attention and his mind took it all in so straightforwardly and calmly; *of course he was to be interviewed as well* his mind meandered and seemed to say, *naturally...of course*!

They were soon seated in the cramped, television studio where the bright, hot lights burned into them; Sam had seen this room many times from the comfort of his own home but it looked so different, provocative and colourful in real life.

The red lights went on and suddenly they were live on national television, Peter Alliss gave a short introduction to the fact that Sam Chester, an unknown, amateur golfer was leading, *The British Open* and then mischievously focussed his attention on, Oliver.

"I understand this is all your fault, Young Man, isn't it...?"

Oliver blinked anxiously and the camera picked up every sense of his youth, innocence and naivety.

Peter Alliss continued, and his mock, stern expression changed into a resonant chuckle and a laugh.

"...I understand you had a dream, My Lad?"

Oliver smiled and relaxed; the man had been joking and teasing him which was a game he knew well and he nodded in happy confirmation!

"Yes... I dreamt my Dad was going to win *The Open*!"

Peter Allis was instantly delighted with him.

"And here you are, Oliver, what do you think now?"

Oliver looked outside at the gathering gloom then at his father's name still at the top of the leader board and he looked cheekily at the old interviewer under his large, brown eyelashes.

"We've got a better chance now... than we had when we started!"

Peter Alliss laughed, markedly enjoying the young man's cheeky and sparky, confident response; it was marvellous television.

"That you have, Oliver...that you have!"

He then turned to Sam and showed him

various high points of his round on the television monitor while Sam looked at himself in awe and genuine surprise; it was as though he was watching someone else.

He'd never seen himself on video and as he watched the edited highlights of his play, he couldn't help but marvel at some of the shots and how they had transposed themselves to the small screen.

The older man picked up the trace and sense of his wonder.

"Sam…how do you feel?"

Sam smiled at the celebrity interviewer uncertainly and cautiously.

"I'm not sure, Peter, happy but strange…it is for sure, more than a little overwhelming."

Peter Allis then took him through a range of questions about the round, some of his amateur career, including Jerry Pate and then, as Sam had seen him do so many times, throw in the final, killer question right at the end.

"So…can you win it, Sam…?"

He glanced outside at the bleak, mucky clouds.

"…The wind is getting up, all the leaders seem

to be struggling and… you might be leading at the end of the day…"

His eyes were dark, intense and deadly serious.

"…Can you actually win it?"

Sam looked at him blankly as if the question was unreasonable but there was only one round to go and inexplicably, somehow out of the blue, the dream was suddenly more than that now.

His head span privately for a moment; *it was possible, was it really, truly, possible*?

"I just don't know Peter, I can only try my best."

Peter Allis returned his attention to Oliver, who had spent the last few minutes looking around the small studio aimlessly, and asked him the same question with the equivalent, comparable force.

"Can your Dad win it, Oliver?"

The boy fixed him with his bright, trusting, hazel eyes and spoke softly and with the beginning of tiredness, as the adrenaline was rapidly being exhausted and running out.

"Of course my Dad will win…!"

His face remained a glowing picture and he spoke words about the future, as if his prediction in itself was enough to make it come true.

"…He's the best and… I dreamed he would!"

Peter Alliss smiled; he'd got the answer he wanted as he looked directly into the lens with his familiar twinkle and a trace of blue in his famous eye.

"Well we've heard it from the horse's mouth… Oliver's Dad, Sam Chester an unknown amateur from Lancaster is going to win the *Open Championship* tomorrow…"

He smiled slyly and his full face was gleeful and merry.

"…And we all wish him the very best of luck…!"

The cameras blinked off and the transmission went live back to the course where somebody had just holed a bunker shot for a birdie.

Peter Alliss went over to Sam and Oliver and shook both of their hands heartily and with real enthusiasm for their fantastical adventure.

"…Well done again…and I genuinely wish you every joy for tomorrow; I'll be rooting for you!"

Sam thanked him for his kindness and departed from the studio in readiness to leave the course for the day; the attention was becoming overpowering and he started to feel the need to have a break.

As he reached the bottom of the steps, Sam found his path blocked by an uptight, young man with light, sandy hair and a broad, American accent.

"Mr Chester…?"

His voice was whiney and grating.

"…Joe Thomas, ABC Sport; may we take a minute of your time?"

Sam looked at him pleadingly. "

"We're tired, Joe can…?"

He was persistent; this was his job and the players needed to co-operate in this difficult business of golf.

"Please, Mr Chester, we've a surprise for you; it will not take long."

Sam shrugged, realised he was under an obligation to the competition and followed the man through yet another maze of television rooms and then up some metal steps and finally into another tiny, illuminated studio.

There was an American presenter in a bright, yellow shirt and a slight, gaunt man with thinning blonde hair waiting for them.

The presenter introduced himself.

"I'm, Danny Thomas…sit down, Sam and Oliver, please…"

He took his breath and smiled.

"…Bit rushed, sorry…just answer a few points for the viewers please…we're live coast to coast in 10…9 seconds…"

Sam felt a small microphone being fitted to his shirt and the same item attached to Oliver; the presenter then brushed back his wavy, black hair smiled into the camera and listened as a voice out of the brightness counted down. "…3, 2, 1…we'…re go…and… live!"

The broadcaster began to burst into animation with sudden enthusiasm and gusto.

"Good morning…"

He continued loudly in an American, *smiley* voice.

"…Welcome to the 3rd round of the *British Open* where we've had a sensation. The leader in the clubhouse is an unknown amateur called, Sam Chester and the way the afternoon rounds and weather's going…he could well be leading going into the last day…."

He laughed, took a breath and continued.

"…We've got Sam and his boy, Oliver… who's the youngest caddy in the history of the championships with us…"

He turned theatrically and waved his arm at them.

"… Well done, Sam…say hello to all the folks in the USA…"

Sam smiled into the convex, refractive glass once more and felt slightly uncomfortable as it focussed on him and then his son, as the man rambled energetically on,

"You must feel great, Sam?"

He replied tiredly.

"I do, Danny!"

The man asked him what was expected and he answered pretty much the same questions posed by Peter Allis as spontaneously as he could the second time around.

Finally, as if in summation, his temporary host

posed to him an unusual, unexpected, innocent query.

"Have you ever had anything happen before like this?"

Sam had no wish to rake up his faded, past, amateur success; it seemed so insignificant and petty compared to the enormity of his present accomplishment and feat.

"No…not really!"

He felt he was being fulsome and honest but the presenter looked at him and gave him a mock, staged, disbelieving look.

"Sam, I've got someone here that can dispute that!"

The silent, sallow man beside him suddenly came to prominence and life, looked teasingly into the camera and spoke softly.

"I seem to remember an extravagant putt at Hoylake that caused a bit of an international commotion."

The man's face instantly emitted a rich, warm smile, in a split second, 25 years disappeared and Sam realised who he was sitting next to and gasped in surprise.

"Jerry…Jerry Pate…!"

Sam forgot all about the cameras, gripped the man's hand excitedly and firmly then smiled broadly, as if full of newly discovered energy.

"How are you, Jerry…it's been so long."

He held his fingers tightly as the man answered him poignantly.

"But it seems like yesterday… doesn't it?"

Sam nodded and relaxed in his seat while Danny explained to the viewers the events that transpired all that time ago.

"Sam beat our own Jerry in the British Amateur when he was just 17 years old and when Jerry had just won the US Amateur."

The former US Open Champion nodded and spoke his piece.

"I had a hard time in the UK those two weeks but I thought I'd beaten, Sam… when he holed this monster putt on the 17th…"

He shook his head and laughed out loud.

"… I've never forgotten it!"

Sam was genuinely surprised.

"Oh, I thought you would have…with all your other victories, I was just lucky…that day"

His partially blonde head nodded.

"You were, Sam…but I remember it…because somehow the match had something special about it… something memorable and even though I lost…"

He smiled and chuckled once more in his reminiscence.

"… It was fantastic to be a part of!"

Danny the commentator interrupted their shared memories.

"Gentlemen …can we get back to today!"

His lairy focus was on Sam once more.

"Can you win…or will the pressure be too much? It would be too onerous for most professionals… never mind an amateur?"

Sam proffered a disarming smile.

"Danny…I have absolutely no idea, it's all a bit of a conundrum and a puzzle at the moment…we will see."

The presenter then melodramatically asked his companion.

"Jerry...what do you think?"

His old adversary shrugged happily.

"Why not, Danny...why not? He beat me and he sure played fantastic today, I hope he does!"

The interviewer saved his best query till last, and murmured to the obviously tired child sitting exhaustedly, almost drifting into a doze by his father.

"And finally to this, Young Man; what do you think, Oliver...can your Dad actually win it?"

The boy came back to life suddenly as if on stage again; he leaned on his arm and wrist until it was supporting his chin and looked as though he was considering the question earnestly.

He made compulsive almost magical viewing and television!

His mother had always taught him always to be polite and respectful and he murmured graciously and appropriately.

"Well, Mr Jones..."

He then spoke coolly and his sparkling eyes showed not the slightest trace of cynicism or shadow of uncertainty.

"…I believed my Dad could win before he'd even entered and…if we're leading going into the last round…"

He giggled deliciously.

"…You surely don't expect me to change my mind?"

Danny, Jerry and Sam all roared at the child's confidence and audacity as the extravagant anchor wound up their apparently, little, private show.

"Well even though we'd all like to see an American win, Oliver, we'll say a prayer for your Dad as well…"

He snickered in spoken hilarity.

"… It would be one hell of a tale!"

The presenter finally looked directly and calmly into the camera as if to meaningfully change the mood and subject.

"…Now out live to the course, we rejoin the coverage to watch Tiger's last few holes!"

The red light died and the people in the small studio all breathed a communal sigh of relief.

"Thanks, Sam…"

Danny Thomas smiled, delighted with his coup; the interview with Jerry Pate, Sam and his son had been a winning combination and had undoubtedly made an impact Stateside.

"…You and your boy were just great."

Jerry Pate handed Sam a small slip of paper.

"This is my address Sam, in Florida; if you visit I'd like a re-match!"

Sam thanked him and reciprocated with his own information and his famous, feted opponent said that if he had time he would love to take up his offer of dinner at his family home.

As he was walking out of the door the slim, blonde man suddenly took Sam to one side and spoke to him seriously.

"You don't quite realise what you're doing…?"

Sam looked at him blankly and he explained.

"…Don't you understand, we all think, even an old has-been like me…"

His pale eyes had a searching, far away, distant look.

"…We dream that we can just walk out and claim a *Masters* or an *Open* again… I want you to win it for me…"

He was genuine and honest.

"…For all of us; show us we can all triumph again… just one more time!"

Sam was surprised but peculiarly, understood his instincts, hopes and thoughts; he smiled in appreciation of his enthusiasm, unexpected feelings and transparent, good wishes.

"Jerry, that's a wonderful thing to say…and you can be sure I'll be trying…my hardest."

The man smiled at him teasingly in dry recollection.

"I remember you trying, Sam, when you try…"

He chuckled a final time and his slim features lit up in sudden, youthful reminiscence and somehow equal pain and discomfort.

"… You're pretty hard to beat!"

Sam dissipated into the crowds once more then saw on the scoreboards that, as had been foretold by the media and his clairvoyant, clever son, all the leaders were stumbling and faltering in the troublesome wind and damp gloominess of the late afternoon.

His nearest challenger was Tiger who had held par through the day and was 10 under for the tournament, with a multitude of other famous professionals packed behind him.

Fatigue suddenly captured him and Sam refused any further interviews and remembered, embarrassed of how he had thought badly of so many professionals that seemed to have little time for the media.

It was a difficult and tiring game to play when you were at the top and demands were placed upon you; and he'd only experienced it for a solitary, singular, good round!

The sanctity of the car was a relief and he guided his estate out of the crowds, through the gates and into the relative obscurity of the traffic moving slowly away from this madness and mayhem.

He felt his son's hand tightly on his as he changed gears and gazed then looked at his gorgeous child who whispered to him.

"Dad..."

He laughed exhaustedly.

"...I was so proud of you today... it was just

unforgettable!"

Sam felt a lump in his throat and knew it was the wrong time for sentimentality; he had to stay level-headed and stable.

"Thanks, Oliver but there's still a long way to go."

He nodded, agreed then closed his eyes.

"I know, Dad...but if you ask me, then even *I*... think you're allowed a small pat on the back."

Sam saw the rain as it started to lash onto his windscreen and knew that in all probability he would in fact be leading *The Open* at the day's end and commented accordingly.

"Maybe you're correct, Son..."

He dwelt for a moment on the unbelievable fact that he was actually leading *The British Open* and suddenly smiled in full agreement with his boy.

"...I suppose you just may be right about that!"

The traffic came to a sudden stop as the squally weather created a small logjam of assorted cars and coaches enabling Sam to open the central compartment then remove his mobile phone; he'd missed eight calls!

He pressed a button and suddenly his wife's voice was at the end of the line screaming at him in her breathless excitement.

"Sam, Sam, Sam! What have *you* done, the world's gone mad."

He was immediately concerned.

"What do you mean?"

She was hysterical and could hardly talk.

"We've been bombarded with the newspapers, television, I watched your round... you and Oliver...you were *fantastic*!"

He smiled wryly as this was so unlike her; before today she had never really understood the power and appeal of golf, or the fact that it was a fascinating and mesmerising game.

"Are you OK?"

Tahnee was happy and that made him overjoyed.

"Sam we're unbelievably great, I never realised that you were so good..."

She laughed then cried and sent her love down the line.

"...Go and win it, Sam! Don't worry about

us...Frankie, your Mum and me, we're just so delighted..."

Sam was so pleased to hear his wife's thrilled, engaged voice and whispered to her as if unable to find the energy to speak loudly.

"...I'll see you tomorrow... whatever happens... give my love to everyone."

Oliver suddenly snatched the phone from his father.

"Hi, Mum, are we great or are we great?"

His mother laughed and teased him with her adoration.

"Can't you get a bigger bag to carry, Oliver...?"

Her voice was fuelled with such joy and emotion.

"...It's hard to tell where it begins and you start, on the television."

The boy murmured disbelievingly.

"Have you really seen me on the television?"

His mother was talking as if she was drunk.

"Are you joking, Son... you're all over it...and the papers."

Oliver pleaded and pressed her.

"Save the papers, Mum, please, I want to fill up…Dad's scrap book!"

She smiled; Sam knew and could see her happy face in his head and it grounded him, somehow bringing everything back into perspective.

This was truly the life he treasured.

"I will, Son… look after your Dad… I love you."

Her tone was trying not to sound concerned, but she spoke as if she wanted to hug him and her son caught her mood.

"I love you too Mum, we'll be fine, just you see!"

He comforted her but pressed the red button on the front panel and it was just his blessed father and him, silent and alone once more.

The traffic was moving again and the two of them said nothing until they reached the relative seclusion of Mrs Mackay's lodgings; it felt to Sam like a haven and refuge from an incredible, all powerful, uncontrollable storm.

Sam had hardly drawn up when the old woman came running out to them squealing excitedly.

"Weel dun, Mah Laddie's… weel dun…Ah could'na believe it when Ah saw the television… ye're both famous!"

Sam kissed the elderly woman gently on the cheek.

"We're still the same as we were this morning, Mrs Mackay, Oliver still likes beans and chips and I'm still… well you know what I mean!"

She laughed and slapped him on his sturdy back.

"Ah understand what ye say, Sam…but…"

Her green, dancing eyes were glinting and glowing.

"…Sometimes ye hae tae take the applause… weel dun, Laddie, weel dun!"

They walked upstairs, both bathed then changed for dinner; Sam sat down briefly in the television room and was shocked to find that he was the second item on the main evening news.

Brief highlights of his round were shown along with the favourites faltering, and it confirmed the fact that he was leading at 11 under with, Tiger Woods 2 back at 9 under.

The dining room was crammed with the guests for dinner and as he walked in with his son the whole room stood up and applauded them, as one single gesture of congratulations.

Remembering his brief lecture from Mrs Mackay he smiled and gave a small bow of acceptance and announced to them humbly.

"Thank you…but there's still a way to go!"

The white haired resident from the previous night rose from his table, crossed to him and shook Oliver's then Sam's hand.

"My name is, Trevor James…"

Unusually he seemed embarrassed and flustered.

"…I'm sorry for what I said last night, Mr Chester, I guess I never believed that an amateur could compete with the likes of Tiger Woods and co."

Sam nodded and understood.

"Don't worry about it, Mr James…but golf, like life… is a funny game, sometimes you never know what is possible… until you try."

The mature man smiled then patted him on the arm as he drew away.

"I wish you all the best tomorrow…"

Another voice called out from small crowd around the tables.

"We all do, Sam, good luck tomorrow!"

Sam waved at all of them, as if he was a King giving a speech from a balcony and addressing his subjects; it was a bizarre and unusual experience but strangely wonderful at the same time.

"Thank you…thank you very much for your positive thoughts…I might need them before too long."

He sat down in sudden fatigue and was grateful for the simple, good food; sausages, beans and chips for Oliver and fish, vegetables and boiled potatoes for him.

It was some return to the sense of routine and normality and Sam felt as though he desperately needed it.

They were finished eating around 9p.m and Sam looked at his son's eyelids, fighting so hard to keep from covering his big, wonderful, sparkling eyes.

He led him up the stairs, let him wash then brush his teeth quickly and tucked him into the pristine, white sheets.

Almost before his head touched the pillow his child was fast asleep!

Sam was equally exhausted or drained but not yet drowsy and he was grateful that the media did not know where he was or could disturb him from his efforts to prepare himself mentally for the challenge ahead tomorrow.

His starting time was 2p.m; he was playing with Tiger Woods in the last pairing in *The Open*, and he was 2 shots ahead.

It was simply undeniable, unbelievable, but as Sam left the house and started to walk leisurely up the quiet road, now muddied by the rain, that led to the open fields behind, he realised and accepted that it was an indisputable fact.

The grey clouds and wild wind had lifted and even at this late hour it was still not yet dark; Sam looked out to sea and admired the celestial, red sky that seemed to be melting into the darkening horizon.

He thought about his round today; he had finally found that missing piece inside himself.

At a certain level of expertise, he now understood, golf became an insular, mind game and he would need to find that separation tomorrow.

Could he cope with the pressure: the media: the expectation?

He laughed out loud to himself

"*What expectation…?*"

Who could possibly believe he could win against Tiger; it was surely and patently impossible?

His eyes looked out at the sky again and it was almost biblical in its panorama and hue; dazzling, spectacular colours of splendour and he whispered out only to the dying embers of the wind.

"*…But it is impossible to be where I am…it is all unbelievable!*"

Instinctively he held out his hands just to clearly see them, and amazingly they remained unaffected, still and calm.

Remarkably under the circumstances he was relaxed, and resolved to enjoy the beauty of the evening, breathe in the re-energising freshness of the warm, Scottish air and let tomorrow take care of itself.

He wanted to revel in what was left of this

precise time and spectacle without any heed, concern or fear of what lay beyond.

Sam leaned on the familiar gate and reflected on his last, incredible 24 hours, his good luck, the amazing round, the favourable weather, Jerry Pate, his sons and his divine and delectable wife.

It had all been life's perfection; it had been a perfect day!

Chapter 27

Sam slept surprisingly well; he had been exhausted and, apart from an initial thought about the momentous day to come before he lost consciousness, he dreamed and dwelt of nothing at all and awoke enlivened, refreshed and regenerated.

His initial instinct was to jump up as if he had an early start but then he remembered; as if how could he forget?

He had plenty of time, he was last off!

It was 7.45a.m but he could not go back to sleep; Oliver was still dormant as if needing to also recharge his batteries and he did not want to disturb him.

He remembered that there was a small newsagent's a few hundred yards down the road in the village and he decided to walk, stretch his legs and buy some papers.

The morning was dry and had a distinct crispness with just a hint of a chill that Sam knew would thaw quickly then naturally into a bright and warm, summer day.

The horizon and sky looked perfectly clear and as he walked along the quiet, sandy path, it was hard for him to imagine the tumult that lay but a few miles up the road.

The shopkeeper in the village store was an old, thin woman with bright, red hair and she was wearing a long, tartan skirt and spoke to him challengingly.

"Good morning to ye, Sir."

Sam responded, enthused by her positive energy.

"Good morning…I'll have a copy of each paper please!"

The woman giggled and smiled as if she was a much more juvenile and younger girl than she appeared.

"Och...it's nae sae often we have such a big spender in here...!"

Her voice trailed away; she saw that the only customer in her tiny shop had picked up one of the tabloids with tears in his eyes and she questioned him in sudden alarm.

"...What's the matter, Laddie?"

Sam showed her a picture on the back pages of the paper, of a small, baby with large, shining, innocent, bright eyes.

It was spread all across the back page of *The Sun*, with the headline, *Best of Luck Today, Dad* across the top.

Sam snivelled and sniffed softly.

"This is a picture of my new, Son..."

He smiled embarrassed at his emotional show but he could not contain or help himself.

"...I'm sorry, but it's the first time I've seen him!"

The wiry, lady's charcoal eyes stared at him incredulously and with some amusement and disbelief.

"Will ye be Sam Chester?"

Sam nodded and she stuck out her skeletal, bony, thin fingers and beamed at him in delight.

"Weel let me shake yer hand, Laddie… an wish ye the very best o' luck today; yon *Tiny* Woods has won enough!"

Sam laughed at the mistake and corrected her.

"It's Tiger!"

The woman just shrugged disinterestedly.

"What's the difference…they're a' Americans are they no…?"

Sam smiled again and her sharp spheres admired the photograph as he did so; she was enigmatic, eccentric and extremely funny!

"…He's a Bonny Wee Boy, Sir!"

Sam nodded and looked once more at his new divine son.

"He is indeed, Madam…now what do I owe you?"

Her grey, granite globes sparkled and shone

like polished marbles for a long moment in mischief.

"Nout...but please sign a wee token fur me!"

Sam held the pen and wrote onto a blank white card as the woman seemingly dictated a small story to her, from him!

His fingers and hand moved patiently as he signed the bottom with a flash and a flourish of his wrist and left her premises armed with the papers, a sense of lightness, well being, and an intense injection of good humour.

He thought to himself that there must be something in the Scottish water...that makes these local people so companionable!

When Sam returned to the house, Oliver was up and waiting for him at the breakfast table; Sam showed him the articles and the photographs of his baby brother, *Frankie*.

The boy looked at them not really comprehending or understanding the magnitude of the media coverage, but Sam was aware, well aware and he felt as though he was suddenly the middle and very epicentre of the world's sporting focus and attention.

The morning drifted by lazily but at 10a.m they both got dressed, Oliver in blue trousers and a white shirt and Sam all in black; it was what he liked to play in as a boy!

The two of them loaded the car with their bags and cases; they turned to say their goodbyes to, Mrs Mackay and Sam spoke first.

"Thank you so much…you have helped more than you could ever imagine."

Purposefully he handed her the cheque for their food and accommodation and the perky woman looked at the small, promissory document and smiled.

"Ah'm no gonna cash it, Laddie; Ah'm gonna frame it and teel a'body that this is where *The Open Champion* stayed!"

Sam laughed at her cheek and positivity.

"Well you'll know that today, one way or the other… but whether I win or not you make sure you bank it; if I win I'll send you a better momento than this little scrap of paper!"

Oliver ran to the old woman and planted a gentle kiss on one of her ruddy cheeks and she flushed up like a heated kettle about to steam.

"Thank you, Mrs Mackay, you're the best cook in the world… almost as good as my Mum!"

The woman was flustered as if unused to such fuss and appreciation.

"Weel an that's a compliment indeed, Laddie...noo away wi ye...ye've got things to do!"

She stood and waved as they drove slowly from the farm and disappeared from her sight; Sam thought he could trace a small tear in her eye as she shouted after them in earnest.

"Best o' luck, Boys...best o' luck!"

The traffic to the course was heavy and both of them sat patiently as they drove along the narrow roads that were so familiar by now; Oliver watched the chaos and murmured absentmindedly.

"Do you think we should go to Ladyburn to practice?"

Sam shook his head determinedly.

"No Oliver we have to face it, to be in the centre of the whirlwind; we have to deal with the madness...as you told me...and you were right..."

He laughed and poked him in his ribs until he chuckled then giggled,

"…As always!"

Oliver listened then watched as the sea came in and out of his vision and then suddenly they had arrived.

The two of them were swiftly ushered into the player's car park and, as Sam opened the car door, twenty photographers and reporters surrounded him instantly and bombarded him with endless questions.

"*How do you feel this morning Sam? Did you sleep well? Are you nervous? Are you going to win?*"

The inquisition came at him in a torrent as he tried to smile but was pleased when a senior official came to assist then guide him and his son to the recorder's caravan.

Michael Bonallack was in the small, well organised vehicle; the older man smiled broadly and warmly as they strode then climbed up the shiny, metal risers to get inside.

He directed an immediate question to the child.

"Hello, My Lad…how are you today?"

Oliver shook the man's hand as if he were a grown up and had known the Secretary all his life.

"We're cool, Sir…all set to go!"

The experienced player and administrator looked at Sam as he handed him his card for the final round then asked him with some concern and sincerity; he knew that going out with his limited experience was bound to be intimidating and daunting.

"Are you OK, Sam?"

Sam looked into the man's dark, blue eyes and knew he empathised and understood exactly how he was feeling.

"It's going to be an *interesting* day, Mr Bonallack…"

He sighed deeply and asked, then answered the rhetorical question to himself.

"… Am I OK…? I am as prepared mentally and physically as I could ever hope to be…and…"

Sam spoke suddenly with a boyish grin and a quirky, emerging smile coming to his face.

"…I do *have* a bit of a secret weapon!"

They both looked at Oliver whose attention was attuned to outside the caravan and the older man nodded.

"He's a special lad, Sam, and him being with

you... who knows? I will be wishing my best thoughts for you but..."

His voice lowered to whisper.

"...Don't tell anyone I'm supposed to be unbiased and independent!"

Sam laughed and armed with his card, he left the tiny space then, after a brief drink and sandwich in the Player's refreshment tent, they walked towards the practice ground.

Everywhere there were crowds, players, spectators, media; people Sam didn't know who kept coming up to him and wanting to shake his hand and wish him luck.

He stepped through the ropes and onto the long, frenetic, preparation area; he was immediately relieved to feel the distance between the maniacal commotion and him once more.

It gave him time and space to reset his buzzing head.

As he had correctly predicted in the car, the only place to be calm and separated was actually in the eye of the storm and, as he rolled out the clean, white balls specially provided for the players, he knew that he had to turn and retune his full attention back to this teasing and testing game of golf.

Sam ignored the countless, famous professionals on the range and started through his normal and familiar warm up routine.

He hit a few wayward shots to start, as his body threw off the distractions of the previous day, but soon he was sensing or feeling the plane and groove that he knew so well.

His full session took him 30 minutes and after hitting a few effortless drives, he went back to his wedge then aimlessly tried to retain that feeling of fluidity and freedom in his swing.

He was suddenly distracted; a face shone out to him in the crowd surrounding the green arena; it was an unexpected vision from the past and he stopped rehearsing and stared again, more intently.

The man was tall, bald and more bowed and weary than he remembered but he still had those distinguished, grey sideburns!

It was Len, Len Thompson and without a further thought Sam walked over to where he was and instantly gestured and beckoned to him.

"Let this person through…"

He muttered his direction urgently to one of the nearby officials.

"….He's my… *my coach!*"

The tall, lofty, impressive figure of the man walked slowly and languidly through the cordon and Sam threw his arms around him as much as he could, given the disparity in their respective sizes.

The old professional was still almost twice his height but his former pupil just gasped up to him in real surprise and pleasure.

"How are you, Len? I'm so pleased to see you…"

Sam guided Oliver towards him; he was undoubtedly old but somehow still imposing and the child seemed a little in awe of him as Sam had been all those years ago.

"…This is my son, Len…Oli…"

The aging colossus finished his introduction.

"Oliver…"

His voice remained as rich, Irish and emotive as ever.

"…You're famous, Young Man."

The boy shook hands with the gentle giant and Sam watched, as the man's palm seemed to consume his son's fingers.

He recalled those first, formative shots with Len and how these very hands had first divided the balls for him, as his former teacher stared down upon his child and chuckled happily.

"I used to instruct your, Dad when he wasn't much older than you, Son!"

Oliver simply gazed up at him with wide, dancing, disbelieving eyes; his father was never that young, surely?

Sam smiled at his coach, patted him on the arm and muttered to his boy in tribute and acclamation to this mercurial, elevated gentleman.

"He taught me all I know!"

Len laughed in his usual, shy and modest manner.

"I wish that were true, Sam…"

His leathery face was more lined, weather beaten, and ravaged with age than he recalled, but undeniably his spirit was forever young.

"…But you've learnt a few things since then…

that were always beyond my capabilities…"

His green globes glinted and eternally shone with life.

"… I saw you on the television and it was as if it was 25 years ago…"

His sighed and smiled almost together.

"… I had to come and wish you all the very best, Son…the very best!"

Sam was touched and a little overcome then replied quietly but with real warmth and affection for him.

"That's so nice of you, Len…I really appreciate it."

His favourite teacher stood straight suddenly and brushed the few, white strands of his hair back onto his bald, patchy, pale head.

"Now…"

He was mocking but serious suddenly.

"…If I'm your coach then… let's concentrate… reminiscences are for later, you've a job to do…!"

Sam smiled and knew that he was correct; as instructed he picked up his 5 iron, set his body and mind and after making the perfect angle then turn, hit a simply divine strike at the far marker post.

The wizened, lofty man simply laughed out loud in gratification and admiration at his mastery and ability.

"...You've definitely discovered a few new tricks, Sam..."

He whistled as he continued to watch the shape and power of the shot.

"...You always had incredible drive and talent but...this is something else, Son..."

He shook his huge head slowly for emphasis.

"...*Something else!*"

Reactively they all felt and heard a sudden murmur from the crowd, a tangible undercurrent of tension, then a tall, imposing slim figure dressed in black trousers and a bright, red top strode to the far side of the practice area; it was Tiger Woods here to prepare for the battle ahead.

Sam remembered the lesson from Jerry Pate all those years ago and he paid the man no heed or attention; he had to concentrate on his own game or he knew for certain the distractions of any prior introduction would overwhelm him.

As if Len knew what Sam was thinking he put his arm around his shoulder and hugged him caringly and lovingly.

"Sam, I see you now with your son and your family and I've got to tell you…that you can't lose today whether you win or not…!"

He looked at the big, enormous, daunting stands surrounding the course and it was as if he remembered every fearful, nervous word he ever said about them.

"…You've had your share of problems from this game and… although I'm past giving you advice…just enjoy yourself today, Son… you deserve it…"

He slipped Sam an address and number, written on a scrap of card, into the palm of his hand and suddenly, like a spirit or a ghost of ancient times, he melted back into the crowd.

"…I'll see you later, Son!"

Then like the mythical, Cheshire cat in, *Alice in Wonderland,* his mesmerising face smiled fully, before he disappeared…completely!

Sam looked at the large, digital, green clock

nearby; there was an hour before his tee off time and he spent the next 20 minutes on the putting green trying to adjust to the greens that seemed to be gaining speed with each passing second.

Finally he felt he had done enough and he walked into the locker room with Oliver to freshen up before their final test, voyage and challenge began.

One of the stewards stopped him and handed him a small sack that was filled with mail; he opened some of the letters and they were from people he had known from the faded past.

He smiled wryly as he did not wish to question the sincerity of the good wishes but it was ironic that as soon as he did well people wanted to make contact and speak to him but, historically, when he really needed them...Well?

Perhaps that was life or just golf as he had experienced it, insincerity and selfishness abounded but that was now firmly an unimportant part of his history.

The truth, as he knew and understood it, was the people that had truly and genuinely been there for him, were very few and far between.

He handed Oliver the bag then gave him the

keys of the car and instructed him gently.

"Just run and put these in the boot please…and don't be long!"

The boy ran out and for the first time in days, Sam was alone; the other professionals and challengers were out on the course and he put his cheeks in his hands and tried to just focus his swirling head.

Sam knew that he had to get to where he had been yesterday, to play the game inside his mind in just shape and rhythm; he had to separate his conscious thought from the innumerable distractions otherwise he would never be able to cope with the stress and … *Tiger*!

As if to disturb his contemplation he heard a familiar voice and he looked up instantly; an incredibly charismatic, handsome, older, sun tanned face beamed down on him.

"I am not disturbing you, Sam?"

He spoke in a rich, Spanish accent; it was Severiano Ballesteros!

"No, Mr…"

His eyes were inky black and his face flushed in eager enthusiasm.

"You can call me, Seve…"

The man smiled almost shyly, as if he himself was just a boy.

"…I had to come and …I don't want to say… wish you luck…"

He stood for a moment and was still, reflective and quiet.

"…It is more than that…"

The incredibly, famous golfer then sat down next to him, then stared and gazed at the polished, changing room floor.

"…The last few years, Sam… they have not been so good. I feel like giving up then I see you and your son…"

He sighed and looked up at him.

"…You play with your heart and your soul and you…you inspire me, Sam…!"

He chuckled and laughed as he reminded him in that instant somehow of the irresistible and charismatic, Len Thompson.

"…You inspire all of us who continue to battle and try!"

Sam looked at him; he seemed so much

smaller and more vulnerable than when he had watched his endless endeavours, misadventures and fabulous exploits on the television.

Seve had always been his hero and he had always played the game and conducted himself with such style; he was very much a genius or legend and Sam could only whisper humbly in his response to him.

"It is so kind of you to say that, Seve…"

Sam was embarrassed at such praise, especially from him.

"…But I have always admired you, rather than the other way around!"

The man smiled again as if suddenly remembering once more who he was, the place he took in the world and the golfing hierarchy within it as he smiled then murmured.

"Then let us say the pupil has taught something to the, *Master*… I will not wish you good luck, Sam because I do not wish to put you under any more pressure."

Oliver suddenly ran back into the locker room as if only to interrupt them and then halted directly in front of this enigmatic stranger, as if he had hit an impenetrable, imaginary, brick wall.

"Seve!"

He spoke and exhaled as if he couldn't believe his eyes but the celebrated *Spanish Matador* took Oliver's hand as if to shake it, then kissed him gently on the cheek as he whispered kindly to him.

"You keep your back straight today, your head held high, Oliver, and help your Dad!"

Oliver looked at him and found it hard to speak.

"I will, Seve…I will!"

The eternal, golfing enigma turned to Sam then wrung his hands instinctively; it was undoubtedly a gesture to indicate and say that he knew and understood, as he did of course, how to labour, toil and suffer at this game.

"I would just tell you one thing, Sam…before I go…"

His tone was deep and sincere; all traces of humour lost from his darkened, striking visage.

"…You play today as you have done this week… with your heart and maybe…"

He smiled almost sadly and with a melancholy lilt to his tone.

"…Maybe the fates will be kind to you…"

He looked away into the distance then whispered to him as if he was imparting a private, special, personal secret and someone else might overhear him.

"…Sometimes when I won…*my heart*… that was the very best club I had in my bag!"

He stroked Oliver's head, smiled at them both and left the locker room silently, leaving father and son alone and shaking like two leaves in the aftermath of a tempestuous and miraculous gale.

Severiano Ballesteros was without doubt a spirit, inspiration and a whirlwind all in one!

Sam finally breathed in deeply, feeling slightly unnerved by his hero's good wishes and he looked at his watch before quickly refocusing then adjusting his brain to the task to come; they were off in 15 minutes and he glanced at his son and smiled.

"Are we ready, Oliver?"

The boy sat closely next to him as Sam suddenly remembered that his caddy was just a child, only 9 years of age but, given the boy's achievements and input, it was almost as if he had misplaced and forgotten the fact once more.

Lovingly he wrapped his arm around his slender shoulders and rubbed them gently as if to prepare them for the days work ahead.

He could physically feel his boy's excitement and his expectation, but perhaps surprisingly, could not sense any fear or trepidation inside his wiry, lithe form.

His special son was supremely confident in his father's talent and ability, which made Sam emotionally flush and fill up with enormous courage and pride.

Oliver looked up at him in determination then brushed back from his hazel eyes, the long hair that had grown during his vacation from his mother's attentions and he seemed to glow contentedly.

"I'm ready if you are, Dad?"

Sam leant down and kissed his child on his soft, silky mane; he felt better, part of his world was with him and he knew for sure it was an unbreakable rock to hold him fast and secure from the unavoidable stresses and pressures waiting for him outside.

"I'm ready, Oliver, as ready as I'll ever be!"

Chapter 28

They walked out of the locker room where Oliver picked up their bag, all the clubs having been cleaned and straightened by his small but diligent hands.

Sam then led them intently through the tunnel of canvas and scaffolding from which they eventually emerged onto the 1st tee, just as the last game but one had departed, to instant, rapt applause, partisan hollering and enthusiastic cheering.

His illustrious playing partner was already waiting on the manicured grass with his gaudy, bright, red shirt on; the man, smiled broadly, walked over to him, shook him firmly by the hand and spoke clearly.

"Hi, Sam…I'm Tiger Woods…"

His dark eyes sparked then sparkled in relish; it was clear he truly lived for these special days as he was trained and used to them!

"… We're going to have some fun today!"

Oliver marched on carrying the bag as Tiger held out his palm to him also, then greeted the child with the same sportsmanship, camaraderie and enthusiasm as he had to his father.

Sam retained a sense of the famous golfer's hands; they had that same supple richness and quality that all the great players he had known possessed, and it was a tad unsettling.

Oliver, after his introduction to the illustrious American, tried his level best not to look intimidated, but their opponent today had a substance, aura and a presence that was hard for either of them to simply ignore.

Tiger went back to his caddy and Sam admired him for not trying to undermine him; spoken congratulations to be where he was in leading the tournament would have been appropriate, but somewhat patronising or condescending as well.

Sam felt, in spite of the enormous gulf of trophies and experience between him and his renowned adversary, the man was treating him with respect, as an equal, and it was noted and appreciated.

His blue eyes looked out and stared vacuously

out to the flat, pale, sea-line and distance; then he closed them tightly for a split second and, with all his spirit, tried to concentrate and focus.

He knew that he had to quickly get inside himself; the cameras, crowds, stands, distractions, noises were inescapable and everywhere!

Instinctively Sam understood that he must collect his previously random thoughts in his often unreliable mind; he had to urgently bring everything he had recently learned to bear!

The announcer called clearly and a hush fell over the assembled crowd.

"On the tee, Tiger Woods…"

The dark figure walked onto the immaculate, green, grass area, waved politely at the masses all around and smiled broadly but was already intent and prepared.

"…At 9 under par for the tournament."

Sam drew in his breath and held it for a moment; they were about to begin on another wild, fantastical adventure!

The crowd fell respectfully hushed; however noisy they had been, the courtesy and etiquette of silence was always paramount and universally respected.

Sam watched him spin, turn then swing and he could see that Tiger was ready; his eyes glazed and concentrated as the iron went off like a cannon shot, powering down the fairway.

"…On the tee, Sam Chester… 11 under par for the tournament!"

Sam felt his heart beating, drumming inside his chest and then felt the softness of his son's small hand on his own once more as he whispered quietly to him.

"We'll be OK, Dad…"

He squeezed his fingers meaningfully.

"…Don't worry…we're together!"

Sam looked out to the far horizon a final time for separation, focussed on an insignificant, small boat that was almost mixed in with the roll of the sea, and finally it withdrew his mind from the madness around him.

In his head he was back home on the course at the bottom of the garden and he breathed in the fresh, salt air, gratefully entering into his separation and fantasy world once more.

"*Relax, Sam...*"

He exhaled and murmured under his heated breath.

"*...Just relax!*"

His calm fingers teed the ball up and his body stood over the shot then looked down the green and inviting surface in the distance.

He had one last practice swing, made the shot in his closed and isolated mind, then turned in his, *inner space* for real and watched as the small globe flew straight and true.

The crowd applauded but Sam did not hear them; he was back in his own private domain, where the sound was muffled, colours were dull and the only thing that was certain was shape and rhythm, pace and timing.

The actual disconnection of the course was truly a relief; he was alone apart from his son, his supporter and inspiration and as he connected solidly with his pitch shot he knew he was settled and would be able to cope with the trials ahead.

Sam missed his *20 foot* putt to gain only a par and Tiger's birdie hardly registered with him; he only had his own round to focus upon!

They both made par at the 2nd and then Tiger birdied the 3rd; they were now level and Sam had not made a mistake or dropped a shot!

The 4th yielded another couple of pars and at the long 5th Sam hit a wonderful second shot to *15 feet* and just missed his eagle attempt.

Tiger however birdied the hole as well and, as the round progressed to the turn, his illustrious, playing companion birdied the 9th and was now one ahead.

The commentators from around the world were already writing the fearsome, irrepressible, Young Lion's coronation speech; everything was going as expected, the courageous amateur was putting up a spirited show but against Tiger?

Was there really any contest?

Sam remained level over the next 3 holes and discovered he was yet a further shot behind.

Tiger had held a *30 footer* on the 11th for a birdie to be 14 under and went into his famous celebration by punching the fresh air with his right arm, as the crowd around the green went into raptures of delirious appreciation and delight.

Sam was the home favourite, but a Champion

in full flow was an irresistible spectacle as everyone embraced the wonderful display of his skill and genius.

There was a slight hold up on the 13th, and as they turned towards home, Oliver stood next to his father and looked at Tiger's, dark, stony, unblinking eyes and was staggered at their incredible intensity.

He whispered up to his parent and murmured up to him in all of his innocence and honesty.

"You can't beat him, Dad…"

His voice was cool and calm as if suddenly realising and appreciating who they were up against.

"…He's unbelievable… like a machine… I won't be upset if we lose to him, Dad…"

He shook his young head in genuine wonder.

"…He's just too good!"

Sam looked at the man as if recognising he *was* the best; Tiger Woods was focussed, unwavering and would give no quarter but, just as he was preparing to mentally accept defeat, he felt a strange, long lost and peculiar, unfamiliar sensation inside him.

It was just a feeling, a sudden surge of anger and a frustration that was tangible and almost physical; the boy he had once been all those years ago was still inside him and exactly as he could never countenance defeat in the distant past, he couldn't and wouldn't accept it now!

He looked far out into the watery expanse a final time then gathered all his mental strength; Tiger was only human, and as he thought about the last few unbelievable months he realised that he had something else working for him, something, almost ethereal and unreal!

Sam had never thought too much about spirituality but, as the warm breeze caressed his brow he sensed for sure that there was more to life, and his life in particular, than just what he could see!

Sam stood over his tee shot on the 13th and allowed his anger to swell inside him; his brain was still focussed and separated from the realities of his situation but suddenly he had harnessed his will and God-given eternal, inbuilt loathing and hatred of defeat.

The tee shot was long and straight and after a pitch shot that nearly hit the hole he birdied to Tiger's par.

At the 14th Sam hit a superb drive and iron to

10 feet and although Tiger made birdie, Sam's eyes didn't flicker as he calmly rolled the putt in for the eagle.

They both got their pars on the 15th and, as Sam hit his second to *15 feet,* on the next hole he watched as Tiger made his only mistake of the day and went through the green.

Sam could see the line clearly and raised his hand to accept the applause as his putt went down for another birdie.

Tiger knelt down behind his *8 footer,* this to stop going 2 behind, and although he struck the shot well, the ball horse-shoed out of the uncooperative void and Sam, walked to the 17th tee now commandingly 2 shots ahead.

Again there was a slight delay and Sam saw fleetingly, the anger and frustration burning in his adversary's eyes; he knew that his famed opponent was also not going to lie down for anyone!

Sam played first and, still in perfect synchronisation, shaped his 3 wood shot around the corner of the hole.

Tiger then stood on the tee and, in spite of himself, Sam was compelled to watch him hit his drive; it was almost as if he saw the man's powerful swing in slow motion.

The turn, then the stretch; straining with every mental or physical part of his dark, muscular body with almost superhuman effort!

His club connected with the ball as a thunderclap and Sam drew in his breath as it seemed to disappear into the clear, blue sky and bounce somewhere near the green, miles down the fairway.

The crowd gasped, whooped or cheered and Sam tried to ignore everything and whispered to himself as he ambled purposely down to where his ball was waiting on the short, cut grass.

"*Stay focussed…concentrate!*"

His eyes peered then looked at his second shot into the dreaded 17th and strangely but thankfully he still felt in control.

He turned his shoulders, made a good shape but watched in dismay as the flighted ball bounced vertically left as it landed, then gathered into the tortuous, *Hell's Bunker*, the graveyard of so many rounds.

Tiger had no more than a wedge to the green and as the grandstands around the green exploded into ecstatic, wild applause, Sam realised that his second shot must have finished close, very close!

The horrible, unfair kick was the first piece of bad fortune Sam had experienced in recent days and as he walked down to the 17th green he sensed that he was beginning to lose the cocoon that had shielded him from the pressure and, from what he was in sight of achieving!

Suddenly he looked at the massive grandstands and saw them for what they were; the cameras and the electrical, media mayhem that was simply everywhere.

As he reached his ball lying poorly on the front right-hand side of the trap, he truly uncomfortably started to feel the stress and tension; those hated, familiar ants and spiders were about to be released and to begin crawling on him once again.

He stared then saw to his disquiet that Tiger was only *5 feet* from the hole and as Sam perused his shot he realised that he had no way towards the pin from his horrible lie against the layered, high, unreasonable lip of the bunker.

His only option and route was to try and land the ball on the very front of the green then attempt to get down in 2!

In frantic panic and anxiety he grabbed at the sand iron and, as he tried to pull it out of the bag, he felt a fierce, solid, restraining force preventing him doing so.

His darting eyes looked and saw that his son was holding his palm over the club and would determinedly not release it as he shouted under his breath at him.

"Dad… I'm sorry but I've seen you like this before, at the first qualifying…step away…"

His words were commands not choices.

"…Take a moment… and get a grip!"

Sam looked at the young boy and although his first instinct in his turmoil was to hit him; he realised that his mind had indeed gone into trauma and he inhaled, took the boys sanguine counsel then temporarily left the glinting, silver club in the bag.

He walked around the green, then the bunker and did not return to take the sand iron into his fingers until he was calm once more.

Sensibly, Sam realised that he could not get back to his abstract state and did not try to as this was not the time.

Now he needed all his courage and raw nerves and he knew for sure that he had always possessed these battling qualities.

He settled in the bunker, grounding his shoes into the soft, fine, delicate sand and looked up the sharp face of the depression or grave he was in.

Sam understood and accepted he had to get the ball up steeply and hope for a 2 putt from the front!

He centred himself, concentrated only on his shot and after taking the club vertically outside the normal plane watched as it just cleared the top of the bunker and ran down the slope to the very front of the green over 40 yards from the stick but mercifully, above ground!

The crowd applauded while the commentators and spectators throughout the world watched on captivated or enthralled as the exquisite drama played out and unfolded.

It looked like there would be a 2 or 3 shot swing as the pendulum of momentum and chance was moving clearly in Tiger's favour.

Sam walked the length of the green; he could see the flag but not the bottom of the hole from where he lay, as it was hidden behind the small, dangerous incline near the bunker.

He squatted and leaned down behind his devilish ball and stared at the impossible, lengthy journey it had to traverse and travel.

In apprehension he realised that it was actually possible, almost probable, to putt and roll the ball back into the sand if he was foolish enough to aim directly at the pin.

It was undoubtedly terrifying and his eyes looked up for an instant to see the cameras on him once more and the whole world watching!

Remembering his son's advice, he stepped away, there was little point trying to read the line as the distance he was away, was too great for such subtleties.

Sam knew this particular shot was simply and purely all about pace and courage.

He waited for the rowing boat in his subconscious mind to stabilise onto calm water, then sensed or tried to feel his gifted hands and fingers as his head willed them to be icy still and relaxed.

His body stood like a stone over the tortuous shot and, as he felt the putter strike the ball so sweetly, he instantly had the strangest, most delicious, miraculous sensation, of déjà-vu!

In confusion he just watched as the white globe spun and commenced on its far journey up the hill, through the contours, slowing until it reached the top and then, only and scarcely avoiding the slope to the bunker it rolled, *just*, over the brow and then down towards the hole.

Sam watched his son pull the flag out excitedly and he remembered instantly where he'd witnessed this scenario before!

Hoylake, the British Amateur, Jerry Pate, surely not again, it just wasn't possible!

The incredible audible roar behind the green and then the sounds of reaction from the grandstands everywhere told Sam that lightning had indeed struck twice and the ball had actually gone in!

He watched as his son then ran around the green waving the large flagpole violently in wild celebration at his father's outrageous, continuing, barely credible, good fortune.

In the commentator's boxes everything was hysteria and Jerry Pate was screaming to his ABC viewers.

"I knew it, I just knew it… I knew….Wow…I knew… he was going to hole it!"

The noise seemed to go on forever; it was an echo from the past magnified a thousand times and, as if captive to his own dreamlike state, Sam raised his arms for quiet in the same professional manner as he'd done at Hoylake all those eons ago.

Tiger was not smiling, his eyes were cold and angry and he had no intention of allowing Sam's luck to rob him of his further place in golfing history and immortality.

He knelt behind the putt, waited for the crowd noise to fade to stillness and then calmly stroked the ball into the hole for a birdie; his fist punched the air and he gritted his teeth as he did so.

This was war and under no circumstances would he be cheated and denied his plunder or prize!

They both walked quietly the short distance to the next tee; there were 40,000 people around the 18th hole but, as Sam hit his 3 wood up the centre of the fairway you could not hear a single, audible sound.

Sam sensed that he would have to make 3 to win and, again he watched almost spellbound, as Tiger used his grace, power and prodigious will to outrageously propel the ball to the very front of the green where it nestled in the legendary *Valley of Sin*.

The noise as they walked down the 18th began as applause; then seemed to grow with each graceful step they took nearer the green until it was a deafening, crescendo and deafening crash of sound.

It was just unbelievable and as Sam crossed the fabled *Swilcan Burn* bridge once more he stopped momentarily with Oliver and simply gazed around them and took the scene and the spectacle in!

The stands on either side of the green were packed and crammed with spectators, everywhere people were standing or screaming and Oliver took his father's hand in his and whispered to him as if they weren't actually, really there at all.

"*Bloomin Hell*, Dad…it's only a game of golf… isn't it?"

Sam, even in this fantastical, pressure cooker couldn't help but chuckle and laugh.

"It's supposed to be, Oliver but…it's also… *The Open…*"

He smiled, tenderly stroked his boy's, soft head and was not scared or fearful anymore with him at his side, as his lips murmured in final explanation to him.

"…It's more than just… golf!"

The boy's hazel eyes sparkled, as if utterly seduced by the sheer, dazzling, colourful, and outlandish show before him.

He resettled the impressive bag on his shoulders then winked cheekily up at his father and smiled in real childish happiness and expressive joy.

He could never have imagined, even in his dream that *The Open* could be like this; it was far better and more fantastical than anything he could have conjured or made up in his pretty head!

"OK, come on, Dad…no more time to look…let's go!"

Chapter 29

In homage to Mrs Mackay's words about taking a bow, Sam raised his arms and acknowledged the applause and noticed, as if for the first time, how much the public loved his son.

The handsome, beautiful, Little Man lugging the large, enormous bag had been equally big news in recent days as the boy also raised his slender hands and wrists and waved to the crowd enthusiastically.

Eventually they reached the ball and quickly Sam concentrated and re-gathered his thoughts.

In keeping with his more experienced manner, he waited for the crowd that had stampeded at the rear of him, to settle behind the temporary ropes and then looked directly at the shot he had left.

It was only 60 yards, but disconcertingly over the fearsome, *Valley of Sin*, where the pin was just a few yards over the sharp brow of the hill.

It was a treacherous, dangerous shot and anything even slightly short would fall back disastrously down the slope.

Sam concentrated intensely, sensing only his timing and nerve; he had to keep relaxed and loose, any tension or jerkiness on such a short shot would spell catastrophe!

Finally he was content as he settled his head over the tiny, white sphere, swung his arm and shoulders and felt the pleasure of a clean, incisive, sweet strike.

The ball pitched just behind the hole, checked and slowed; abruptly finishing about *12 feet* behind the flag.

The crowd exploded into incredible colour then noise and Sam marvelled as he walked up to the green and waved further to the gallery, that he extraordinarily had a putt for *The Open*!

After all the years of effort, exasperation, failure and his premature, early retirement from the game; he *actually* had a putt for the *British Open*; it was simply unbelievable and seemingly, beyond all realms of credibility.

That was if Tiger did not hole from the bottom of the demanding, divisive hill and everyone held their breath as the young American surveyed his final approach and attempt.

He seemed to slowly analyse his long putt from every conceivable angle then finally, theatrically stood and settled down to hit the shot.

Tiger's body was perfectly still and, with a minimum of further fuss he hit the ball and watched as it ran up the slope energetically towards the hole.

The crowd began to yell, cheer, squeal and shriek excitedly as it followed the break and began to bear down ever closer to the empty cup.

Oliver reflexively closed his eyes, unable to watch and only re-opened them as he heard the communal exhalation of breath that signified that the putt had thankfully missed.

It had agonisingly finished 3 inches behind the hole and, as Tiger touched his white, peaked cap and tapped the ball in, all that stood between Sam and victory was a *12 foot* left to right putt, downhill, with seemingly only the whole universe watching!

There was hardly any pressure at all!

Instinctively he crouched then kneeled down behind his ball but could literally, actually and physically feel his body start to tremble and shake for the first time since this tournament had begun in earnest

In different ways, and at variable levels, he had maintained control over himself throughout, but now started to question if he could honestly hold his nerve for this one, final time.

He finally and anxiously stood over the putt, shaped to hit it then remembered how he had missed the self same shot at the last qualifying round; instantly he stepped away and knew he could and would not strike it until his mind was absolutely clear.

Peter Alliss was having a field day, fiesta and an epileptic fit in the commentary box.

"Oh my goodness…"

He was making quips, moaning and gasping as he passed commentary or judgement; this was history being made whatever happened and, although he genuinely felt the tension, he professionally *milked* the situation for all it was worth.

"…Memories of dear old…Doug Sanders… he should never have stepped away…it's not a good sign…!"

The combined strain, stress, trauma and obvious drama was vivid, raw and real as were his comments which were well taken and founded.

"…Oh dear, oh dear… my old nerves can't… take it!"

Sam called Oliver over to him and made him kneel down behind the short distance to the tiny, teasing, intended refuge.

"Tell me which way it goes, Son…will you!"

Oliver peered, examined and looked at the putt from either side of the hole; he then rose up to his father close beside him and whispered seriously.

"I can only tell you one thing, Dad."

Sam was grateful for any advice; the line of this put was so difficult to read and he was in a dilemma and a quandary.

"What's that, Oliver?"

The child leaned up and whispered directly in his father's ear.

"I haven't got a clue…"

He sniggered suddenly.

"…I haven't been able to read a single putt since we started…it's too complicated for me…!"

Sam smiled, laughed and felt himself relax just a little; his perfect child always seemed to know just what to say to soothe and settle him as he continued to speak.

"…Dad…"

He was still pretending to read the *borrow*.

"…One thing I do know…"

Oliver paused, as if for affect.

"…Whether you hole it or miss it… I'll love you just the same…"

His small fingers stroked his father's precious

hands in way of good luck.

"...I'm proud of you either way, Dad!"

Sam, there, in front of the world-wide audience, put his arm around his son and kissed him gently on the cheek.

"Thanks, Oliver...I needed to hear that!"

His boy looked over at Tiger's, dark eyes that were staring and looking fiercely and impassively at them.

"One other thing though..."

He muttered wryly, cheekily but honestly.

"....I'd try your best to hole it..."

Oliver glanced at their opponent once again.

"... I don't fancy our chances in a play off!"

The boy walked back to the bag as Sam felt an easing of his tension then an infusion of confidence and direction return to him once more.

Instinctively, although he knew that his son was only teasing him as normal, he was also probably right, and Sam could sense this divisive putt was the ultimate and final test.

He truly doubted that he could beat Tiger in any play off!

It was something that he seemed to realise and knew in his soul that such a further challenge would prove to be a bridge too far.

This was it!

Intuitively he sensed that the coming moment was all or nothing and he had to give this putt and shot every part of himself; his skill, his courage and all of his heart!

Sam focussed his mind again, picturing the boat; it needed to be so becalmed, on such perfectly still waters.

He was that small craft, calm, steady in the liquid, mercury pool with not so much as a movement or even a ripple to distract him.

Finally, after an interminable time he was ready; the line was left lip and after picking a spot just ahead of his ball, easily drew the blade of the putter back and sent it on its way to the hole with perfect topspin.

The small, white sphere rolled smoothly, took the gentle slope and then, agonisingly and painfully seemed to die on the very tortuous edge and sharp lip of the hole.

Everything suddenly went into slow motion, the crowd seemed to inhale in a single breath and, as if in an actual dream, he heard his son's small, sharp, voice pierce the quietness of communal apprehension and expectation as he screamed with ferocious, vicious energy.

"Get in you, *Little Bastard*...get in!"

As if the, almost inert object heard him, Sam saw that the ball was not as yet quite spent and, almost imperceptibly, it moved fractionally, then again and suddenly, magically and magnificently it tumbled, fell and disappeared into the tiny chasm and abyss!

The whole arena exploded into a maniacal crescendo of noise; everywhere people were screaming, crying and through the commotion Tiger walked up to Sam and his serious expression changed into a big, juvenile, boyish grin.

"Man..."

His gravelly voice chuckled then laughed and repeated himself in his disorientation.

"...*Man*...that was something to be a part of...!"

He shook his opposition's hand then hugged him around his shoulders and ridiculously it felt to Sam as if somehow he was incredibly pleased for him.

"…I feel like I've won it myself…"

The famous golfer was laughing at what had just transpired; he'd finished 3, 3 and lost!

"…It was so *unbelievable*!"

Tiger sought out, Oliver and shook his hand as well.

"…If you want to work on the States tour…"

He tempted and teased him at the same time.

"…You can work for me… *anytime*!"

Tiger Woods left the green with a big, winning smile on his face and Sam marvelled at how all the truly great, immortal sportsmen seemed to be blessed with such a wonderful dignity in winning or losing.

It was as if the two, diametrically opposite things were almost compatible and complimentary.

Sam was jostled to the recorder's caravan and after he had checked and signed his score card he sat in the black, plastic seat as if suddenly aware of what he had achieved.

He was *Open Champion*; Sam closed his eyes

in shock and wonder for a second as he tried to drink the absurd thought in.

It was fully 20 minutes before the presentation ceremony could begin and after a couple of brief interviews, Sam sat in one of the green chairs laid out by the 18th hole as he waited patiently and tried to accept that this was real.

The evening was mild and calm and the stands were still crammed, bustling and bursting with life; they remained full to overflowing and it was as if no one wanted to miss the celebration, merriment or party.

Sam sat and thought about his life and his father, how much he would have given for him to have been there watching; then he smiled to himself as he realised that in some way he definitely was!

He looked at his son waiting steadfastly by the side of the green with his giant bag still beside him; he thought about his wife and his new son and how he longed to see them both.

Michael Bonallack came to the microphone and the surrounding, immense audience respectfully went quiet.

"The winner of *The Open Championship*…"

Out of normal tradition the man smiled

markedly and then put in an unusual line in his speech and announcement.

"...*As his son, Oliver, so bravely and confidently predicted to me*...is the amateur, Sam Chester!"

The crowd spontaneously exploded into delirium and further wild, unprompted applause.

Sam rose from his chair and walked the few yards to the table where the famous, *Claret Jug* was sparkling and waiting to be presented to him.

Eventually the crowd went quiet again but, as the secretary offered him the trophy, Sam suddenly stepped back and gently beckoned to his son standing so proudly like a miniature, puffed-up peacock at the side and edge of the green.

As the boy walked towards them, Michael Bonallack started to clap him slowly, rhythmically in time to his short stride; Sam joined him and in an instant, the whole arena was applauding in evocative sound and energy to the boy's diminutive gait.

It was a loud, deafening, resonant, celebratory pulse of dreams, life and improbable, fantastical achievement!

As he reached his father they took the silver, resplendent trophy together and the arena once again exploded into wild applause then unbridled screaming and thunderous cheering.

Sam handed the boy the precious, gleaming, shining jug and raised him in a single movement onto his shoulder where Oliver lifted the trophy towards the late, blue, summer sky in a gesture of joy, jubilation and triumph and screamed out to the world and the unpredictable winds that covered it.

"You did it, Dad…"

He shouted, yelled and cried in his glee and joy above the deafening, raucous noise.

"…You actually did it!"

Sam smiled and laughed shaking his head from side to side as if in some type of mistrust or mental rejection of what had already transpired and passed.

But it was undeniable, a fact, although he did correct his child, as if for the first time since they had arrived in Scotland at the commencement of their unlikely adventure and quest.

"No, Oliver…*we* did it…"

He chuckled, laughed and raised him up ever higher on his shoulder in pure ecstasy and awe.

"...*We* surely did!"

And there in the stillness of the late summer afternoon a sudden, mystical zephyr blew in from the sea and showered them both with a thousand, silver, shimmering, grass cuttings.

Sam acknowledged the sensations and embraced them; they reminded him of his boyhood, of the beginning, of a long, green, pristine, practice area and an old, greenkeeper's shed. It was as if the golfing Gods themselves were rejoicing, honouring and recognising the fruition and fulfilment of a fateful prophecy and a rare, singular promise.

A promise by them made in purity and innocence to one of the chosen few, so many years ago!

The End

Printed in Great Britain
by Amazon